S.F.    Asimov, Isaac

        The robots of
dawn

| DATE DUE | | |
|---|---|---|
| JUN 7 1984 | JUN 1 9 1987 | |
| JUL 6 1984 | DEC 1 1 1987 | |
| JUL 2 3 1984 | DEC 3 0 1987 | |
| AUG 2 8 1984 | SEP 5 '88 | |
| JAN 1 1 1985 | SEP 2 7 '88 | |
| FEB 6 1985 | NOV 3 0 '88 | |
| MAR 2 0 1985 | MAY | |
| APR 2 5 1985 | | |
| JUN 7 1985 | SEP 1 9 | |
| MAR 4 1986 | FEB 1 4 1990 | |
| JUL 1 2 1986 | JUL 1 2 1991 | |
| OCT 2 1 1986 | AUG 2 6 1991 | |

# The Robots of Dawn

*Science Fiction by Isaac Asimov*

# ISAAC ASIMOV

# The Robots of Dawn

1983

DOUBLEDAY & COMPANY, INC.

GARDEN CITY, NEW YORK

*36,303*

*S.F*

Library of Congress Cataloging in Publication Data
Asimov, Isaac, 1920–
The robots of dawn.
I. Title.
PS3551.S5R6   1983      813'.54
ISBN 0-385-18400-X
Library of Congress Catalog Card Number 83–8960

*Dedicated to Marvin Minsky and
Joseph F. Engelberger, who epitomize
(respectively) the theory and practice
of robotics*

# Contents

# The Robots of Dawn

# 1

## Baley

*1.*

Elijah Baley found himself in the shade of the tree and muttered to himself, "I knew it. I'm sweating."

He paused, straightened up, wiped the perspiration from his brow with the back of his hand, then looked dourly at the moisture that covered it.

"I *hate* sweating," he said to no one, throwing it out as a cosmic law. And once again he felt annoyance with the Universe for making something both essential and unpleasant.

One *never* perspired (unless one wished to, of course) in the City, where temperature and humidity were absolutely controlled and where it was never absolutely necessary for the body to perform in ways that made heat production greater than heat removal.

Now *that* was civilized.

He looked out into the field, where a straggle of men and women were, more or less, in his charge. They were mostly youngsters in their late teens, but included some middle-aged people like himself. They were hoeing inexpertly and doing a variety of other things that robots were designed to do—and could do much more efficiently had they not been ordered to stand aside and wait while the human beings stubbornly practiced.

There were clouds in the sky and the sun, at the moment, was going behind one of them. He looked up uncertainly. On the one hand, it meant the direct heat of the sun (and the sweating) would be cut down. On the other hand, was there a chance of rain?

That was the trouble with the Outside. One teetered forever between unpleasant alternatives.

It always amazed Baley that a relatively small cloud could cover the sun completely, darkening Earth from horizon to horizon yet leaving most of the sky blue.

He stood beneath the leafy canopy of the tree (a kind of primitive wall and ceiling, with the solidity of the bark comforting to the touch) and looked again at the group, studying it. Once a week they were out there, whatever the weather.

They were gaining recruits, too. They were definitely more in number than the stout-hearted few who had started out. The City government, if not an actual partner in the endeavor, was benign enough to raise no obstacles.

To the horizon on Baley's right—eastward, as one could tell by the position of the late-afternoon sun—he could see the blunt, many-fingered domes of the City, enclosing all that made life worthwhile. He saw, as well, a small moving speck that was too far off to be made out clearly.

From its manner of motion and from indications too subtle to describe, Baley was quite sure it was a robot, but that did not surprise him. The Earth's surface, outside the Cities, was the domain of robots, not of human beings—except for those few, like himself, who were dreaming of the stars.

Automatically, his eyes turned back toward the hoeing star-dreamers and went from one to the other. He could identify and name each one. All working, all learning how to endure the Outside, and—

He frowned and muttered in a low voice, "Where's Bentley?"

And another voice, sounding behind with a somewhat breathless exuberance, said, "Here I am, Dad."

Baley whirled. "Don't *do* that, Ben."

"Do what?"

"Sneak up on me like that. It's hard enough trying to keep my equilibrium in the Outside without my having to worry about surprises, too."

"I wasn't trying to surprise you. It's tough to make much noise walking on the grass. One can't help that. —But don't you think you ought to go in, Dad? You've been out two hours now and I think you've had enough."

"Why? Because I'm forty-five and you're a punk kid of nineteen? You think you have to take care of your decrepit father, do you?"

Ben said, "Yes, I guess that's it. And a bit of good detective work on your part, too. You cut right through to the nub."

Ben smiled broadly. His face was round, his eyes sparkling. There was a lot of Jessie in him, Baley thought, a lot of his mother. There was little trace of the length and solemnity of Baley's own face.

And yet Ben had his father's way of thinking. He could at times furrow into a grave solemnity that made it quite clear that he was of perfectly legitimate origin.

"I'm doing very well," said Baley.

"You are, Dad. You're the best of us, considering—"

"Considering what?"

"Your age, of course. And I'm not forgetting that you're the one who started this. Still, I saw you take cover under the tree and I thought—well, maybe the old man has had enough."

"I'll 'old man' you," said Baley. The robot he had noted in the direction of the City was now close enough to be made out clearly, but Baley dismissed it as unimportant. He said, "It makes sense to get under a tree once in a while when the sun's too bright. We've got to learn to use the advantages of the Outside, as well as learning to bear its disadvantages. —And there's the sun coming out from behind that cloud."

"Yes, it will do that. —Well, then, don't you want to go in?"

"I can stick it out. Once a week, I have an afternoon off and I spend it here. That's my privilege. It goes with my C-7 rating."

"It's not a question of privilege, Dad. It's a question of getting overtired."

"I feel fine, I tell you."

"Sure. And when you get home, you'll go straight to bed and lie in the dark."

"Natural antidote to overbrightness."

"And Mom worries."

"Well, let her worry. It will do her good. Besides, what's the harm in being out here? The worst part is I *sweat,* but I just have to get used to it. I can't run away from it. When I started, I couldn't even walk this far from the City without having to turn back—and you were the only one with me. Now look at how many we've got and how far I can come without trouble. I can do plenty of work, too. I can last another hour. Easy. —I tell you, Ben, it would do your mother good to come out here herself."

"Who? Mom? Surely you jest."

"Some jest. When the time comes to take off, I won't be able to go along—because she won't."

"And you'll be glad of it. Don't kid yourself, Dad. It won't be for quite a while—and if you're not too old now, you'll be too old then. It's going to be a game for young people."

"You know," said Baley, half-balling his fist, "you are such a wise guy with your 'young people.' Have you ever been off Earth? Have any of those people in the field been off Earth? *I* have. Two years ago. That was before I had any of this acclimatization—and I survived."

"I know, Dad, but that was briefly, and in the line of duty, and you were taken care of in a going society. It's not the same."

"It *was* the same," said Baley stubbornly, knowing in his heart that it wasn't. "And it won't take us so long to be able to leave. If I could get permission to go to Aurora, we could get this act off the ground."

"Forget it. It's not going to happen that easily."

"We've got to try. The government won't let us go without Aurora giving us the go-ahead. It's the largest and strongest of the Spacer worlds and what it says—"

"Goes! I know. We've all talked this over a million times. But you don't have to go there to get permission. There are such things as hyper-relays. You can talk to them from here. I've said that any number of times before."

"It's not the same. We'll need face-to-face contact—and I've said *that* any number of times before."

"In any case," said Ben, "we're not ready yet."

"We're not ready because Earth won't give us the ships. The Spacers will, together with the necessary technical help."

"Such faith! Why should the Spacers do it? When did they start feeling kindly toward us short-lived Earthpeople?"

"If I could talk to them—"

Ben laughed. "Come on, Dad. You just want to go to Aurora to see that woman again."

Baley frowned and his eyebrows beetled over his deep-set eyes. "Woman? Jehoshaphat, Ben, what are you talking about?"

"Now, Dad, just between us—and not a word to Mom—what *did* happen with that woman on Solaria? I'm old enough. You can tell me."

"*What* woman on Solaria?"

"How can you look at me and deny any knowledge of the woman everyone on Earth saw in the hyperwave dramatization? Gladia Delmarre. *That* woman!"

"*Nothing* happened. That hyperwave thing was nonsense. I've told you that a thousand times. She didn't look that way. *I* didn't look that way. It was all made up and you know it was produced over my protests, just because the government thought it would put Earth in a good light with the Spacers. —And you make sure you don't imply anything different to your mother."

"Wouldn't dream of it. Still, this Gladia went to Aurora and you keep wanting to go there, too."

"Are you trying to tell me that you honestly think the reason I want to go to Aurora— Oh, *Jehoshaphat!*"

His son's eyebrows raised. "What's the matter?"

"The robot. That's R. Geronimo."

"Who?"

"One of our Department messenger robots. And it's out here! I'm off-time and I *deliberately* left my receiver at home because I didn't want them to get at me. That's my C-7 privilege and yet they send for me by robot."

"How do you know it's coming to you, Dad?"

"By very clever deduction. One: there's no one else here who has any connection with the Police Department; and two: that miserable thing is heading right toward me. From that I deduce that it wants me. I should get on the other side of the tree and stay there."

"It's not a wall, Dad. The robot can walk around the tree."

And the robot called out, "Master Baley, I have a message for you. You are wanted at Headquarters."

The robot stopped, waited, then said again, "Master Baley, I have a message for you. You are wanted at Headquarters."

"I hear and understand," Baley said tonelessly. He had to say that or the robot would have continued to repeat.

Baley frowned slightly as he studied the robot. It was a new model, a little more humaniform than the older models were. It had been uncrated and activated only a month before and with some degree of fanfare. The government was always trying for something—anything—that might produce more acceptance of robots.

It had a grayish surface with a dull finish and a somewhat re-silient touch (perhaps like soft leather). The facial expression, while largely changeless, was not quite as idiotic as that of most robots. It was, though, in actual fact, quite as idiotic, mentally, as all the rest.

For a moment, Baley thought of R. Daneel Olivaw, the Spacer robot who had been on two assignments with him, one on Earth and one on Solaria, and whom he had last encountered when Daneel had consulted him in the mirror-image case. Daneel was a robot who was so human that Baley could treat him as a friend and could still miss him, even now. If all robots were like that—

Baley said, "This is my day off, boy. There is no necessity for me to go to Headquarters."

R. Geronimo paused. There was a trifling vibration in his hands. Baley noticed that and was quite aware that it meant a certain amount of conflict in the robot's positronic pathways. They had to obey human beings, but it was quite common for two human beings to want two different types of obedience.

The robot made a choice. It said, "It is your day off, master. —You are wanted at Headquarters."

Ben said uneasily, "If they want you, Dad—"

Baley shrugged. "Don't be fooled, Ben. If they really wanted me badly, they'd have sent an enclosed car and probably used a human volunteer, instead of ordering a robot to do the walking —and irritate me with one of its messages."

Ben shook his head. "I don't think so, Dad. They wouldn't know where you were or how long it would take to find you. I don't think they would want to send a human being on an uncertain search."

"Yes? Well, let's see how strong the order is. —R. Geronimo, go back to Headquarters and tell them I'll be at work at 0900." Then sharply, "Go back! That's an order!"

The robot hesitated perceptibly, then turned, moved away, turned again, made an attempt to come back toward Baley, and finally remained in one spot, its whole body vibrating.

Baley recognized it for what it was and muttered to Ben, "I may have to go. Jehoshaphat!"

What was troubling the robot was what the roboticists called an equipotential of contradiction on the second level. Obedience was the Second Law and R. Geronimo was now suffering from two roughly equal and contradictory orders. Robot-block was what the general population called it or, more frequently, roblock for short.

Slowly, the robot turned. Its original order was the stronger, but not by much, so that its voice was slurred. "Master, I was told you might say that. If so I was to say—" It paused, then added hoarsely, "I was to say—if you are alone."

Baley nodded curtly to his son and Ben didn't wait. He knew when his father was Dad and when he was a policeman. Ben retreated hastily.

For a moment, Baley played irritably with the notion of strengthening his own order and making the roblock more nearly complete, but that would surely cause the kind of damage that would require positronic analysis and reprogramming. The expense of that would be taken out of his salary and it might easily amount to a year's pay.

He said, "I withdraw my order. What were you told to say?"

R. Geronimo's voice at once cleared. "I was told to say that you are wanted in connection with Aurora."

Baley turned toward Ben and called out, "Give them another half hour and then say I want them back in. I've got to leave now."

And as he walked off with long strides, he said petulantly to the robot, "Why couldn't they tell you to say that at once? And why can't they program you to use a car so that I wouldn't have to walk?"

He knew very well why that wasn't done. Any accident involving a robot-driven car would set off another antirobot riot.

He did not slacken his pace. There were two kilometers to walk before they even got to the City wall and, thereafter, they would have to reach Headquarters through heavy traffic.

Aurora? What kind of crisis was brewing now?

2.

It took half an hour for Baley to reach the entranceway into the City and he stiffened himself for what he suspected ahead. Perhaps—*perhaps*—it wouldn't happen this time.

He reached the dividing plane between Outside and City, the wall that marked off chaos from civilization. He placed his hand over the signal patch and an opening appeared. As usual, he didn't wait for the opening to be completed, but slipped in as soon as it was wide enough. R. Geronimo followed.

The police sentry on duty looked startled, as he always did when someone came in from Outside. Each time there was the same look of disbelief, the same coming to attention, the same sudden hand upon the blaster, the same frown of uncertainty.

Baley presented his identity card with a scowl and the sentry saluted. The door closed behind him—and it happened.

Baley was inside the City. The walls closed around him and the City became the Universe. He was again immersed in the endless, eternal hum and odor of people and machinery that would soon fade below the threshold of consciousness; in the soft, indirect artificial light that was nothing at all like the partial and varying glare of the Outside, with its green and brown and blue and white and its interruptions of red and yellow. Here there was no erratic wind, no heat, no cold, no threat of rain; here there was instead the quiet permanence of unfelt air currents that kept everything fresh. Here was a designed combination of temperature and humidity so perfectly adjusted to humans it remained unsensed.

Baley felt his breath drawn in tremulously and he gladdened in the realization that he was home and safe with the known and *knowable*.

That was what always happened. Again he had accepted the City as the womb and moved back into it with glad relief. He knew that such a womb was something from which humanity must emerge and be born. Why did he always sink back this way?

And would that always be? Would it really be that, though he might lead countless numbers out of the City and off the Earth and out to the stars, he would not, in the end, be able to go himself? Would he always feel at home only in the City?

He clenched his teeth—but there was no use thinking about it.

He said to the robot, "Were you brought to this point by car, boy?"

"Yes, master."

"Where is it now?"

"I do not know, master."

Baley turned to the sentry. "Officer, this robot was brought to this spot two hours ago. What has happened to the car that brought him?"

"Sir, I went on duty less than an hour ago."

Actually, it was foolish to ask. Those in the car did not know how long it would take the robot to find him, so they would not wait. Baley had a brief impulse to call in, but they would tell him to take the Expressway; it would be quicker.

The only reason he hesitated was the presence of R. Geronimo. He didn't want its company on the Expressway and yet he could not expect the robot to make its way back to Headquarters through hostile crowds.

Not that he had a choice. Undoubtedly, the Commissioner

was not eager to make this easy for him. He would be annoyed at not having had him on call, free time or not.

Baley said, "This way, boy."

The City covered over five thousand square kilometers and contained over four hundred kilometers of Expressway, plus hundreds of kilometers of Feederway, to serve its well over twenty million people. The intricate net of movement existed on eight levels and there were hundreds of interchanges of varying degrees of complexity.

As a plainclothesman, Baley was expected to know them all—and he did. Put him down blindfolded in any corner of the City, whip off the blindfold, and he could make his way flawlessly to any other designated portion.

There was no question then but that he knew how to get to Headquarters. There were eight reasonable routes he could follow, however, and for a moment he hesitated over which might be least crowded at this time.

Only for a moment. Then he decided and said, "Come with me, boy." The robot followed docilely at his heels.

They swung onto a passing Feeder and Baley seized one of the vertical poles: white, warm, and textured to give a good grip. Baley did not want to sit down; they would not be on for long. The robot had waited for Baley's quick gesture before placing its hand upon the same pole. It might as well have remained standing without a grip—it would not have been difficult to maintain balance—but Baley wanted to take no chance of being separated. He was responsible for the robot and did not wish to risk being asked to replace the financial loss to the City should anything happen to R. Geronimo.

The Feeder had a few other people on board and the eyes of each turned curiously—and inevitably—to the robot. One by one, Baley caught those glances. Baley had the look of one used to authority and the eyes he caught turned uneasily away.

Baley gestured again as he swung off the Feeder. It had reached the strips now and was moving at the same speed as the nearest strip, so that there was no necessity for it to slow down. Baley stepped onto that nearest strip and felt the whipping of air once they were no longer protected by plastic enclosure.

He leaned into the wind with the ease of long practice, lifting one arm to break the force at eye level. He ran the strips downward to the intersection with the Expressway and then began the run upward to the speed-strip that bordered the Expressway.

He heard the teenage cry of "Robot!" (he had been a teenager himself once) and knew exactly what would happen. A group of them—two or three or half a dozen—would swarm up or down the strips and somehow the robot would be tripped and would go clanging down. Then, if it ever came before a magistrate, any teenager taken into custody would claim the robot had collided with him and was a menace on the strips—and would undoubtedly be let go.

The robot could neither defend itself in the first instance, nor testify in the second.

Baley moved rapidly and was between the first of the teenagers and the robot. He sidestepped onto a faster strip, brought his arm higher, as though to adjust to the increase in wind speed, and somehow the young man was nudged off course and onto a slower strip for which he was not prepared. He called out wildly, "Hey!" as he went sprawling. The others stopped, assessed the situation quickly, and veered away.

Baley said, "Onto the Expressway, boy."

The robot hesitated briefly. Robots were not allowed, unaccompanied, on the Expressway. Baley's order had been a firm one, however, and it moved aboard. Baley followed, which relieved the pressure on the robot.

Baley moved brusquely through the crowd of standees, forcing R. Geronimo ahead of him, making his way up to the less crowded upper level. He held on to a pole and kept one foot firmly on the robot's, again glaring down all eye contact.

Fifteen and a half kilometers brought him to the close-point for the Police Headquarters and he was off. R. Geronimo came off with him. It hadn't been touched, not a scuff. Baley delivered it at the door and accepted a receipt. He carefully checked the date, the time, and the robot's serial number, then placed the receipt in his wallet. Before the day was over, he would check and make certain that the transaction had been computer-registered.

Now he was going to see the Commissioner—and he knew the

Commissioner. Any failing on Baley's part would be suitable
cause for demotion. He was a harsh man, the Commissioner. He
considered Baley's past triumphs a personal offense.

3.

The Commissioner was Wilson Roth. He had held the post for
two and a half years, since Julius Enderby had resigned once the
furor roused by the murder of a Spacer had subsided and the
resignation could be safely offered.

Baley had never quite reconciled himself to the change. Julius,
with all his shortcomings, had been a friend as well as a superior; Roth was merely a superior. He was not even City-bred.
Not *this* City. He had been brought in from outside.

Roth was neither unusually tall nor unusually fat. His head
was large, though, and seemed to be set on a neck that slanted
slightly forward from his torso. It made him appear heavy:
heavy-bodied and heavy-headed. He even had heavy lids half-
obscuring his eyes.

Anyone would think him sleepy, but he never missed anything. Baley had found that out very soon after Roth had taken
over the office. He was under no illusion that Roth liked him. He
was under less illusion that he liked Roth.

Roth did not sound petulant—he never did—but his words
did not exude pleasure, either. "Baley, why is it so hard to find
you?" he said.

Baley said in a carefully respectful voice, "It is my afternoon
off, Commissioner."

"Yes, your C-7 privilege. You've heard of a Waver, haven't
you? Something that receives official messages? You are subject
to recall, even on your off-time."

"I know that very well, Commissioner, but there are no longer
any regulations concerning the wearing of a Waver. We can be
reached without one."

"Inside the City, yes, but you were Outside—or am I mistaken?"

"You are not mistaken, Commissioner. I was Outside. The

regulations do not state that, in such a case, I am to wear a Waver."

"You hide behind the letter of the statute, do you?"

"Yes, Commissioner," said Baley calmly.

The Commissioner rose, a powerful and vaguely threatening man, and sat on the desk. The window to the Outside, which Enderby had installed, had long been closed off and painted over. In the closed-in room (warmer and more comfortable for that), the Commissioner seemed the larger.

He said, without raising his voice, "You rely, Baley, on Earth's gratitude, I think."

"I rely on doing my job, Commissioner, as best I can and in accord with the regulations."

"And on Earth's gratitude when you bend the spirit of those regulations."

Baley said nothing to that.

The Commissioner said, "You are considered as having done well in the Sarton murder case three years ago."

"Thank you, Commissioner," said Baley. "The dismantling of Spacetown was a consequence, I believe."

"It was—and that was something applauded by all Earth. You are also considered as having done well on Solaria two years ago and, before you remind me, the result was a revision in the terms of the trade treaties with the Spacer worlds, to the considerable advantage of Earth."

"I believe that is on record, sir."

"And you are very much the hero as a result."

"I make no such claim."

"You have received two promotions, one in the aftermath of each affair. There has even been a hyperwave drama based on the events on Solaria."

"Which was produced without my permission and against my will, Commissioner."

"Which nevertheless made you a kind of hero."

Baley shrugged.

The Commissioner, having waited for a spoken comment for a few seconds, went on, "But you have done nothing of importance in nearly two years."

"It is natural for Earth to ask what I have done for it lately."

"Exactly. It probably does ask. It knows that you are a leader in this new fad of venturing Outside, in fiddling with the soil, and in pretending to be a robot."

"It is permitted."

"Not all that is permitted is admired. It is possible that more people think of you as peculiar than as heroic."

"That is, perhaps, in accord with my own opinion of myself," said Baley.

"The public has a notoriously short memory. The heroic is vanishing rapidly behind the peculiar in your case, so that if you make a mistake you will be in serious trouble. The reputation you rely on—"

"With respect, Commissioner, I do not rely on it."

"The reputation the Police Department *feels* you rely on will not save you and *I* will not be able to save you."

The shadow of a smile seemed to pass for one moment over Baley's dour features. "I would not want you, Commissioner, to risk your position in a wild attempt to save me."

The Commissioner shrugged and produced a smile precisely as shadowy and fleeting. "You need not worry about that."

"Then why are you telling me all this, Commissioner?"

"To warn you. I am not trying to destroy you, you understand, so I am warning you *once*. You are going to be involved in a very delicate matter, in which you may easily make a mistake, and I am warning you that you must not make one." Here his face relaxed into an unmistakable smile.

Baley did not respond to the smile. He said, "Can you tell me what the very delicate matter is?"

"I do not know."

"Does it involve Aurora?"

"R. Geronimo was instructed to tell you that it did, if it had to, but I know nothing about it."

"Then how can you tell, Commissioner, that it is a very delicate matter?"

"Come, Baley, you are an investigator of mysteries. What brings a member of the Terrestrial Department of Justice to the City, when you might easily have been asked to go to Washing-

ton, as you did two years ago in connection with the Solaria incident? And what makes the person from Justice frown and seem
ill-tempered and grow impatient at the fact that you were not
reached instantly? Your decision to make yourself unavailable
was a mistake, one that was in no way my responsibility. It is
perhaps not fatal in itself, but you are off on the wrong foot, I
believe."

"You are delaying me further, however," said Baley, frowning.

"Not really. The official from Justice is having some light
refreshment—you know the perks that the Terries allow themselves. We will be joined when that is done. The news of your
arrival has been transmitted, so just continue to wait, as I am
doing."

Baley waited. He had known, at the time, that the hyperwave
drama, forced upon him against his will, however it might have
helped Earth's position, had ruined him in the Department. It
had cast him in three-dimensional relief against the two-dimen-
sional flatness of the organization and had made him a marked
man.

He had risen to higher rank and greater privileges, but that,
too, had increased Department hostility against him. And the
higher he rose, the more easily he would shatter in case of a fall.

If he made a mistake—

4.

The official from Justice entered, looked about casually,
walked to the other side of Roth's desk, and took the seat. As
highest-classified individual, the official behaved properly. Roth
calmly took a secondary seat.

Baley remained standing, laboring to keep his face un-
surprised.

Roth might have warned him, but he had not. He had clearly
chosen his words deliberately, in order to give no sign.

The official was a woman.

There was no reason for this not to be. Any official might be a
woman. The Secretary-General might be a woman. There were

women on the police force, even a woman with the rank of captain.

It was just that, without warning, one didn't expect it in any given case. There were times in history when women entered administrative posts in considerable numbers. Baley knew that; he knew history well. But this wasn't one of those times.

She was quite tall and sat stiffly upright in the chair. Her uniform was not very different from that of a man, nor was her hair styling or facial adornment. What gave her sex away immediately were her breasts, the prominence of which she made no attempt to hide.

She was fortyish, her facial features regular and cleanly chiseled. She had middle-aged attractively, with, as yet, no visible gray in her dark hair.

She said, "You are Plainclothesman Elijah Baley, Classification C-7." It was a statement, not a question.

"Yes, ma'am," Baley answered, nevertheless.

"I am Undersecretary Lavinia Demachek. You don't look very much as you did in that hyperwave drama concerning you."

Baley had been told that often. "They couldn't very well portray me as I am and collect much of an audience, ma'am," said Baley dryly.

"I'm not sure of that. You look stronger than the baby-faced actor they used."

Baley hesitated a second or so and decided to take the chance —or perhaps felt he couldn't resist taking it. Solemnly, he said, "You have a cultivated taste, ma'am."

She laughed and Baley let out his breath very gently. She said, "I like to think I have. —Now what do you mean by keeping me waiting?"

"I was not informed you would come, ma'am, and it was off-time for me."

"Which you spent Outside, I understand."

"Yes, ma'am."

"You are one of those cranks, as I would say were my taste not a cultivated one. Let me ask, instead, if you are one of those enthusiasts."

"Yes, ma'am."

"You expect to emigrate some day and found new worlds in the wildernesses of the Galaxy?"

"Perhaps not I, ma'am. I may prove to be too old, but—"

"How old are you?"

"Forty-five, ma'am."

"Well, you look it. I am forty-five also, as it happens."

"You do not look it, ma'am."

"Older or younger?" She broke into laughter again, then said, "But let's not play games. Do you imply I am too old to be a pioneer?"

"No one can be a pioneer in our society, without training Outside. The training works best with the young. My son, I hope, will someday stand on another world."

"Indeed? You know, of course, that the Galaxy belongs to the Spacer worlds."

"There are only fifty of them, ma'am. There are millions of worlds in the Galaxy that are habitable—or can be made habitable—and that probably do not possess indigenous intelligent life."

"Yes, but not one ship can leave Earth without Spacer permission."

"That might be granted, ma'am."

"I do not share your optimism, Mr. Baley."

"I have spoken to Spacers who—"

"I know you have," said Demachek. "My superior is Albert Minnim, who, two years ago, sent you to Solaria." She permitted herself a small curve of the lips. "An actor portrayed him in a bit role on that hyperwave drama, one that resembled him closely, as I recall. He was not pleased, as I also recall."

Baley changed the subject. "I asked Undersecretary Minnim—"

"He has been promoted, you know."

Baley thoroughly understood the importance of grades in classification. "His new title, ma'am?"

"Vice-Secretary."

"Thank you. I asked Vice-Secretary Minnim to request permission for me to visit Aurora to deal with this subject."

"When?"

"Not very long after my return from Solaria. I have renewed the request twice since."

"But have not received a favorable reply?"

"No, ma'am."

"Are you surprised?"

"I am disappointed, ma'am."

"No point in that." She leaned back a trifle in the chair. "Our relationship with the Spacer worlds is very touchy. You may feel that your two feats of detection have eased the situation—and so they have. That awful hyperwave drama has also helped. The total easing, however, has been this much"—she placed her thumb and forefinger close together—"out of this much," and she spread her hands far apart.

"Under those circumstances," she went on, "we could scarcely take the risk of sending you to Aurora, the leading Spacer world, and having you perhaps do something that could create inter- stellar tension."

Baley's eyes met hers. "I have been on Solaria and have done no harm. On the contrary—"

"Yes, I know, but you were there at Spacer request, which is parsecs distant from being there at our request. You cannot fail to see that."

Baley was silent.

She made a soft snorting sound of nonsurprise and said, "The situation has grown worse since your requests were placed with —and very correctly ignored by—the Vice-Secretary. It has grown particularly worse in the last month."

"Is that the reason for this conference, ma'am?"

"Do you grow impatient, sir?" She addressed him sardonically in the to-a-superior intonation. "Do you direct me to come to the point?"

"No, ma'am."

"Certainly you do. And why not? I grow tedious. Let me ap- proach the point by asking if you know Dr. Han Fastolfe."

Baley said carefully, "I met him once, nearly three years ago, in what was then Spacetown."

"You liked him, I believe."

"He was friendly—for a Spacer."

She made another soft snorting sound. "I imagine so. Are you aware that he has been an important political power on Aurora over the last two years?"

"I had heard he was in the government from a—a partner I once had."

"From R. Daneel Olivaw, your Spacer robot friend?"

"My ex-partner, ma'am."

"On the occasion when you solved a small problem concerning two mathematicians on board a Spacer ship?"

Baley nodded. "Yes, ma'am."

"We keep informed, you see. Dr. Han Fastolfe has been, more or less, the guiding light of the Auroran government for two years, an important figure in their World Legislature, and he is even spoken of as a possible future Chairman. —The Chairman, you understand, is the closest thing to a chief executive that the Aurorans have."

Baley said, "Yes, ma'am," and wondered when she would get to the very delicate matter of which the Commissioner had spoken.

Demachek seemed in no hurry. She said, "Fastolfe is a—moderate. That's what he calls himself. He feels Aurora—and the Spacer worlds generally—have gone too far in their direction, as you, perhaps, feel that we on Earth have gone too far in ours. He wishes to step backward to less robotry, to a more rapid turnover of generations, and to alliance and friendship with Earth. Naturally, we support him—but very quietly. If we were too demonstrative in our affection, that might well be the kiss of death for him."

Baley said, "I believe he would support Earth's exploration and settlement of other worlds."

"I believe so, too. I am of the opinion he said as much to you."

"Yes, ma'am, when we met."

Demachek steepled her hands and put the tips of her fingers to her chin. "Do you think he represents public opinion on the Spacer worlds?"

"I don't know, ma'am."

"I'm afraid he does not. Those who are with him are lukewarm. Those who are against him are an ardent legion. It is only his political skills and his personal warmth that have kept him as close to the seats of power as he is. His greatest weakness, of course, is his sympathy for Earth. That is constantly used against him and it influences many who would share his views in every other respect. If you were sent to Aurora, any mistake you made would help strengthen anti-Earth feeling and would therefore weaken him, possibly fatally. Earth simply cannot take that risk."

Baley muttered, "I see."

"Fastolfe is willing to take the risk. It was he who arranged to have you sent to Solaria at a time when his political power was barely beginning and when he was very vulnerable. But then, he has only his personal power to lose, whereas we must be concerned with the welfare of over eight billion Earthpeople. That is what makes the present political situation almost unbearably delicate."

She paused and, finally, Baley was forced to ask the question. "What is the situation that you are referring to, ma'am?"

"It seems," said Demachek, "that Fastolfe has become implicated in a serious and unprecedented scandal. If he is clumsy, the chances are that he will undergo political destruction in a matter of weeks. If he is superhumanly clever, perhaps he will hold out for some months. A little sooner, a little later, he could be destroyed as a political force on Aurora—and *that* would be a real disaster for Earth, you see."

"May I ask what he is accused of? Corruption? Treason?"

"Nothing that small. His personal integrity is, in any case, unquestioned even by his enemies."

"A crime of passion, then? Murder?"

"Not *quite* murder."

"I don't understand, ma'am."

"There are human beings on Aurora, Mr. Baley. And there are robots, too, most of them something like ours, not very much more advanced in most cases. However, there are a few humaniform robots, robots so humaniform that they can be taken for human."

Baley nodded. "I know that very well."

"I suppose that destroying a humaniform robot is not exactly murder in the strict sense of the word."

Baley leaned forward, eyes widening. He shouted, "Jehoshaphat, woman! Stop playing games. Are you telling me that Dr. Fastolfe has killed R. Daneel?"

Roth leaped to his feet and seemed about to advance on Baley, but Undersecretary Demachek waved him back. She seemed unruffled.

She said, "Under the circumstances, I excuse your disrespect, Baley. No, R. Daneel has *not* been killed. He is not the only humaniform robot on Aurora. Another such robot, *not* R. Daneel, has been killed, if you wish to use the term loosely. To be more precise, its mind has been totally destroyed; it was placed into permanent and irreversible roblock."

Baley said, "And they say that Dr. Fastolfe did it?"

"His enemies are saying so. The extremists, who wish only Spacers to spread through the Galaxy and who wish Earthpeople to vanish from the Universe, are saying so. If these extremists can maneuver another election within the next few weeks, they will surely gain total control of the government, with incalculable results."

"Why is this roblock so important politically? I don't understand."

"I am not myself certain," said Demachek. "I do not pretend to understand Auroran politics. I gather that the humaniforms were in some way involved with the extremist plans and that the destruction has infuriated them." She wrinkled her nose. "I find their politics very confusing and I will only mislead you if I try to interpret it."

Baley labored to control himself under the Undersecretary's level stare. He said in a low voice, "Why am I here?"

"Because of Fastolfe. Once before you went out into space in order to solve a murder and succeeded. Fastolfe wants you to try again. You are to go to Aurora and discover who was responsible for the roblock. He feels that to be his only chance of turning back the extremists."

"I am not a roboticist. I know nothing about Aurora—"

"You knew nothing about Solaria, either, yet you managed. The point is, Baley, we are as eager to find out what really happened as Fastolfe is. We don't want him destroyed. If he is, Earth will be subject to a kind of hostility from these Spacer extremists that will probably be greater than anything we have yet experienced. We don't want that to happen."

"I can't take on this responsibility, ma'am. The task is—"

"Next to impossible. We know that, but we have no choice. Fastolfe insists—and behind him, for the moment, stands the Auroran government. If you refuse to go or if we refuse to let you go, we will have to face the Auroran fury. If you do go and are successful, we'll be saved and you will be suitably rewarded."

"And if I go—and fail?"

"We will do our best to see to it that the blame will be yours and not Earth's."

"The skins of officialdom will be saved, in other words."

Demachek said, "A kinder way of putting it is that you will be thrown to the wolves in the hope that Earth will not suffer too badly. One man is not a bad price to pay for our planet."

"It seems to me that, since I am sure to fail, I might as well not go."

"You know better than that," said Demachek softly. "Aurora has asked for you and you cannot refuse. —And why should you want to refuse? You've been trying to go to Aurora for two years and you've been bitter over your failure to get our permission."

"I've wanted to go in peace to arrange for help in the settlement of other worlds, not to—"

"You might still try to get their help for your dream of settling other worlds, Baley. After all, suppose you *do* succeed. It's possible, after all. In that case, Fastolfe will be much beholden to you and he may do far more for you than he ever would have otherwise. And we ourselves will be sufficiently grateful to you to help. Isn't that worth a risk, even a large one? However small your chances of success are if you go, those chances are zero if you do not go. Think of that, Baley, but please—not too long."

Baley's lips tightened and, finally, realizing there was no alternative, he said, "How much time do I have to—"

And Demachek said calmly, "Come. Haven't I been explaining that we have no choice—and no time, either? You leave," she looked at the timeband on her wrist, "in just under six hours."

## 5.

The spaceport was at the eastern outskirts of the City in an all-but-deserted Sector that was, strictly speaking, Outside. This was palliated by the fact that the ticket offices and the waiting rooms were actually in the City and that the approach to the ship itself was by vehicle through a covered path. By tradition, all takeoffs were at night, so that a pall of darkness further deadened the effect of Outside.

The spaceport was not very busy, considering the populous character of Earth. Earthmen very rarely left the planet and the traffic consisted entirely of commercial activity organized by robots and Spacers.

Elijah Baley, waiting for the ship to be ready for boarding, felt already cut off from Earth.

Bentley sat with him and there was a glum silence between the two. Finally, Ben said, "I didn't think Mom would want to come."

Baley nodded. "I didn't think so, either. I remember how she was when I went to Solaria. This is no different."

"Did you manage to calm her down?"

"I did what I could, Ben. She thinks I'm bound to be in a space crash or that the Spacers will kill me once I'm on Aurora."

"You got back from Solaria."

"That just makes her the less eager to risk me a second time. She assumes the luck will run out. However, she'll manage. —You rally round, Ben. Spend some time with her and, whatever you do, don't talk about heading out to settle a new planet. That's what really bothers her, you know. She feels you'll be leaving her one of these years. She knows she won't be able to go and so she'll never see you again."

"She may not," said Ben. "That's the way it might work out."

"You can face that easily, maybe, but she can't, so just don't discuss it while I'm gone. All right?"

"All right. —I think she's a little upset about Gladia."

Baley looked up sharply. "Have you been—"

"I haven't said a word. But she saw that hyperwave thing, too, you know, and she knows Gladia's on Aurora."

"What of it? It's a big planet. Do you think Gladia Delmarre will be waiting at the spaceport for me? —Jehoshaphat, Ben, doesn't your mother *know* that hyperwave axle grease was nine-tenths fiction?"

Ben changed the subject with a tangible effort. "It seems funny—you sitting here with no luggage of any kind."

"I'm sitting here with too much. I've got the clothes I'm wearing, don't I? They'll get rid of those as soon as I'm on board. Off they go—to be chemically treated, then dumped into space. After that, they'll give me a totally new wardrobe, after I have been personally fumigated and cleaned and polished, inside and out. I've been through that once before."

Again silence and then Ben said, "You know, Dad—" and stopped suddenly. He tried again, "You know Dad—" and did no better.

Baley looked at him steadily. "What are you trying to say, Ben?"

"Dad, I feel like an awful jackass saying this, but I think I'd better. You're not the hero type. Even I never thought you were. You're a nice guy and the best father there could be, but not the hero type."

Baley grunted.

"Still," said Ben, "when you stop to think of it, it was you who got Spacetown off the map; it was you who got Aurora on our side; it was you who started this whole project of settling other worlds. Dad, you've done more for Earth than everyone in the government put together. So why aren't you appreciated more?"

Baley said, "Because I'm not the hero type and because this stupid hyperwave drama was foisted on me. It has made an enemy of every man in the Department, it's unsettled your mother, and it's given me a reputation I can't live up to." The light flashed on his wrist-caller and he stood up. "I've got to go now, Ben."

"I know. But what I want to say, Dad, is that *I* appreciate you. And this time when you come back, you'll get that from everybody and not just from me."

Baley felt himself melting. He nodded rapidly, put a hand on his son's shoulder, and muttered, "Thanks. Take care of yourself —and your mother—while I'm gone."

He walked away, not looking back. He had told Ben that he was going to Aurora to discuss the settlement project. If that were so, he *might* come back in triumph. As it was—

He thought: I'll come back in disgrace—if I come back at all.

# 2

## Daneel

6.

It was Baley's third time on a spaceship and the passage of two years had in no way dimmed his memory of the first two times. He knew exactly what to expect.

There would be the isolation—the fact that no one would see him or have anything to do with him, with the exception (perhaps) of a robot. There would be the constant medical treatment—the fumigation and sterilization. (No other way of putting it.) There would be the attempt to make him fit to approach the disease-conscious Spacers who thought of Earthpeople as walking bags of multifarious infections.

There would be differences, too, however. He would not, this time, be quite so afraid of the process. Surely the feeling of loss at being out of the womb would be less dreadful.

He would be prepared for the wider surroundings. This time, he told himself boldly (but with a small knot in his stomach, for all that), he might even be able to insist on being given a view of space.

Would it look different from photographs of the night sky as seen from Outside? he wondered.

He remembered his first view of a planetarium dome (safely within the City, of course). It had given him no sensation of being Outside, no discomfort at all.

Then there were the two times—no, three—that he had been in the open at night and saw the real stars in the real dome of the sky. That had been far less impressive than the planetarium dome had been, but there had been a cool wind each time and a feeling of distance, which made it more frightening than the dome—but less frightening than daytime, for the darkness was a comforting wall about him.

Would, then, the sight of the stars through a spaceship viewing window seem more like a planetarium or more like Earth's night sky? Or would it be a different sensation altogether?

He concentrated on that, as though to wash out the thought of leaving Jessie, Ben, and the City.

With nothing less than bravado, he refused the car and insisted on walking the short distance from the gate to the ship in the company of the robot who had come for him. It was just a roofed-over arcade, after all.

The passage was slightly curved and he looked back while he could still see Ben at the other end. He lifted his hand casually, as though he were taking the Expressway to Trenton, and Ben waved both arms wildly, holding up the first two fingers of each hand outspread in the ancient symbol of victory.

Victory? A useless gesture, Baley was certain.

He switched to another thought that might serve to fill and occupy him. What would it be like to board a spaceship by day, with the sun shining brightly on its metal and with himself and the others who were boarding all exposed to the Outside.

How would it feel to be entirely aware of a tiny cylindrical world, one that would detach itself from the infinitely larger world to which it was temporarily attached and that would then lose itself in an Outside infinitely larger than any Outside on Earth, until after an endless stretch of Nothingness it would find another—

He held himself grimly to a steady walk, letting no change in expression show—or so he thought, at least. The robot at his side, however, brought him to a halt.

"Are you ill, sir?" (Not "master," merely "sir." It was an Auroran robot.)

"I'm all right, boy," said Baley hoarsely. "Move on."

He kept his eyes turned to the ground and did not lift them again till the ship itself was towering above him.

An Auroran ship!

He was sure of that. Outlined by a warm spotlight, it soared taller, more gracefully, and yet more powerfully than the Solarian ships had.

Baley moved inside and the comparison remained in favor of Aurora. His room was larger than the ones two years before had been: more luxurious, more comfortable.

He knew exactly what was coming and removed all his clothes without hesitation. (Perhaps they would be disintegrated by plasma torch. Certainly, he would not get them back on returning to Earth—if he returned. He hadn't the first time.)

He would receive no other clothes till he had been thoroughly bathed, examined, dosed, and injected. He almost welcomed the humiliating procedures imposed on him. After all, it served to keep his mind off what was taking place. He was scarcely aware of the initial acceleration and scarcely had time to think of the moment during which he left Earth and entered space.

When he was finally dressed again, he surveyed the results unhappily in a mirror. The material, whatever it was, was smooth and reflective and shifted color with any change in angle. The trouser legs hugged his ankles and were, in turn, covered by the tops of shoes that molded themselves softly to his feet. The sleeves of his blouse hugged his wrists and his hands were covered by thin, transparent gloves. The top of the blouse covered his neck and an attached hood could, if desired, cover his head. He was being so covered, not for his own comfort, he knew, but to reduce his danger to the Spacers.

He thought, as he looked at the outfit, that he should feel uncomfortably enclosed, uncomfortably hot, uncomfortably damp. But he did not. He wasn't, to his enormous relief, even sweating.

He made the reasonable deduction. He said to the robot that had walked him to the ship and was still with him, "Boy, are these clothes temperature-controlled?"

The robot said, "Indeed they are, sir. It is all-weather clothing and is considered very desirable. It is also exceedingly expensive. Few on Aurora are in a position to wear it."

"That so? Jehoshaphat!"

He stared at the robot. It seemed a fairly primitive model, not very much different from Earth models, in fact. Still, there was a certain subtlety of expression that Earth models lacked. It could change expression in a limited way, for instance. It had smiled very slightly when it indicated that Baley had been given that which few on Aurora could afford.

The structure of its body resembled metal and yet had the look of something woven, something shifting slightly with movement, something with colors that matched and contrasted pleasingly. In short, unless one looked very closely and steadily, the robot, though definitely nonhumaniform, seemed to be wearing clothing.

Baley said, "What ought I to call you, boy?"

"I am Giskard, sir."

"R. Giskard?"

"If you wish, sir."

"Do you have a library on this ship?"

"Yes, sir."

"Can you get me book-films on Aurora?"

"What kind, sir?"

"Histories—political science—geographies—anything that will let me know about the planet."

"Yes, sir."

"And a viewer."

"Yes, sir."

The robot left through the double door and Baley nodded grimly to himself. On his trip to Solaria, it had never occurred to him to spend the useless time crossing space in learning something useful. He had come along a bit in the last two years.

He tried the door the robot had just passed through. It was locked and utterly without give. He would have been enormously surprised at anything else.

He investigated the room. There was a hyperwave screen. He handled the controls idly, received a blast of music, managed to lower the volume eventually, and listened with disapproval. Tinkly and discordant. The instruments of the orchestra seemed vaguely distorted.

He touched other contacts and finally managed to change the view. What he saw was a space-soccer game that was played, obviously, under conditions of zero-gravity. The ball flew in straight lines and the players (too many of them on each side— with fins on backs, elbows, and knees that must serve to control movement) soared in graceful sweeps. The unusual movements made Baley feel dizzy. He leaned forward and had just found and used the off-switch when he heard the door open behind him.

He turned and, because he thoroughly expected to see R. Giskard, he was aware at first only of someone who was *not* R. Giskard. It took a blink or two to realize that he saw a thoroughly human shape, with a broad, high-cheekboned face and with short, bronze hair lying flatly backward, someone dressed in clothing with a conservative cut and color scheme.

"Jehoshaphat!" said Baley in a nearly strangled voice.

"Partner Elijah," said the other, stepping forward, a small, grave smile on his face.

"Daneel!" cried Baley, throwing his arms around the robot and hugging tightly. "Daneel!"

## 7.

Baley continued to hold Daneel, the one unexpected familiar object on the ship, the one strong link to the past. He clung to Daneel in a gush of relief and affection.

And then, little by little, he collected his thoughts and knew that he was hugging not Daneel but R. Daneel—*Robot* Daneel Olivaw. He was hugging a robot and the robot was holding him lightly, allowing himself to be hugged, judging that the action gave pleasure to a human being and enduring that action because the positronic potentials of his brain made it impossible to repel the embrace and so cause disappointment and embarrassment to the human being.

The insurmountable First Law of Robotics states: "A robot may not injure a human being—" and to repel a friendly gesture would do injury.

Slowly, so as to reveal no sign of his own chagrin, Baley released his hold. He even gave each upper arm of the robot a final squeeze, so that there might seem to be no shame to the release.

"Haven't seen you, Daneel," said Baley, "since you brought that ship to Earth with the two mathematicians. Remember?"

"Of a certainty, Partner Elijah. It is a pleasure to see you."

"You feel emotion, do you?" said Baley lightly.

"I cannot say what I feel in any human sense, Partner Elijah. I can say, however, that the sight of you seems to make my thoughts flow more easily, and the gravitational pull on my body seems to assault my senses with lesser insistence, and that there are other changes I can identify. I imagine that what I sense corresponds in a rough way to what it is that you may sense when you feel pleasure."

Baley nodded. "Whatever it is you sense when you see me, old partner, that makes it seem preferable to the state in which you are when you don't see me, suits me well—if you follow my meaning. But how is it you are here?"

"Giskard Reventlov, having reported you—" R. Daneel paused.

"Purified?" asked Baley sardonically.

"Disinfected," said R. Daneel. "I felt it appropriate to enter then."

"Surely you would not fear infection otherwise?"

"Not at all, Partner Elijah, but others on the ship might then be reluctant to have me approach them. The people of Aurora are sensitive to the chance of infection, sometimes to a point beyond a rational estimate of the probabilities."

"I understand, but I wasn't asking why you were here at this moment. I meant why are you here at all?"

"Dr. Fastolfe, of whose establishment I am part, directed me to board the ship that had been sent to pick you up for several reasons. He felt it desirable that you have one immediate item of the known in what he was certain would be a difficult mission for you."

"That was a kindly thought on his part. I thank him."

R. Daneel bowed gravely in acknowledgment. "Dr. Fastolfe

also felt that the meeting would give me"—the robot paused—
"appropriate sensations."

"Pleasure, you mean, Daneel."

"Since I am permitted to use the term, yes. And as a third
reason—and the most important—"

The door opened again at that point and R. Giskard walked
in.

Baley's head turned toward it and he felt a surge of displeasure. There was no mistaking R. Giskard as a robot and its
presence emphasized, somehow, the robotism of Daneel (R.
Daneel, Baley suddenly thought again), even though Daneel was
far the superior of the two. Baley didn't *want* the robotism of
Daneel emphasized; he didn't want himself humiliated for his
inability to regard Daneel as anything but a human being with a
somewhat stilted way with the language.

He said impatiently, "What is it, boy?"

R. Giskard said, "I have brought the book-films you wished to
see, sir, and the viewer."

"Well, put them down. Put them down. —And you needn't
stay. Daneel will be here with me."

"Yes, sir." The robot's eyes—faintly glowing, Baley noticed, as
Daneel's were not—turned briefly to R. Daneel, as though seeking orders from a superior being.

R. Daneel said quietly, "It will be appropriate, friend Giskard,
to remain just outside the door."

"I shall, friend Daneel," said R. Giskard.

It left and Baley said with some discontent, "Why does it have
to stay just outside the door? Am I a prisoner?"

"In the sense," said R. Daneel, "that it would not be permitted
for you to mingle with the ship's company in the course of this
voyage, I regret to be forced to say you are indeed a prisoner.
Yet that is not the reason for the presence of Giskard. —And I
should tell you at this point that it might well be advisable,
Partner Elijah, if you did not address Giskard—or any robot—as
'boy.'"

Baley frowned. "Does it resent the expression?"

"Giskard does not resent any action of a human being. It is
simply that 'boy' is not a customary term of address for robots

on Aurora and it would be inadvisable to create friction with the Aurorans by unintentionally stressing your place of origin through habits of speech that are nonessential."

"How do I address it, then?"

"As you address me, by the use of his accepted identifying name. That is, after all, merely a sound indicating the particular person you are addressing—and why should one sound be preferable to another? It is merely a matter of convention. And it is also the custom on Aurora to refer to a robot as 'he'—or sometimes 'she'—rather than as 'it.' Then, too, it is not the custom on Aurora to use the initial 'R.' except under formal conditions where the entire name of the robot is appropriate—and even then the initial is nowadays often left out."

"In that case—Daneel," (Baley repressed the sudden impulse to say "R. Daneel") "how do you distinguish between robots and human beings?"

"The distinction is usually self-evident, Partner Elijah. There would seem to be no need to emphasize it unnecessarily. At least that is the Auroran view and, since you have asked Giskard for films on Aurora, I assume you wish to familiarize yourself with things Auroran as an aid to the task you have undertaken."

"The task which has been dumped on me, yes. And what if the distinction between robot and human being is *not* self-evident, Daneel? As in your case?"

"Then why make the distinction, unless the situation is such that it is essential to make it?"

Baley took a deep breath. It was going to be difficult to adjust to this Auroran pretense that robots did not exist. He said, "But then, if Giskard is not here to keep me prisoner, why is it—he—outside the door?"

"Those are according to the instructions of Dr. Fastolfe, Partner Elijah. Giskard is to protect you."

"Protect me? Against what? —Or against whom?"

"Dr. Fastolfe was not precise on that point, Partner Elijah. Still, as human passions are running high over the matter of Jander Panell—"

"Jander Panell?"

"The robot whose usefulness was terminated."

"The robot, in other words, who was killed?"

"Killed, Partner Elijah, is a term that is usually applied to human beings."

"But on Aurora distinctions between robots and human beings are avoided, are they not?"

"So they are! Nevertheless, the possibility of distinction or lack of distinction in the particular case of the ending of functioning has never arisen—to my knowledge. I do not know what the rules are."

Baley pondered the matter. It was a point of no real importance, purely a matter of semantics. Still, he wanted to probe the manner of thinking of the Aurorans. He would get nowhere otherwise.

He said slowly, "A human being who is functioning is alive. If that life is violently ended by the deliberate action of another human being, we call that 'murder' or 'homicide.' 'Murder' is, somehow, the stronger word. To be witness, suddenly, to an attempted violent end to the life of a human being, one would shout 'Murder!' It is not at all likely that one would shout 'Homicide!' It is the more formal word, the less emotional word."

R. Daneel said, "I do not understand the distinction you are making, Partner Elijah. Since 'murder' and 'homicide' are both used to represent the violent ending of the life of a human being, the two words must be interchangeable. Where, then, is the distinction?"

"Of the two words, one screamed out will more effectively chill the blood of a human being than the other will, Daneel."

"Why is that?"

"Connotations and associations; the subtle effect, not of dictionary meaning, but of years of usage; the nature of the sentences and conditions and events in which one has experienced the use of one word as compared with that of the other."

"There is nothing of this in my programming," said Daneel, with a curious sound of helplessness hovering over the apparent lack of emotion with which he said this (the same lack of emotion with which he said everything).

Baley said, "Will you accept my word for it, Daneel?"

Quickly, Daneel said, almost as though he had just been presented with the solution to a puzzle, "Without doubt."

"Now, then, we might say that a robot that is functioning is alive," said Baley. "Many might refuse to broaden the word so far, but we are free to devise definitions to suit ourselves if it is useful. It is easy to treat a functioning robot as alive and it would be unnecessarily complicated to try to invent a new word for the condition or to avoid the use of the familiar one. *You* are alive, for instance, Daneel, aren't you?"

Daneel said, slowly and with emphasis, "I am functioning!"

"Come. If a squirrel is alive, or a bug, or a tree, or a blade of grass, why not you? I would never remember to say—or to think—that I am alive but that you are merely functioning, especially if I am to live for a while on Aurora, where I am to try not to make unnecessary distinctions between a robot and myself. Therefore, I tell you that we are both alive and I ask you to take my word for it."

"I will do so, Partner Elijah."

"And yet can we say that the ending of robotic life by the deliberate violent action of a human being is also 'murder'? We might hesitate. If the crime is the same, the punishment should be the same, but would that be right? If the punishment of the murder of a human being is death, should one actually execute a human being who puts an end to a robot?"

"The punishment of a murderer is psychic-probing, Partner Elijah, followed by the construction of a new personality. It is the personal structure of the mind that has committed the crime, not the life of the body."

"And what is the punishment on Aurora for putting a violent end to the functioning of a robot?"

"I do not know, Partner Elijah. Such an incident has never occurred on Aurora, as far as I know."

"I suspect the punishment would not be psychic-probing," said Baley. "How about 'roboticide'?"

"Roboticide?"

"As the term used to describe the killing of a robot."

Daneel said, "But what about the verb derived from the noun,

Partner Elijah? One never says 'to homicide' and it would therefore not be proper to say 'to roboticide.'"

"You're right. You would have to say 'to murder' in each case."

"But murder applies specifically to human beings. One does not murder an animal, for instance."

Baley said, "True. And one does not murder even a human being by accident, only by deliberate intent. The more general term is 'to kill.' That applies to accidental death as well as to deliberate murder—and it applies to animals as well as human beings. Even a tree may be killed by disease, so why may not a robot be killed, eh, Daneel?"

"Human beings and other animals and plants as well, Partner Elijah, are all living things," said Daneel. "A robot is a human artifact, as much as this viewer is. An artifact is 'destroyed,' 'damaged,' 'demolished,' and so on. It is never 'killed.'"

"Nevertheless, Daneel, I shall say 'killed.' Jander Panell was killed."

Daneel said, "Why should a difference in a word make any difference to the thing described?"

"'That which we call a rose by any other name would smell as sweet.' Is that it, Daneel?"

Daneel paused, then said, "I am not certain what is meant by the smell of a rose, but if a rose on Earth is the common flower that is called a rose on Aurora, and if by its 'smell' you mean a property that can be detected, sensed, or measured by human beings, then surely calling a rose by another sound-combination —and holding all else equal—would not affect the smell or any other of its intrinsic properties."

"True. And yet changes in name do result in changes in perception where human beings are concerned."

"I do not see why, Partner Elijah."

"Because human beings are often illogical, Daneel. It is not an admirable characteristic."

Baley sank deeper into his chair and fiddled with his viewer, allowing his mind, for a few minutes, to retreat into private thought. The discussion with Daneel was useful in itself, for while Baley played with the question of words, he managed to forget that he was in space, to forget that the ship was moving forward until it was far enough from the mass centers of the Solar System to make the Jump through hyperspace; to forget that he would soon be several million kilometers from Earth and, not long after that, several light-years from Earth.

More important, there were positive conclusions to be drawn. It was clear that Daneel's talk about Aurorans making no distinction between robots and human beings was misleading. The Aurorans might virtuously remove the initial "R.," the use of "boy" as a form of address, and the use of "it" as the customary pronoun, but from Daneel's resistance to the use of the same word for the violent ends of a robot and of a human being (a resistance inherent in his programming which was, in turn, the natural consequence of Auroran assumptions about how Daneel ought to behave) one had to conclude that these were merely superficial changes. In essence, Aurorans were as firm as Earthmen in their belief that robots were machines that were infinitely inferior to human beings.

That meant that his formidable task of finding a useful resolution of the crisis (if that were possible at all) would not be hampered by at least one particular misperception of Auroran society.

Baley wondered if he ought to question Giskard, in order to confirm the conclusions he reached from his conversation with Daneel—and, without much hesitation, decided not to. Giskard's simple and rather unsubtle mind would be of no use. He would "Yes, sir" and "No, sir" to the end. It would be like questioning a recording.

Well, then, Baley decided, he would continue with Daneel, who was at least capable of responding with something approaching subtlety.

He said, "Daneel, let us consider the case of Jander Panell, which I assume, from what you have said so far, is the first case of roboticide in the history of Aurora. The human being responsible—the killer—is, I take it, not known."

"If," said Daneel, "one assumes that a human being was responsible, then his identity is not known. In that, you are right, Partner Elijah."

"What about the motive? Why was Jander Panell killed?"

"That, too, is not known."

"But Jander Panell was a humaniform robot, one like yourself and not one like, for instance, R. Gis— I mean, Giskard."

"That is so. Jander was a humaniform robot like myself."

"Might it not be, then, that no case of roboticide was intended?"

"I do not understand, Partner Elijah."

Baley said, a little impatiently, "Might not the killer have thought this Jander was a human being, that the intention was homicide, not roboticide?"

Slowly, Daneel shook his head. "Humaniform robots are quite like human beings in appearance, Partner Elijah, down to the hairs and pores in our skin. Our voices are thoroughly natural, we can go through the motions of eating, and so on. And yet, in our behavior there are noticeable differences. There may be fewer such differences with time and with refinement of technique, but as yet they are many. You—and other Earthmen not used to humaniform robots—may not easily note these differences, but Aurorans would. No Auroran would mistake Jander—or me —for a human being, not for a moment."

"Might some Spacer, other than an Auroran, make the mistake?"

Daneel hesitated. "I do not think so. I do not speak from personal observation or from direct programmed knowledge, but I do have the programming to know that all the Spacer worlds are as intimately acquainted with robots as Aurora is—some, like Solaria, even more so—and I deduce, therefore, that no Spacer would miss the distinction between human and robot."

"Are there humaniform robots on the other Spacer worlds?"

"No, Partner Elijah, they exist only on Aurora so far."

"Then other Spacers would not be intimately acquainted with humaniform robots and might well miss the distinctions and mistake them for human beings."

"I do not think that is likely. Even humaniform robots will behave in robotic fashion in certain definite ways that any Spacer would recognize."

"And yet surely there are Spacers who are not as intelligent as most, not as experienced, not as mature. There are Spacer children, if nothing else, who would miss the distinction."

"It is quite certain, Partner Elijah, that the—roboticide—was not committed by anyone unintelligent, inexperienced, or young. Completely certain."

"We're making eliminations. Good. If no Spacer would miss the distinction, what about an Earthman? Is it possible that—"

"Partner Elijah, when you arrive in Aurora, you will be the first Earthman to set foot on the planet since the period of original settlement was over. All Aurorans now alive were born on Aurora or, in a relatively few cases, on other Spacer worlds."

"The first Earthman," muttered Baley. "I am honored. Might not an Earthman be present on Aurora without the knowledge of Aurorans?"

"No!" said Daneel with simple certainty.

"Your knowledge, Daneel, might not be absolute."

"No!" came the repetition, in tones precisely similar to the first.

"We conclude, then," said Baley with a shrug, "that the roboticide was intended to be roboticide and nothing else."

"That was the conclusion from the start."

Baley said, "Those Aurorans who concluded this at the start had all the information to begin with. I am getting it now for the first time."

"My remark, Partner Elijah, was not meant in any pejorative manner. I know better than to belittle your abilities."

"Thank you, Daneel. I know there was no intended sneer in your remark. —You said just a while ago that the roboticide was not committed by anyone unintelligent, inexperienced, or young and that this is completely certain Let us consider your remark—"

Baley knew that he was taking the long route. He had to. Considering his lack of understanding of Auroran ways and of their manner of thought, he could not afford to make assumptions and skip steps. If he were dealing with an intelligent human being in this way, that person would be likely to grow impatient and blurt out information—and consider Baley an idiot into the bargain. Daneel, however, as a robot, would follow Baley down the winding road with total patience.

That was one type of behavior that gave away Daneel as a

robot, however humaniform he might be. An Auroran might be able to judge him a robot from a single answer to a single question. Daneel was right as to the subtle distinctions.

Baley said, "One might eliminate children, perhaps also most women, and many male adults by presuming that the method of roboticide involved great strength—that Jander's head was perhaps crushed by a violent blow or that his chest was smashed inward. This would not, I imagine, be easy for anyone who was not a particularly large and strong human being." From what Demachek had said on Earth, Baley knew that this was not the manner of the roboticide, but how was he to tell that Demachek herself had not been misled?

Daneel said, "It would not be possible at all for any human being."

"Why not?"

"Surely, Partner Elijah, you are aware that the robotic skeleton is metallic in nature and much stronger than human bone. Our movements are more strongly powered, faster, and more delicately controlled. The Third Law of Robotics states: 'A robot must protect its own existence.' An assault by a human being could easily be fended off. The strongest human being could be immobilized. Nor is it likely that a robot can be caught unaware. We are always aware of human beings. We could not fulfill our functions otherwise."

Baley said, "Come, now, Daneel. The Third Law states: 'A robot must protect its own existence, as long as such protection does not conflict with the First or Second Law.' The Second Law states: 'A robot must obey the orders given it by a human being, except where such orders would conflict with the First Law.' And the First Law states: 'A robot may not injure a human being or, through inaction, allow a human being to come to harm.' A human being could order a robot to destroy himself —and a robot would then use his own strength to smash his own skull. And if a human being attacked a robot, that robot could not fend off the attack without harming the human being, which would violate First Law."

Daneel said, "You are, I suppose, thinking of Earth's robots. On Aurora—or on any of the Spacer worlds—robots are regarded more highly than on Earth and are, in general, more complex, versatile, and valuable. The Third Law is distinctly stronger in comparison to the Second Law on Spacer worlds than it is on Earth. An order for self-destruction would be questioned and there would have to be a truly legitimate reason for it to be carried through—a clear and present danger. And in fending off an attack, the First Law would not be violated, for Auroran robots are deft enough to immobilize a human being without hurting him."

"Suppose, though, that a human being maintained that, unless a robot destroyed himself, he—the human being—would be destroyed? Would not the robot then destroy himself?"

"An Auroran robot would surely question a mere statement to that effect. There would have to be clear evidence of the possible destruction of a human being."

"Might not a human being be sufficiently subtle to so arrange matters in such a way as to make it seem to a robot that that human being was indeed in great danger? Is it the ingenuity that would be required that makes you eliminate the unintelligent, inexperienced, and young?"

And Daneel said, "No, Partner Elijah, it is not."

"Is there an error in my reasoning?"

"None."

"Then the error may lie in my assumption that he was physically damaged. He was not, in actual fact, physically damaged. Is that right?"

"Yes, Partner Elijah."

(That meant Demachek had had her facts straight, Baley thought.)

"In that case, Daneel, Jander was mentally damaged. Roblock! Total and irreversible!"

"Roblock?"

"Short for robot-block, the permanent shutdown of the functioning of the positronic pathways."

"We do not use the word 'roblock' on Aurora, Partner Elijah."

"What do you say?"

"We say 'mental freeze-out.'"

"Either way, it is the same phenomenon being described."

"It might be wise, Partner Elijah, to use our expression or the Aurorans you speak to may not understand; conversation may be impeded. You stated a short while ago that different words make a difference."

"Very well. I will say 'freeze-out.' —Could such a thing happen spontaneously?"

"Yes, but the chances are infinitesimally small, roboticists say. As a humaniform robot, I can report that I have never myself experienced any effect that could even approach mental freeze-out."

"Then one must assume that a human being deliberately set up a situation in which mental freeze-out would take place."

"That is precisely what Dr. Fastolfe's opposition contends, Partner Elijah."

"And since this would take robotic training, experience, and skill, the unintelligent, the inexperienced, and the young cannot have been responsible."

"That is the natural reasoning, Partner Elijah."

"It might even be possible to list the number of human beings on Aurora with sufficient skill and thus set up a group of suspects that might not be very large in number."

"That has, in actual fact, been done, Partner Elijah."

"And how long is the list?"

"The longest list suggested contains only one name."

It was Baley's turn to pause. His brows drew together in an angry frown and he said, quite explosively, "Only one name?"

Daneel said quietly, "Only one name, Partner Elijah. That is the judgment of Dr. Han Fastolfe, who is Aurora's greatest theoretical roboticist."

"But what is, then, the mystery in all this? Whose is the one name?"

R. Daneel said, "Why, that of Dr. Han Fastolfe, of course. I have just stated that he is Aurora's greatest theoretical roboticist and, in Dr. Fastolfe's professional opinion, he himself is the only one who could possibly have maneuvered Jander Panell into total mental freeze-out without leaving any sign of the process. However, Dr. Fastolfe also states that he did not do it."

"But that no one else could have, either?"

"Indeed, Partner Elijah. There lies the mystery."

"And what if Dr. Fastolfe—" Baley paused. There would be no point in asking Daneel if Dr. Fastolfe was lying or was somehow mistaken, either in his own judgment that no one but he could have done it or in the statement that he himself had not done it. Daneel had been programmed by Fastolfe and there would be no chance that the programming included the ability to doubt the programmer.

Baley said, therefore, with as close an approach to mildness as he could manage, "I will think about this, Daneel, and we will talk again."

"That is well, Partner Elijah. It is, in any case, time for sleep. Since it is possible that, on Aurora, the pressure of events may force an irregular schedule upon you, it would be wise to seize the opportunity for sleep now. I will show you how one produces a bed and how one manages the bedclothes."

"Thank you, Daneel," muttered Baley. He was under no illusion that sleep would come easily. He was being sent to Aurora for the specific purpose of demonstrating that Fastolfe was innocent of roboticide—and success in that was required for Earth's continued security and (much less important but equally dear to Baley's heart) for the continued prospering of Baley's own career—yet, even before reaching Aurora, he had discovered that Fastolfe had virtually confessed to the crime.

8.

Baley did sleep—eventually, after Daneel demonstrated how to reduce the field intensity that served as a form of pseudo-gravity. This was not true antigravity and it consumed so much energy that the process could only be used at restricted times and under unusual conditions.

Daneel was not programmed to be able to explain the manner in which this worked and, if he had, Baley was quite certain he would not have understood it. Fortunately, the controls could be operated without any understanding of the scientific justification.

Daneel said, "The field intensity cannot be reduced to zero—at least, not by these controls. Sleeping under zero-gravity is not, in any case, comfortable, certainly not for those inexperienced in space travel. What one needs is an intensity low enough to give one a feeling of freedom from the pressure of one's own weight, but high enough to maintain an up-down orientation. The level varies with the individual. Most people would feel most comfortable at the minimum intensity allowed by the control, but you might find that, on first use, you would wish a higher intensity, so that you might retain the familiarity of the weight sensation to a somewhat greater extent. Simply experiment with different levels and find the one that suits."

Lost in the novelty of the sensation, Baley found his mind drifting away from the problem of Fastolfe's affirmation/denial, even as his body drifted away from wakefulness. Perhaps the two were one process.

He dreamed he was back on Earth (of course), moving along an Expressway but not in one of the seats. Rather, he was floating along beside the high-speed strip, just over the head of the moving people, gaining on them slightly. None of the ground-bound people seemed surprised; none looked up at him. It was a rather pleasant sensation and he missed it upon waking.

After breakfast the following morning—

Was it morning actually? Could it be morning—or any other time of day—in space?

Clearly, it couldn't. He thought awhile and decided he would define morning as the time after waking, and he would define breakfast as the meal eaten after waking, and abandon specific timekeeping as objectively unimportant. —For him, at least, if not for the ship.

After breakfast, then, the following morning, he studied the news sheets offered him only long enough to see that they said nothing about the roboticide on Aurora and then turned to those book-films that had been brought to him the previous day ("wake period"?) by Giskard.

He chose those whose titles sounded historical and, after viewing through several hastily, he decided that Giskard had brought him books for adolescents. They were heavily illustrated and simply written. He wondered if that was Giskard's estimate of Baley's intelligence—or, perhaps, of his needs. After some thought, Baley decided that Giskard, in his robotic innocence, had chosen well and that there was no point in brooding over a possible insult.

He settled down to viewing with greater concentration and noted at once that Daneel was viewing the book-film with him. Actual curiosity? Or just to keep his eyes occupied?

Daneel did not once ask to have a page repeated. Nor did he stop to ask a question. Presumably, he merely accepted what he read with robotic trust and did not permit himself the luxury of either doubt or curiosity.

Baley did not ask Daneel any questions concerning what he read, though he did ask for instructions on the operation of the print-out mechanism of the Auroran viewer, with which he was not familiar.

Occasionally, Baley stopped to make use of the small room that adjoined his room and could be used for the various private physiological functions, so private that the room was referred to as "the Personal," with the capital letter always understood, both on Earth and—as Baley discovered when Daneel referred to it— on Aurora. It was just large enough for one person—which made it bewildering to a City-dweller accustomed to huge banks of urinals, excretory seats, washbasins, and showers.

In viewing the book-films, Baley did not attempt to memorize details. He had no intention of becoming an expert on Auroran society, nor even of passing a high school test on the subject. Rather, he wished to get the feel of it.

He noticed, for instance, even through the hagiographic attitude of historians writing for young people, that the Auroran pioneers—the founding fathers, the Earthpeople who had first come to Aurora to settle in the early days of interstellar travel— had been very much Earthpeople. Their politics, their quarrels, every facet of their behavior had been Earthish; what happened on Aurora was, in ways, similar to the events that took place when the relatively empty sections of Earth had been settled a couple of thousand years before.

Of course, the Aurorans had no intelligent life to encounter and to fight, no thinking organisms to puzzle the invaders from Earth with questions of treatment, humane or cruel. There was

precious little life of any kind, in fact. So the planet was quickly
settled by human beings, by their domesticated plants and animals, and by the parasites and other organisms that were adven-
titiously brought along. And, of course, the settlers brought robots with them.

The first Aurorans quickly felt the planet to be theirs, since it
fell into their laps with no sense of competition, and they had
called the planet New Earth to begin with. That was natural,
since it was the first extrasolar planet—the first Spacer world—to
be settled. It was the first fruit of interstellar travel, the first
dawn of an immense new era. They quickly cut the umbilical
cord, however, and renamed the planet Aurora after the Roman
goddess of the dawn.

It was the World of the Dawn. And so did the settlers from
the start self-consciously declare themselves the progenitors of a
new kind. All previous history of humanity was a dark Night
and only for the Aurorans on this new world was the Day finally
approaching.

It was this great fact, this great self-praise, that made itself
felt over all the details: all the names, dates, winners, losers. It
was the essential.

Other worlds were settled, some from Earth, some from
Aurora, but Baley paid no attention to that or to any of the details. He was after the broad brushstrokes and he noted the two
massive changes that took place and pushed the Aurorans ever
farther away from their Earthly origins. These were first, the increasing integration of robots into every facet of life and second,
the extension of the life-span.

As the robots grew more advanced and versatile, the Aurorans
grew more dependent on them. But never helplessly so. Not like
the world of Solaria, Baley remembered, on which a very few
human beings were in the collective womb of very many robots.
Aurora was not like that.

And yet they grew more dependent.

Viewing as he did for intuitive feel—for trend and generality
—every step in the course of human/robot interaction seemed to
depend on dependence. Even the manner in which a consensus
of robotic rights was reached—the gradual dropping of what
Daneel would call "unnecessary distinctions"—was a sign of the

dependence. To Baley, it seemed not that the Aurorans were growing more humane in their attitude out of a liking for the humane, but that they were denying the robotic nature of the objects in order to remove the discomfort of having to recognize the fact that human beings were dependent upon objects of artificial intelligence.

As for the extended life-span, that was accompanied by a slowing of the pace of history. The peaks and troughs smoothed out. There was a growing continuity and a growing consensus.

There was no question but that the history he was viewing grew less interesting as it went along; it became almost soporific. For those living through it, this had to be good. History was interesting to the extent that it was catastrophic and, while that might make absorbing viewing, it made horrible living. Undoubtedly, personal lives continued to be interesting for the vast majority of Aurorans and, if the collective interaction of lives grew quiet, who would mind?

If the World of the Dawn had a quiet sunlit Day, who on that world would clamor for storm?

—Somewhere in the course of his viewing, Baley felt an indescribable sensation. If he had been forced to attempt a description, he would have said it was that of a momentary inversion. It was as though he had been turned inside out— and then back as he had been—in the course of a small fraction of a second.

So momentary had it been that he almost missed it, ignoring it as though it had been a tiny hiccup inside himself.

It was only perhaps a minute later, suddenly going over the feeling in retrospect, that he remembered the sensation as something he had experienced twice before: once when traveling to Solaria and once when returning to Earth from that planet.

It was the "Jump," the passage through hyperspace that, in a timeless, spaceless interval, sent the ship across the parsecs and defeated the speed-of-light limit of the Universe. (No mystery in words, since the ship merely left the Universe and traversed something which involved no speed limit. Total mystery in concept, however, for there was no way of describing what hyperspace was, unless one made use of mathematical symbols which

could, in any case, not be translated into anything compre-
hensible.)

If one accepted the fact that human beings had learned to manipulate hyperspace without understanding the thing they
manipulated, then the effect was clear. At one moment, the ship
had been within microparsecs of Earth and, at the next moment,
it was within microparsecs of Aurora.

Ideally, the Jump took zero-time—literally zero—and, if it
were carried through with perfect smoothness, there would
not, could not be any biological sensation at all. Physicists maintained, however, that perfect smoothness required infinite energy
so that there was always an "effective time" that was not quite
zero, though it could be made as short as desired. It was that
which produced that odd and essentially harmless feeling of inversion.

The sudden realization that he was very far from Earth and
very close to Aurora filled Baley with a desire to see the Spacer
world.

Partly, it was the desire to see somewhere people lived. Partly,
it was a natural curiosity to see something that had been filling
his thoughts as a result of the book-films he had been viewing.

Giskard entered just then with the middle meal between waking and sleeping (call it "lunch") and said, "We are approaching
Aurora, sir, but it will not be possible for you to observe it from
the bridge. There would, in any case, be nothing to see. Aurora's
sun is merely a bright star and it will be several days before we
are near enough to Aurora itself to see any detail." Then he
added, as though in afterthought, "It will not be possible for you
to observe it from the bridge at that time, either."

Baley felt strangely abashed. Apparently, it was assumed he
would want to observe and that want was simply squashed. His
presence as a viewer was not desired.

He said, "Very well, Giskard," and the robot left.

Baley looked after him somberly. How many other constraints
would be placed on him? Improbable as successful completion
of his task was, he wondered in how many different ways
Aurorans would conspire to make it impossible.

# 3

## Giskard

9.

Baley turned and said to Daneel, "It annoys me, Daneel, that I must remain a prisoner here because the Aurorans on board this ship fear me as a source of infection. This is pure superstition. I have been treated."

Daneel said, "It is not because of Auroran fears that you are being asked to remain in your cabin, Partner Elijah."

"No? What other reason?"

"Perhaps you remember that, when we first met on this ship, you asked me my reasons for being sent to escort you. I said it was to give you something familiar as an anchor and to please me. I was then about to tell you the third reason, when Giskard interrupted us with your viewer and viewing material—and thereafter we launched into a discussion of roboticide."

"And you never told me the third reason. What is it?"

"Why, Partner Elijah, it is merely that I might help protect you."

"Against what?"

"Unusual passions have been stirred by the incident we have agreed to call roboticide. You are being called to Aurora to help demonstrate Dr. Fastolfe's innocence. And the hyperwave drama—"

"Jehoshaphat, Daneel," said Baley in outrage. "Have they seen that thing on Aurora, too?"

"They have seen it throughout the Spacer worlds, Partner Elijah. It was a most popular program and has made it quite plain that you are a most extraordinary investigator."

"So that whoever might be behind the roboticide may well have exaggerated fears of what I might accomplish and might therefore risk a great deal to prevent my arrival—or to kill me."

"Dr. Fastolfe," said Daneel calmly, "is quite convinced that no one is behind the roboticide, since no human being other than himself could have carried it through. It was a purely fortuitous occurrence, in Dr. Fastolfe's view. However, there are those who are trying to capitalize on the occurrence and it would be to their interest to keep you from proving that. For that reason, you must be protected."

Baley took a few hasty steps to one wall of the room and then back to the other, as though to speed his thought processes by physical example. Somehow he did not feel any sense of personal danger.

He said, "Daneel, how many humaniform robots are there all together on Aurora?"

"Do you mean now that Jander no longer functions?"

"Yes, now that Jander is dead."

"One, Partner Elijah."

Baley stared at Daneel in shock. Soundlessly, he mouthed the word: One?

Finally, he said, "Let me understand this, Daneel. You are the only humaniform robot on Aurora?"

"Or on any world, Partner Elijah. I thought you were aware of this. I was the prototype and then Jander was constructed. Since then, Dr. Fastolfe has refused to construct any more and no one else has the skill to do it."

"But in that case, since of two humaniform robots, one has been killed, does it not occur to Dr. Fastolfe that the remaining humaniform—you, Daneel—might be in danger."

"He recognizes the possibility. But the chance that the fantastically unlikely occurrence of mental freeze-out would take place a second time is remote. He doesn't take it seriously. He feels, however, that there might be a chance of other misadventure. That, I think, played some small part in his sending me to Earth to get you. It kept me away from Aurora for a week or so."

"And you are now as much a prisoner as I am, aren't you, Daneel?"

"I am a prisoner," said Daneel gravely, "only in the sense, Partner Elijah, that I am expected not to leave this room."

"In what other sense is one a prisoner?"

"In the sense that the person so restricted in his movements resents the restriction. A true imprisonment has the implication of being involuntary. I quite understand the reason for being here and I concur in the necessity."

"*You* do," grumbled Baley. "I do not. I am a prisoner in the full sense. And what keeps us safe here, anyway?"

"For one thing, Partner Elijah, Giskard is on duty outside."

"Is he intelligent enough for the job?"

"He understands his orders entirely. He is rugged and strong and quite realizes the importance of his task."

"You mean he is prepared to be destroyed to protect the two of us?"

"Yes, of course, just as I am prepared to be destroyed to protect you."

Baley felt abashed. He said, "You do not resent the situation in which you may be forced to give up your existence for me?"

"It is my programming, Partner Elijah," said Daneel in a voice that seemed to soften, "yet somehow it seems to me that, even were it not for my programming, saving you makes the loss of my own existence seem quite trivial in comparison."

Baley could not resist this. He held out his hand and closed it on Daneel's with a fierce grip. "Thank you, Partner Daneel, but please do not allow it to happen. I do not wish the loss of your existence. The preservation of my own would be inadequate compensation, it seems to me."

And Baley was amazed to discover that he really meant it. He was faintly horrified to realize that he would be ready to risk his life for a robot. —No, not for a robot. For Daneel.

10.

Giskard entered without signaling. Baley had come to accept that. The robot, as his guard, had to be able to come and go as he pleased. And Giskard was *only* a robot, in Baley's eyes, however much he might be a "he" and however much one did not mention the "R." If Baley were scratching himself, picking his nose, engaged in any messy biological function, it seemed to him that Giskard would be indifferent, nonjudgmental, incapable of reacting in any way, but coldly recording the observation in some inner memory bank.

It made Giskard simply a piece of mobile furniture and Baley felt no embarrassment in his presence. —Not that Giskard had ever intruded on him at an inconvenient moment, Baley thought idly.

Giskard brought a small cubicle with him. "Sir, I suspect that you still wish to observe Aurora from space."

Baley started. No doubt, Daneel had noted Baley's irritation and had deduced its cause and taken this way of dealing with it. To have Giskard do it and present it as an idea of his simple-minded own was a touch of delicacy on Daneel's part. It would free Baley of the necessity of expressing gratitude. Or so Daneel would think.

Baley had, as a matter of fact, been more irritated at being, to his way of thinking, needlessly kept from the view of Aurora than at being kept imprisoned generally. He had been fretting over the loss of the view during the two days since the Jump. —So he turned and said to Daneel, "Thank you, my friend."

"It was Giskard's idea," said Daneel.

"Yes, of course," said Baley with a small smile. "I thank him, too. What is this, Giskard?"

"It is an astrosimulator, sir. It works essentially like a trimensional receiver and is connected to the viewroom. If I might add—"

"Yes?"

"You will not find the view particularly exciting, sir. I would not wish you to be unnecessarily disappointed."

"I will try not to expect too much, Giskard. In any case, I will not hold you responsible for any disappointment I might feel."

"Thank you, sir. I must return to my post, but Daneel will be able to help you with the instrument if any problem arises."

He left and Baley turned to Daneel with approval. "Giskard handled that very well, I thought. He may be a simple model, but he's well-designed."

"He, too, is a Fastolfe robot, Partner Elijah. —This astrosimulator is self-contained and self-adjusted. Since it is already focused on Aurora, it is only necessary to touch the control-edge. That will put it in operation and you need do nothing more. Would you care to set it going yourself?"

Baley shrugged. "No need. You may do it."

"Very well."

Daneel had placed the cubicle upon the table on which Baley had done his book-film viewing.

"This," he said, indicating a small rectangle in his hand, "is the control, Partner Elijah. You need only hold it by the edges in this manner and then exert a small inward pressure to turn the mechanism on—and then another to turn it off."

Daneel pressed the control-edge and Baley shouted in a strangled way.

Baley had expected the cubicle to light up and to display within itself a holographic representation of a star field. That was not what happened. Instead, Baley found himself in space—*in* space—with bright, unblinking stars in all directions.

It lasted for only a moment and then everything was back as it was: the room and, within it, Baley, Daneel, and the cubicle.

"My regrets, Partner Elijah," said Daneel. "I turned it off as soon as I understood your discomfort. I did not realize you were not prepared for the event."

"Then prepare me. What happened?"

"The astrosimulator works directly on the visual center of the human brain. There is no way of distinguishing the impression it leaves from three-dimensional reality. It is a comparatively recent device and so far it has been used only for astronomical scenes which are, after all, low in detail."

"Did you see it, too, Daneel?"

"Yes, but very poorly and without the realism a human being experiences. I see the dim outline of a scene superimposed upon the still-clear contents of the room, but it has been explained to me that human beings see the scene only. Undoubtedly, when the brains of those such as myself are still more finely tuned and adjusted—"

Baley had recovered his equilibrium. "The point is, Daneel, that I was aware of *nothing* else. I was not aware of myself. I did not see my hands or sense where they were. I felt as though I were a disembodied spirit or—er—as I imagine I would feel if I were dead but were consciously existing in some sort of immaterial afterlife."

"I see now why you would find that rather disturbing."

"Actually, I found it *very* disturbing."

"My regrets, Partner Elijah. I shall have Giskard take this away."

"No. I'm prepared now. Let me have that cube. —Will I be able to turn it off, even though I am not conscious of the existence of my hands?"

"It will cling to your hand, so that you will not drop it, Partner Elijah. I have been told by Dr. Fastolfe, who has experienced this phenomenon, that the pressure is automatically applied when the human being holding it wills an end. It is an automatic phenomenon based on nerve manipulation, as the vision itself is. At least, that is how it works with Aurorans and I imagine—"

"That Earthmen are sufficiently similar to Aurorans, physiologically, for it to work with us as well. —Very well, give me the control and I will try."

With a slight internal wince, Baley squeezed the control-edge and was in space again. He was expecting it this time and, once he found he could breathe without difficulty and did not feel in any way as though he were immersed in a vacuum, he labored to accept it all as a visual illusion. Breathing rather stertorously (perhaps to convince himself he was actually breathing), he stared about curiously in all directions.

Suddenly aware he was hearing his breath rasp in his nose, he said, "Can you hear me, Daneel?"

He heard his own voice—a little distant, a little artificial—but he heard it.

And then he heard Daneel's, different enough to be distinguishable.

"Yes, I can," said Daneel. "And you should be able to hear me, Partner Elijah. The visual and kinesthetic senses are interfered with for the sake of a greater illusion of reality, but the auditory sense remains untouched. Largely so, at any rate."

"Well, I see only stars—ordinary stars, that is. Aurora has a sun. We are close enough to Aurora, I imagine, to make the star that is its sun considerably brighter than the others."

"Entirely too bright, Partner Elijah. It is blanked out or you might suffer retinal damage."

"Then where is the planet Aurora?"

"Do you see the constellation of Orion?"

"Yes, I do. —Do you mean we still see the constellations as we see them in Earth's sky, as in the City planetarium?"

"Just about. As stellar distances go, we are not far from Earth and the Solar System of which it is part, so that they have the starview in common. Aurora's sun is known as Tau Ceti on Earth and is only 3.67 parsecs from there. —Now if you'll imagine a line from Betelgeuse to the middle star of Orion's belt and continue it for an equal length and a bit more, the middling-bright star you see is actually the planet Aurora. It will become increasingly unmistakable over the next few days, as we approach it rapidly."

Baley regarded it gravely. It was just a bright starlike object. There was no luminous arrow, going on and off, pointing to it. There was no carefully lettered inscription arced over it.

He said, "Where's the sun? Earth's star, I mean."

"It's in the constellation Virgo, as seen from Aurora. It is a second-magnitude star. Unfortunately, the astrosimulator we have is not properly computerized and it would not be easy to point it out to you. It would, in any case, just appear to be a star, quite an ordinary one."

"Never mind," said Baley. "I am going to turn off this thing now. If I have trouble—help out."

He didn't have trouble. It flicked off just as he thought of doing so and he sat blinking in the suddenly harsh light of the room.

It was only then, when he had returned to his normal senses, that it occurred to him that for some minutes he had seemed to himself to have been out in space, without a protecting wall of any kind, and yet his Earthly agoraphobia had not been activated. He had been perfectly comfortable, once he had accepted his own nonexistence.

The thought puzzled him and distracted him from his book-film viewing for a while.

Periodically, he returned to the astrosimulator and took another look at space as seen from a vantage point just outside the spaceship, with himself nowhere present (apparently). Sometimes it was just for a moment, to reassure himself that he was still not made uneasy by the infinite void. Sometimes he found himself lost in the pattern of the stars and he began lazily counting them or forming geometrical figures, rather luxuriating in the ability to do something which, on Earth, he would never have been able to do because the mounting agoraphobic uneasiness would quickly have overwhelmed everything else.

Eventually, it grew quite obvious that Aurora was brightening. It soon became easy to detect among the other dots of light, then unmistakable, and finally unavoidable. It began as a tiny sliver of light and, thereafter, it enlarged rapidly and began to show phases.

It was almost precisely a half-circle of light when Baley became aware of the existence of phases.

Baley inquired and Daneel said, "We are approaching from outside the orbital plane, Partner Elijah. Aurora's south pole is more or less in the center of its disk, somewhat into the lighted half. It is spring in the southern hemisphere."

Baley said, "According to the material I have been reading, Aurora's axis is tipped sixteen degrees." He had glanced over the physical description of the planet with insufficient attention in his anxiety to get to the Aurorans, but he remembered that.

"Yes, Partner Elijah. Eventually, we will move into orbit about Aurora and the phases will then change rapidly. Aurora revolves more rapidly than Earth does—"

"It has a 22-hour day. Yes."

"A day of 22.3 traditional hours. The Auroran day is divided into 10 Auroran hours, with each hour divided into 100 Auroran minutes, which are, in turn, divided into 100 Auroran seconds. An Auroran second is thus roughly equal to 0.8 Earth seconds."

"Is that what the books mean when they refer to metric hours, metric minutes, and so on?"

"Yes. It was difficult to persuade the Aurorans, at first, to abandon the time units to which they were accustomed and both systems—the standard and the metric—were in use. Eventually, of course, the metric won out. At present we speak only of hours, minutes, and seconds, but the decimalized versions are invariably meant. The same system has been adopted throughout the Spacer worlds, even though, on the other worlds, it does not tie in with the natural rotation of the planet. Each planet also uses a local system, of course."

"As Earth does."

"Yes, Partner Elijah, but Earth uses *only* the original standard time units. That inconveniences the Spacer worlds where trade is concerned, but they allow Earth to go its way in this."

"Not out of friendliness, I imagine. I suspect they wish to emphasize Earth's difference. —How does decimalization fit in with the year? After all, Aurora must have a natural period of revolution about its sun that controls the cycle of its seasons. How is that measured?"

Daneel said, "Aurora revolves about its sun in 373.5 Auroran days or in about 0.95 Earth years. That is not considered a vital matter in chronology. Aurora accepts 30 of its days as equaling a month and 10 months as equaling a metric year. The metric year is equal to about 0.8 seasonal years or about three-quarters of an Earth year. The relationship is different on each world, of course. Ten days is usually referred to as a decimonth. All the Spacer worlds use this system."

"Surely, there must be some convenient way of following the cycle of the seasons?"

"Each world has its seasonal year, too, but it is little regarded. One can, by computer, convert any day—past or present—into its position in the seasonal year if, for any reason, such informa-

tion is desired. And this is true on any world, where conversion
to and from the local days is also as easily possible. And, of
course, Partner Elijah, any robot can do the same and can guide
human activity where the seasonal year or local time is relevant.
The advantage of metricized units is that it supplies humanity
with a unified chronometry that involves little more than deci-
mal point shifts."

It bothered Baley that the books he viewed made none of this
clear. But then, from his own knowledge of Earth's history, he
knew that, at one time, the lunar month had been the key to the
calendar and that there had come a time when, for ease of
chronometry, the lunar month came to be ignored and was never
missed. Yet if he had given books on Earth to some stranger,
that stranger would have very likely found no mention of the
lunar month or any historical change in calendars. Dates would
have been given without explanation.

What else would be given without explanation?

How far could he rely, then, on the knowledge he was gaining? He would have to ask questions constantly, take nothing for
granted.

There would be so many opportunities to miss the obvious, so
many chances to misunderstand, so many ways of taking the
wrong path.

11.

Aurora filled his vision now when he used the astrosimulator
and it looked like Earth. (Baley had never seen Earth in the
same way, but there had been photographs in astronomy texts
and he had seen those.)

Well, what Baley saw on Aurora were the same cloud patterns, the same glimpse of desert areas, the same large stretches
of day and night, the same pattern of twinkling light in the expanse of the night hemisphere as the photographs showed on
Earth's globe.

Baley watched raptly and thought: What if, for some reason,
he had been taken into space, told he was being brought to

Aurora, and was in reality being returned to Earth for some reason—for some subtle and insane reason. How could he tell the difference before landing?

Was there reason to be suspicious? Daneel had carefully told him that the constellations were the same in the sky of both planets, but wouldn't that be naturally so for planets circling neighboring stars? The gross appearance of both planets from space was identical, but wouldn't that be expected if both were habitable and comfortably suited to human life?

Was there any reason to suppose such a farfetched deception would be played upon him? What purpose would it serve? And yet why shouldn't it be made to appear farfetched and useless? If there were an obvious reason to do such a thing, he would have seen through it at once.

Would Daneel be party to such a conspiracy? Surely not, if he were a human being. But he was only a robot; might there not be a way to order him to behave appropriately?

There was no way of coming to a decision. Baley found himself watching for glimpses of continental outlines that he could recognize as Earthly or as non-Earthly. That would be the telling test—except that it didn't work.

The glimpses that came and went hazily through the clouds were of no use to him. He was not sufficiently knowledgeable about Earth's geography. What he really knew of Earth were its underground Cities, its caves of steel.

The bits of coastline he saw were unfamiliar to him—whether Aurora or Earth, he did not know.

Why this uncertainty, anyway? When he had gone to Solaria, he had never doubted his destination; he had never suspected that they might be bringing him back to Earth. —Ah, but then he had gone on a clear-cut mission in which there was reasonable chance for success. Now he felt there was no chance at all.

Perhaps it was, then, that he *wanted* to be returned to Earth and was building a false conspiracy in his mind so that he could imagine it possible.

The uncertainty in his mind had come to have a life of its own. He couldn't let go. He found himself watching Aurora with an almost mad intensity, unable to come back to the cabin-reality.

Aurora was moving, turning slowly—

He had watched long enough to see that. While he had been viewing space, everything had seemed motionless, like a painted backdrop, a silent and static pattern of dots of light, with, later on, a small half-circle included. Was it the motionlessness that had enabled him to be nonagoraphobic?

But now he could see Aurora moving and he realized that the ship was spiraling down in the final stage before landing. The clouds were bellying upward—

No, not the clouds; the ship was spiraling downward. The *ship* was moving. *He* was moving. He was suddenly aware of his own existence. He was hurtling downward through the clouds. He was falling, unguarded, through thin air toward solid ground.

His throat constricted; it was becoming very hard to breathe.

He told himself desperately: You are enclosed. The walls of the ship are around you.

But he sensed no walls.

He thought: Even without considering the walls, you are still enclosed. You are wrapped in skin.

But he sensed no skin.

The sensation was worse than simple nakedness—he was an unaccompanied personality, the essence of identity totally uncovered, a living point, a singularity surrounded by an open and infinite world, and he was falling.

He wanted to close off the vision, contract his fist upon the control-edge, but nothing happened. His nerve-endings had so abnormalized that the automatic contraction at an effort of will did not work. He had no will. Eyes would not close, fist would not contract. He was caught and hypnotized by terror, frightened into immobility.

All he sensed before him were clouds, white—not quite white —off-white—a slight golden-orange cast—

And all turned to gray—and he was drowning. He could not

breathe. He struggled desperately to open his clogged throat, to call to Daneel for help—

He could make no sound—

## 12.

Baley was breathing as though he had just breasted the tape at the end of a long race. The room was askew and there was a hard surface under his left elbow.

He realized he was on the floor.

Giskard was on his knees beside him, his robot's hand (firm but somewhat cold) closed on Baley's right fist. The door to the cabin, visible to Baley just beyond Giskard's shoulder, stood ajar.

Baley knew, without asking, what had happened. Giskard had seized that helpless human hand and clenched it upon the control-edge to end the astrosimulation. Otherwise—

Daneel was there as well, his face close to Baley's, with a look on it that might well have been pain.

He said, "You said nothing, Partner Elijah. Had I been more quickly aware of your discomfort—"

Baley tried to gesture that he understood, that it did not matter. He was still unable to speak.

The two robots waited until Baley made a feeble movement to get up. Arms were under him at once, lifting him. He was placed in a chair and the control was gently taken away from him by Giskard.

Giskard said, "We will be landing soon. You will have no further need of the astrosimulator, I believe."

Daneel added gravely, "It would be best to remove it, in any case."

Baley said, "Wait!" His voice was a hoarse whisper and he was not sure the word could be made out. He drew a deep breath, cleared his throat feebly, and said again, "Wait!"—and then, "Giskard."

Giskard turned back. "Sir?"

Baley did not speak at once. Now that Giskard knew he was

wanted, he would wait a lengthy interval, perhaps indefinitely. Baley tried to gather his scattered wits. Agoraphobia or not, there still remained his uncertainty about their destination. That had existed first and it might well have intensified the agoraphobia.

He had to find out. Giskard would not lie. A robot could not lie—unless very carefully instructed to do so. And why instruct Giskard? It was Daneel who was his companion, who was to be in his company at all times. If there was lying to be done, that would be Daneel's job. Giskard was merely a fetcher and carrier, a guard at the door. Surely there was no need to undergo the task of carefully instructing *him* in the web of lies.

"Giskard!" said Baley, almost normally now.

"Sir?"

"We are about to land, are we?"

"In a little less than two hours, sir."

That was two metric hours, thought Baley. More than two real hours? Less? It didn't matter. It would only confuse. Forget it.

Baley said, as sharply as he could manage, "Tell me right now the name of the planet we are about to land on."

A human being, if he had answered at all, would have done so only after a pause—and then with an air of considerable surprise.

Giskard answered at once, with a flat and uninflected assertion, "It is Aurora, sir."

"How do you know?"

"It is our destination. Then, too, it could not be Earth, for instance, since Aurora's sun, Tau Ceti, is only ninety percent the mass of Earth's sun. Tau Ceti is a little cooler, therefore, and its light has a distinct orange tinge to fresh and unaccustomed Earth eyes. You may have already seen the characteristic color of Aurora's sun in the reflection upon the upper surface of the cloud bank. You will certainly see it in the appearance of the landscape—until your eyes grow accustomed to it."

Baley's eyes left Giskard's impassive face. He *had* noticed the color difference, Baley thought, and had attached no importance to it. A bad error.

"You may go, Giskard."

"Yes, sir."

Baley turned bitterly to Daneel. "I've made a fool of myself, Daneel."

"I gather you wondered if perhaps we were deceiving you and taking you somewhere that was not Aurora. Did you have a reason for suspecting this, Partner Elijah?"

"None. It may have been the result of the uneasiness that arose from subliminal agoraphobia. Staring at seemingly motionless space, I felt no perceptible illness, but it may have lain just under the surface, creating a gathering uneasiness."

"The fault was ours, Partner Elijah. Knowing of your dislike for open spaces, it was wrong to subject you to astrosimulation or, having done so, to subject you to no closer supervision."

Baley shook his head in annoyance. "Don't say that, Daneel. I have supervision enough. The question in my mind is how closely I am to be supervised on Aurora itself."

Daneel said, "Partner Elijah, it seems to me it will be difficult to allow you free access to Aurora and Aurorans."

"That is just what I must be allowed, nevertheless. If I'm to get to the truth of this case of roboticide, I must be free to seek information directly on the site—and from the people involved."

Baley was, by now, feeling quite himself though a bit weary. Embarrassingly enough, the intense experience he had passed through left him with a keen desire for a pipe of tobacco, something he thought he had done away with altogether better than a year before. He could feel the taste and odor of the tobacco smoke making its way through his throat and nose.

He would, he knew, have to make do with the memory. On Aurora, he would on no account be allowed to smoke. There was no tobacco on any of the Spacer worlds and, if he had had any on him to begin with, it would have been removed and destroyed.

Daneel said, "Partner Elijah, this must be discussed with Dr. Fastolfe once we land. I have no power to make any decisions in this matter."

"I'm aware of that, Daneel, but how do I speak to Fastolfe? Through the equivalent of an astrosimulator? With controls in my hand?"

"Not at all, Partner Elijah. You will speak face-to-face. He plans to meet you at the spaceport."

## 13.

Baley listened for the noises of landing. He did not know what they might be, of course. He did not know the mechanism of the ship, how many men and women it carried, what they would have to do in the process of landing, what in the way of noise would be involved.

Shouts? Rumbles? A dim vibration?

He heard nothing.

Daneel said, "You seem to be under tension, Partner Elijah. I would prefer that you did not wait to tell me of any discomfort you might feel. I must help you at the very moment you are, for any reason, unhappy."

There was a faint stress on the word "must."

Baley thought absently: The First Law drives him. He surely suffered as much in his way as I suffered in mine when I collapsed and he did not foresee it in time. A forbidden imbalance of positronic potentials may have no meaning to me, but it may produce in him the same discomfort and the same reaction as acute pain would to me.

He thought further: How can I tell what exists inside the pseudoskin and pseudoconsciousness of a robot, any more than Daneel can tell what exists inside me.

And then, feeling remorse at having thought of Daneel as a robot, Baley looked into the other's gentle eyes (when did he start thinking of their expression as gentle?) and said, "I would tell you of any discomfort at once. There is none. I am merely trying to hear any noise that might tell me of the progress of the landing procedure, Partner Daneel."

"Thank you, Partner Elijah," said Daneel gravely. He bowed his head slightly and went on, "There should be no discomfort in the landing. You will feel acceleration, but that will be minimal, for this room will yield, to a certain extent, in the direction of the acceleration. The temperature may go up, but not more than two degrees Celsius. As for sonic effects, there may be a low hiss as we pass through the thickening atmosphere. Will any of this disturb you?"

"It shouldn't. What does disturb me is not being free to participate in the landing. I would like to know about such things. I do not want to be imprisoned and to be kept from the experience."

"You have already discovered, Partner Elijah, that the nature of the experience does not suit your temperament."

"And how am I to get over that, Daneel?," he said strenuously. "That is not enough reason to keep me here?"

"Partner Elijah, I have already explained that you are kept here for your own safety."

Baley shook his head in clear disgust. "I have thought of that and I say it's nonsense. My chances of straightening out this mess are so small, with all the restrictions being placed on me and with the difficulty I will have in understanding anything about Aurora, that I don't think anyone in his right mind would bother to take the trouble to try to stop me. And if they did, why bother attacking me personally? Why not sabotage the ship? If we imagine ourselves to be facing no-holds-barred villains, they should find a ship—and the people aboard it—and you and Giskard—and myself, of course—to be a small price to pay."

"This has, in point of fact, been considered, Partner Elijah. The ship has been carefully studied. Any signs of sabotage would be detected."

"Are you sure? One hundred percent certain?"

"Nothing of this sort can be absolutely certain. Giskard and I were comfortable, however, with the thought that the certainty was quite high and that we might proceed with minimal expectation of disaster."

"And if you were wrong?"

Something like a small sign of spasm crossed Daneel's face, as though he were being asked to consider something that interfered with the smooth working of the positronic pathways in his brain. He said, "But we have not been wrong."

"You cannot say that. We are approaching the landing and that is sure to be the danger moment. In fact, at this point there is no need to sabotage the ship. My personal danger is greatest now—right now. I can't hide in this room if I'm to disembark at Aurora. I will have to pass through the ship and be within reach of others. Have you taken precautions to keep the landing safe?" (He was being petty—striking out at Daneel needlessly because he was chafing at his long imprisonment—and at the indignity of his moment of collapse.)

But Daneel said calmly, "We have, Partner Elijah. And, incidentally, we have landed. We are now resting on the surface of Aurora."

For a moment, Baley was bewildered. He looked around wildly, but of course there was nothing to see but an enclosing room. He had felt and heard nothing of what Daneel had described. None of the acceleration, or heat, or wind whistle. —Or had Daneel deliberately brought up the matter of his personal danger once again, in order to make sure he would not think of other unsettling—but minor—matters.

Baley said, "And yet there's still the matter of getting off the ship. How do I do that without being vulnerable to possible enemies?"

Daneel walked to one wall and touched a spot upon it. The wall promptly split in two, the two halves moving apart. Baley found himself looking into a long cylinder, a tunnel.

Giskard had entered the room at that moment from the other side and said, "Sir, the three of us will move through the exit tube. Others have it under observation from without. At the other end of the tube, Dr. Fastolfe is waiting."

"We have taken every precaution," said Daneel.

Baley muttered, "My apologies, Daneel—Giskard." He moved into the exit tube somberly. Every effort to assure that precautions had been taken also assured him that those precautions were thought necessary.

Baley liked to think he was no coward, but he was on a strange planet, with no way of telling friend from enemy, with no way of taking comfort in anything familiar (except, of course, Daneel). At crucial moments, he thought with a shiver, he would be without enclosure to warm him and to give him relief.

# 4

## Fastolfe

*14.*

Dr. Han Fastolfe was indeed waiting—and smiling. He was tall and thin, with light brown hair that was not very thick, and there were, of course, his ears. It was the ears that Baley remembered, even after three years. Large ears, standing away from his head, giving him a vaguely humorous appearance, a pleasant homeliness. It was the ears that made Baley smile, rather than Fastolfe's welcome.

Baley wondered briefly if Auroran medical technology did not extend to the minor plastic surgery required to correct the ungainliness of those ears. —But then, it might well be that Fastolfe liked their appearance as Baley himself (rather to his surprise) did. There is something to be said about a face that makes one smile.

Perhaps Fastolfe valued being liked at first glance. Or was it that he found it useful to be underestimated? Or just different?

Fastolfe said, "Plainclothesman Elijah Baley. I remember you well, even though I persist in thinking of you as possessing the face of the actor who portrayed you."

Baley's face turned grim. "That hyperwave dramatization haunts me, Dr. Fastolfe. If I knew where I could go to escape it—"

"Nowhere," said Fastolfe genially. "At least ordinarily. So if you don't like it, we'll expunge it from our conversations right now. I shall never mention it again. Agreed?"

"Thank you." With calculated suddenness, he thrust out his hand at Fastolfe.

Fastolfe hesitated perceptibly. Then he took Baley's hand, holding it gingerly—and not for long—and said, "I shall assume you are not a walking sack of infection, Mr. Baley."

Then he said ruefully, staring at his hands, "I must admit, though, that my hands have been treated with an inert film that doesn't feel entirely comfortable. I'm a creature of the irrational fears of my society."

Baley shrugged. "So are we all. I do not relish the thought of being Outside—in the open air, that is. For that matter, I do not relish having had to come to Aurora under the circumstances in which I find myself."

"I understand that well, Mr. Baley. I have a closed car for you here and, when we come to my establishment, we will do our best to continue to keep you enclosed."

"Thank you, but in the course of my stay on Aurora, I feel that it will be necessary for me to stay Outside on occasion. I am prepared for that—as best I can be."

"I understand, but we will inflict the Outside on you only when it is necessary. That is not now the case, so please consent to be enclosed."

The car was waiting in the shadow of the tunnel and there would scarcely be a trace of Outside in passing from the latter to the former. Behind him, Baley was aware of both Daneel and Giskard, quite dissimilar in appearance but both identical in grave and waiting attitude—and both endlessly patient.

Fastolfe opened the back door and said, "Please to get in."

Baley entered. Quickly and smoothly, Daneel entered behind him, while Giskard, virtually simultaneously, in what seemed almost like a well-choreographed dance movement, entered on the other side. Baley found himself wedged, but not oppressively so, between them. In fact, he welcomed the thought that, between himself and the Outside, on both sides, was the thickness of a robotic body.

But there was no Outside. Fastolfe climbed into the front seat and, as the door closed behind him, the windows blanked out and a soft, artificial light suffused the interior.

Fastolfe said, "I don't generally drive this way, Mr. Baley, but I don't mind a great deal and you may find it more comfortable. The car is completely computerized, knows where it's going, and can deal with any obstructions or emergencies. We need interfere in no way."

There was the faintest feeling of acceleration and then a vague, barely noticeable sensation of motion.

Fastolfe said, "This is a secure passage, Mr. Baley. I have gone to considerable trouble to make certain that as few people as possible know you will be in this car and certainly you will not be detected within it. The trip by car—which rides on air-jets, by the way, so that it is an airfoil, actually—will not take long, but, if you wish, you can seize the opportunity to rest. You are quite safe now."

"You speak," said Baley, "as though you think I'm in danger. I was protected to the point of imprisonment on the ship—and again now." Baley looked about the small, enclosed interior of the car, within which he was hemmed by the frame of metal and opacified glass, to say nothing of the metallic frame of two robots.

Fastolfe laughed lightly. "I am overreacting, I know, but feeling runs high on Aurora. You arrive here at a time of crisis for us and I would rather be made to look silly by overreacting than to run the terrible risk that underreacting entails."

Baley said, "I believe you understand, Dr. Fastolfe, that my failure here would be a blow to Earth."

"I understand that well. I am as determined as you are to prevent your failure. Believe me."

"I do. Furthermore, my failure here, for whatever reason, will also be my personal and professional ruin on Earth."

Fastolfe turned in his seat to look at Baley with a shocked expression. "Really? That would not be warranted."

Baley shrugged. "I agree, but it will happen. I will be the obvious target for a desperate Earth government."

"This was not in my mind when I asked for you, Mr. Baley.

You may be sure I will do what I can. Though, in all honesty"—his eyes fell away—"that will be little enough, if we lose."

"I know that," said Baley dourly. He leaned back against the soft upholstery and closed his eyes. The motion of the car was limited to a gentle lulling sway, but Baley did not sleep. Instead, he thought hard—for what that was worth.

15.

Baley did not experience the Outside at the other end of the trip, either. When he emerged from the airfoil, he was in an underground garage and a small elevator brought him up to ground level (as it turned out).

He was ushered into a sunny room and, as he passed through the direct rays of the sun (yes, faintly orange), he shrank away a bit.

Fastolfe noticed. He said, "The windows are not opacifiable, though they can be darkened. I will do that, if you like. In fact, I should have thought of that—"

"No need," said Baley gruffly. "I'll just sit with my back to it. I must acclimate myself."

"If you wish, but let me know if, at any time, you grow too uncomfortable. —Mr. Baley, it is late morning here on this part of Aurora. I don't know your personal time on the ship. If you have been awake for many hours and would like to sleep, that can be arranged. If you are wakeful but not hungry, you need not eat. However, if you feel you can manage it, you are welcome to have lunch with me in a short while."

"That would fit in well with my personal time, as it happens."

"Excellent. I'll remind you that our day is about seven percent shorter than Earth's. It shouldn't involve you in too much biorhythmic difficulties, but if it does, we will try to adjust ourselves to your needs."

"Thank you."

"Finally— I have no clear idea what your food preferences might be."

"I'll manage to eat whatever is put before me."

"Nevertheless, I won't feel offended if anything seems—not palatable."

"Thank you."

"And you won't mind if Daneel and Giskard join us?"

Baley smiled faintly. "Will they be eating, too?"

There was no answering smile from Fastolfe. He said seriously, "No, but I want them to be with you at all times."

"Still danger? Even here?"

"I trust nothing entirely. Even here."

A robot entered. "Sir, lunch is served."

Fastolfe nodded. "Very good, Faber. We will be at the table in a few moments."

Baley said, "How many robots do you have?"

"Quite a few. We are not at the Solarian level of ten thousand robots to a human being, but I have more than the average number—fifty-seven. The house is a large one and it serves as my office and my workshop as well. Then, too, my wife, when I have one, must have space enough to be insulated from my work in a separate wing and must be served independently."

"Well, with fifty-seven robots, I imagine you can spare two. I feel the less guilty at your having sent Giskard and Daneel to escort me to Aurora."

"It was no casual choice, I assure you, Mr. Baley. Giskard is my majordomo and my right hand. He has been with me all my adult life."

"Yet you sent him on the trip to get me. I am honored," said Baley.

"It is a measure of your importance, Mr. Baley. Giskard is the most reliable of my robots, strong and sturdy."

Baley's eye flickered toward Daneel and Fastolfe added, "I don't include my friend Daneel in these calculations. He is not my servant, but an achievement of which I have the weakness to be extremely proud. He is the first of his class and, while Dr. Roj Nemennuh Sarton was his designer and model, the man who—"

He paused delicately, but Baley nodded brusquely and said, "I understand."

He did not require the phrase to be completed with a reference to Sarton's murder on Earth.

"While Sarton supervised the actual construction," Fastolfe went on, "it was I whose theoretical calculations made Daneel possible."

Fastolfe smiled at Daneel, who bowed his head in acknowledgment.

Baley said, "There was Jander, too."

"Yes." Fastolfe shook his head and looked downcast. "I should perhaps have kept him with me, as I do Daneel. But he *was* my second humaniform and that makes a difference. It is Daneel who is my first-born, so to speak—a special case."

"And you construct no more humaniform robots now?"

"No more. But come," said Fastolfe, rubbing his hands. "We must have our lunch. —I do not think, Mr. Baley, that on Earth the population is accustomed to what I might term natural food. We are having shrimp salad, together with bread and cheese, milk, if you wish, or any of an assortment of fruit juices. It's all very simple. Ice cream for dessert."

"All traditional Earth dishes," said Baley, "which exist now in their original form only in Earth's ancient literature."

"None of it is entirely common here on Aurora, but I didn't think it made sense to subject you to our own version of gourmet dining, which involves food items and spices of Auroran varieties. The taste would have to be acquired."

He rose. "Please come with me, Mr. Baley. There will just be the two of us and we will not stand on ceremony or indulge in unnecessary dining ritual."

"Thank you," said Baley. "I accept that as a kindness. I have relieved the tedium of the trip here by a rather intensive viewing of material relating to Aurora and I know that proper politeness requires many aspects to a ceremonial meal that I would dread."

"You need not dread."

Baley said, "Could we break ceremony even to the extent of talking business over the meal, Dr. Fastolfe? I must not lose time unnecessarily."

"I sympathize with that point of view. We will indeed talk business and I imagine I can rely on you to say nothing to anyone concerning that lapse. I would not want to be expelled from polite society." He chuckled, then said, "Though I should not laugh. It is nothing to laugh at. Losing time may be more than an inconvenience alone. It could easily be fatal."

## 16.

The room that Baley left was a spare one: several chairs, a chest of drawers, something that looked like a piano but had brass valves in the place of keys, some abstract designs on the walls that seemed to shimmer with light. The floor was a smooth checkerboard of several shades of brown, perhaps designed to be reminiscent of wood, and although it shone with highlights as though freshly waxed, it did not feel slippery underfoot.

The dining room, though it had the same floor, was like it in no other way. It was a long rectangular room, overburdened with decoration. It contained six large square tables that were clearly modules that could be assembled in various fashions. A bar was to be found along one short wall, with gleaming bottles of various colors standing before a curved mirror that seemed to lend a nearly infinite extension to the room it reflected. Along the other short wall were four recesses, in each of which a robot waited.

Both long walls were mosaics, in which the colors slowly changed. One was a planetary scene, though Baley could not tell if it were Aurora, or another planet, or something completely imaginary. At one end there was a wheat field (or something of that sort) filled with elaborate farm machinery, all robot-controlled. As one's eye traveled along the length of the wall, that gave way to scattered human habitations, becoming, at the other end, what Baley felt to be the Auroran version of a City.

The other long wall was astronomical. A planet, blue-white, lit by a distant sun, reflected light in such a manner that not the closest examination could free one from the thought that it was slowly rotating. The stars that surrounded it—some faint, some bright—seemed also to be changing their patterns, though when the eye concentrated on some small grouping and remained fixed there, the stars seemed immobile.

Baley found it all confusing and repellent.

Fastolfe said, "Rather a work of art, Mr. Baley. Far too expensive to be worth it, though, but Fanya would have it. —Fanya is my current partner."

"Will she be joining us, Dr. Fastolfe?"

"No, Mr. Baley. As I said, just the two of us. For the duration, I have asked her to remain in her own quarters. I do not want to subject her to this problem we have. You understand, I hope?"

"Yes, of course."

"Come. Please take your seat."

One of the tables was set with dishes, cups, and elaborate cutlery, not all of which were familiar to Baley. In the center was a tall, somewhat tapering cylinder that looked as though it might be a gigantic chess pawn made out of a gray rocky material.

Baley, as he sat down, could not resist reaching toward it and touching it with a finger.

Fastolfe smiled. "It's a spicer. It possesses simple controls that allows one to use it to deliver a fixed amount of any of a dozen different condiments on any portion of a dish. To do it properly, one picks it up and performs rather intricate evolutions that are meaningless in themselves but that are much valued by fashionable Aurorans as symbols of the grace and delicacy with which meals should be served. When I was younger, I could, with my thumb and two fingers, do the triple genuflection and produce salt as the spicer struck my palm. Now if I tried it, I'd run a good risk of braining my guest. I trust you won't mind if I do not try."

"I urge you not to try, Dr. Fastolfe."

A robot placed the salad on the table, another brought a tray of fruit juices, a third brought the bread and cheese, a fourth adjusted the napkins. All four operated in close coordination, weaving in and out without collision or any sign of difficulty. Baley watched them in astonishment.

They ended, without any apparent sign of prearrangements, one at each side of the table. They stepped back in unison, bowed in unison, turned in unison, and returned to the recesses along the wall at the far end of the room. Baley was suddenly aware of Daneel and Giskard in the room as well. He had not seen them come in. They waited in two recesses that had somehow appeared along the wall with the wheat field. Daneel was the closer.

Fastolfe said, "Now that they've gone—" He paused and shook his head slowly in rueful conclusion. "Except that they haven't. Ordinarily, it is customary for the robots to leave before lunch actually begins. Robots do not eat, while human beings do. It therefore makes sense that those who eat do so and that those who do not leave. And it has ended by becoming one more ritual. It would be quite unthinkable to eat until the robots left. In this case, though—"

"They have not left," said Baley.

"No. I felt that security came before etiquette and I felt that, not being an Auroran, you would not mind."

Baley waited for Fastolfe to make the first move. Fastolfe lifted a fork, so did Baley. Fastolfe made use of it, moving slowly and allowing Baley to see exactly what he was doing.

Baley bit cautiously into a shrimp and found it delightful. He recognized the taste, which was like the shrimp paste produced on Earth but enormously more subtle and rich. He chewed slowly and, for a while, despite his anxiety to get on with the investigation while dining, he found it quite unthinkable to do anything but give his full attention to the lunch.

It was, in fact, Fastolfe who made the first move. "Shouldn't we make a beginning on the problem, Mr. Baley?"

Baley felt himself flush slightly. "Yes. By all means. I ask your pardon. Your Auroran food caught me by surprise, so that it was difficult for me to think of anything else. —The problem, Dr. Fastolfe, is of your making, isn't it?"

"Why do you say that?"

"Someone has committed roboticide in a manner that requires great expertise—as I have been told."

"Roboticide? An amusing term." Fastolfe smiled. "Of course, I understand what you mean by it. —You have been told correctly; the manner requires *enormous* expertise."

"And only you have the expertise to carry it out—as I have been told."

"You have been told correctly there, too."

"And even you yourself admit—in fact, you insist—that only you could have put Jander into a mental freeze-out."

"I maintain what is, after all, the truth, Mr. Baley. It would do me no good to lie, even if I could bring myself to do so. It is notorious that I am the outstanding theoretical roboticist in all the Fifty Worlds."

"Nevertheless, Dr. Fastolfe, might not the second-best theoretical roboticist in all the worlds—or the third-best, or even the fifteenth-best—nevertheless possess the necessary ability to commit the deed? Does it really require all the ability of the very best?"

Fastolfe said calmly, "In my opinion, it really requires all the ability of the very best. Indeed, again in my opinion, I, myself, could only accomplish the task on one of my good days. Remember that the best brains in robotics—including mine—have specifically labored to design positronic brains that could *not* be driven into mental freeze-out."

"Are you certain of all that? Really certain?"

"Completely."

"And you stated so publicly?"

"Of course. There was a public inquiry, my dear Earthman. I was asked the questions you are now asking and I answered truthfully. It is an Auroran custom to do so."

Baley said, "I do not, at the moment, question that you were convinced you were answering truthfully. But might you not have been swayed by a natural pride in yourself? That might also be typically Auroran, might it not?"

"You mean that my anxiety to be considered the best would make me willingly put myself in a position where everyone would be forced to conclude I had mentally frozen Jander?"

"I picture you, somehow, as content to have your political and social status destroyed, provided your scientific reputation remained intact."

"I see. You have an interesting way of thinking, Mr. Baley. This would not have occurred to me. Given a choice between admitting I was second-best and admitting I was guilty of, to use your phrase, a roboticide, you are of the opinion I would knowingly accept the latter."

"No, Dr. Fastolfe, I do not wish to present the matter quite so simplistically. Might it not be that you deceive yourself into thinking you are the greatest of all roboticists and that you are completely unrivaled, clinging to that at all costs, because you unconsciously—*unconsciously*, Dr. Fastolfe—realize that, in fact, you are being overtaken—or have even already been overtaken —by others."

Fastolfe laughed, but there was an edge of annoyance in it. "Not so, Mr. Baley. Quite wrong."

"Think, Dr. Fastolfe! Are you certain that none of your roboticist colleagues can approach you in brilliance?"

"There are only a few who are capable of dealing at all with humaniform robots. Daneel's construction created virtually a new profession for which there is not even a name—humaniformicists, perhaps. Of the theoretical roboticists on Aurora, not one, except for myself, understands the workings of Daneel's positronic brain. Dr. Sarton did, but he is dead—and he did not understand it as well as I do. The basic theory is *mine*."

"It may have been yours to begin with, but surely you can't expect to maintain exclusive ownership. Has no one learned the theory?"

Fastolfe shook his head firmly. "Not one. I have taught no one and I defy any other living roboticist to have developed the theory on his own."

Baley said, with a touch of irritation, "Might there not be a bright young man, fresh out of the university, who is cleverer than anyone yet realizes, who—"

"*No*, Mr. Baley, no. I would have known such a young man. He would have passed through my laboratories. He would have worked with me. At the moment, no such young man exists. Eventually, one will; perhaps many will. At the moment, *none!*"

"If you died, then, the new science dies with you?"

"I am only a hundred and sixty-five years old. That's metric years, of course, so it is only a hundred and twenty-four of your Earth years, more or less. I am still quite young by Auroran standards and there is no medical reason why my life should be considered even half over. It is not entirely unusual to reach an age of four hundred years—metric years. There is yet plenty of time to teach."

They had finished eating, but neither man made any move to leave the table. Nor did any robot approach to clear it. It was as though they were transfixed into immobility by the intensity of the back and forth flow of talk.

Baley's eyes narrowed. He said, "Dr. Fastolfe, two years ago I was on Solaria. There I was given the clear impression that the Solarians were, on the whole, the most skilled roboticists in all the worlds."

"On the whole, that's probably true."

"And not one of them could have done the deed?"

"Not one, Mr. Baley. Their skill is with robots who are, at best, no more advanced than my poor, reliable Giskard. The Solarians know nothing of the construction of humaniform robots."

"How can you be sure of that?"

"Since you were on Solaria, Mr. Baley, you know very well that Solarians can approach each other with only the greatest of difficulty, that they interact by trimensional viewing—except where sexual contact is absolutely required. Do you think that any of them would dream of designing a robot so human in appearance that it would activate their neuroses? They would so avoid the possibility of approaching him, since he would look so human, that they could make no reasonable use of him."

"Might not a Solarian here or there display a surprising tolerance for the human body? How can you be sure?"

"Even if a Solarian could, which I do not deny, there are no Solarian nationals on Aurora this year."

"None?"

"None! They do not like to be thrown into contact even with Aurorans and, except on the most urgent business, none will come here—or to any other world. Even in the case of urgent business, they will come no closer than orbit and then they deal with us only by electronic communication."

Baley said, "In that case, if you are—literally and actually—

the only person in all the worlds who could have done it, *did* you kill Jander?"

Fastolfe said, "I cannot believe that Daneel did not tell you I have denied this deed."

"He did tell me so, but I want to hear it from *you.*"

Fastolfe crossed his arms and frowned. He said, through clenched teeth, "Then I'll tell you so. I did *not* do it."

Baley shook his head. "I believe you believe that statement."

"I do. And most sincerely. I am telling the truth. I did *not* kill Jander."

"But if you did not do it, and if no one else can possibly have done it, then— But wait. I am, perhaps, making an unwarranted assumption. Is Jander really dead or have I been brought here under false pretenses?"

"The robot is really destroyed. It will be quite possible to show him to you, if the Legislature does not bar my access to him before the day is over—which I don't think they will do."

"In that case, if you did not do it, and if no one else could possibly have done it, and if the robot is actually dead—who committed the crime?"

Fastolfe sighed. "I'm sure Daneel told you what I have maintained at the inquiry—but you want to hear it from my own lips."

"That is right, Dr. Fastolfe."

"Well, then, *no one* committed the crime. It was a spontaneous event in the positronic flow along the brain paths that set up the mental freeze-out in Jander."

"Is that likely?"

"No, it is not. It is extremely unlikely—but if I did not do it, then that is the only thing that can have happened."

"Might it not be argued that there is a greater chance that you are lying than that a spontaneous mental freeze-out took place."

"Many *do* so argue. But I happen to know that I did *not* do it and that leaves only the spontaneous event as a possibility."

"And you have had me brought here to demonstrate—to *prove* —that the spontaneous event did, in fact, take place?"

"Yes."

"But how does one go about proving the spontaneous event? Only by proving it, it seems, can I save you, Earth, and myself."

"In order of increasing importance, Mr. Baley?"

Baley looked annoyed. "Well, then, you, me, and Earth."

"I'm afraid," said Fastolfe, "that after considerable thought, I have come to the conclusion that there is no way of obtaining such a proof."

## 17.

Baley stared at Fastolfe in horror. "No way?"

"No way. None." And then, in a sudden fit of apparent abstraction, he seized the spicer and said, "You know, I am curious to see if I can still do the triple genuflection."

He tossed the spicer into the air with a calculated flip of the wrist. It somersaulted and, as it came down, Fastolfe caught the narrow end on the side of his right palm (his thumb tucked down). It went up slightly and swayed and was caught on the side of the left palm. It went up again in reverse and was caught on the side of the right palm and then again on the left palm. After this third genuflection, it was lifted with sufficient force to produce a flip. Fastolfe caught it in his right fist, with his left hand nearby, palm upward. Once the spicer was caught, Fastolfe displayed his left hand and there was a fine sprinkling of salt in it.

Fastolfe said, "It is a childish display to the scientific mind and the effort is totally disproportionate to the end, which is, of course, a pinch of salt, but the good Auroran host is proud of being able to put on a display. There are some experts who can keep the spicer in the air for a minute and a half, moving their hands almost more rapidly than the eye can follow.

"Of course," he added thoughtfully, "Daneel can perform such actions with greater skill and speed than any human. I have tested him in this manner in order to check on the workings of his brain paths, but it would be totally wrong to have him display such talents in public. It would needlessly humiliate human spicists—a popular term for them, you understand, though you won't find it in dictionaries."

Baley grunted.

Fastolfe sighed. "But we must get back to business."

"You brought me through several parsecs of space for that purpose."

"Indeed, I did. —Let us proceed!"

Baley said, "Was there a reason for that display of yours, Dr. Fastolfe?"

Fastolfe said, "Well, we seem to have come to an impasse. I've brought you here to do something that can't be done. Your face was rather eloquent and, to tell you the truth, I felt no better. It seemed, therefore, that we could use a breathing space. And now—let us proceed."

"On the impossible task?"

"Why should it be impossible for you, Mr. Baley? Your reputation is that of an achiever of the impossible."

"The hyperwave drama? You believe that foolish distortion of what happened on Solaria?"

Fastolfe spread his arms. "I have no other hope."

Baley said, "And I have no choice. I must continue to try; I cannot return to Earth a failure. That has been made clear to me. —Tell me, Dr. Fastolfe, how could Jander have been killed? What sort of manipulation of his mind would have been required?"

"Mr. Baley, I don't know how I could possibly explain that, even to another roboticist, which you certainly are not, and even if I were prepared to publish my theories, which I certainly am not. However, let me see if I can't explain something. —You know, of course, that robots were invented on Earth."

"Very little concerning robotics is dealt with on Earth—"

"Earth's strong antirobot bias is well-known on the Spacer worlds."

"But the Earthly origin of robots is obvious to any person on Earth who thinks about it. It is well-known that hyperspatial travel was developed with the aid of robots and, since the Spacer worlds could not have been settled without hyperspatial travel, it follows that robots existed before settlement had taken place and while Earth was still the only inhabited planet. Robots were therefore invented on Earth by Earthpeople."

"Yet Earth feels no pride in that, does it?"

"We do not discuss it," said Baley shortly.

"And Earthpeople know nothing about Susan Calvin?"

"I have come across her name in a few old books. She was one of the early pioneers in robotics."

"Is that all you know of her?"

Baley made a gesture of dismissal. "I suppose I could find out more if I searched the records, but I have had no occasion to do so."

"How strange," said Fastolfe. "She's a demigod to all Spacers, so much so that I imagine that few Spacers who are not actually roboticists think of her as an Earthwoman. It would seem a profanation. They would refuse to believe it if they were told that she died after having lived scarcely more than a hundred metric years. And yet you know her only as an early pioneer."

"Has she got something to do with all this, Dr. Fastolfe?"

"Not directly, but in a way. You must understand that numerous legends cluster about her name. Most of them are undoubtedly untrue, but they cling to her, nonetheless. One of the most famous legends—and one of the least likely to be true— concerns a robot manufactured in those primitive days that, through some accident on the production lines, turned out to have telepathic abilities—"

"What!"

"A legend! I told you it was a legend—and undoubtedly untrue! Mind you, there is some theoretical reason for supposing this might be possible, though no one has ever presented a plausible design that could even begin to incorporate such an ability. That it could have appeared in positronic brains as crude and simple as those in the prehyperspatial era is totally unthinkable. That is why we are quite certain that this particular tale is an invention. But let me go on anyway, for it points out a moral."

"By all means, go on."

"The robot, according to the tale, could read minds. And when asked questions, he read the questioner's mind and told the questioner what he wanted to hear. Now the First Law of Robotics states quite clearly that a robot may not injure a human being or, through inaction, allow a person to come to harm, but to robots generally that means physical harm. A robot who can read minds, however, would surely decide that disappointment or anger or any violent emotion would make the human being feeling those emotions unhappy and the robot would interpret the inspiring of such emotions under the heading of 'harm.' If, then, a telepathic robot knew that the truth might disappoint or enrage a questioner or cause that person to feel envy or unhappiness, he would tell a pleasing lie, instead. Do you see that?"

"Yes, of course."

"So the robot lied even to Susan Calvin herself. The lies could not long continue, for different people were told different things that were not only inconsistent among themselves but unsupported by the gathering evidence of reality, you see. Susan Calvin discovered she had been lied to and realized that those lies had led her into a position of considerable embarrassment. What would have disappointed her somewhat to begin with had now, thanks to false hopes, disappointed her unbearably. —You never heard the story?"

"I give you my word."

"Astonishing! Yet it certainly wasn't invented on Aurora, for it is equally current on all the worlds. —In any case, Calvin took her revenge. She pointed out to the robot that, whether he told the truth or told a lie, he would equally harm the person with whom he dealt. He could not obey the First Law, whatever action he took. The robot, understanding this, was forced to take refuge in total inaction. If you want to put it colorfully, his positronic pathways burned out. His brain was irrecoverably destroyed. The legend goes on to say that Calvin's last word to the destroyed robot was '*Liar!*'"

Baley said, "And something like this, I take it, was what happened to Jander Panell. He was faced with a contradiction in terms and his brain burned out?"

"It's what *appears* to have happened, though that is not as easy to bring about as it would have been in Susan Calvin's day.

Possibly because of the legend, roboticists have always been careful to make it as difficult as possible for contradictions to arise. As the theory of positronic brains has grown more subtle and as the practice of positronic brain design has grown more intricate, increasingly successful systems have been devised to have all situations that might arise resolve into nonequality, so that some action can always be taken that will be interpreted as obeying the First Law."

"Well, then, you can't burn out a robot's brain. Is that what you're saying? Because if you are, what happened to Jander?"

"It's *not* what I'm saying. The increasingly successful systems I speak of, are never *completely* successful. They cannot be. No matter how subtle and intricate a brain might be, there is always some way of setting up a contradiction. That is a fundamental truth of mathematics. It will remain forever impossible to produce a brain so subtle and intricate as to reduce the chance of contradiction to zero. Never quite to zero. However, the systems have been made so close to zero that to bring about a mental freeze-out by setting up a suitable contradiction would require a deep understanding of the particular positronic brain being dealt with—and *that* would take a clever theoretician."

"Such as yourself, Dr. Fastolfe?"

"Such as myself. In the case of humaniform robots, *only* myself."

"Or no one at all," said Baley, heavily ironic.

"Or no one at all. Precisely," said Fastolfe, ignoring the irony. "The humaniform robots have brains—and, I might add, bodies —constructed in conscious imitation of the human being. The positronic brains are extraordinarily delicate and they take on some of the fragility of the human brain, naturally. Just as a human being may have a stroke, though some chance event within the brain and without the intervention of any external effect, so a humaniform brain might, through chance alone—the occasional aimless drifting of positrons—go into mental freeze."

"Can you prove that, Dr. Fastolfe?"

"I can demonstrate it mathematically, but of those who could follow the mathematics, not all would agree that the reasoning was valid. It involves certain suppositions of my own that do not fit into the accepted modes of thinking in robotics."

"And how likely is spontaneous mental freeze-out?"

"Given a large number of humaniform robots, say a hundred thousand, there is an even chance that one of them might undergo spontaneous mental freeze-out in an average Auroran lifetime. And yet it could happen much sooner, as it did to Jander, although then the odds would be very greatly against it."

"But look here, Dr. Fastolfe, even if you were to prove conclusively that a spontaneous mental freeze-out *could* take place in robots generally, that would not be the same as proving that such a thing happened to Jander in particular at this particular time."

"No," admitted Fastolfe, "you are quite right."

"You, the greatest expert in robotics, cannot prove it in the specific case of Jander."

"Again, you are quite right."

"Then what do you expect me to be able to do, when I know nothing of robotics."

"There is no need to *prove* anything. It would surely be sufficient to present an ingenious suggestion that would make spontaneous mental freeze-out plausible to the general public."

"Such as—"

"I don't know."

Baley said harshly, "Are you sure you don't know, Dr. Fastolfe?"

"What do you mean? I have just said I don't know."

"Let me point out something. I assume that Aurorans, generally, know that I have come to the planet for the purpose of tackling this problem. It would be difficult to manage to get me here secretly, considering that I am an Earthman and this is Aurora."

"Yes, certainly, and I made no attempt to do that. I consulted the Chairman of the Legislature and persuaded him to grant me permission to bring you here. It is how I've managed to win a stay in judgment. You are to be given a chance to solve the mystery before I go on trial. I doubt that they'll give me a very long stay."

"I repeat, then— Aurorans, in general, know I'm here and I imagine they know precisely why I am here—that I am supposed to solve the puzzle of the death of Jander."

"Of course. What other reason could there be?"

"And from the time I boarded the ship that brought me here, you have kept me under close and constant guard because of the danger that your enemies might try to eliminate me—judging me to be some sort of wonderman who just might solve the puzzle in such a way as to place you on the winning side, even though all the odds are against me."

"I fear that as a possibility, yes."

"And suppose someone who does not want to see the puzzle solved and you, Dr. Fastolfe, exonerated should actually succeed in killing me. Might that not swing sentiment in your favor? Might not people reason that your enemies felt you were, in actual fact, innocent or they would not fear the investigation so much that they would want to kill me?"

"Rather complicated reasoning, Mr. Baley. I suppose that, properly exploited, your death might be used to such a purpose, but it's not going to happen. You are being protected and you will not be killed."

"But *why* protect me, Dr. Fastolfe? Why not let them kill me and use my death as a way of winning?"

"Because I would rather you remained alive and succeeded in actually demonstrating my innocence."

Baley said, "But surely you know that I *can't* demonstrate your innocence."

"Perhaps you can. You have every incentive. The welfare of Earth hangs on your doing so and, as you have told me, your own career."

"What good is incentive? If you ordered me to fly by flapping my arms and told me further that if I failed, I would be promptly killed by slow torture and that Earth would be blown up and all its population destroyed, I would have enormous incentive to flap my wings and fly—and yet still be unable to do so."

Fastolfe said uneasily, "I know the chances are small."

"You know they are nonexistent," said Baley violently, "and that only my death can save you."

"Then I will not be saved, for I am seeing to it that my enemies cannot reach you."

"But *you* can reach me."

"What?"

"I have the thought in my head, Dr. Fastolfe, that you yourself might kill me in such a way as to make it appear that your enemies have done the deed. You would then use my death against them—and that that is why you have brought me to Aurora."

For a moment, Fastolfe looked at Baley with a kind of mild surprise and then, in an excess of passion both sudden and extreme, his face reddened and twisted into a snarl. Sweeping up the spicer from the table, he raised it high and brought his arm down to hurl it at Baley.

And Baley, caught utterly by surprise, barely managed to cringe back against his chair.

# 5

# Daneel and Giskard

## 18.

If Fastolfe had acted quickly, Daneel had reacted far more quickly still.

To Baley, who had all but forgotten Daneel's existence, there seemed a vague rush, a confused sound, and then Daneel was standing to one side of Fastolfe, holding the spicer, and saying, "I trust, Dr. Fastolfe, that I did not in any way hurt you."

Baley noted, in a dazed sort of way, that Giskard was not far from Fastolfe on the other side and that every one of the four robots at the far wall had advanced almost to the dining room table.

Panting slightly, Fastolfe, his hair quite disheveled, said, "No, Daneel. You did very well, indeed." He raised his voice. "You all did well, but remember, you must allow nothing to slow you down, even my own involvement."

He laughed softly and took his seat once more, straightening his hair with his hand.

"I'm sorry," he said, "to have startled you so, Mr. Baley, but I felt the demonstration might be more convincing than any words of mine would have been."

Baley, whose moment of cringing had been purely a matter of reflex, loosened his collar and said, with a touch of hoarseness, "I'm afraid I expected words, but I agree the demonstration was convincing. I'm glad that Daneel was close enough to disarm you."

"Any one of them was close enough to disarm me, but Daneel was the closest and got to me first. He got to me quickly enough to be gentle about it. Had he been farther away, he might have had to wrench my arm or even knock me out."

"Would he have gone that far?"

"Mr. Baley," said Fastolfe. "I have given instructions for your protection and I *know* how to give instructions. They would not have hesitated to save you, even if the alternative was harm to me. They would, of course, have labored to inflict minimum harm, as Daneel did. All he harmed was my dignity and the neatness of my hair. And my fingers tingle a bit." Fastolfe flexed them ruefully.

Baley drew a deep breath, trying to recover from that short period of confusion. He said, "Would not Daneel have protected me, even without your specific instruction?"

"Undoubtedly. He would have had to. You must not think, however, that robotic response is a simple yes or no, up or down, in or out. It is a mistake the layman often makes. There is the matter of speed of response. My instructions with regard to you were so phrased that the potential built up within the robots of my establishment, including Daneel, is abnormally high, as high as I can reasonably make it, in fact. The response, therefore, to a clear and present danger to you is extraordinarily rapid. I knew it would be and it was for that reason that I could strike out at you as rapidly as I did—knowing I could give you a *most* convincing demonstration of my inability to harm you."

"Yes, but I don't entirely thank you for it."

"Oh, I was entirely confident in my robots, especially Daneel. It did occur to me, though, a little too late, that if I had not instantly released the spicer, he might, quite against his will—or the robotic equivalent of will—have broken my wrist."

Baley said, "It occurs to me that it was a foolish risk for you to have undertaken."

"It occurs to me, as well—after the fact. Now if you had prepared yourself to hurl the spicer at me, Daneel would have at once countered your move, but not with quite the same speed, for he has received no special instructions as to my safety. I can hope he would have been fast enough to save me, but I'm not sure—and I would prefer not to test that matter." Fastolfe smiled genially.

Baley said, "What if some explosive device were dropped on the house from some airborne vehicle?"

"Or if a gamma beam were trained upon us from a neighboring hilltop. —My robots do not represent infinite protection, but such radical terrorist attempts are unlikely in the extreme here on Aurora. I suggest we do not worry about them."

"I am willing not to worry about them. Indeed, I did not seriously suspect that you were a danger to me, Dr. Fastolfe, but I needed to eliminate the possibility altogether if I were to continue. We can now proceed."

Fastolfe said, "Yes, we can. Despite this additional and very dramatic distraction, we still face the problem of proving that Jander's mental freeze-out was spontaneous chance."

But Baley had been made aware of Daneel's presence and he now turned to him and said uneasily, "Daneel, does it pain you that we discuss this matter?"

Daneel, who had deposited the spicer on one of the farther of the empty tables, said, "Partner Elijah, I would prefer that past-friend Jander were still operational, but since he is not and since he cannot be restored to proper functioning, the best of what is left is that action be taken to prevent similar incidents in the future. Since the discussion now has that end in view, it pleases rather than pains me."

"Well, then, just to settle another matter, Daneel, do *you* believe that Dr. Fastolfe is responsible for the end of your fellow-robot Jander? —You'll pardon my inquiring, Dr. Fastolfe?"

Fastolfe gestured his approval and Daneel said, "Dr. Fastolfe has stated that he was not responsible, so he, of course, was not."

"You have no doubts on the matter, Daneel?"

"None, Partner Elijah."

Fastolfe seemed a little amused. "You are cross-examining a robot, Mr. Baley."

"I know that, but I cannot quite think of Daneel as a robot and so I have asked."

"His answers would have no standing before any Board of Inquiry. He is compelled to believe me by his positronic potentials."

"I am not a Board of Inquiry, Dr. Fastolfe, and I am clearing out the underbrush. Let me go back to where I was. Either you burned out Jander's brain or it happened by random circumstance. You assure me that I cannot prove random circumstance and that leaves me only with the task of disproving any action by you. In other words, if I can show that it is *impossible* for you to have killed Jander, we are left with random circumstance as the only alternative."

"And how can you do that?"

"It is a matter of means, opportunity, and motive. You had the means of killing Jander—the theoretical ability to so manipulate him that he would end in a mental freeze-out. But did you have the opportunity? He was your robot, in that you designed his brain paths and supervised his construction, but was he in your actual possession at the time of the mental freeze-out?"

"No, as a matter of fact. He was in the possession of another."

"For how long?"

"About eight months—or a little over half of one of your years."

"Ah. It's an interesting point. Were you with him—or near him—at the time of his destruction? Could you have reached him? In short, can we demonstrate the fact that you were so far from him—or so out of touch with him—that it is not reasonable to suppose that you could have done the deed at the time it is supposed to have been done?"

Fastolfe said, "That, I'm afraid, is impossible. There is a rather broad interval of time during which the deed might have been done. There are no robotic changes after destruction equivalent to rigor mortis or decay in a human being. We can only say that, at a certain time, Jander was known to be in operation and, at a certain other time, he was known not to be in operation. Between the two was a stretch of about eight hours. For that period, I have no alibi."

"None? During that time, Dr. Fastolfe, what were you doing?"

"I was here in my establishment."

"Your robots were surely aware, perhaps, that you were here and could bear witness."

"They were certainly aware, but they cannot bear witness in any legal sense and on that day Fanya was off on business of her own."

"Does Fanya share your knowledge of robotics, by the way?"

Fastolfe indulged in a wry smile. "She knows less than you do. —Besides, none of this matters."

"Why not?"

Fastolfe's patience was clearly beginning to stretch to the cracking point. "My dear Mr. Baley, this was not a matter of close-range physical assault, such as my recent pretended attack on you. What happened to Jander did not require my physical presence. As it happens, although not actually in my establishment, Jander was not far away geographically, but it wouldn't have mattered if he were on the other side of Aurora. I could always reach him electronically and could, by the orders I gave him and the responses I could educe, send him into mental freeze-out. The crucial step would not even necessarily require much in the way of time—"

Baley said at once, "It's a short process, then, one that someone else might move through by chance, while intending something perfectly routine?"

"No!" said Fastolfe. "For Aurora's sake, Earthman, let me talk. I've already told you that's not the case. Inducing mental freeze-out in Jander would be a long and complicated and tortuous process, requiring the greatest understanding and wit, and could be done by *no one* accidentally, without incredible and long-continued coincidence. There would be far less chance of accidental progress over that enormously complex route than of spontaneous mental freeze-out, if my mathematical reasoning were only accepted.

"However, if *I* wished to induce mental freeze-out, I could carefully produce changes and reactions, little by little, over a period of weeks, months, even years, until I had brought Jander to the very point of destruction. And at no time in that process would he show any signs of being at the edge of catastrophe, just as you could approach closer and closer to a precipice in the dark and yet feel no loss in firmness of footing whatever, even at the very edge. Once I had brought him to the very brink, how-ever—the lip of the precipice—a single remark from me would send him over. It is that final step that would take but a moment of time. You see?"

Baley tightened his lips. There was no use trying to mask his disappointment. "In short, then, you had the opportunity."

"*Anyone* would have had the opportunity. Anyone on Aurora, provided he or she had the necessary ability."

"And only you have the necessary ability."

"I'm afraid so."

"Which brings us to motive, Dr. Fastolfe."

"Ah."

"And it's there that we might be able to make a good case. These humaniform robots are yours. They are based on your theory and you were involved in their construction at every step of the way, even if Dr. Sarton supervised that construction. They exist because of you and *only* because of you. You have spoken of Daneel as your 'first-born.' They are your creations, your chil-dren, your gift to humanity, your hold on immortality." (Baley felt himself growing eloquent and, for a moment, imagined him-self to be addressing a Board of Inquiry.) "Why on Earth—or Aurora, rather—why on Aurora should you undo this work? Why should you destroy a life you have produced by a miracle of mental labor?"

Fastolfe looked wanly amused. "Why, Mr. Baley, you know nothing about it. How can you possibly know that my theory was the result of a miracle of mental labor? It might have been the very dull extension of an equation that anyone might have accomplished but which none had bothered to do before me."

"I think not," said Baley, endeavoring to cool down. "If no one but you can understand the humaniform brain well enough to destroy it, then I think it likely that no one but you can under-stand it well enough to create it. Can you deny that?"

Fastolfe shook his head. "No, I won't deny that. And yet, Mr. Baley"—his face grew grimmer than it had been since they had met—"your careful analysis is succeeding only in making mat-ters far worse for us. We have already decided that I am the only one with the means and the opportunity. As it happens, I also have a motive—the best motive in the world—and my enemies know it. How on Earth, then, to quote you—or on Aurora, or on anywhere—are we going to prove I didn't do it?"

### 19.

Baley's face crumpled into a furious frown. He stepped hastily away, making for the corner of the room, as though seeking enclosure. Then he turned suddenly and said sharply, "Dr. Fastolfe, it seems to me that you are taking some sort of pleasure in frustrating me."

Fastolfe shrugged. "No pleasure. I'm merely presenting you with the problem as it is. Poor Jander died the robotic death by the pure uncertainty of positronic drift. Since I know I had nothing to do with it, I know that's how it must be. However, no one else can be sure I'm innocent and all the indirect evidence points to me—and this must be faced squarely in deciding what, if anything, we can do."

Baley said, "Well, then, let's investigate your motive. What seems like an overwhelming motive to you may be nothing of the sort."

"I doubt that. I am no fool, Mr. Baley."

"You are also no judge, perhaps, of yourself and your motives. People sometimes are not. You may be dramatizing yourself for some reason."

"I don't think so."

"Then tell me your motive. What is it? Tell me!"

"Not so quickly, Mr. Baley. It's not easy to explain it. —Could you come outside with me?"

Baley looked quickly toward the window. Outside?

The sun had sunk lower in the sky and the room was the sunnier for it. He hesitated, then said, rather more loudly than was necessary, "Yes, I will!"

"Excellent," said Fastolfe. And then, with an added note of amiability, he added, "But perhaps you would care to visit the Personal first."

Baley thought for a moment. He felt no immediate urgency, but he did not know what might await him Outside, how long he would be expected to stay, what facilities there might or might not be there. Most of all, he did not know Auroran customs in this respect and he could not recall anything in the book-films he had viewed on the ship that served to enlighten him in this respect. It was safest, perhaps, to acquiesce in whatever one's host suggested.

"Thank you," he said, "if it will be convenient for me to do so."

Fastolfe nodded. "Daneel," he said, "show Mr. Baley to the Visitors' Personal."

Daneel said, "Partner Elijah, would you come with me?"

As they stepped together into the next room, Baley said, "I am sorry, Daneel, that you were not part of the conversation between myself and Dr. Fastolfe."

"It would not have been fitting, Partner Elijah. When you asked me a direct question, I answered, but I was not invited to take part fully."

"I would have issued the invitation, Daneel, if I did not feel constrained by my position as guest. I thought it might be wrong to take the initiative in this respect."

"I understand. —This is the Visitors' Personal, Partner Elijah. The door will open at a touch of your hand anywhere upon it if the room is unoccupied."

Baley did not enter. He paused thoughtfully, then said, "If you *had* been invited to speak, Daneel, is there anything you would have said? Any comment you would have cared to make? I would value your opinion, my friend."

Daneel said, with his usual gravity, "The one remark I care to make is that Dr. Fastolfe's statement that he had an excellent motive for placing Jander out of operation was unexpected to me. I do not know what the motive might be. Whatever he states to be his motive, however, you might ask why he would not have the same motive to put me in mental freeze-out. If they can believe he had a motive to put Jander out of operation, why would the same motive not apply to me? I would be curious to know."

Baley looked at the other sharply, seeking automatically for expression in a face not given to lack of control. He said, "Do you feel insecure, Daneel? Do you feel Fastolfe is a danger to you?"

Daneel said, "By the Third Law, I must protect my own existence, but I would not resist Dr. Fastolfe or any human being if it were their considered opinion that it was necessary to end my existence. That is the Second Law. However, I know that I am of great value, both in terms of investment of material, labor, and time, and in terms of scientific importance. It would therefore be necessary to explain to me carefully the reasons for the necessity of ending my existence. Dr. Fastolfe has never said anything to me—*never*, Partner Elijah—that would sound as though such a thing were in his mind. I do not believe it is remotely in his mind to end my existence or that it ever was in his mind to end Jander's existence. Random positronic drift must have ended Jander and may, someday, end me. There is always an element of chance in the Universe."

Baley said, "You say so, Fastolfe says so, and I believe so—but the difficulty is to persuade people generally to accept this view of the matter." He turned gloomily to the door of the Personal and said, "Are you coming in with me, Daneel?"

Daneel's expression contrived to seem amused. "It is flattering, Partner Elijah, to be taken for human to this extent. I have no need, of course."

"Of course. But you can enter anyway."

"It would not be appropriate for me to enter. It is not the custom for robots to enter the Personal. The interior of such a room is purely human. —Besides, this is a one-person Personal."

"One person!" Momentarily, Baley was shocked. He rallied, however. Other worlds, other customs! And this one he did not recall being described in the book-films. He said, "That's what you meant, then, by saying that the door would open only if it were unoccupied. What if it is occupied, as it will be in a moment?"

"Then it will *not* open at a touch from outside, of course, and your privacy will be protected. Naturally, it will open at a touch from the inside."

"And what if a visitor fell into a faint, had a stroke or a heart seizure while in there and could not touch the door from inside. Wouldn't that mean no one could enter to help him?"

"There are emergency ways of opening the door, Partner Elijah, if that should seem advisable." Then, clearly disturbed, "Are you of the opinion that something of this sort will occur?"

"No, of course not. —I am merely curious."

"I will be immediately outside the door," said Daneel uneasily. "If I hear a call, Partner Elijah, I will take action."

"I doubt that you'll have to." Baley touched the door, casually and lightly, with the back of his hand and it opened at once. He waited a moment or two to see if it would close. It didn't. He stepped through and the door then closed promptly.

While the door was open, the Personal had seemed like a room that flatly served its purpose. A sink, a stall (presumably equipped with a shower arrangement), a tub, a translucent half-door with a toilet seat beyond in all likelihood. There were several devices that he did not quite recognize. He assumed they were intended for the fulfillment of personal services of one sort or another.

He had little chance to study any of these, for in a moment it was all gone and he was left to wonder if what he had seen had really been there at all or if the devices had seemed to exist because they were what he had expected to see.

As the door closed, the room darkened, for there was no window. When the door was completely closed, the room lit up again, but nothing of what he had seen returned. It was daylight and he was Outside—or so it appeared.

There was open sky above, with clouds drifting across it in a fashion just regular enough to seem clearly unreal. On every side there seemed an outstretching of greenery moving in equally repetitive fashion.

He felt the familiar knotting of his stomach that arose whenever he found himself Outside—but he was *not* Outside. He had walked into a windowless room. It had to be a trick of the lighting.

He stared directly ahead of him and slowly slid his feet forward. He put his hands out before him. Slowly. Staring hard.

His hands touched the smoothness of a wall. He followed the

flatness to either side. He touched what he had seen to be a sink in that moment of original vision and, guided by his hands, he could see it now—faintly, faintly against the overpowering sensation of light.

He found the faucet, but no water came from it. He followed its curve backward and found nothing that was the equivalent of the familiar handles that would control the flow of water. He did find an oblong strip whose slight roughness marked it off from the surrounding wall. As his fingers slid along it, he pushed slightly and experimentally against it and at once the greenery, which stretched far beyond the plane along which his fingers told him the wall existed, was parted by a rivulet of water, falling quickly from a height toward his feet with a loud noise of splashing.

He jumped backward in automatic panic, but the water ended before it reached his feet. It didn't stop coming, but it didn't reach the floor. He put his hand out. It was not water, but a light-illusion of water. It did not wet his hand; he felt nothing. But his eyes stubbornly resisted the evidence. They saw water.

He followed the rivulet upward and eventually came to something that *was* water—a thinner stream issuing from the faucet. It was cold.

His fingers found the oblong again and experimented, pushing here and there. The temperature shifted quickly and he found the spot that produced water of suitable tepidity.

He did not find any soap. Somewhat reluctantly, he began to rub his unsoaped hands against each other under what seemed a natural spring that should have been soaking him from head to foot but did not. And as though the mechanism could read his mind or, more likely, was guided by the rubbing together of his hands, he felt the water grow soapy, while the spring he did/ didn't see grew bubbles and developed into foam.

Still reluctant, he bent over the sink and rubbed his face with the same soapy water. He felt the bristles of his beard, but knew that there was no way in which he could translate the equipment of this room into a shave without instruction.

He finished and held his hands helplessly under the water. How did he stop the soap? He did not have to ask. Presumably, his hands, no longer rubbing either themselves or his face, controlled that. The water lost its soapy feel and the soap was rinsed from his hands. He splashed the water against his face—without rubbing—and that was rinsed too. Without the help of vision and with the clumsiness of one unused to the process, he managed to soak his shirt badly.

Towels? Paper?

He stepped back, eyes closed, holding his head forward to avoid dripping more water on his clothes. Stepping back was, apparently, the key action, for he felt the warm flow of an air current. He placed his face within it and then his hands.

He opened his eyes and found the spring no longer flowing. He used his hands and found that he could feel no real water.

The knot in his stomach had long since dissolved into irritation. He recognized that Personals varied enormously from world to world, but somehow this nonsense of simulated Outside went too far.

On Earth, a Personal was a huge community chamber restricted to one gender, with private cubicles to which one had a key. On Solaria, one entered a Personal through a narrow corridor appended to one side of a house, as though Solarians hoped that it would not be considered a part of their home. In both worlds, however, though so different in every possible way, the Personals were clearly defined and the function of everything in them could not be mistaken. Why should there be, on Aurora, this elaborate pretense of rusticity that totally masked every part of a Personal?

Why?

At any rate, his annoyance gave him little emotional room in which to feel uneasy over the pretense of Outside. He moved in the direction in which he recalled having seen the translucent half-door.

It was not the correct direction. He found it only by following the wall slowly and after barking various parts of his body against protuberances.

In the end, he found himself urinating into the illusion of a small pond that did not seem to be receiving the stream properly. His knees told him that he was aiming correctly between the sides of what he took to be a urinal and he told himself that if he were using the wrong receptacle or misjudging his aim, the fault was not his.

For a moment, when done, he considered finding the sink again for a final hand rinse and decided against it. He just couldn't face the search and that false waterfall.

Instead, he found, by groping, the door through which he had entered, but he did not know he had found it until his hand touch resulted in its opening. The light died out at once and the normal nonillusory gleam of day surrounded him.

Daneel was waiting for him, along with Fastolfe and Giskard.

Fastolfe said, "You took nearly twenty minutes. We were beginning to fear for you."

Baley felt himself grow warm with rage. "I had problems with your foolish illusions," he said in a tightly controlled fashion.

Fastolfe's mouth pursed and his eyebrows rose in a silent: Oh-h!

He said, "There is a contact just inside the door that controls the illusion. It can make it dimmer and allow you to see reality through it—or it can wipe out the illusion altogether, if you wish."

"I was not told. Are all your Personals like this?"

Fastolfe said, "No. Personals on Aurora commonly possess illusory qualities, but the nature of the illusion varies with the individual. The illusion of natural greenery pleases me and I vary its details from time to time. One grows tired of anything, you know, after a while. There are some people who make use of erotic illusions, but that is not to my taste.

"Of course, when one is familiar with Personals, the illusions offer no trouble. The rooms are quite standard and one knows where everything is. It's no worse than moving about a well-known place in the dark. —But tell me, Mr. Baley, why didn't you find your way out and ask for directions?"

Baley said, "Because I didn't wish to. I admit that I was extremely irritated over the illusions, but I accepted them. After all, it was Daneel who led me to the Personal and he gave me no instructions, nor any warning. He would certainly have instructed me at length, if he had been left to his own devices, for he would surely have foreseen harm to me otherwise. I had to assume, therefore, that you had carefully instructed him not to warn me and, since I didn't really expect you to play a practical joke on me, I had to assume that you had a serious purpose in doing so."

"Oh?"

"After all, you had asked me to come Outside and, when I agreed, you immediately asked me if I wished to visit the Personal. I decided that the purpose of sending me into an illusion of Outside was to see whether I could endure it—or if I would come running out in panic. If I could endure it, I might be trusted with the real thing. Well, I endured it. I'm a little wet, thank you, but that will dry soon enough."

Fastolfe said, "You are a clear-thinking person, Mr. Baley. I apologize for the nature of the test and for the discomfort I caused you. I was merely trying to ward off the possibility of far greater discomfort. Do you still wish to come out with me?"

"I not only wish it, Dr. Fastolfe. I insist on it."

### 20.

They made their way through a corridor, with Daneel and Giskard following close behind.

Fastolfe said chattily, "I hope you won't mind the robots accompanying us. Aurorans never go anywhere without at least one robot in attendance and, in your case in particular, I must insist that Daneel and Giskard be with you at all times."

He opened a door and Baley tried to stand firm against the beat of sunshine and wind, to say nothing of the envelopment of the strange and subtly alien smell of Aurora's land.

Fastolfe stayed to one side and Giskard went out first. The robot looked keenly about for a few moments. One had the impression that all his senses were intently engaged. He looked back and Daneel joined him and did the same.

"Leave them for a moment, Mr. Baley," said Fastolfe, "and they will tell us when they think it safe for us to emerge. Let me take the opportunity of once again apologizing for the scurvy trick I played on you with respect to the Personal. I assure you we would have known if you were in trouble—your various vital signs were being recorded. I am very pleased, though not entirely surprised, that you penetrated my purpose." He smiled and, with almost unnoticeable hesitation, placed his hand upon Baley's left shoulder and gave it a friendly squeeze.

Baley held himself stiffly. "You seem to have forgotten your earlier scurvy trick—your apparent attack on me with the spicer. If you will assure me that we will now deal with each other frankly and honestly, I will consider these matters as having been of reasonable intent."

"Done!"

"Is it safe to leave now?" Baley looked out to where Giskard and Daneel had moved farther and had separated from each other to right and left, still watching and sensing.

"Not quite yet. They will move all around the establishment. —Daneel tells me that you invited him into the Personal with you. Was that seriously meant?"

"Yes. I knew he had no need, but I felt it might be impolite to exclude him. I wasn't sure of Auroran custom in that respect, despite all the reading I did on Auroran matters."

"I suppose that isn't one of those things Aurorans feel necessary to mention and of course one can't expect the books to make any attempt to prepare visiting Earthmen concerning these subjects—"

"Because there are so few visiting Earthmen?"

"Exactly. The point is, of course, that robots never visit Personals. It is the one place where human beings can be free of them. I suppose there is the feeling that one should feel free of them at some periods and in some places."

Baley said, "And yet when Daneel was on Earth on the occasion of Sarton's death three years ago, I tried to keep him out of the Community Personal by saying he had no need. Still, he insisted on entering."

"And rightly so. He was, on that occasion, strictly instructed to give no indication he was not human, for reasons you well remember. Here on Aurora, however— Ah, they are done."

The robots were coming toward the door and Daneel gestured them outward.

Fastolfe held out his arm to bar Baley's way. "If you don't mind, Mr. Baley, I will go out first. Count to one hundred patiently and then join us."

21.

Baley, on the count of one hundred, stepped out firmly and walked toward Fastolfe. His face was perhaps too stiff, his jaws too tightly clenched, his back too straight.

He looked about. The scene was not very different from that which had been presented in the Personal. Fastolfe had, perhaps, used his own grounds as a model. Everywhere there was green and in one place there was a stream filtering down a slope. It was, perhaps, artificial, but it was not an illusion. The water was real. He could feel the spray when he passed near it.

There was somehow a tameness to it all. The Outside on Earth seemed wilder and more grandly beautiful, what little Baley had seen of it.

Fastolfe said, with a gentle touch on Baley's upper arm and a motion of his hand, "Come in this direction. Look there!"

A space between two trees revealed an expanse of lawn.

For the first time, there was a sense of distance and on the horizon one could see a dwelling place: low-roofed, broad, and so green in color that it almost melted into the countryside.

"This is a residential area," said Fastolfe. "It might not seem so to you, since you are accustomed to Earth's tremendous hives, but we are in the Auroran city of Eos, which is actually the administrative center of the planet. There are twenty thousand human beings living here, which makes it the largest city, not only on Aurora but on all the Spacer worlds. There are as many people in Eos as on all of Solaria." Fastolfe said it with pride.

"How many robots, Dr. Fastolfe?"

"In this area? Perhaps a hundred thousand. On the planet as a whole, there are fifty robots to each human being on the average, not ten thousand per human as on Solaria. Most of our robots are on our farms, in our mines, in our factories, in space. If anything, we suffer from a shortage of robots, particularly of household robots. Most Aurorans make do with two or three such robots, some with only one. Still, we don't want to move in the direction of Solaria."

"How many human beings have no household robots at all?"

"None at all. That would not be in the public interest. If a human being, for any reason, could not afford a robot, he or she would be granted one which would be maintained, if necessary, at public expense."

"What happens as the population rises? Do you add more robots?"

Fastolfe shook his head. "The population does not rise. Aurora's population is two hundred million and that has remained stable for three centuries. It is the number desired. Surely you have read that in the books you viewed."

"Yes, I have," admitted Baley, "but I found it difficult to believe."

"Let me assure you it's true. It gives each of us ample land, ample space, ample privacy, and an ample share of the world's resources. There are neither too many people as on Earth, nor too few as on Solaria." He held out his arm for Baley to take, so they might continue walking.

"What you see," Fastolfe said, "is a tame world. It is what I have brought you out to show you, Mr. Baley?"

"There is no danger in it?"

"Always *some* danger. We do have storms, rock slides, earthquakes, blizzards, avalanches, a volcano or two— Accidental death can never be entirely done away with. And there are even the passions of angry or envious persons, the follies of the immature, and the madness of the shortsighted. These things are very minor irritants, however, and do not much affect the civilized quiet that rests upon our world."

Fastolfe seemed to ruminate over his words for a moment, then he sighed and said, "I can scarcely want it to be any other way, but I have certain intellectual reservations. We have brought here to Aurora only those plants and animals we felt

would be useful, ornamental, or both. We did our best to eliminate anything we would consider weeds, vermin, or even less
than standard. We selected strong, healthy, and attractive
human beings, according to our own views, of course. We have
tried— But you smile, Mr. Baley."

Baley had not. His mouth had merely twitched. "No no," he
said. "There is nothing to smile about."

"There is, for I know as well as you do that I myself am not
attractive by Auroran standards. The trouble is that we cannot
altogether control gene combinations and intrauterine influences.
Nowadays, of course, with ectogenesis becoming more common
—though I hope it shall never be as common as it is on Solaria
—I would be eliminated in the late fetal stage."

"In which case, Dr. Fastolfe, the worlds would have lost a
great theoretical roboticist."

"Perfectly correct," said Fastolfe, without visible embarrassment, "but the worlds would never have known that, would
they? —In any case, we have labored to set up a very simple but
completely workable ecological balance, an equable climate, a
fertile soil, and resources as evenly distributed as is possible.
The result is a world that produces all of everything that we
need and that is, if I may personify, considerate of our wants.
—Shall I tell you the ideal for which we have striven?"

"Please do," said Baley.

"We have labored to produce a planet which, taken as a
whole, would obey the Three Laws of Robotics. It does nothing
to harm human beings, either by commission or omission. It
does what we want it to do, as long as we do not ask it to harm
human beings. And it protects itself, except at times and in
places where it must serve us or save us even at the price of
harm to itself. Nowhere else, neither on Earth nor in the other
Spacer worlds, is this so nearly true as here on Aurora."

Baley said sadly, "Earthmen, too, have longed for this, but we
have long since grown too numerous and we have too greatly
damaged our planet in the days of our ignorance to be able to
do very much about it now. —But what of Aurora's indigenous
life-forms? Surely you did not come to a dead planet."

Fastolfe said, "You know we didn't, if you have viewed books on our history. Aurora had vegetation and animal life when we arrived—and a nitrogen-oxygen atmosphere. This was true of all the fifty Spacer worlds. Peculiarly, in every case, the life-forms were sparse and not very varied. Nor were they particularly tenacious in their hold on their own planet. We took over, so to speak, without a struggle—and what is left of the indigenous life is in our aquaria, our zoos, and in a few carefully maintained primeval areas.

"We do not really understand why the life-bearing planets that human beings have encountered have been so feebly life-bearing, why only Earth itself has been overflowing with madly tenacious varieties of life filling every environmental niche, and why only Earth has developed any sign of intelligence whatever."

Baley said, "Maybe it is coincidence, the accident of incomplete exploration. We know so few planets so far."

"I admit," said Fastolfe, "that that is the most likely explanation. Somewhere there may be an ecological balance as complex as that of Earth. Somewhere there may be intelligent life and a technological civilization. Yet Earth's life and intelligence has spread outward for parsecs in every direction. If there is life and intelligence elsewhere, why have they not spread out as well—and why have we not encountered each other?"

"That might happen tomorrow, for all we know."

"It might. And if such an encounter is imminent, all the more reason why we should not be passively waiting. For we are growing passive, Mr. Baley. No new Spacer world has been settled in two and a half centuries. Our worlds are so tame, so delightful, we do not wish to leave them. This world was originally settled, you see, because Earth had grown so unpleasant that the risks and dangers of new and empty worlds seemed preferable by comparison. By the time our fifty Spacer worlds were developed—Solaria last of all—there was no longer any push, any need to move out elsewhere. And Earth itself had retreated to its underground caves of steel. The End. Finis."

"You don't really mean that."

"If we stay as we are? If we remain placid and comfortable and unmoving? Yes, I do mean that. Humanity must expand its range somehow if it is to continue to flourish. One method of expansion is through space, through a constant pioneering reach toward other worlds. If we fail in this, some other civilization that is undergoing such expansion will reach us and we will not be able to stand against its dynamism."

"You expect a space war—like a hyperwave shoot-'em-up."

"No, I doubt that that would be necessary. A civilization that is expanding through space will not need our few worlds and will probably be too intellectually advanced to feel the need to batter its way into hegemony here. If, however, we are surrounded by a more lively, a more vibrant civilization, we will wither away by the mere force of the comparison; we will die of the realization of what we have become and of the potential we have wasted. Of course, we might substitute other expansions— an expansion of scientific understanding or of cultural vigor, for instance. I fear, however, that these expansions are not separable. To fade in one is to fade in all. Certainly, we are fading in all. We live too long. We are too comfortable."

Baley said, "On Earth, we think of Spacers as all-powerful, as totally self-confident. I cannot believe I'm hearing this from one of you."

"You won't from any other Spacer. My views are unfashionable. Others would find them intolerable and I don't often speak of such things to Aurorans. Instead, I simply talk about a new drive for further settlement, without expressing my fears of the catastrophes which will result if we abandon colonization. In that, at least, I have been winning. Aurora has been seriously— even enthusiastically—considering a new era of exploration and settlement."

"You say that," said Baley, "without any noticeable enthusiasm. What's wrong?"

"It's just that we are approaching my motive for the destruction of Jander Panell."

Fastolfe paused, shook his head, and continued, "I wish, Mr. Baley, I could understand human beings better. I have spent six decades in studying the intricacies of the positronic brain and I expect to spend fifteen to twenty more on the problem. In this time, I have barely brushed against the problem of the *human* brain, which is enormously more intricate. Are there Laws of Humanics as there are Laws of Robotics? How many Laws of Humanics might there be and how can they be expressed mathematically? I don't know.

"Perhaps, though, there may come a day when someone will work out the Laws of Humanics and then be able to predict the broad strokes of the future, and *know* what might be in store for humanity, instead of merely guessing as I do, and *know* what to do to make things better, instead of merely speculating. I dream sometimes of founding a mathematical science which I think of as 'psychohistory,' but I know I can't and I fear no one ever will."

He faded to a halt.

Baley waited, then said softly, "And your motive for the destruction of Jander Panell, Dr. Fastolfe?"

Fastolfe did not seem to hear the question. At any rate, he did not respond. He said, instead, "Daneel and Giskard are again signaling that all is clear. Tell me, Mr. Baley, would you consider walking with me farther afield?"

"Where?" asked Baley cautiously.

"Toward a neighboring establishment. In that direction, across the lawn. Would the openness disturb you?"

Baley pressed his lips together and looked in that direction, as though attempting to measure its effect. "I believe I could endure it. I anticipate no trouble."

Giskard, who was close enough to hear, now approached still closer, his eyes showing no glow in the daylight. If his voice was without human emotion, his words marked his concern. "Sir, may I remind you that on the journey here you suffered serious discomfort on the descent to the planet?"

Baley turned to face him. However he might feel toward Daneel, whatever warmth of past association might paper over his attitude toward robots, there was none here. He found the more primitive Giskard distinctly repellent. He labored to fight down the touch of anger he felt and said, "I was incautious aboard ship, boy, because I was overly curious. I faced a vision I had never experienced before and I had no time for adjustment. This is different."

"Sir, do you feel discomfort now? May I be assured of that?"

"Whether I do or not," said Baley firmly (reminding himself that the robot was helplessly in the grip of the First Law and trying to be polite to a lump of metal who, after all, had Baley's welfare as his only care) "doesn't matter. I have my duty to perform and that cannot be done if I am to hide in enclosures."

"Your duty?" Giskard said it as though he had not been programmed to understand the word.

Baley looked quickly in Fastolfe's direction, but Fastolfe stood quietly in his place and made no move to intervene. He seemed to be listening with abstracted interest, as though weighing the reaction of a robot of a given type to a new situation and comparing it with relationships, variables, constants, and differential equations only he understood.

Or so Baley thought. He felt annoyed at being part of an observation of that type and said (perhaps too sharply, he knew), "Do you know what 'duty' means?"

"That which should be done, sir," said Giskard.

"Your duty is to obey the Laws of Robotics. And human beings have their laws, too—as your master, Dr. Fastolfe, was only this moment saying—which must be obeyed. I must do that which I have been assigned to do. It is important."

"But to go into the open when you are not—"

"It must be done, nevertheless. My son may someday go to another planet, one much less comfortable than this one, and expose himself to the Outside for the rest of his life. And if I could, I would go with him."

"But why would you do that?"

"I have told you. I consider it my duty."

"Sir, I cannot disobey the Laws. Can you disobey yours? For I must urge you to—"

"I can choose not to do my duty, but I do not choose to—and that is sometimes the stronger compulsion, Giskard."

There was silence for a moment and then Giskard said, "Would it do you harm if I were to succeed in persuading you not to walk into the open?"

"Insofar as I would then feel I have failed in my duty, it would."

"More harm than any discomfort you might feel in the open?"

"Much more."

"Thank you for explaining this, sir," said Giskard and Baley imagined there was a look of satisfaction on the robot's largely expressionless face. (The human tendency to personify was irrepressible.)

Giskard stepped back and now Dr. Fastolfe spoke. "That was interesting, Mr. Baley. Giskard needed instructions before he could quite understand how to arrange the positronic potential response to the Three Laws or, rather, how those potentials were to arrange themselves in the light of the situation. Now he knows how to behave."

Baley said, "I notice that Daneel asked no questions."

Fastolfe said, "Daneel knows you. He has been with you on Earth and on Solaria. —But come, shall we walk? Let us move slowly. Look about carefully and, if at any time you should wish to rest, to wait, even to turn back, I will count on you to let me know."

"I will, but what is the purpose of this walk? Since you anticipate possible discomfort on my part, you cannot be suggesting it idly."

"I am not," said Fastolfe. "I think you will want to see the inert body of Jander."

"As a matter of form, yes, but I rather think it will tell me nothing."

"I'm sure of that, but then you might also have the opportunity to question the one who was Jander's quasi-owner at the time of the tragedy. Surely you would like to speak to some human being other than myself concerning the matter."

22.

Fastolfe moved slowly forward, plucking a leaf from a shrub that he passed, bending it in two, and nibbling at it.

Baley looked at him curiously, wondering how Spacers could put something untreated, unheated, even unwashed into their mouths, when they feared infection so badly. He remembered that Aurora was free (*entirely* free?) of pathogenic microorganisms, but found the action repulsive anyway. Repulsion did not have to have a rational basis, he thought defensively—and suddenly found himself on the edge of excusing the Spacers their attitude toward Earthmen.

He drew back! That was different! Human beings were involved there!

Giskard moved ahead, forward and toward the right. Daneel lagged behind and toward the left. Aurora's orange sun (Baley scarcely noted the orange tinge now) was mildly warm on his back, lacking the febrile heat that Earth's sun had in summer (but, then, what was the climate and season on this portion of Aurora right now?).

The grass or whatever it was (it looked like grass) was a bit stiffer and springier than he recalled it being on Earth and the ground was hard, as though it had not rained for a while.

They were moving toward the house up ahead, presumably the house of Jander's quasi-owner.

Baley could hear the rustle of some animal in the grass to the right, the sudden chirrup of a bird somewhere in a tree behind him, the small unplaceable clatter of insects all about. These, he told himself, were all animals with ancestors that had once lived on Earth. They had no way of knowing that this patch of ground they inhabited was not all there was—forever and forever back in time. The very trees and grass had arisen from other trees and grass that had once grown on Earth.

Only human beings could live on this world and know that they were not autochthonous but had stemmed from Earthmen—and yet did the Spacers really know it or did they simply put it out of their mind? Would the time come, perhaps, when they would not know it at all? When they would not remember which world they had come from or whether there was a world of origin at all?

"Dr. Fastolfe," he said suddenly, in part to break the chain of thought that he found to be growing oppressive, "you still have not told me your motive for the destruction of Jander."

"True! I have not! —Now why do you suppose, Mr. Baley, I

have labored to work out the theoretical basis for the positronic brains of humaniform robots?"

"I cannot say."

"Well, think. The task is to design a robotic brain as close to the human as possible and that would require, it would seem, a certain reach into the poetic—" He paused and his small smile became an outright grin. "You know it always bothers some of my colleagues when I tell them that, if a conclusion is not poetically balanced, it cannot be scientifically true. They tell me they don't know what that means."

Baley said, "I'm afraid I don't, either."

"But I know what it means. I can't explain it, but I feel the explanation without being able to put it into words, which may be why I have achieved results my colleagues have not. However, I grow grandiose, which is a good sign I should become prosaic. To imitate a human brain, when I know almost nothing about the workings of the human brain, needs an intuitive leap—something that feels to me like poetry. And the same intuitive leap that would give me the humaniform positronic brain should surely give me a new access of knowledge about the human brain itself. That was my belief—that through humaniformity I might take at least a small step toward the psychohistory I told you about."

"I see."

"And if I succeeded in working out a theoretical structure that would imply a humaniform positronic brain, I would need a humaniform body to place it in. The brain does not exist by itself, you understand. It interacts with the body, so that a humaniform brain in a nonhumaniform body would become, to an extent, itself nonhuman."

"Are you sure of that?"

"Quite. You have only to compare Daneel with Giskard."

"Then Daneel was constructed as an experimental device for furthering the understanding of the human brain?"

"You have it. I labored two decades at the task with Sarton. There were numerous failures that had to be discarded. Daneel was the first true success and, of course, I kept him for further study—and out of"—he grinned lopsidedly, as though admitting to something silly—"affection. After all, Daneel can grasp the notion of human duty, while Giskard, with all his virtues, has trouble doing so. You saw."

"And Daneel's stay on Earth with me, three years ago, was his first assigned task?"

"His first of any importance, yes. When Sarton was murdered, we needed something that was a robot and could withstand the infectious diseases of Earth and yet looked enough like a man to get around the antirobotic prejudices of Earth's people."

"An astonishing coincidence that Daneel should be right at hand at that time."

"Oh? Do you believe in coincidences? It is my feeling that any time at which a development as revolutionary as the humaniform robot came into being, some task that would require its use would present itself. Similar tasks had probably been presenting themselves regularly in all the years that Daneel did not exist— and because Daneel did not exist, other solutions and devices had to be used."

"And have your labors been successful, Dr. Fastolfe? Do you now understand the human brain better than you did?"

Fastolfe had been moving more and more slowly and Baley had been matching his progress to the other's. They were now standing still, about halfway between Fastolfe's establishment and the other's. It was the most difficult point for Baley, since it was equally distant from protection in either direction, but he fought down the growing uneasiness, determined not to provoke Giskard. He did not wish by some motion or outcry—or even expression—to activate the inconvenience of Giskard's desire to save him. He did not want to have himself lifted up and carried off to shelter.

Fastolfe showed no sign of understanding Baley's difficulty. He said, "There's no question but that advances in mentology have been carried through. There remain enormous problems and perhaps these will always remain, but there has been progress. Still—"

"Still?"

"Still, Aurora is not satisfied with a purely theoretical study of the human brain. Uses for humaniform robots have been advanced that I do not approve of."

"Such as the use on Earth."

"No, that was a brief experiment that I rather approved of and was even fascinated by. Could Daneel fool Earthpeople? It turned out he could, though, of course, the eyes of Earthmen for robots are not very keen. Daneel cannot fool the eyes of Aurorans, though I dare say future humaniform robots could be improved to the point where they would. There are other tasks that have been proposed, however."

"Such as?"

Fastolfe gazed thoughtfully into the distance. "I told you this world was tame. When I began my movement to encourage a renewed period of exploration and settlement, it was not to the supercomfortable Aurorans—or Spacers generally—that I looked for leadership. I rather thought we ought to encourage Earthmen to take the lead. With their horrid world—excuse me—and short life-span, they have so little to lose, I thought that they would surely welcome the chance, especially if we were to help them technologically. I spoke to you about such a thing when I saw you on Earth three years ago. Do you remember?" He looked sidelong at Baley.

Baley said stolidly, "I remember quite well. In fact, you started a chain of thought in me that has resulted in a small movement on Earth in that very direction."

"Indeed? It would not be easy, I imagine. There is the claustrophilia of you Earthmen, your dislike of leaving your walls."

"We are fighting it, Dr. Fastolfe. Our organization is planning to move out into space. My son is a leader in the movement and I hope the day may come when he leaves Earth at the head of an expedition to settle a new world. If we do indeed receive the technological help you speak of—" Baley let that dangle.

"If we supplied the ships, you mean?"

"And other equipment. Yes, Dr. Fastolfe."

"There are difficulties. Many Aurorans do not want Earthmen to move outward and settle new worlds. They fear the rapid spread of Earthish culture, its beehive Cities, its chaoticism." He stirred uneasily and said, "Why are we standing here, I wonder? Let's move on."

He walked slowly forward and said, "I have argued that that would not be the way it would be. I have pointed out that the settlers from Earth would not be Earthmen in the classical mode. They would not be enclosed in Cities. Coming to a new world, they would be like the Auroran Fathers coming here. They would develop a manageable ecological balance and would be closer to Aurorans than to Earthmen in attitude."

"Would they not then develop all the weaknesses you find in Spacer culture, Dr. Fastolfe?"

"Perhaps not. They would learn from our mistakes. —But that is academic, for something has developed which makes the argument moot."

"And what is that?"

"Why, the humaniform robot. You see, there are those who see the humaniform robot as the perfect settler. It is they who can build the new worlds."

Baley said, "You've always had robots. Do you mean this idea was never advanced before?"

"Oh, it was, but it was always clearly unworkable. Ordinary nonhumaniform robots, without immediate human supervision, building a world that would suit their own nonhumaniform selves, could not be expected to tame and build a world that would be suitable for the more delicate and flexible minds and bodies of human beings."

"Surely the world they would build would serve as a reasonable first approximation."

"Surely it would, Mr. Baley. It is a sign of Auroran decay, however, that there is an overwhelming feeling among our people that a reasonable first approximation is unreasonably insufficient. —A group of humaniform robots, on the other hand, as closely resembling human beings in body and mind as possible, would succeed in building a world which, in suiting themselves, would also inevitably suit Aurorans. Do you follow the reasoning?"

"Completely."

"They would build a world so well, you see, that when they are done and Aurorans are finally willing to leave, our human beings will step out of Aurora and into another Aurora. They will never have left home; they will simply have another newer home, exactly like the older one, in which to continue their decay. Do you follow that reasoning, too?"

"I see your point, but I take it that Aurorans do not."

"*May* not. I think I can argue the point effectively, if the opposition does not destroy me politically via this matter of the destruction of Jander. Do you see the motive attributed to me? I am supposed to have embarked on a program of the destruction of humaniform robots rather than allow them to be used to settle other planets. Or so my enemies say."

It was Baley now who stopped walking. He looked thoughtfully at Fastolfe and said, "You understand, Dr. Fastolfe, that it is to Earth's interest that your point of view win out completely."

"And to your own interests as well, Mr. Baley."

"And to mine. But if I put myself to one side for the moment, it still remains vital to my world that our people be allowed, encouraged, and helped to explore the Galaxy; that we retain as much of our own ways as we are comfortable with; that we not be condemned to imprisonment on Earth forever, since there we can only perish."

Fastolfe said, "Some of you, I think, will insist on remaining imprisoned."

"Of course. Perhaps almost all of us will. However, at least some of us—as many of us as possible—will escape if given permission. —It is therefore my duty, not only as a representative of the law of a large fraction of humanity but as an Earthman, plain and simple, to help you clear your name, whether you are guilty or innocent. Nevertheless, I can throw myself wholeheartedly into this task only if I know that, in fact, the accusations against you are unjustified."

"Of course! I understand."

"In the light, then, of what you have told me of the motive attributed to you, assure me once again that you did not do this thing."

Fastolfe said, "Mr. Baley, I understand completely that you have no choice in this matter. I am quite aware that I can tell you, with impunity, that I am guilty and that you would still be compelled by the nature of your needs and those of your world to work with me to mask that fact. Indeed, if I were actually guilty, I would feel compelled to tell you so, so that you could take that fact into consideration and, knowing the truth, work the more efficiently to rescue me—and yourself. But I cannot do so, because the fact is I am innocent. However much appearances may be against me, I did not destroy Jander. Such a thing never entered my mind."

"Never?"

Fastolfe smiled sadly. "Oh, I may have thought once or twice that Aurora would have been better off if I had never worked out the ingenious notions that led to the development of the humaniform positronic brain—or that it would be better off if such brains proved unstable and readily subject to mental freeze-out. But those were fugitive thoughts. Not for a split second did I contemplate bringing about Jander's destruction for this reason."

"Then we must destroy this motive that they attribute to you."

"Good. But how?"

"We could show that it serves no purpose. What good does it do to destroy Jander? More humaniform robots can be built. Thousands. Millions."

"I'm afraid that's not so, Mr. Baley. None can be built. I alone know how to design them, and, as long as robot colonization is a possible destiny, I refuse to build any more. Jander is gone and only Daneel is left."

"The secret will be discovered by others."

Fastolfe's chin went up. "I would like to see the roboticist capable of it. My enemies have established a Robotics Institute with no other purpose than to work out the methods behind the construction of a humaniform robot, but they won't succeed. They certainly haven't succeeded so far and I know they won't succeed."

Baley frowned. "If you are the only man who knows the secret of the humaniform robots, and if your enemies are desperate for it, will they not try to get it out of you?"

"Of course. By threatening my political existence, by perhaps maneuvering some punishment that will forbid my working in the field and thus putting an end to my professional existence as well, they hope to have me agree to share the secret with them. They may even have the Legislature direct me to share the secret on the pain of confiscation of property, imprisonment—who knows what? However, I have made up my mind to submit to anything—anything—rather than give in. But I don't want to have to, you understand."

"Do they know of your determination to resist?"

"I hope so. I have told them plainly enough. I presume they think I'm bluffing, that I'm not serious. —But I am."

"But if they believe you, they might take more serious steps."

"What do you mean?"

"Steal your papers. Kidnap you. Torture you."

Fastolfe broke into a loud laugh and Baley flushed. He said, "I hate to sound like a hyperwave drama, but have you considered that?"

Fastolfe said, "Mr. Baley— First, my robots can protect me. It would take full-scale war to capture me or my work. Second, even if somehow they succeeded, not one of the roboticists opposed to me could bear to make it plain that the only way he could obtain the secret of the humaniform positronic brain is to steal it or force it from me. His or her professional reputation would be completely wiped out. Third, such things on Aurora are unheard of. The merest hint of an unprofessional attempt upon me would swing the Legislature—*and* public opinion—in my favor at once."

"Is that so?" muttered Baley, silently damning the fact of having to work in a culture whose details he simply didn't understand.

"Yes. Take my word for it. I wish they would try something of this melodramatic sort. I wish they were so incredibly stupid as to do so. In fact, Mr. Baley, I wish I could persuade you to go to them, worm your way into their confidence, and cajole them into mounting an attack on my establishment or waylaying me on an empty road—or anything of the sort that, I imagine, is common on Earth."

Baley said stiffly, "I don't think that would be my style."

"I don't think so, either, so I have no intention of trying to implement my wish. And believe me, that is too bad, for if we cannot persuade them to try the suicidal method of force, they will continue to do something much better, from their standpoint. They will destroy me by falsehoods."

"What falsehoods?"

"It is not just the destruction of one robot they attribute to me. That is bad enough and just might suffice. They are whispering—it is only a whisper as yet—that the death is merely an experiment of mine and a dangerous, successful one. They whisper that I am working out a system for destroying humaniform brains rapidly and efficiently, so that when my enemies *do* create their own humaniform robots, I, together with members of my party, will be able to destroy them all, thus preventing Aurora from settling new worlds and leaving the Galaxy to my Earthmen confederates."

"Surely there can be no truth in this."

"Of course not. I told you these are lies. And ridiculous lies, too. No such method of destruction is even theoretically possible and the Robotics Institute people are not on the point of creating their own humaniform robots. I cannot conceivably indulge in an orgy of mass destruction even if I wanted to. I *cannot*."

"Doesn't the whole thing fall by its own weight, then?"

"Unfortunately, it's not likely to do so in time. It may be silly nonsense, but it will probably last long enough to sway public opinion against me to the point of swinging just enough votes in the Legislature to defeat me. Eventually, it will all be recognized as nonsense, but by then it will be too late. And please notice that Earth is being used as a whipping boy in this. The charge that I am laboring on behalf of Earth is a powerful one and many will choose to believe the whole farrago, against their own better sense, because of their dislike of Earth and Earthpeople."

Baley said, "What you're telling me is that active resentment against Earth is being built up."

Fastolfe said, "Exactly, Mr. Baley. The situation grows worse for me—and for Earth—every day and we have very little time."

"But isn't there an easy way of knocking this thing on its head?" (Baley, in despair, decided it was time to fall back on Daneel's point.) "If you were indeed anxious to test a method for the destruction of a humaniform robot, why seek out one in another establishment, one with which it might be inconvenient to experiment? You had Daneel, himself, in your own establishment. He was at hand and convenient. Would not the experiment have been conducted upon him if there were any truth at all in the rumor?"

"No no," said Fastolfe. "I couldn't get anyone to believe that. Daneel was my first success, my triumph. I wouldn't destroy him under any circumstances. Naturally, I would turn to Jander. Everyone would see that and I would be a fool to try to persuade them that it would have made more sense for me to sacrifice Daneel."

They were walking again, nearly at their destination. Baley was in deep silence, his face tight-lipped.

Fastolfe said, "How do you feel, Mr. Baley?"

Baley said in a low voice, "If you mean as far as being Outside is concerned, I am not even aware of it. If you mean as far as our dilemma is concerned, I think I am as close to giving up as I can possibly be without putting myself into an ultrasonic brain-dissolving chamber." Then passionately, "Why did you send for me, Dr. Fastolfe? Why have you given me this job? What have I ever done to you to be treated so?"

"Actually," said Fastolfe, "it was not my idea to begin with and I can only plead my desperation."

"Well, whose idea was it?"

"It was the owner of this establishment we have now reached who suggested it originally—and I had no better idea."

"The owner of this establishment? Why would he—"

"She."

"Well, then, why would she suggest anything of the sort?"

"Oh! I haven't explained that she knows you, have I, Mr. Baley? There she is, waiting for us now."

Baley looked up, bewildered.

"Jehoshaphat," he whispered.

# 6

---

# Gladia

*23.*

The young woman who faced them said with a wan smile, "I knew that when I met you again, Elijah, that would be the first word I would hear."

Baley stared at her. She had changed. Her hair was shorter and her face was even more troubled now than it had been two years ago and seemed more than two years older, somehow. She was still unmistakably Gladia, however. There was still the triangular face, with its pronounced cheekbones and small chin. She was still short, still slight of figure, still vaguely childlike.

He had dreamed of her frequently—though not in an overtly erotic fashion—after returning to Earth. His dreams were always stories of not being able to quite reach her. She was always there, a little too far off to speak to easily. She never quite heard when he called her. She never grew nearer when he approached her.

It was not hard to understand why the dreams had been as they were. She was a Solarian-born person and, as such, was rarely supposed to be in the physical presence of other human beings.

Elijah had been forbidden to her because he was human—and beyond that (of course) because he was from Earth. Though the exigencies of the murder case he was investigating forced them to meet, throughout their relationship she was completely covered, when physically together, to prevent actual contact. And yet, at their last meeting, she had, in defiance of good sense, fleetingly touched his cheek with her bare hand. She must have known she could be infected as a result. He cherished the touch the more, for every aspect of her upbringing combined to make it unthinkable.

The dreams had faded in time.

Baley said, rather stupidly, "It was *you* who owned the—"

He paused and Gladia finished the sentence for him. "The robot. And two years ago, it was I who possessed the husband. Whatever I touch is destroyed."

Without really knowing what he was doing, Baley reached up to place his hand on his cheek. Gladia did not seem to notice.

She said, "You came to rescue me that first time. Forgive me, but I had to call on you again. —Come in, Elijah. Come in, Dr. Fastolfe."

Fastolfe stepped back to allow Baley to walk in first. He followed. Behind Fastolfe came Daneel and Giskard—and they, with the characteristic self-effacement of robots, stepped to unoccupied wall niches on opposite sides and remained silently standing, backs to the wall.

For one moment, it seemed that Gladia would treat them with the indifference with which human beings commonly treated robots. After a glance at Daneel, however, she turned away and said to Fastolfe in a voice that choked a little, "That one. Please. Ask him to leave."

Fastolfe said, with a small motion of surprise, "Daneel?"

"He's too—too Janderlike!"

Fastolfe turned to look at Daneel and a look of clear pain crossed his face momentarily. "Of course, my dear. You must forgive me. I did not think. —Daneel, move into another room and remain there while we are here."

Without a word, Daneel left.

Gladia glanced a moment at Giskard, as though to judge whether he, also, was too Janderlike, and turned away with a small shrug.

She said, "Would either of you like refreshment of any kind? I have an excellent coconut drink, fresh and cold."

"No, Gladia," said Fastolfe. "I have merely brought Mr. Baley here as I promised I would. I will not stay long."

"If I may have a glass of water," said Baley, "I won't trouble you for anything more."

Gladia raised one hand. Undoubtedly, she was under observation, for, in a moment, a robot moved in noiselessly, with a glass of water on a tray and a small dish of what looked like crackers with a pinkish blob on each.

Baley could not forbear taking one, even though he was not certain what it might be. It had to be something Earth-descended, for he could not believe that on Aurora, he—or anyone —would be eating any portion of the planet's sparse indigenous biota or anything synthetic either. Nevertheless, the descendants of Earthly food species might change with time, either through deliberate cultivation or the action of a strange environment— and Fastolfe, at lunchtime, *had* said that much of the Auroran diet was an acquired taste.

He was pleasantly surprised. The taste was sharp and spicy, but he found it delightful and took a second almost at once. He said, "Thank you" to the robot (who would not have objected to standing there indefinitely) and took the entire dish, together with the glass of water.

The robot left.

It was late afternoon now and the sunlight came ruddily through the western windows. Baley had the impression that this house was smaller than Fastolfe's, but it would have been more cheerful had not the sad figure of Gladia standing in its midst provoked a dispiriting effect.

That might, of course, be Baley's imagination. Cheer, in any case, seemed to him impossible in any structure purporting to house and protect human beings that yet remained exposed to the Outside beyond each wall. Not one wall, he thought, had the warmth of human life on the other side. In no direction could one look for companionship and community. Through every outer wall, every side, top and bottom, there was inanimate world. Cold! Cold!

And coldness flooded back upon Baley himself as he thought again of the dilemma in which he found himself. (For a moment, the shock of meeting Gladia again had driven it from his mind.)

Gladia said, "Come. Sit down, Elijah. You must excuse me for not quite being myself. I am, for a second time, the center of a planetary sensation—and the first time was more than enough."

"I understand, Gladia. Please do not apologize," said Baley.

"And as for you, dear Doctor, please don't feel you need go."

"Well—" Fastolfe looked at the time strip on the wall. "I will stay for a short while, but then, my dear, there is work that must be done though the skies fall. All the more so, since I must look forward to a near future in which I may be restrained from doing any work at all."

Gladia blinked rapidly, as though holding back tears. "I know, Dr. Fastolfe. You are in deep trouble because of—of what happened here and I don't seem to have time to think of anything but my own—discomfort."

Fastolfe said, "I'll do my best to take care of my own problem, Gladia, and there is no need for you to feel guilt over the matter. —Perhaps Mr. Baley will be able to help us both."

Baley pressed his lips together at that, then said heavily, "I was not aware, Gladia, that you were in any way involved in this affair."

"Who else would be?" she said with a sigh.

"You are—were—in possession of Jander Panell?"

"Not truly in possession. I had him on loan from Dr. Fastolfe."

"Were you with him when he—" Baley hesitated over some way of putting it.

"Died? Mightn't we say died? —No, I was not. And before you ask, there was no one else in the house at the time. I was alone. I am usually alone. Almost always. That is my Solarian upbringing, you remember. Of course, that is not obligatory. You two are here and I do not mind—very much."

"And you were definitely alone at the time Jander died? No mistake?"

"I have said so," said Gladia, sounding a little irritated. "No,

never mind, Elijah. I know you must have everything repeated
and repeated. I *was* alone. Honestly."

"There were robots present, though."

"Yes, of course. When I say 'alone,' I mean there were no
other human beings present."

"How many robots do you possess, Gladia? Not counting
Jander."

Gladia paused as though she were counting internally. Finally,
she said, "Twenty. Five in the house and fifteen on the grounds.
Robots move freely between my house and Dr. Fastolfe's, too, so
that it isn't always possible to judge, when a robot is quickly
seen at either establishment, whether it is one of mine or one of
his."

"Ah," said Baley, "and since Dr. Fastolfe has fifty-seven robots
in his establishment, that means, if we combine the two, that
there are seventy-seven robots available, altogether. Are there
any other establishments whose robots may mingle with yours
indistinguishably?"

Fastolfe said, "There's no other establishment near enough to
make that practical. Nor is the practice of mixing robots really
encouraged. Gladia and I are a special case because she is not
Auroran and because I have taken rather a—responsibility for
her."

"Even so. Seventy-seven robots," said Baley.

"Yes," said Fastolfe, "but why are you making this point?"

Baley said, "Because it means you can have any of seventy-
seven moving objects, each vaguely human in form, that you are
used to seeing out of the corner of the eye and to which you
would pay no particular attention. Isn't it possible, Gladia, that
if an actual human being were to penetrate the house, for whatever purpose, you would scarcely be aware of it? It would be
one more moving object, vaguely human in form, and you would
pay no attention."

Fastolfe chuckled softly and Gladia, unsmiling, shook her
head.

"Elijah," she said, "one can tell you are an Earthman. Do you
imagine that any human being, even Dr. Fastolfe here, could

possibly approach my house without my being informed of the fact by my robots. I might ignore a moving form, assuming it to be a robot, but no robot ever would. I was waiting for you just now when you arrived, but that was because my robots had informed me you were approaching. No, no, when Jander died, there was no other human being in the house."

"Except yourself?"

"Except myself. Just as there was no one in the house except myself when my husband was killed."

Fastolfe interposed gently. "There is a difference, Gladia. Your husband was killed with a blunt instrument. The physical presence of the murderer was necessary and, if you were the only one present, that was serious. In this case, Jander was put out of operation by a subtle spoken program. Physical presence was not necessary. Your presence here alone means nothing, especially since you do not know how to block the mind of a humaniform robot."

They both turned to look at Baley, Fastolfe with a quizzical look on his face, Gladia with a sad one. (It irritated Baley that Fastolfe, whose future was as bleak as Baley's own, nevertheless seemed to face it with humor. What on Earth is there to the situation to cause one to laugh like an idiot? Baley thought morosely.)

"Ignorance," said Baley slowly, "may mean nothing. A person may not know how to get to a certain place and yet may just happen to reach it while walking blindly. One might talk to Jander and, all unknowingly, push the button for mental freeze-out."

Fastolfe said, "And the chances of that?"

"You're the expert, Dr. Fastolfe, and I suppose you will tell me they are very small."

"Incredibly small. A person may not know how to get to a certain place, but if the only route is a series of tight ropes stretched in sharply changing directions, what are the chances of reaching it by walking randomly while blindfolded?"

Gladia's hands fluttered in extreme agitation. She clenched her fists, as though to hold them steady, and brought them down on her knees. "I didn't do it, accident or not. I wasn't with him when it happened. I *wasn't*. I spoke to him in the morning. He was well, perfectly normal. Hours later, when I summoned him, he never came. I went in search of him and he was standing in his accustomed place, seeming quite normal. The trouble was, he didn't respond to me. He didn't respond at all. He has never responded since."

Baley said, "Could something you had said to him, quite in passing, have produced mind-freeze only after you had left him —an hour after, perhaps?"

Fastolfe interposed sharply, "Quite impossible, Mr. Baley. If mind-freeze is to take place, it takes place at once. Please do not badger Gladia in this fashion. She is incapable of producing mind-freeze deliberately and it is unthinkable that she would produce it accidentally."

"Isn't it unthinkable that it would be produced by random positronic drift, as you say it must have?"

"Not quite as unthinkable."

"Both alternatives are extremely unlikely. What is the difference in unthinkability?"

"A great one. I imagine that a mental freeze-out through positronic drift might have a probability of 1 in $10^{12}$; that by accidental pattern-building 1 in $10^{100}$. That is just an estimate, but a reasonable one. The difference is greater than that between a single electron and the entire Universe—and it is in favor of the positronic drift."

There was silence for a while.

Baley said, "Dr. Fastolfe, you said earlier that you couldn't stay long."

"I have stayed too long already."

"Good. Then would you leave now?"

Fastolfe began to rise, then said, "Why?"

"Because I want to speak to Gladia alone."

"To badger her?"

"I must question her without your interference. Our situation is entirely too serious to worry about politeness."

Gladia said, "I am not afraid of Mr. Baley, dear Doctor." She added wistfully, "My robots will protect me if his impoliteness becomes extreme."

Fastolfe smiled and said, "Very well, Gladia." He rose and held out his hand to her. She took it briefly.

He said, "I would like to have Giskard remain here for general protection—and Daneel will continue to be in the next room, if you don't mind. Could you lend me one of your own robots to escort me back to my establishment?"

"Certainly," said Gladia, raising her arms. "You know Pandion, I believe."

"Of course! A sturdy and reliable escort." He left, with the robot following closely.

Baley waited, watching Gladia, studying her. She sat there, her eyes on her hands, which were folded limply together in her lap.

Baley was certain there was more for her to tell. How he could persuade her to talk, he couldn't say, but of one thing more he was certain. While Fastolfe was there, she would not tell the whole truth.

### 24.

Finally, Gladia looked up, her face like a little girl's. She said in a small voice, "How are you, Elijah? How do you feel?"

"Well enough, Gladia."

She said, "Dr. Fastolfe said he would lead you here across the open and see to it that you would have to wait some time in the worst of it."

"Oh? Why was that? For the fun of it?"

"No, Elijah. I had told him how you reacted to the open. You remember the time you fainted and fell into the pond?"

Elijah shook his head quickly. He could not deny the event or his memory thereof, but neither did he approve of the reference. He said gruffly, "I'm not quite like that anymore. I've improved."

"But Dr. Fastolfe said he would test you. Was it all right?"

"It was sufficiently all right. I didn't faint." He remembered the episode aboard the spaceship during the approach to Aurora and ground his teeth faintly. That was different and there was no call to discuss the matter.

He said, in a deliberate change of subject, "What do I call you here? How do I address you?"

"You've been calling me Gladia."

"It's inappropriate, perhaps. I could say Mrs. Delmarre, but you may have—"

She gasped and interrupted sharply, "I haven't used that name since arriving here. Please don't you use it."

"What do the Aurorans call you, then?"

"They say Gladia Solaria, but that's just an indication that I'm an alien and I don't want that either. I am simply Gladia. One name. It's not an Auroran name and I doubt that there's another one on this planet, so it's sufficient. I'll continue to call you Elijah, if you don't mind."

"I don't mind."

Gladia said, "I would like to serve tea." It was a statement and Baley nodded.

He said, "I didn't know that Spacers drank tea."

"It's not Earth tea. It's a plant extract that is pleasant but is not considered harmful in any way. We call it tea."

She lifted her arm and Baley noted that the sleeve held tightly at the wrist and that joining it were thin, flesh-colored gloves. She was still exposing the minimum of body surface in his presence. She was still minimizing the chance of infection.

Her arm remained in the air for a moment and, after a few more moments, a robot appeared with a tray. He was patently even more primitive than Giskard, but he distributed the tea-cups, the small sandwiches, and the bite-sized bits of pastry smoothly. He poured tea with what amounted to grace.

Baley said curiously, "How do you do that, Gladia?"

"Do what, Elijah?"

"You lift your arm whenever you want something and the robots always know what it is. How did this one know you wanted tea served?"

"It's not difficult. Every time I lift my arm, it distorts a small electromagnetic field that is maintained continuously across the room. Slightly different positions of my hand and fingers produce different distortions and my robots can interpret these distortions as orders. I only use it for simple orders: Come here! Bring tea! and so on."

"I haven't noticed Dr. Fastolfe using the system at his establishment."

"It's not really Auroran. It's our system in Solaria and I'm used to it. —Besides, I always have tea at this time. Borgraf expects it."

"This is Borgraf?" Baley eyed the robot with some interest, aware that he had only glanced at him before. Familiarity was quickly breeding indifference. Another day and he would not notice robots at all. They would flutter about him unseen and chores would appear to do themselves.

Nevertheless, he did not want to fail to notice them. He wanted them to fail to be there. He said, "Gladia, I want to be alone with you. Not even robots. —Giskard, join Daneel. You can stand guard from there."

"Yes, sir," said Giskard, brought suddenly to awareness and response by the sound of his name.

Gladia seemed distantly amused. "You Earthpeople are so odd. I know you have robots on Earth, but you don't seem to know how to handle them. You *bark* your orders, as though they're deaf."

She turned to Borgraf and, in a low voice, said, "Borgraf, none of you are to enter the room until summoned. Do not interrupt us for anything short of a clear and present emergency."

Borgraf said, "Yes, ma'am." He stepped back, glanced over the table as though checking whether he had omitted anything, turned, and left the room.

Baley was amused, in his turn. Gladia's voice had been soft, but her tone had been as crisp as though she were a sergeant-major addressing a recruit. But then, why should he be surprised? He had long known that it was easier to see another's follies than one's own.

Gladia said, "We are now alone, Elijah. Even the robots are gone."

Baley said, "You are not afraid to be alone with me?"

Slowly, she shook her head. "Why should I be? A raised arm, a gesture, a startled outcry—and several robots would be here promptly. No one on any Spacer world has any reason to fear any other human being. This is not Earth. Whyever should you ask, anyway?"

"Because there are other fears than physical ones. I would not offer you violence of any kind or mistreat you physically in any way. But are you not afraid of my questioning and what it might uncover about you? Remember that this is not Solaria, either. On Solaria, I sympathized with you and was intent on demonstrating your innocence."

She said in a low voice, "Don't you sympathize with me now?"

"It's not a husband dead this time. You are not suspected of murder. It's only a robot that has been destroyed and, as far as I know, you are suspected of nothing. Instead, it is Dr. Fastolfe who is my problem. It is of the highest importance to me—for reasons I need not go into—that I be able to demonstrate *his* innocence. If the process turns out to be damaging to you, I will not be able to help it. I do not intend to go out of my way to save you pain. It is only fair that I tell you this."

She raised her head and fixed her eyes on his arrogantly. "Why should anything be damaging to me?"

"Perhaps we will now proceed to find out," said Baley coolly, "without Dr. Fastolfe present to interfere." He plucked one of the small sandwiches out of the dish with a small fork (there was no point in using his fingers and perhaps making the entire dish unusable to Gladia), scraped it off onto his own plate, popped it into his mouth, and then sipped at his tea.

She matched him sandwich for sandwich, sip for sip. If he were going to be cool, so was she, apparently.

"Gladia," said Baley, "it is important that I know, exactly, the relationship between you and Dr. Fastolfe. You live near him and the two of you form what is virtually a single robotic household. He is clearly concerned for you. He has made no effort to defend his own innocence, aside from the mere statement that he is innocent, but he defends you strongly the moment I harden my questioning."

Gladia smiled faintly. "What do you suspect, Elijah?"

Baley said, "Don't fence with me. I don't want to suspect. I want to know."

"Has Dr. Fastolfe mentioned Fanya?"

"Yes, he has."

"Have you asked him whether Fanya is his wife or merely his companion? Whether he has children?"

Baley stirred uneasily. He might have asked such questions, of course. In the close quarters of crowded Earth, however, privacy was cherished, precisely because it had all but perished. It was virtually impossible on Earth not to know all the facts about the family arrangements of others, so one never asked and pretended ignorance. It was a universally maintained fraud.

Here on Aurora, of course, the Earth ways would not hold, yet Baley automatically held with them. Stupid!

He said, "I have not yet asked. Tell me."

Gladia said, "Fanya is his wife. He has been married a number of times, consecutively of course, though simultaneous marriage for either or both sexes is not entirely unheard of on Aurora." The bit of mild distaste with which she said that brought an equally mild defense. "It *is* unheard of on Solaria.

"However, Dr. Fastolfe's current marriage will probably soon be dissolved. Both will then be free to make new attachments, though often either or both parties do not wait for dissolution to do that. —I don't say I understand this casual way of treating the matter, Elijah, but it is how Aurorans build their relationships. Dr. Fastolfe, to my knowledge, is rather straitlaced. He always maintains one marriage or another and seeks nothing outside of it. On Aurora, that is considered old-fashioned and rather silly."

Baley nodded. "I've gathered something of this in my reading. Marriage takes place when there's the intention to have children, I understand."

"In theory, that is so, but I'm told hardly anyone takes that seriously these days. Dr. Fastolfe already has two children and can't have any more, but he still marries and applies for a third. He gets turned down, of course, and knows he will. Some people don't even bother to apply."

"Then why bother marrying?"

"There are social advantages to it. It's rather complicated and, not being an Auroran, I'm not sure I understand it."

"Well, never mind. Tell me about Dr. Fastolfe's children."

"He has two daughters by two different mothers. Neither of the mothers was Fanya, of course. He has no sons. Each daughter was incubated in the mother's womb, as is the fashion on Aurora. Both daughters are adults now and have their own establishments."

"Is he close with his daughters?"

"I don't know. He never talks about them. One is a roboticist and I suppose he *must* keep in touch with her work. I believe the other is running for office on the council of one of the cities or that she is actually in possession of the office. I don't really know."

"Do you know if there are family strains?"

"None that I am aware of, which may not go for much, Elijah. As far as I know, he is on civil terms with all his past wives. None of the dissolutions were carried through in anger. For one thing, Dr. Fastolfe is not that kind of person. I can't imagine him greeting anything in life with anything more extreme than a good-natured sigh of resignation. He'll joke on his deathbed."

That, at least, rang true, Baley thought. He said, "And Dr. Fastolfe's relationship to you. The truth, please. We are not in a position to dodge the truth in order to avoid embarrassment."

She looked up and met his eyes levelly. She said, "There is no embarrassment to avoid. Dr. Han Fastolfe is my friend, my very good friend."

"How good, Gladia?"

"As I said—very good."

"Are you waiting for the dissolution of his marriage so that you may be his next wife?"

"No." She said it very calmly.

"Are you lovers, then?"

"No."

"Have you been?"

"No. —Are you surprised?"

"I merely need information," said Baley.

"Then let me answer your questions connectedly, Elijah, and don't bark them at me as though you expected to surprise me into telling you something I would otherwise keep secret." She said it without noticeable anger. It was almost as though she were amused.

Baley, flushing slightly, was about to say that this was not at all his intention, but, of course, it was and he would gain nothing by denying it. He said in a soft growl, "Well, then, go ahead."

The remains of the tea littered the table between them. Baley wondered if, under ordinary conditions, she would not have lifted her arm and bent it just so—and if the robot, Borgraf, would not have then entered silently and cleared the table.

Did the fact that the litter remained upset Gladia—and would it make her less self-controlled in her response? If so, it had better remain—but Baley did not really hope for much, for he could see no signs of Gladia being disturbed over the mess or even of her being aware of it.

Gladia's eyes had fallen to her lap again and her face seemed to sink lower and to become a touch harsh, as though she were reaching into a past she would much rather obliterate.

She said, "You caught a glimpse of my life on Solaria. It was not a happy one, but I knew no other. It was not until I experienced a touch of happiness that I suddenly knew exactly to what an extent—and how intensively—my earlier life was not happy. The first hint came through you, Elijah."

"Through me?" Baley was caught by surprise.

"Yes, Elijah. Our last meeting on Solaria—I hope you remember it, Elijah—taught me something. I touched you! I removed my glove, one that was similar to the glove I am wearing now, and I touched your cheek. The contact did not last long. I don't know what it meant to you—no, don't tell me, it's not important—but it meant a great deal to me."

She looked up, meeting his eyes defiantly. "It meant *everything* to me. It changed my life. Remember, Elijah, that until then, after my few years of childhood, I had never touched a man—or any human being, actually—except for my husband. And I touched my husband very rarely. I had *viewed* men on trimensic, of course, and in the process I had become entirely familiar with every physical aspect of males, every part of them. I had nothing to learn, in that respect.

"But I had no reason to think that one man felt much different from another. I knew what my husband's skin felt like, what his hands felt like when he could bring himself to touch me, what—everything. I had no reason to think that anything would be different with any man. There was no pleasure in contact with my husband, but why should there be? Is there particular pleasure in the contact of my fingers with this table, except to the extent that I might appreciate its physical smoothness?

"Contact with my husband was part of an occasional ritual that he went through because it was expected of him and, as a good Solarian, he therefore carried it through by the calendar and clock and for the length of time and in the manner prescribed by good breeding. Except that, in another sense, it wasn't good breeding, for although this periodic contact was for the precise purpose of sexual intercourse, my husband had not applied for a child and was not interested, I believe, in producing one. And I was too much in awe of him to apply for one on my own initiative, as would have been my right.

"As I look back on it, I can see that the sexual experience was perfunctory and mechanical. I never had an orgasm. Not once. That such a thing existed I gathered from some of my reading, but the descriptions merely puzzled me and—since they were to be found only in imported books—Solarian books never dealt with sex—I could not trust them. I thought they were merely exotic metaphors.

"Nor could I experiment—successfully, at least—with autoeroticism. Masturbation is, I think, the common word. At least, I have heard that word used on Aurora. On Solaria, of course, no aspect of sex is ever discussed, nor is any sex-related word used in polite society. —Nor is there any other kind of society on Solaria.

"From something I occasionally read, I had an idea of how one might go about masturbating and, on a number of occasions, I made a halfhearted attempt to do what was described. I could not carry it through. The taboo against touching human flesh made even my own seem forbidden and unpleasant to me. I could brush my hand against my side, cross one leg over another, feel the pressure of thigh against thigh, but these were casual touches, unregarded. To make the process of touch an instrument of deliberate pleasure was different. Every fiber of me knew it shouldn't be done and, because I knew that, the pleasure wouldn't come.

"And it never occurred to me, never once, that there might be pleasure in touching under other circumstances. Why should it occur to me? How could it occur to me?

"Until I touched you that time. Why I did, I don't know. I felt a gush of affection for you because you had saved me from being a murderess. And besides, you were not altogether forbidden. You were not a Solarian. You were not—forgive me—altogether a man. You were a creature of Earth. You were human in appearance, but you were short-lived and infection-prone, something to be dismissed as semihuman at best.

"So because you had saved me and were not really a man, I could touch you. And what's more, you looked at me not with the hostility and repugnance of my husband—or with the carefully schooled indifference of someone viewing me on trimensic. You were right there, palpable, and your eyes were warm and concerned. You actually trembled when my hand approached your cheek. I saw that.

"Why it was, I don't know. The touch was so fugitive and there was no way in which the physical sensation was different from what it would have been if I had touched my husband or any other man—or, perhaps, even any woman. But there was more to it than the physical sensation. You were there, you welcomed it, you showed me every sign of what I accepted as—affection. And when our skins—my hand, your cheek—made contact, it was as though I had touched gentle fire that made its way up my hand and arm instantaneously and set me all in flame.

"I don't know how long it lasted—it couldn't be for more than a moment or two—but for me time stood still. Something happened to me that had never happened to me before and, looking back on it long afterward, when I had learned about it, I realized that I had very nearly experienced an orgasm.

"I tried not to show it—"

(Baley, not daring to look at her, shook his head.)

"Well, then, I didn't show it. I said, 'Thank you, Elijah.' I said it for what you had done for me in connection with my husband's death. But I said it much more for lighting my life and showing me, without even knowing it, what there was in life; for opening a door; for revealing a path; for pointing out a horizon. The physical act was nothing in itself. Just a touch. But it was the beginning of everything."

Her voice had faded out and, for a moment, she said nothing, remembering.

Then one finger lifted. "No. Don't say anything. I'm not done yet.

"I had had imaginings before, very vague uncertain things. A man and I, doing what my husband and I did, but somehow different—I didn't even know different in what way—and feeling something different—something I could not even imagine when imagining with all my might. I might conceivably have gone through my whole life trying to imagine the unimaginable and I might have died as I suppose women on Solaria—and men, too—often do, never knowing, even after three or four centuries. Never knowing. Having children, but never knowing.

"But one touch of your cheek, Elijah, and I knew. Isn't that amazing? You taught me what I might imagine. Not the mechanics of it, not the dull, reluctant approach of bodies, but something that I could never have conceived as having anything to do with it. The look on a face, the sparkle in an eye, the feeling of—gentleness—kindness—something I can't even describe —acceptance—a lowering of the terrible barrier between individuals. Love, I suppose—a convenient word to encompass all of that and more.

"I felt love for you, Elijah, because I thought you could feel love for me. I don't say you loved me, but it seemed to me you could. I never had that and, although in ancient literature they talked of it, I didn't know what they meant any more than when men in those same books talked about 'honor' and killed each other for its sake. I accepted the word, but never made out its meaning. I still haven't. And so it was with 'love' until I touched you.

"After that I could imagine—and I came to Aurora remembering you, and thinking of you, and talking to you endlessly in my mind, and thinking that in Aurora I would meet a million Elijahs."

She stopped, lost in her own thoughts for a moment, then suddenly went on:

"I didn't. Aurora, it turned out, was, in its way, as bad as Solaria. In Solaria, sex was *wrong*. It was hated and we all turned away from it. We could not love for the hatred that sex aroused.

"In Aurora, sex was *boring*. It was accepted calmly, easily—as easily as breathing. If one felt the impulse, one reached out toward anyone who seemed suitable and, if that suitable person was not at the moment engaged in something that could not be put aside, sex followed in any fashion that was convenient. Like breathing. —But where is the ecstasy in breathing? If one were choking, then perhaps the first shuddering breath that followed upon deprivation might be an overwhelming delight and relief. But if one never choked?

"And if one never unwillingly went without sex? If it were taught to youngsters on an even basis with reading and programming? If children were expected to experiment as a matter of course, and if older children were expected to help out?

"Sex—permitted and free as water—has nothing to do with love on Aurora, just as sex—forbidden and a thing of shame—has nothing to do with love on Solaria. In either case, children are few and must come about only after formal application. —And then, if permission is granted, there must be an interlude of sex designed for childbearing only, dull and brackish. If, after a reasonable time, impregnation doesn't follow, the spirit rebels and artificial insemination is resorted to.

"In time, as on Solaria, ectogenesis will be the thing, so that fertilization and fetal development will take place in genotaria and sex will be left to itself as a form of social interaction and play that has no more to do with love than space-polo does.

"I could not move into the Auroran attitude, Elijah. I had not been brought up to it. With terror, I had reached out for sex and no one refused—and no one mattered. Each man's eyes were blank when I offered myself and remained blank as they accepted. Another one, they said, what matter? They were willing, but no more than willing.

"And touching them meant nothing. I might have been touching my husband. I learned to go through with it, to follow their lead, to accept their guidance—and it all still meant nothing. I gained not even the urge to do it to myself and by myself. The feeling you had given me never returned and, in time, I gave up.

"In all this, Dr. Fastolfe was my friend. He alone, on all Aurora, knew everything that happened on Solaria. At least, so I think. You know that the full story was not made public and certainly did not appear in that dreadful hyperwave program that I've heard of—I refused to watch it.

"Dr. Fastolfe protected me against the lack of understanding on the part of Aurorans and against their general contempt for Solarians. He protected me also against the despair that filled me after a while.

"No, we were not lovers. I would have offered myself, but by the time it occurred to me that I might do so, I no longer felt that the feeling you had inspired, Elijah, would ever recur. I thought it might have been a trick of memory and I gave up. I did not offer myself. Nor did he offer himself. I do not know why he did not. Perhaps he could see that my despair arose over my failure to find anything useful in sex and did not want to accentuate the despair by repeating the failure. It would be typically kind of him to be careful of me in this way—so we were not lovers. He was merely my friend at a time when I needed that so much more.

"There you are, Elijah. You have the whole answer to the questions you asked. You wanted to know my relationship with Dr. Fastolfe and said you needed information. You have it. Are you satisfied?"

Baley tried not let his misery show. "I am sorry, Gladia, that life has been so hard for you. You have given me the information I needed. You have given me more information than, perhaps, you think you have."

Gladia frowned. "In what way?"

Baley did not answer directly. He said, "Gladia, I am glad that your memory of me has meant so much to you. It never occurred to me at any time on Solaria, that I was impressing you so and, even if it had, I would not have tried— You know."

"I know, Elijah," she said, softening. "Nor would it have availed you if you had tried. I couldn't have."

"And I know that. —Nor do I take what you have told me as an invitation now. One touch, one moment of sexual insight, need be no more than that. Very likely, it can never be repeated and that onetime existence ought not to be spoiled by foolish attempts at resurrection. That is a reason why I do not now—offer myself. My failure to do so is not to be interpreted as one more blank ending for you. Besides—"

"Yes."

"You have, as I said earlier, told me perhaps more than you realize you did. You have told me that the story does not end with your despair."

"Why do you say that?"

"In telling me of the feeling that was inspired by the touch upon my cheek, you said something like 'looking back on it long afterward, when I had learned, I realized that I had very nearly experienced an orgasm.' —But then you went on to explain that sex with Aurorans was never successful and, I presume, you did not then experience orgasm either. Yet you *must* have, Gladia, if you recognized the sensation you experienced that time on Solaria. You could not look back and recognize it for what it was, unless you had learned to love successfully. In other words, you *have* had a lover and you *have* experienced love. If I am to believe that Dr. Fastolfe is not your lover and has not been, then it follows that someone else is—or was."

"And if so? Why is that your concern, Elijah?"

"I don't know if it is or is not, Gladia. Tell me who it is and, if it proves to be not my concern, that will be the end of it."

Gladia was silent.

Baley said, "If you don't tell me, Gladia, I will have to tell you. I told you earlier that I am not in a position to spare your feelings."

Gladia remained silent, the corners of her lips whitening with pressure.

"It must be someone, Gladia, and your sorrow over Jander's loss is extreme. You sent Daneel out because you could not bear to look at him for the reminder of Jander that his face brought. If I am wrong in deciding that it was Jander Panell—" He paused a moment, then said harshly, "If the robot, Jander Panell, was not your lover, say so."

And Gladia whispered, "Jander Panell, the robot, was not my lover." Then, loudly and firmly, she said, "He was my husband!"

25.

Baley's lips moved soundlessly, but there was no mistaking the tetrasyllabic exclamation.

"Yes," said Gladia. "Jehoshaphat! You are startled. Why? Do you disapprove?"

Baley said tonelessly, "It is not my place either to approve or disapprove."

"Which means you disapprove."

"Which means I seek only information. How does one distinguish between a lover and a husband on Aurora?"

"If two people live together in the same establishment for a period of time, they may refer to each other as 'wife' or 'husband,' rather than as 'lover.'"

"How long a period of time?"

"That varies from region to region, I understand, according to local option. In the city of Eos, the period of time is three months."

"Is it also required that during this period of time one refrain from sexual relations with others?"

Gladia's eyebrows lifted in surprise. "Why?"

"I merely ask."

"Exclusivity is unthinkable on Aurora. Husband or lover, it makes no difference. One engages in sex at pleasure."

"And did you please while you were with Jander?"

"As it happens I did not, but that was my choice."

"Others offered themselves?"

"Occasionally."

"And you refused?"

"I can always refuse at will. That is part of the nonexclusivity."

"But did you refuse?"

"I did."

"And did those whom you refused know why you refused?"

"What do you mean?"

"Did they know that you had a robot husband?"

"I had a *husband*. Don't call him a robot husband. There is no such expression."

"Did they know?"

She paused. "I don't know if they knew."

"Did you tell them?"

"What reason was there to tell them?"

"Don't answer my questions with questions. Did you tell them?"

"I did not."

"How could you avoid that? Don't you think an explanation for your refusal would have been natural?"

"No explanation is ever required. A refusal is simply a refusal and is always accepted. I don't understand you."

Baley stopped to gather his thoughts. Gladia and he were not at cross-purposes; they were running down parallel tracks.

He started again. "Would it have seemed natural on Solaria to have a robot for a husband?"

"On Solaria, it would have been unthinkable and I would never have thought of such a possibility. On Solaria, everything was unthinkable. —And on Earth, too, Elijah. Would your wife ever have taken a robot for a husband?"

"That's irrelevant, Gladia."

"Perhaps, but your expression was answer enough. We may not be Aurorans, you and I, but we are on Aurora. I have lived here for two years and I accept its mores."

"Do you mean that human-robot sexual connections are common here on Aurora?"

"I don't know. I merely know that they are accepted because

everything is accepted where sex is concerned—everything that is voluntary, that gives mutual satisfaction, and that does no physical harm to anyone. What conceivable difference would it make to anyone else how an individual or any combination of individuals found satisfaction? Would anyone worry about which books I viewed, what food I ate, what hour I went to sleep or awoke, whether I was fond of cats or disliked roses? Sex, too, is a matter of indifference—on Aurora."

"On Aurora," echoed Baley. "But you were not born on Aurora and were not brought up in its ways. You told me just a while ago that you couldn't adjust to this very indifference to sex that you now praise. Earlier, you expressed your distaste for multiple marriages and for easy promiscuity. If you did not tell those whom you refused why you refused, it might have been because, in some hidden pocket of your being, you were ashamed of having Jander as a husband. You might have known—or suspected, or even merely supposed—that you were unusual in this—unusual even on Aurora—and you were ashamed."

"No, Elijah, you won't talk me into being ashamed. If having a robot as a husband is unusual even on Aurora, that would be because robots like Jander are unusual. The robots we have on Solaria, or on Earth—or on Aurora, except for Jander and Daneel—are not designed to give any but the most primitive sexual satisfaction. They might be used as masturbation devices, perhaps, as a mechanical vibrator might be, but nothing much more. When the new humaniform robot becomes widespread, so will human-robot sex become widespread."

Baley said, "How did you come to possess Jander in the first place, Gladia? Only two existed—both in Dr. Fastolfe's establishment. Did he simply give one of them—half of the total—to you?"

"Yes."

"Why?"

"Out of kindness, I suppose. I was lonely, disillusioned, wretched, a stranger in a strange land. He gave me Jander for company and I will never be able to thank him enough for it. It only lasted for half a year, but that half-year may be worth all my life beside."

"Did Dr. Fastolfe know that Jander was your husband?"

"He never referred to it, so I don't know."

"Did *you* refer to it?"

"No."

"Why not?"

"I saw no need. —And no, it was not because I felt shame."

"How did it happen?"

"That I saw no need?"

"No. That Jander became your husband."

Gladia stiffened. She said in a hostile voice, "Why do I have to explain that?"

Baley said, "Gladia, it's getting late. Don't fight me every step of the way. Are you distressed that Jander is—is gone?"

"Need you ask?"

"Do you want to find out what happened?"

"Again, need you ask?"

"Then help me. I need all the information I can get if I am to begin—even begin—to make progress in working out an apparently insoluble problem. How did Jander become your husband?"

Gladia sat back in her chair and her eyes were suddenly brimming with tears. She pushed at the plate of crumbs that had once been pastry and said in a choked voice:

"Ordinary robots do not wear clothes, but they are so designed as to give the effect of wearing clothes. I know robots well, having lived on Solaria, and I have a certain amount of artistic talent—"

"I remember your light-forms," said Baley softly.

Gladia nodded in acknowledgment. "I constructed a few designs for new models that would possess, in my opinion, more style and more interest than some of those in use in Aurora. Some of my paintings, based on those designs, are on the walls here. Others I have in other places in this establishment."

Baley's eyes moved to the paintings. He had seen them. They were of robots, unmistakably. They were not naturalistic, but seemed elongated and unnaturally curved. He noted now that the distortions were so designed as to stress, quite cleverly, those portions which, now that he looked at them from a new perspective, suggested clothing. Somehow there was an impression of servants' costumes he had once viewed in a book devoted to the Victorian England of medieval times. Did Gladia know of these things or was it a merely chance, if circumstantial, similarity? It was a question of no account, probably, but not something (perhaps) to be forgotten.

When he had first noticed them, he had thought it was Gladia's way of surrounding herself with robots in imitation of life on Solaria. She hated that life, she said, but that was only a product of her thinking mind. Solaria had been the only home she had really known and that is not easily sloughed off—perhaps not at all. And perhaps that remained a factor in her painting, even if her new occupation gave her a more plausible motive.

She was speaking. "I was successful. Some of the robot-manufacturing concerns paid well for my designs and there were numerous cases of existing robots being resurfaced according to my directions. There was a certain satisfaction in all this that, in a small measure, compensated for the emotional emptiness of my life.

"When Jander was given me by Dr. Fastolfe, I had a robot who, of course, wore ordinary clothing. The dear doctor was, indeed, kind enough to give me a number of changes of clothing for Jander.

"None of it was in the least imaginative and it amused me to buy what I considered more appropriate garb. That meant measuring him quite accurately, since I intended to have my designs made to order—and *that* meant having him remove his clothing in stages.

"He did so—and it was only when he was completely unclothed that I quite realized how close to human he was. Nothing was lacking and those portions which might be expected to be erectile were, indeed, erectile. Indeed, they were under what, in a human, would be called conscious control. Jander could tumesce and detumesce on order. He told me so when I asked him if his penis was functional in that respect. I was curious and he demonstrated.

"You must understand that, although he looked very much

like a man, I knew he was a robot. I have a certain hesitation about touching men—you understand—and I have no doubt that played a part in my inability to have satisfactory sex with Aurorans. But this was not a man and I had been with robots all my life. I could touch Jander freely.

"It didn't take me long to realize that I enjoyed touching him and it didn't take Jander long to realize that I enjoyed it. He was a finely tuned robot who followed the Three Laws carefully. To have failed to give joy when he could would have been to disappoint. Disappointment could be reckoned as harm and he could not harm a human being. He took infinite care then to give me joy and, because I saw in him the desire to give joy, something I never saw in Auroran men, I was indeed joyful and, eventually, I found out, to the full, I think, what an orgasm is."

Baley said, "You were, then, completely happy?"

"With Jander? Of course. Completely."

"You never quarreled?"

"With Jander? How could I? His only aim, his only reason for existence, was to please me."

"Might that not disturb you? He only pleased you because he had to."

"What motive would anyone have to do anything but that, for one reason or another, he had to?"

"And you never had the urge to try real—to try Aurorans after you had learned to experience orgasm?"

"It would have been an unsatisfactory substitute. I wanted only Jander. —And do you understand, now, what I have lost?"

Baley's naturally grave expression lengthened into solemnity. He said, "I understand, Gladia. If I gave you pain earlier, please forgive me, for I did not entirely understand then."

But she was weeping and he waited, unable to say anything more, unable to think of a reasonable way to console her.

Finally, she shook her head and wiped her eyes with the back of her hand. She whispered, "Is there anything more?"

Baley said apologetically, "A few questions on another subject and then I will be through annoying you." He added cautiously, "For now."

"What is it?" She seemed very tired.

"Do you know that there are people who seem to think that Dr. Fastolfe was responsible for the killing of Jander?"

"Yes."

"Do you know that Dr. Fastolfe himself admits that only he possesses the expertise to kill Jander in the way that he was killed?"

"Yes. The dear doctor told me so himself."

"Well, then, Gladia, do *you* think Dr. Fastolfe killed Jander?"

She looked up at him, suddenly and sharply, and then said angrily, "Of course not. Why should he? Jander was *his* robot to begin with and he was full of care for him. You don't know the dear doctor as I do, Elijah. He is a gentle person who would hurt no one and who would never hurt a robot. To suppose he would kill one is to suppose that a rock would fall upward."

"I have no further questions, Gladia, and the only other business I have here, at the moment, is to see Jander—what remains of Jander—if I have your permission."

She was suspicious again, hostile. "Why? *Why?*"

"Gladia! Please! I don't expect it to be of any use, but I must see Jander and *know* that seeing him is of no use. I will try to do nothing that will offend your sensibilities."

Gladia stood up. Her gown, so simple as to be nothing more than a closely fitting sheath, was not black (as it would have been on Earth) but of a dull color that showed no sparkle anywhere in it. Baley, no connoisseur of clothing, realized how well it represented mourning.

"Come with me," she whispered.

26.

Baley followed Gladia through several rooms, the walls of which glowed dully. On one or two occasions, he caught a hint of movement, which he took to be a robot getting rapidly out of the way, since they had been told not to intrude.

Through a hallway, then, and up a short flight of stairs into a small room in which one part of one wall gleamed to give the effect of a spotlight.

The room held a cot and a chair—and no other furnishings.

"This was his room," said Gladia. Then, as though answering Baley's thought, she went on to say, "It was all he needed. I left him alone as much as I could—all day if I could. I did not want to ever grow tired of him." She shook her head. "I wish now I had stayed with him every second. I didn't know our time would be so short. —Here he is."

Jander was lying on the cot and Baley looked at him gravely. The robot was covered with a smooth and shiny material. The spotlighted wall cast its glow on Jander's head, which was smooth and almost inhuman in its serenity. The eyes were wide open, but they were opaque and lusterless. He looked enough like Daneel to give ample point to Gladia's discomfort at Daneel's presence. His neck and bare shoulders showed above the sheet.

Baley said, "Has Dr. Fastolfe inspected him?"

"Yes, thoroughly. I came to him in despair and, if you had seen him rush here, the concern he felt, the pain, the—the panic, you would never think he could have been responsible. There was nothing he could do."

"Is he unclothed?"

"Yes. Dr. Fastolfe had to remove the clothing for a thorough examination. There was no point in replacing them."

"Would you permit me to remove the covering, Gladia?"

"Must you?"

"I do not wish to be blamed for having missed some obvious point of examination."

"What can you possibly find that Dr. Fastolfe didn't?"

"Nothing, Gladia, but I must *know* that there is nothing for me to find. Please cooperate."

"Well, then, go ahead, but *please* put the covering back exactly as it is now when you are done."

She turned her back on him and on Jander, put her left arm against the wall, and rested her forehead on it. There was no sound from her—no motion—but Baley knew that she was weeping again.

The body was, perhaps, not quite human. The muscular contours were somehow simplified and a bit schematic, but all the parts were there: nipples, navel, penis, testicles, pubic hair, and so on. Even fine, light hair on the chest.

How many days was it since Jander had been killed? It struck Baley that he didn't know, but it had been sometime before his trip to Aurora had begun. Over a week had passed and there was no sign of decay, either visually or olfactorily. A clear robotic difference.

Baley hesitated and then thrust one arm under Jander's shoulders and another under his hips, working them through to the other side. He did not consider asking for Gladia's help—*that* would be impossible. He heaved and, with some difficulty, turned Jander over without throwing him off the cot.

The cot creaked. Gladia must know what he was doing, but she did not turn around. Though she did not offer to help, she did not protest either.

Baley withdrew his arms. Jander felt warm to the touch. Presumably, the power unit continued to do so simple a thing as to maintain temperature, even with the brain inoperative. The body felt firm and resilient, too. Presumably, it never went through any stage analogous to rigor mortis.

One arm was now dangling off the cot in quite a human fashion. Baley moved it gently and released it. It swung to and fro slightly and came to a halt. He bent one leg at the knee and studied the foot, then the other. The buttocks were perfectly formed and there was even an anus.

Baley could not get rid of the feeling of uneasiness. The notion that he was violating the privacy of a human being would not go away. If it were a human corpse, its coldness and its stiffness would have deprived it of humanity.

He thought uncomfortably: A robot corpse is much more human than a human corpse.

Again he reached under Jander, lifted, and turned him over.

He smoothed out the sheet as best he could, then replaced the cover as it had been and smoothed that. He stepped back and decided it was as it had been at first—or as near to that as he could manage.

"I'm finished, Gladia," he said.

She turned, looked at Jander with wet eyes, and said, "May we go, then?"

"Yes, of course, but Gladia—"

"Well?"

"Will you be keeping him this way? I imagine he won't decay."

"Does it matter if I do?"

"In some ways, yes. You must give yourself a chance to recover. You can't spend three centuries mourning. What is over is over." (His statements sounded hollowly sententious in his own ear. What must they have sounded like in hers?)

She said, "I know you mean it kindly, Elijah. I have been requested to keep Jander till the investigation is done. He will then be torched at my request."

"Torched?"

"Put under a plasma torch and reduced to his elements, as human corpses are. I will have holograms of him—and memories. Will that satisfy you?"

"Of course. I must return to Dr. Fastolfe's house now."

"Yes. Have you learned anything from Jander's body?"

"I did not expect to, Gladia."

She faced him full. "And Elijah, I want you to find who did this and why. I must know."

"But Gladia—"

She shook her head violently, as though keeping out anything she wasn't ready to hear. "I *know* you can do this."

# 7

---

# Again Fastolfe

## 27.

Baley emerged from Gladia's house into the sunset. He turned toward what he assumed must be the western horizon and found Aurora's sun, a deep scarlet in color, topped by thin strips of ruddy clouds set in an apple-green sky.

"Jehoshaphat," he murmured. Clearly, Aurora's sun, cooler and more orange than Earth's sun, accentuated the difference at setting, when its light passed through a greater thickness of Aurora.

Daneel was behind him; Giskard, as before, well in front.

Daneel's voice was in his ear. "Are you well, Partner Elijah?"

"Quite well," said Baley, pleased with himself. "I'm handling the Outside well, Daneel. I can even admire the sunset. Is it always like this?"

Daneel gazed dispassionately at the setting sun and said, "Yes. But let us move quickly toward Dr. Fastolfe's establishment. At this time of year, the twilight does not last long, Partner Elijah, and I would wish you there while you can still see easily."

"I'm ready. Let's go." Baley wondered if it might not be better to wait for the darkness. It would not be pleasant not to see, but, then, it would give him the illusion of being enclosed—and he was not, in his heart, sure as to how long this euphoria induced by admiring a sunset (a sunset, mind you, Outside) would last.

But that was a cowardly uncertainty and he would not own up to it.

Giskard noiselessly drifted backward toward him and said, "Would you prefer to wait, sir? Would the darkness suit you better? We ourselves will not be discommoded."

Baley became aware of other robots, farther off, on every side. Had Gladia marked off her field robots for guard duty or had Fastolfe sent his?

It accentuated the way they were all caring for him and, perversely, he would not admit to weakness. He said, "No, we'll go now," and struck off at a brisk walk toward Fastolfe's establishment, which he could just see through the distant trees.

Let the robots follow or not, as they wished, he thought boldly. He knew that, if he let himself think about it, there would be something within him that would still quail at the thought of himself on the outer skin of a planet with no protection but air between himself and the great void, but he would *not* think of it.

It was the exhilaration at being free of the fear that made his jaws tremble and his teeth click. Or it was the cool wind of evening that did it—and that also set the gooseflesh to appearing on his arms.

It was *not* the Outside.

It was *not*.

He said, trying to unclench his teeth, "How well did you know Jander, Daneel?"

Daneel said, "We were together for some time. From the time of friend Jander's construction, till he passed into the establishment of Miss Gladia, we were together steadily."

"Did it bother you, Daneel, that Jander resembled you so closely?"

"No, sir. He and I each knew ourselves apart, Partner Elijah, and Dr. Fastolfe did not mistake us either. We were, therefore, two individuals."

"And could you tell them apart, too, Giskard?" They were closer to him now, perhaps because the other robots had taken over the long-distance duties.

Giskard said, "There was no occasion, as I recall, on which it was important that I do so."

"And if there had been, Giskard?"

"Then I could have done so."

"What was your opinion of Jander, Daneel?"

Daneel said, "My opinion, Partner Elijah? Concerning what aspect of Jander do you wish my opinion?"

"Did he do his work well, for instance?"

"Certainly."

"Was he satisfactory in every way?"

"In every way, to my knowledge."

"How about you, Giskard? What is your opinion?"

Giskard said, "I was never as close to friend Jander as friend Daneel was and it would not be proper for me to state an opinion. I can say that, to my knowledge, Dr. Fastolfe was uniformly pleased with friend Jander. He seemed equally pleased with friend Jander and with friend Daneel. However, I do not think my programming is such as to allow me to offer certainty in such matters."

Baley said, "What about the period after Jander entered the household of Miss Gladia? Did you know him then, Daneel?"

"No, Partner Elijah. Miss Gladia kept him at her establishment. On those occasions when she visited Dr. Fastolfe, he was never with her, as far as I was aware. On occasions when I accompanied Dr. Fastolfe on a visit to Miss Gladia's establishment, I did not see friend Jander."

Baley felt a little surprised at that. He turned to Giskard in order to ask the same question, paused, and then shrugged. He was not really getting anywhere and, as Dr. Fastolfe had indicated earlier, there is not really much use in cross-examining a robot. They would not knowingly say anything that would harm a human being, nor could they be badgered, bribed, or cajoled into it. They would not openly lie, but they would remain stubbornly—if politely—insistent on giving useless answers.

And—perhaps—it no longer mattered.

They were at Fastolfe's doorstep now and Baley felt his breath quickening. The trembling of his arms and lower lip, he was confident, was, indeed, only because of the cool wind.

The sun had gone now, a few stars were visible, the sky was darkening to an odd greenish-purple that made it seem bruised, and he passed through the door into the warmth of the glowing walls.

He was safe.

Fastolfe greeted him. "You are back in good time, Mr. Baley. Was your session with Gladia fruitful?"

Baley said, "Quite fruitful, Dr. Fastolfe. It is even possible that I hold the key to the answer in my hand."

### 28.

Fastolfe merely smiled politely, in a way that signaled neither surprise, elation, nor disbelief. He led the way into what was obviously a dining room, a smaller and friendlier one than the one in which they had had lunch.

"You and I, my dear Mr. Baley," said Fastolfe pleasantly, "will eat an informal dinner alone. Merely the two of us. We will even have the robots absent if that will please you. Nor shall we talk business unless you desperately want to."

Baley said nothing, but paused to look at the walls in astonishment. They were a wavering, luminous green, with differences in brightness and in tint that were slowly progressive from bottom to top. There was a hint of fronds of deeper green and shadowy flickers this way and that. The walls made the room appear to be a well-lit grotto at the bottom of a shallow arm of the sea. The effect was vertiginous—at least, Baley found it so.

Fastolfe had no trouble interpreting Baley's expression. He said, "It's an acquired taste, Mr. Baley, I admit. —Giskard, subdue the wall illumination. —Thank you."

Baley drew a breath of relief. "And thank *you*, Dr. Fastolfe. May I visit the Personal, sir?"

"But of course."

Baley hesitated. "Could you—"

Fastolfe chuckled. "You'll find it perfectly normal, Mr. Baley. You will have no complaints."

Baley bent his head. "Thank you *very much*."

Without the intolerable make-believe, the Personal—he believed it to be the same one he had used earlier in the day—was merely what it was, a much more luxurious and hospitable one than he had ever seen. It was incredibly different from those on Earth, which were rows of identical units stretching indefinitely, each ticked off for use by one—and only one—individual at a time.

It *gleamed* somehow with hygienic cleanliness. Its outermost molecular layer might have been peeled off after every use and a new layer laid on. Obscurely, Baley felt that, if he stayed on Aurora long enough, he would find it difficult to readjust himself to Earth's crowds, which forced hygiene and cleanliness into the background—something to pay a distant obeisance to—a not quite attainable ideal.

Baley, standing there surrounded by conveniences of ivory and gold (not real ivory, no doubt, nor real gold), gleaming and smooth, suddenly found himself shuddering at Earth's casual exchange of bacteria and wincing at its richness in infectivity. Was that not what the Spacers felt? Could he blame them?

He washed his hands thoughtfully, playing with the tiny touches here and there along the control-strip in order to change the temperature. And yet these Aurorans were so unnecessarily garish in their interior decorations, so insistent in pretending they were living in a state of nature when they had tamed nature and broken it. —Or was that only Fastolfe?

After all, Gladia's establishment had been far more austere. —Or was that only because she had been brought up on Solaria?

The dinner that followed was an unalloyed delight. Again, as at lunch, there was the distinct feeling of being closer to nature. The dishes were numerous—each different, each in small portions—and, in a number of cases, it was possible to see that they had once been part of plants and animals. He was beginning to look upon the inconveniences—the occasional small bone, bit of gristle, strand of fiber, which might have repelled him earlier—as a bit of adventure.

The first course was a little fish—a little fish that one ate whole, with whatever internal organs it might have—and that struck

him, at first sight, as another foolish way of rubbing one's nose
in Nature with a capital "N." But he swallowed the little fish
anyway, as Fastolfe did, and the taste converted him at once. He
had never experienced anything like it. It was as though taste
buds had suddenly been invented and inserted in his tongue.

Tastes changed from dish to dish and some were distinctly
odd and not entirely pleasant, but he found it didn't matter. The
thrill of a distinct taste, of *different* distinct tastes (at Fastolfe's
instruction, he took a sip of faintly flavored water between
dishes) was what counted—and not the inner detail.

He tried not to gobble, nor to concentrate his attention entirely on the food, nor to lick his plate. Desperately, he continued to observe and imitate Fastolfe and to ignore the other's
kindly but definitely amused glance.

"I trust," said Fastolfe, "you find this to your taste."

"Quite good," Baley managed to choke out.

"Please don't force yourself into useless politeness. Do not eat
anything that seems strange or unpalatable to you. I will have
additional helpings of anything you do like brought in its place."

"Not necessary, Dr. Fastolfe. It is all rather satisfactory."

"Good."

Despite Fastolfe's offer to eat without robots present, it was a
robot who served. (Fastolfe, accustomed to this, probably did
not even notice the fact, Baley thought—and he did not bring
the matter up.)

As was to be expected, the robot was silent and his motions
were flawless. His handsome livery seemed to be out of historical dramas that Baley had seen on hyperwave. It was only at
very close view that one could see how much the costume was
an illusion of the lighting and how close the robot exterior was
to a smooth metal finish—and no more.

Baley said, "Has the waiter's surface been designed by Gladia?"

"Yes," said Fastolfe, obviously pleased. "How complimented
she will feel to know that you recognized her touch. She is good,
isn't she? Her work is coming into increasing popularity and she
fills a useful niche in Auroran society."

Conversation throughout the meal had been pleasant but

unimportant. Baley had had no urge to "talk business" and had, in fact, preferred to be largely silent while enjoying the meal and leaving it to his unconscious—or whatever faculty took over in the absence of hard thought—to decide on how to approach the matter that seemed to him now to be the central point of the Jander problem.

Fastolfe took the matter out of his hands, rather, by saying, "And now that you've mentioned Gladia, Mr. Baley, may I ask how it came about that you left for her establishment rather deep in despair and have returned almost buoyant and speaking of perhaps having the key to the whole affair in your hand? Did you learn something new—and unexpected, perhaps—at Gladia's?"

"That I did," said Baley absently—but he was lost in the dessert, which he could not recognize at all, and of which (after some yearning in his eyes had acted to inspire the waiter) a second small helping was placed before him. He felt replete. He had never in his life so enjoyed the act of eating and for the first time found himself resenting the physiological limits that made it impossible to eat forever. He felt rather ashamed of himself that he should feel so.

"And what was it learned that was new and unexpected?" asked Fastolfe with quiet patience. "Presumably something I didn't know myself?"

"Perhaps. Gladia told me that you had given Jander to her about half a year ago."

Fastolfe nodded. "I knew *that*. So I did."

Baley said sharply, "Why?"

The amiable look on Fastolfe's face faded slowly. Then he said, "Why not?"

Baley said, "I don't know why not, Dr. Fastolfe. I don't care. My question is: Why?"

Fastolfe shook his head slightly and said nothing.

Baley said, "Dr. Fastolfe, I am here in order to straighten out what seems to be a miserable mess. Nothing you have done— *nothing*—has made things simple. Rather, you have taken what seems to be pleasure in showing me how bad a mess it is and in destroying any speculation I may advance as a possible solution.

Now, I don't expect others to answer my questions. I have no official standing on this world and have no right to ask questions, let alone force answers.

"You, however, are different. I am here at your request and I am trying to save your career as well as mine and, according to your own account of matters, I am trying to save Aurora as well as Earth. Therefore, I expect you to answer my questions fully and truthfully. Please don't indulge in stalemating tactics, such as asking me why not when I ask why. Now, once again—and for the last time: Why?"

Fastolfe thrust out his lips and looked grim. "My apologies, Mr. Baley. If I hesitated to answer, it is because, looking back on it, it seems there is no very dramatic reason. Gladia Delmarre —no, she doesn't want her surname used—Gladia is a stranger on this planet; she has undergone traumatic experiences on her home world, as you know, and traumatic experiences on this one, as perhaps you don't know—"

"I do know. Please be more direct."

"Well, then, I was sorry for her. She was alone and Jander, I thought, would make her feel less alone."

"Sorry for her? Just that. Are you lovers? Have you been?"

"No, not at all. I did not offer. Nor did she. —Why? Did she tell you we were lovers?"

"No, she did not, but I need independent confirmation, in any case. I'll let you know when there is a contradiction; you needn't concern yourself about that. How is it that with you sympathizing so with her and—from what I gather from Gladia, she feeling so grateful to you—that neither of you offered yourself? I gather that on Aurora offering sex is about on a par with commenting upon the weather."

Fastolfe frowned. "You know nothing about it, Mr. Baley. Don't judge us by the standards of your own world. Sex is not a matter of great importance to us, but we are careful as to how we use it. It may not seem so to you, but none of us offer it lightly. Gladia, unused to our ways and sexually frustrated on Solaria, perhaps did offer it lightly—or desperately might be the better word—and it may not be surprising, therefore, that she did not enjoy the results."

"Didn't you try to improve matters?"

"By offering myself? I am not what she needs and, for that matter, she is not what I need. I was *sorry* for her. I like her. I admire her artistic talent. And I want her to be happy. —After all, Mr. Baley, surely you'll agree that the sympathy of one human being for another need not rest on sexual desire or on anything but decent human feeling. Have you never felt sympathy for anyone? Have you never wanted to help someone for no reason other than the good feeling it gave you to relieve another's misery? What kind of planet do you come from?"

Baley said, "What you say is justified, Dr. Fastolfe. I do not question the fact that you are a decent human being. Still, bear with me. When I first asked you why you had given Jander to Gladia, you did not tell me then what you have told me just now —and with considerable emotion, too, I might add. Your first impulse was to duck, to hesitate, to play for time by asking why not.

"Granted that what you finally told me is so, what is it about the question that embarrassed you at first? What reason—that you did *not* want to admit—came to you before you settled on the reason you *did* want to admit? Forgive me for insisting, but I must know—and not out of personal curiosity, I assure you. If what you tell me is of no use in this sorry business, then you may consider it thrown into a black hole."

Fastolfe said in a low voice, "In all honesty, I am not sure why I parried your question. You surprised me into something that, perhaps, I don't want to face. Let me think, Mr. Baley."

They sat there together quietly. The server cleared the table and left the room. Daneel and Giskard were elsewhere (presumably, they were guarding the house). Baley and Fastolfe were at last alone in a robot-free room.

Finally, Fastolfe said, "I don't know what I ought to tell you, but let me go back some decades. I have two daughters. Perhaps you know that. They are by two different mothers—"

"Would you rather have had sons, Dr. Fastolfe?"

Fastolfe looked genuinely surprised. "No. Not at all. The mother of my second daughter wanted a son, I believe, but I wouldn't give my consent to artificial insemination with selected sperm—not even with my own sperm—but insisted on the natural throw of the genetic dice. Before you ask why, it is because I prefer a certain operation of chance in life and because I think, on the whole, I wanted a chance to have a daughter. I would have accepted a son, you understand, but I didn't want to abandon the chance of a daughter. I approve of daughters, somehow. Well, my second proved a daughter and that may have been one of the reasons that the mother dissolved the marriage soon after the birth. On the other hand, a sizable percentage of marriages are dissolved after a birth in any case, so perhaps I needn't look for special reasons."

"She took the child with her, I take it."

Fastolfe bent a puzzled glance at Baley. "Why should she do that? —But I forget. You're from Earth. No, of course not. The child would have been brought up in a nursery, where she could be properly cared for, of course. Actually, though"—he wrinkled his nose as though in sudden embarrassment over a peculiar memory—"she wasn't put there. I decided to bring her up myself. It was legal to do so but very unusual. I was quite young, of course, not yet having attained the century mark, but already I had made my mark in robotics."

"Did you manage?"

"You mean to bring her up successfully? Oh yes. I grew quite fond of her. I named her Vasilia. It was my mother's name, you see." He chuckled reminiscently. "I get these odd streaks of sentiment—like my affection for my robots. I never met my mother, of course, but her name was on my charts. And she's still alive, as far as I know, so I could see her—but I think there's something queasy about meeting someone in whose womb you once were. —Where was I?"

"You named your daughter Vasilia."

"Yes—and I did bring her up and actually grew fond of her. Very fond of her. I could see where the attraction lay in doing something like that, but, of course, I was an embarrassment to my friends and I had to keep her out of their way when there was contact to be made, either social or professional. I remember once—" He paused.

"Yes?"

"It's something I haven't thought of for decades. She came running out, weeping for some reason, and threw herself into my arms when Dr. Sarton was with me, discussing one of the very earliest design programs for humaniform robots. She was only seven years old, I think and, of course, I hugged her, and kissed her, and ignored the business at hand, which was quite unforgivable of me. Sarton left, coughing and choking—and *most* indignant. It was a full week before I could renew contact with him and resume deliberation. Children shouldn't have that effect on people, I suppose, but there are so few children and they are so rarely encountered."

"And your daughter—Vasilia—was fond of you?"

"Oh yes—at least, until— She was very fond of me. I saw to her schooling and made sure her mind was allowed to expand to the fullest."

"You said she was fond of you until—something. You did not finish the sentence. There came a time, then, when she was no longer fond of you. When was that?"

"She wanted to have her own establishment once she grew old enough. It was only natural."

"And you did not want it?"

"What do you mean I did not want it? Of course, I wanted it. You keep assuming I'm a monster, Mr. Baley."

"Am I to assume, instead, that once she reached the age when she was to have her own establishment, she no longer felt the same affection for you that she naturally had when she was actively your daughter, living in *your* establishment as a dependent?"

"Not quite that simple. In fact, it was rather complicated. You see—" Fastolfe seemed embarrassed. "I refused her when she offered herself to me."

"She offered herself to *you?*" said Baley, horrified.

"That part was only natural," said Fastolfe indifferently. "She knew me best. I had instructed her in sex, encouraged her experimentation, taken her to the Games of Eros, done my best for her. It was something to be expected and I was foolish for not expecting it and letting myself be caught."

"But *incest?*"

Fastolfe said, "Incest? Oh yes, an Earthly term. On Aurora, there's no such thing, Mr. Baley. Very few Aurorans know their immediate family. Naturally, if marriage is in question and children are applied for, there is a genealogical search, but what has that to do with social sex? No no, the unnatural thing is that I refused my own daughter." He reddened—his large ears most of all.

"I should hope so," muttered Baley.

"I had no decent reasons for it, either—at least none that I could explain to Vasilia. It was criminal of me not to foresee the matter and prepare a foundation for a rational rejection of one so young and inexperienced, if that were necessary, that would not wound her and subject her to a fearful humiliation. I am really unbearably ashamed that I took the unusual responsibility of bringing up a child, only to subject her to such an unpalatable experience. It seemed to me that we could continue our relationship as father and daughter—as friend and friend—but she did not give up. Whenever I rejected her, no matter how affectionately I tried to do so, matters grew worse between us."

"Until finally—"

"Finally, she wanted her own establishment. I opposed it at first, not because I didn't want her to have one, but because I wanted to reestablish our loving relationship before she left. Nothing I did helped. It was, perhaps, the most trying time of my life. Eventually, she simply—and rather violently—insisted on leaving and I could hold out no longer. She was a professional roboticist by then—I am grateful that she didn't abandon the profession out of distaste for me—and she was able to found an establishment without any help from me. She did so, in fact, and since then there has been little contact between us."

Baley said, "It might be, Dr. Fastolfe, that, since she did *not* abandon robotics, she does not feel wholly estranged."

"It is what she does best and is most interested in. It has nothing to do with me. I know that, for to begin with, I thought as you did and I made friendly overtures, but they were not received."

"Do you miss her, Dr. Fastolfe?"

"Of course I miss her, Mr. Baley. —That is an example of the mistake of bringing up a child. You give into an irrational impulse—an atavistic desire—and it leads to inspiring the child with the strongest possible feeling of love and then subject yourself to the possibility of having to refuse that same child's first offer of herself and scarring her emotionally for life. And, to add to that, you subject yourself to this thoroughly irrational feeling of regret-of-absence. It's something I never felt before and have never felt since. She and I have both suffered needlessly and the fault is entirely mine."

Fastolfe fell into a kind of rumination and Baley said gently, "And what has all this to do with Gladia?"

Fastolfe started. "Oh! I had forgotten. Well, it's rather simple. Everthing I've said about Gladia is true. I liked her. I sympathized with her. I admired her talent. But, in addition, she resembles Vasilia. I noticed the similarity when I saw the first hyperwave account of her arrival from Solaria. It was quite startling and it made me take an interest." He sighed. "When I realized that she, like Vasilia, had been sex-scarred, it was more than I could endure. I arranged to have her established near me, as you see. I have been her friend and done my best to cushion the difficulties of adapting to a strange world."

"She is a daughter-substitute, then."

"After a fashion, yes, I suppose you could call it that, Mr. Baley. —And you have no idea how glad I am she never took it into her head to offer herself to me. To have rejected her would have been to relive my rejection of Vasilia. To have accepted her out of an inability to repeat the rejection would have embittered my life, for then I would have felt that I was doing for this stranger—this faint reflection of my daughter—what I would not do for my daughter herself. Either way— But, never mind, you can see now why I hesitated to answer you at first. Somehow, thinking about it led my mind back to this tragedy in my life."

"And your other daughter?"

"Lumen?" said Fastolfe indifferently. "I never had any contact with her, though I hear of her from time to time."

"She's running for political office, I understand."

"A local one. On the Globalist ticket."

"What is that?"

"The Globalists? They favor Aurora alone—just our own globe, you see. Aurorans are to take the lead in settling the Galaxy. Others are to be barred, as far as possible, particularly Earthmen. 'Enlightened self-interest' they call it."

"This is not your view, of course."

"Of course not. I am heading the Humanist party, which believes that all human beings have a right to share in the Galaxy. When I refer to 'my enemies,' I mean the Globalists."

"Lumen, then, is one of your enemies."

"Vasilia is one, also. She is, indeed, a member of the Robotics Institute of Aurora—the RIA—that was founded a few years ago and which is run by roboticists who view me as a demon to be defeated at all costs. As far as I know, however, my various ex-wives are apolitical, perhaps even Humanist." He smiled wryly and said, "Well, Mr. Baley, have you asked all the questions you wanted to ask?"

Baley's hands aimlessly searched for pockets in his smooth, loose Auroran breeches—something he had been doing periodically since he had begun wearing them on the ship—and found none. He compromised, as he sometimes did, by folding his arms across his chest.

He said, "Actually, Dr. Fastolfe. I'm not at all sure you have yet answered the first question. It seems to me that you never tire of evading that. *Why did you give Jander to Gladia?* Let's get all of it into the open, so that we may be able to see light in what now seems darkness."

29.

Fastolfe reddened again. It might have been anger this time, but he continued to speak softly.

He said, "Do not bully me, Mr. Baley. I have given you your answer. I was sorry for Gladia and I thought Jander would be company for her. I have spoken more frankly to you than I would to anyone else, partly because of the position I am in and partly because you are not an Auroran. In return, I demand a reasonable respect."

Baley bit his lower lip. He was not on Earth. He had no official authority behind him and he had more at stake than his professional pride.

He said, "I apologize, Dr. Fastolfe, if I have hurt your feelings. I do not mean to imply you are being untruthful or uncooperative. Nevertheless, I cannot operate without the whole truth. Let me suggest the possible answer I am looking for and you can then tell me if I am correct, or nearly correct, or totally wrong. Can it be that you have given Jander to Gladia, in order that he might serve as a focus for her sexual drive and so that she might not have occasion to offer herself to *you?* Perhaps that was not your conscious reason, but think about it now. Is it possible that such a feeling contributed to the gift?"

Fastolfe's hand picked up a light and transparent ornament that had been resting on the dining room table. It turned it over and over, over and over. Except for that motion, Fastolfe seemed frozen. Finally, he said, "That might be so, Mr. Baley. Certainly, after I loaned her Jander—it was never an outright gift, incidentally—I was less concerned about her offering herself to me."

"Do you know whether Gladia made use of Jander for sexual purposes?"

"Did you ask Gladia if she made use of him, Mr. Baley?"

"That has nothing to do with my question. Do *you* know? Did you witness any overt sexual actions between them? Did any of your robots inform you of such? Did she herself tell you?"

"The answer to all those questions, Mr. Baley, is no. If I stop to think about it, there is nothing particularly unusual about the use of robots for sexual purposes by either men or women. Ordinary robots are not particularly adapted to it, but human beings are ingenious in this respect. As for Jander, he is adapted to it because he is as humaniform as we could make him—"

"So that he might take part in sex."

"No, that was never in our minds. It was the abstract problem of building a totally humaniform robot that exercised the late Dr. Sarton and myself."

"But such humaniform robots are ideally designed for sex, are they not?"

"I suppose they are and, now that I allow myself to think of it —and I admit I may have had it hidden in my mind from the start—Gladia might well have used Jander so. If she did, I hope the process gave her pleasure. I would consider my loan to her a good deed, if it had."

"Could it have been more of a good deed than you counted upon?"

"In what way?"

"What would you say if I told you that Gladia and Jander were wife and husband?"

Fastolfe's hand, still holding the ornament, closed convulsively upon it, held it tightly for a moment, then let it drop. "What? That's ridiculous. It is legally impossible. There is no question of children, so there can't conceivably be an application for any. Without the intention of such an application, there can be no marriage."

"This is not a matter of legality, Dr. Fastolfe. Gladia is a Solarian, remember, and doesn't have the Auroran outlook. It is a matter of emotion. Gladia herself told me that she considered Jander to have been her husband. I think she considers herself now his widow and that she has had another sexual trauma— and a very severe one. If, in any way, you knowingly contributed to this event—"

"By all the stars," said Fastolfe with unwonted emotion, "I didn't. Whatever else was in my mind, I never imagined that Gladia could fantasize *marriage* to a robot, however humaniform he might be. No Auroran could have imagined that."

Baley nodded and raised his hand. "I believe you. I don't think you are actor enough to be drowning me in a faked sincerity. But I had to know. It was, after all, just possible that—"

"No, it was not. Possible that I foresaw this situation? That I deliberately created this abominable widowhood, for some reason? Never. It was not conceivable, so I did not conceive it. Mr. Baley, whatever I meant in placing Jander in her establishment, I meant well. I did not mean *this*. Meaning well is a poor defense, I know, but it is all that I have to offer."

"Dr. Fastolfe, let us refer to that no more," said Baley. "What *I* have now to offer is a possible solution to the mystery."

Fastolfe breathed deeply and sat back in his chair. "You hinted as much when you returned from Gladia's." He looked at Baley with a hint of savagery in his eyes. "Could you not have told me this 'key' you have at the start? Need we have gone through all—this?"

"I'm sorry, Dr. Fastolfe. The key makes no sense without all—this."

"Well, then. Get on with it."

"I will. Jander was in a position that you, the greatest robotics theoretician in all the world, did not foresee, by your own admission. He was pleasing Gladia so well that she was deeply in love with him and considered him her husband. What if it turns out that, in pleasing her, he was also displeasing her?"

"I'm not sure as to your meaning."

"Well, see here, Dr. Fastolfe. She was rather secretive about the matter. I gather that on Aurora sexual matters are not something one hides at all costs."

"We don't broadcast it over the hyperwave," said Fastolfe dryly, "but we don't make a greater secret of it than we do of any other strictly personal matter. We generally know who's been whose latest partner and, if one is dealing with friends, we often get an idea of how good, or how enthusiastic, or how much the reverse one or the other partner—or both—might be. It's a matter of small talk on occasion."

"Yes, but you knew nothing of Gladia's connection with Jander."

"I suspected—"

"Not the same thing. She told you nothing. You saw nothing. Nor could any robots report anything. She kept it secret even from you, her best friend on Aurora. Clearly, her robots were given careful instructions never to discuss Jander and Jander himself must have been thoroughly instructed to give nothing away."

"I suppose that's a fair conclusion."

"Why should she do that, Dr. Fastolfe?"

"A Solarian sense of privacy about sex?"

"Isn't that the same as saying she was ashamed of it?"

"She had no cause to be, although the matter of considering Jander a husband would have made her a laughingstock."

"She might have concealed that portion very easily without concealing everything. Suppose, in her Solarian way, she was ashamed."

"Well, then?"

"No one enjoys being ashamed—and she might have blamed Jander for it, in the rather unreasonable way people have of seeking to attribute to others the blame for unpleasantness that is clearly their own fault."

"Yes?"

"There might have been times when Gladia, who has a short-fused temper, might have burst into tears, let us say, and upbraided Jander for being the source of her shame and her misery. It might not have lasted long and she might have shifted quickly to apologies and caresses, but would not Jander have clearly gotten the idea that he was actually the source of her shame and her misery?"

"Perhaps."

"And might this not have meant to Jander that if he continued the relationship, he would make her miserable, and that if he ended the relationship, he would make her miserable. Whatever he did, he would be breaking the First Law and, unable to act in any way without such a violation, he could only find refuge in not acting at all—and so went into mental freeze-out. —Do you remember the story you told me earlier today of the legendary mind-reading robot who was driven into stasis by that robotics pioneer?"

"By Susan Calvin, yes. I see! You model your scenario on that old legend. Very ingenious, Mr. Baley, but it won't work."

"Why not? When you said only you could bring about a mental freeze-out in Jander, you did not have the faintest idea that he was involved so deeply in so unexpected a situation. It runs exactly parallel to the Susan Calvin situation."

"Let's suppose that the story about Susan Calvin and the mind-reading robot is not merely a totally fictitious legend. Let's take it seriously. There would still be no parallel between that story and the Jander situation. In the case of Susan Calvin, we would be dealing with an incredibly primitive robot, one that today would not even achieve the status of a toy. It could deal only qualitatively with such matters: A creates misery; not-A creates misery; therefore mental freeze-out."

Baley said, "And Jander?"

"Any modern robot—any robot of the last century—would weigh such matters quantitatively. Which of the two situations, A or not-A, would create the *most* misery? The robot would come to a rapid decision and opt for minimum misery. The chance that he would judge the two mutually exclusive alternatives to produce precisely equal quantities of misery is small and, even if that should turn out to be the case, the modern robot is supplied with a randomization factor. If A and not-A are precisely equal misery-producers according to his judgment, he chooses one or the other in a completely unpredictable way and then follows that unquestioningly. He does *not* go into mental freeze-out."

"Are you saying it is impossible for Jander to go into mental freeze-out? You have been saying *you* could have produced it."

"In the case of the humaniform positronic brain, there is a way of sidetracking the randomization factor that depends entirely on the way in which that brain is constructed. Even if you know the basic theory, it is a very difficult and long-sustained process to so lead the robot down the garden path, so to speak, by a skillful succession of questions and orders as to finally induce the mental freeze-out. It is unthinkable that it be done by accident and the mere existence of an apparent contradiction as that produced by simultaneous love and shame could not do the trick without the most careful quantitative adjustment under the most unusual conditions. —Which leaves us, as I keep saying, with indeterministic chance as the only possible way in which it happened."

"But your enemies will insist that your own guilt is the more likely. —Could we not, in our turn, insist that Jander was brought to mental freeze-out by the conflict brought on by Gladia's love and shame? Would this not sound plausible? And would it not win public opinion to your side?"

Fastolfe frowned. "Mr. Baley, you are too eager. Think about it seriously. If we were to try to get out of our dilemma in this rather dishonest fashion, what would be the consequence? I say nothing of the shame and misery it would bring to Gladia, who would suffer not only the loss of Jander but the feeling that she herself had brought about that loss if, in fact, she had really felt and had somehow revealed her shame. I would not want to do that, but let us put that to one side, if we can. Consider, instead, that my enemies would say that I had loaned her Jander precisely to bring about what had happened. I would have done it, they would say, in order to develop a method for mental freeze-out in humaniform robots while escaping all apparent responsibility myself. We would be worse off than we are now, for I would not only be accused of being an underhanded intriguer, as I am now, but, in addition, of having behaved monstrously toward an unsuspecting woman whom I had pretended to befriend, something I have so far been spared."

Baley was staggered. He felt his jaw drop and his voice degenerate to a stutter. "Surely they would not—"

"But they would. You yourself were at least half-inclined to think so not very many minutes ago."

"Merely as a remote—"

"My enemies would not find it remote and they would not publicize it as remote."

Baley knew he had reddened. He felt the wave of heat and found he could not look Fastolfe in the face. He cleared his throat and said, "You are right. I jumped for a way out without thinking and I can only ask your pardon. I am deeply ashamed. —There's no way out, I suppose, but the truth—if we can find it."

Fastolfe said, "Don't despair. You have already uncovered events in connection with Jander that I never dreamed of. You may uncover more and, eventually, what seems altogether a mystery to us now may unfold and become plain. What do you plan to do next?"

But Baley could think of nothing through the shame of his fiasco. He said, "I don't really know."

"Well, then, it was unfair of me to ask. You have had a long day and not an easy one. It is not surprising that your brain is a bit sluggish now. Why not rest, view a film, go to sleep? You will be better off in the morning."

Baley nodded and mumbled, "Perhaps you're right."

But, at the moment, he didn't think he'd be any better off in the morning at all.

### 30.

The bedroom was cold, both in temperature and ambience. Baley shivered slightly. So low a temperature within a room gave it the unpleasant feeling of being Outside. The walls were faintly off-white and (unusual for Fastolfe's establishment) were not decorated. The floor seemed to the sight to be of smooth ivory, but to the bare feet it felt carpeted. The bed was white and the smooth blanket was cold to the touch.

He sat down at the edge of the mattress and found it yielded very slightly to the pressure of his weight.

He said to Daneel, who had entered with him, "Daneel, does it disturb you when a human being tells a lie?"

"I am aware that human beings lie on occasion, Partner Elijah. Sometimes, a lie might be useful or even mandatory. My feeling about a lie depends upon the liar, the occasion, and the reason."

"Can you always tell when a human being lies?"

"No, Partner Elijah."

"Does it seem to you that Dr. Fastolfe often lies?"

"It has never seemed to me that Dr. Fastolfe has told a lie."

"Even in connection with Jander's death?"

"As far as I can tell, he tells the truth in every respect."

"Perhaps he has instructed you to say that—were I to ask?"

"He has not, Partner Elijah."

"But perhaps he instructed you to say that, too—"

He paused. Again—of what use was it to cross-examine a robot? And in this particular case, he was inviting infinite regression.

He was suddenly aware that the mattress had been yielding slowly under him until it now half-enfolded his hips. He rose suddenly and said, "Is there any way of warming the room, Daneel?"

"It will feel warmer when you are under the cover with the light out, Partner Elijah."

"Ah." He looked about suspiciously. "Would you put the light out, Daneel, and remain in the room when you have done so?"

The light went out almost at once and Baley realized that his supposition that this room, at least, was undecorated was totally wrong. As soon as it was dark, he felt he was Outside. There was the soft sound of wind in trees and the small, sleepy mutters of distant life-forms. There was also the illusion of stars overhead, with an occasional drifting cloud that was just barely visible.

"Put the light back on, Daneel!"

The room flooded with light.

"Daneel," said Baley. "I don't want any of that. I want no stars, no clouds, no sounds, no trees, no wind—no scents, either. I want darkness—featureless darkness. Could you arrange that?"

"Certainly, Partner Elijah."

"Then do so. And show me how I may myself put out the light when I am ready to sleep."

"I am here to protect you, Partner Elijah."

Baley said grumpily, "You can do that, I am sure, from just the other side of the door. Giskard, I imagine, will be just outside the windows, if, indeed, there are windows beyond the draperies."

"There are. —If you cross that threshold, Partner Elijah, you will find a Personal reserved for yourself. That section of the wall is not material and you will move easily through it. The light will turn on as you enter and it will go out as you leave— and there are no decorations. You will be able to shower, if you wish, or do anything else that you care to before retiring or after waking."

Baley turned in the indicated direction. He saw no break in the wall, but the floor molding in that spot did show a thickening as though it were a threshold.

"How do I see it in the dark, Daneel?" he asked.

"That section of the wall—which is not a wall—will glow faintly. As for the room light, there is this depression in the headboard of your bed which, if you place your finger within it, will darken the room if light—or lighten it if dark."

"Thank you. You may leave now."

Half an hour later, he was through with the Personal and found himself huddling beneath the blanket, with the light out, enveloped by a warm spirit-hugging darkness.

As Fastolfe had said, it had been a long day. It was almost unbelievable that it had been only that morning that he had arrived on Aurora. He had learned a great deal and yet none of it had done him any good.

He lay in the dark and went over the events of the day in quiet succession, hoping that something might occur to him that had eluded him before—but nothing like that happened.

So much for the quietly thoughtful, keen-eyed, subtle-brained Elijah Baley of the hyperwave drama.

The mattress was again half-enfolding him and it was like a warm enclosure. He moved slightly and it straightened beneath him, then slowly molded itself to fit his new position.

There was no point in trying, with his worn, sleep-seeking mind, to go over the day again, but he could not help trying a second time, following his own footsteps on this, his first day on Aurora—from the spaceport to Fastolfe's establishment, then to Gladia's, then back to Fastolfe.

Gladia—more beautiful than he remembered but hard—something hard about her—or has she just grown a protective shell—poor woman. He thought warmly of her reaction to the touch of her hand against his cheek—if he could have remained with her, he could have taught her—stupid Aurorans—disgustingly casual atttitude toward sex—anything goes—which means nothing really goes—not worthwhile—stupid—to Fastolfe, to Gladia, back to Fastolfe—back to Fastolfe.

He moved a little and then abstractedly felt the mattress remold again. Back to Fastolfe. What happened on the way back to Fastolfe? Something said? Something not said? And on the ship before he ever got to Aurora—something that fit in—

Baley was in the never-never world of half-sleep, when the mind is liberated and follows a law of its own. It is like the body flying, soaring through the air and liberated of gravity.

Of its own accord, it was taking the events—little aspects he had not noted—putting them together—one thing adding to another—clicking into place—forming a web—a fabric—

And then, it seemed to him, he heard a sound and he roused himself to a level of wakefulness. He listened, heard nothing, and sank once more into the half-sleep to take up the line of thought—and it eluded him.

It was like a work of art sinking into a morass. He could still see its outlines, the masses of color. They got dimmer, but he still knew it was there. And even as he scrambled desperately for it, it was gone altogether and he remembered nothing of it. Nothing at all.

Had he actually thought of anything or was the memory of having done so itself an illusion born of some drifting nonsense in a mind asleep? And he was, indeed, asleep.

When he woke briefly during the night, he thought to himself: I had an idea. An important idea.

But he remembered nothing, except that something had been there.

He remained awake a while, staring into the darkness. If, in fact, something had been there—it would come back in time.

Or it might not! (Jehoshaphat!)

—And he slept again.

# 8

---

# Fastolfe and Vasilia

### 31.

Baley woke with a start and drew in his breath with sharp suspicion. There was a faint and unrecognizable odor in the air that vanished by his second breath.

Daneel stood gravely at the side of the bed. He said, "I trust, Partner Elijah, that you have slept well."

Baley looked around. The drapes were still closed, but it was clearly daylight Outside. Giskard was laying out clothing, totally different, from shoes to jacket, from anything he had worn the day before.

He said, "Quite well, Daneel. Did something awaken me?"

"There was an injection of antisomnin in the room's air circulation, Partner Elijah. It activates the arousal system. We used a smaller than normal amount, since we were uncertain of your reaction. Perhaps we should have used a smaller amount still."

Baley said, "It did seem to be rather like a paddle over the rear. What time is it?"

Daneel said, "It is 0705, by Auroran measure. Physiologically, breakfast will be ready in half an hour." He said it without a trace of humor, though a human being might have found a smile appropriate.

Giskard said, his voice stiffer and a trifle less intoned than Daneel's, "Sir, friend Daneel and I may not enter the Personal. If you will do so and let us know if there is anything you will need, we will supply it at once."

"Yes, of course." Baley raised himself, swung around, and got out of bed.

Giskard began stripping the bed at once. "May I have your pajamas, sir?"

Baley hesitated for a moment only. It was a robot who asked, nothing more. He disrobed and handed the garment to Giskard, who took it with a small, grave nod of acceptance.

Baley looked at himself with distaste. He was suddenly conscious of a middle-aged body that was very likely in less good condition than Fastolfe's, which was nearly three times as old.

Automatically, he looked for his slippers and found there were none. Presumably, he needed none. The floor seemed warm and soft to his feet.

He stepped into the Personal and called out for instructions. From the other side of the illusory section of the wall, Giskard solemnly explained the working of the shaver, of the toothpaste dispenser, explained how to put the flushing device on automatic, how to control the temperature of the shower.

Everything was on a grander and more elaborate scale than anything Earth had to offer and there were no partitions on the other side of which he could hear the movements and involuntary sounds of someone else, something he had to ignore rigidly to maintain the illusion of privacy.

It was effete, thought Baley somberly as he went through the luxurious ritual, but it was an effeteness that (he already knew) he could become accustomed to. If he stayed here on Aurora any length of time, he would find the culture shock of returning to Earth painfully intense, *particularly* with respect to the Personal. He hoped that the readjustment would not take long, but he also hoped that any Earthpeople who settled new worlds would not feel impelled to cling to the concept of Community Personals.

Perhaps, thought Baley, that was how one ought to define "effete": That to which one can become easily accustomed.

Baley stepped out of the Personal, various functions com-

pleted, chin new-cropped, teeth glistening, body showered and
dry. He said, "Giskard, where do I find the deodorant?"

Giskard said, "I do not understand, sir."

Daneel said quickly, "When you activated the lathering control, Partner Elijah, that introduced a deodorant effect. I ask
pardon for friend Giskard's failure to understand. He lacks my
experience on Earth."

Baley lifted his eyebrows dubiously and began to dress with
Giskard's help.

He said, "I see that you and Giskard are still with me every
step of the way. Has there been any sign of any attempt at putting me out of the way?"

Daneel said, "None thus far, Partner Elijah. Nevertheless, it
would be wise to have friend Giskard and myself with you at all
times, if that can possibly be managed."

"Why is that, Daneel?"

"For two reasons, Partner Elijah. First, we can help you with
any aspect of Auroran culture or folkways with which you are
unfamiliar. Second, friend Giskard, in particular, can record and
reproduce every word of every conversation you may have. This
may be of value to you. You will recall that there were times in
your conversations with both Dr. Fastolfe and with Miss Gladia
when friend Giskard and I were at a distance or in another
room—"

"So that conversations were not recorded by Giskard?"

"Actually, they were, Partner Elijah, but with low fidelity—and
there may be portions that will not be as clear as we would want
them to be. It would be better if we stayed as close to you as is
convenient."

Baley said, "Daneel, are you of the opinion that I will be more
at ease if I think of you as guides and as recording devices,
rather than as guards? Why not simply come to the conclusion
that, as guards, you two are completely unnecessary. Since there
have been no attempts at me so far, why isn't it possible to conclude that there will be no attempts at me in the future?"

"No, Partner Elijah, that would be incautious. Dr. Fastolfe
feels that you are viewed with great apprehension by his ene-

mies. They had made attempts to persuade the Chairman not to give Dr. Fastolfe permission to call you in and they will surely continue to attempt to persuade him to have you ordered back to Earth at the earliest possible moment."

"That sort of peaceful opposition requires no guards."

"No, sir, but if the opposition has reason to fear that you may exculpate Dr. Fastolfe, it is possible that they may feel driven to extremes. You are, after all, not an Auroran and the inhibitions against violence on our world would therefore be weakened in your case."

Baley said dourly, "The fact that I've been here a whole day and that nothing has happened should relieve their minds greatly and reduce the threat of violence considerably."

"It would indeed seem so," said Daneel, showing no signs that he recognized the irony in Baley's voice.

"On the other hand," said Baley, "if I seem to make progress, then the danger to me immediately increases."

Daneel paused to consider, then said, "That would seem to be a logical consequence."

"And, therefore, you and Giskard will come with me wherever I go, just in case I manage to do my job a little too well."

Daneel paused again, then said, "Your way of putting it, Partner Elijah, puzzles me, but you seem to be correct."

"In that case," said Baley, "I'm ready for breakfast, though it does take the edge off my appetite to be told that the alternative to failure is attempted assassination."

### 32.

Fastolfe smiled at Baley across the breakfast table. "Did you sleep well, Mr. Baley?"

Baley studied the slice of ham with fascination. It had to be cut with a knife. It was grainy. It had a discrete strip of fat running down one side. It had, in short, not been processed. The result was that it tasted hammier, so to speak.

There were also fried eggs, with the yolk a flattened semisphere in the center, rimmed by white, rather like some daisies that Ben had pointed out to him in the field back on Earth. Intellectually, he knew what an egg looked like before it was processed and he knew that it contained both a yolk and a white, but he had never seen them still separate when ready to eat. Even on the ship coming here and even on Solaria, eggs, when served, were scrambled.

He looked up sharply at Fastolfe. "Pardon me?"

Fastolfe said patiently, "Did you sleep well?"

"Yes. Quite well. I would probably still be sleeping if it hadn't been for the antisomnin."

"Ah yes. Not quite the hospitality a guest has the right to expect, but I felt you might want an early start."

"You are entirely right. And I'm not exactly a guest, either."

Fastolfe ate in silence for a moment or two. He sipped at his hot drink, then said, "Has any enlightenment come overnight? Have you awakened, perhaps, with a new perspective, a new thought?"

Baley looked at Fastolfe suspiciously, but the other's face reflected no sarcasm. As Baley lifted his drink to his lips, he said, "I'm afraid not. I am as ineffectual now as I was last night." He sipped and involuntarily made a face.

Fastolfe said, "I'm sorry. You find the drink unpalatable?"

Baley grunted and cautiously tasted it again.

Fastolfe said, "It is simply coffee, you know. Decaffeinated."

Baley frowned. "It doesn't taste like coffee and— Pardon me, Dr. Fastolfe, I don't want to begin to sound paranoid, but Daneel and I have just had a half-joking exchange on the possibility of violence against me—half-joking on my part, of course, not on Daneel's—and it is in my mind that one way they might get at me is—"

His voice trailed away.

Fastolfe's eyebrows moved upward. He reached for Baley's coffee with a murmur of apology and smelled it. He then ladled out a small portion by spoon and tasted it. He said, "Perfectly normal, Mr. Baley. This is not an attempt at poisoning."

Baley said, "I'm sorry to behave so foolishly, since I know this has been prepared by your own robots—but are you certain?"

Fastolfe smiled. "Robots have been tampered with before

now. —However, there has been no tampering this time. It is just that coffee, although universally popular on the various worlds, comes in different strains. It is notorious that each human being prefers the coffee of his own world. I'm sorry, Mr. Baley, I have no Earth strain to give you. Would you prefer milk? That is relatively constant from world to world. Fruit juice? Aurora's grape juice is considered superior throughout the worlds, generally. There are some who hint, darkly, that we allow it to ferment somewhat, but that, of course, is not true. Water?"

"I'll try your grape juice." Baley looked at the coffee dubiously. "I suppose I ought to try to get used to this."

"Not at all," said Fastolfe. "Why seek out the unpleasant if that is unnecessary? —And so"—his smile seemed a bit strained as he returned to his earlier remark—"night and sleep have brought no useful reflection to you?"

"I'm sorry," said Baley. Then, frowning at a dim memory, "Although—"

"Yes?"

"I have the impression that just before falling asleep, in the free-association limbo between sleep and waking, it seemed to me that I had something."

"Indeed? What?"

"I don't know. The thought drove me into wakefulness but didn't follow me there. Or else some imagined sound distracted me. I don't remember. I snatched at the thought, but didn't retrieve it. It's gone. I *think* that this sort of thing is not uncommon."

Fastolfe looked thoughtful. "Are you sure of this?"

"Not really. The thought grew so tenuous so rapidly I couldn't even be sure that I had actually had it. And even if I had, it may have seemed to make sense to me only because I was half-asleep. If it were repeated to me now in broad daylight, it might make no sense at all."

"But whatever it was and however fugitive, it would have left a trace, surely."

"I imagine so, Dr. Fastolfe. In which case, it will come to me again. I'm confident of that."

"Ought we to wait?"

"What else can we do?"

"There's such a thing as a Psychic Probe."

Baley sat back in his chair and stared at Fastolfe for a moment. He said, "I've heard of it, but it isn't used in police work on Earth."

"We're not on Earth, Mr. Baley," said Fastolfe softly.

"It can do brain damage. Am I not right?"

"Not likely, in the proper hands."

"Not impossible, even in the proper hands," said Baley. "It's my understanding that it cannot be used on Aurora except under sharply defined conditions. Those it is used on must be guilty of a major crime or must—"

"Yes, Mr. Baley, but that refers to Aurorans. You are not an Auroran."

"You mean because I'm an Earthman I'm to be treated as inhuman?"

Fastolfe smiled and spread his hands. "Come, Mr. Baley. It was just a thought. Last night you were desperate enough to suggest trying to solve our dilemma by placing Gladia in a horrible and tragic position. I was wondering if you were desperate enough to risk yourself?"

Baley rubbed his eyes and, for a minute or so, remained silent. Then, in an altered voice, he said, "I was wrong last night. I admitted it. As for this matter now, there is no assurance that what I thought of, when half-asleep, had any relevance to the problem. It may have been pure fantasy—illogical nonsense. There may have been no thought at all. Nothing. Would you consider it wise, for so small a likelihood of gain, to risk damage to my brain, when it is upon that for which you say you depend for a solution to the problem?"

Fastolfe nodded. "You plead your case eloquently—and I was not really serious."

"Thank you, Dr. Fastolfe."

"But where are we to go from here?"

"For one thing, I wish to speak to Gladia again. There are points concerning which I need clarification."

"You should have taken them up last night."

"So I should, but I had more than I could properly absorb last night and there were points that escaped me. I am an investigator and not an infallible computer."

Fastolfe said, "I was not imputing blame. It's just that I hate to see Gladia unnecessarily disturbed. In view of what you told me last night, I can only assume she must be in a state of deep distress."

"Undoubtedly. But she is also desperately anxious to find out what happened—who, if anyone, killed the one she viewed as her husband. That's understandable, too. I'm sure she'll be willing to help me. —And I wish to speak to another person as well."

"To whom?"

"To your daughter Vasilia."

"To Vasilia? Why? What purpose will that serve?"

"She is a roboticist. I would like to talk to a roboticist other than yourself."

"I do not wish that, Mr. Baley."

They had finished eating. Baley stood up. "Dr. Fastolfe, once again I must remind you that I am here at your request. I have no formal authority to do police work. I have no connection with any Auroran authorities. The only chance I have of getting to the bottom of this miserable mess is to hope that various people will voluntarily cooperate with me and answer my questions.

"If you stop me from attempting this, then it is clear that I can get no farther than I am right now, which is nowhere. It will also look extremely bad for you—and therefore for Earth—so I urge you not to stand in my way. If you make it possible for me to interview anyone I wish—or even simply *try* to make it possible by interceding on my behalf—then the people of Aurora will surely consider that to be a sign of self-conscious innocence on your part. If you hamper my investigation, on the other hand, to what conclusion can they come but that you are guilty and fear exposure?"

Fastolfe said, with poorly suppressed annoyance, "I understand that, Mr. Baley. But why Vasilia? There are other roboticists."

"Vasilia is your daughter. She knows you. She might have

strong opinions concerning the likelihood of your destroying a robot. Since she is a member of the Robotics Institute and on the side of your political enemies, any favorable evidence she may give would be persuasive."

"And if she testifies against me?"

"We'll face that when it comes. Would you get in touch with her and ask her to receive me?"

Fastolfe said resignedly, "I will oblige you, but you are mistaken if you think I can easily persuade her to see you. She may be too busy—or think she is. She may be away from Aurora. She may simply not wish to be involved. I tried to explain last night that she has reason—thinks she has reason—to be hostile to me. My asking her to see you may indeed impel her to refuse, merely as a sign of her displeasure with me."

"Would you try, Dr. Fastolfe?"

Fastolfe sighed. "I will try while you are at Gladia's. —I presume you wish to see her directly? I might point out that a trimensional viewing would do. The image is high enough in quality so that you will not be able to tell it from personal presence."

"I'm aware of that, Dr. Fastolfe, but Gladia is a Solarian and has unpleasant associations with trimensional viewing. And, in any case, I am of the opinion that there is an intangible additional effectiveness in being within touching distance. The present situation is too delicate and the difficulties too great for me to want to give up that additional effectiveness."

"Well, I'll alert Gladia." He turned away, hesitated, and turned back. "But, Mr. Baley—"

"Yes, Dr. Fastolfe?"

"Last night you told me that the situation was serious enough for you to disregard any convenience it might cause Gladia. There were, you pointed out, greater things at stake."

"That's so, but you can rely on me not to disturb her if I can help it."

"I am not talking about Gladia now. I merely warn you that this essentially proper view of yours should be extended to myself. I don't expect you to worry about my convenience or pride if you should get a chance to talk to Vasilia. I don't look forward to the results, but if you do talk to her, I will have to endure any ensuing embarrassment and you must not seek to spare me. Do you understand?"

"To be perfectly honest, Dr. Fastolfe, it was never my attention to spare you. If I have to weigh your embarrassment or shame against the welfare of your policies and against the welfare of my world, I would not hesitate a moment to shame you."

"Good! —And Mr. Baley, we must extend that attitude also to yourself. *Your* convenience must not be allowed to stand in the way."

"It wasn't allowed to do so when you decided to have me brought here without consulting me."

"I'm referring to something else. If, after a reasonable time—not a long time, but a reasonable time—you make no progress toward a solution, we will have to consider the possibilities of psychic-probing, after all. Our last chance might be to find out what it is your mind knows that you do not know it knows."

"It may know nothing, Dr. Fastolfe."

Fastolfe looked at Baley sadly. "Agreed. But, as you said concerning the possibility of Vasilia testifying against me—we'll face that when it comes."

He turned away again and walked out of the room.

Baley looked after him thoughtfully. It seemed to him now that if he made progress he would face physical reprisals of an unknown—but possibly dangerous—kind. And if he did not make progress, he would face the Psychic Probe, which could scarcely be better.

"Jehoshaphat!" he muttered softly to himself.


33·


The walk to Gladia's seemed shorter than it had on the day before. The day was sunlit and pleasant again, but the vista looked not at all the same. The sunlight slanted from the opposite direction, of course, and the coloring seemed slightly different.

It could be that the plant life looked a bit different in the morning than in the evening—or smelled different. Baley had, on occasion, thought that of Earth's plant life as well, he remembered.

Daneel and Giskard accompanied him again, but they traveled more closely to him and seemed less intensely alert.

Baley said idly, "Does the sun shine here all the time?"

"It does not, Partner Elijah," said Daneel. "Were it to do so, that would be disastrous for the plant world and, therefore, for humanity. The prediction is, in fact, for the sky to cloud over in the course of the day."

"What was that?" asked Baley, startled. A small and gray-brown animal was crouched in the grass. Seeing them, it hopped away in leisurely fashion.

"A rabbit, sir," said Giskard.

Baley relaxed. He had seen them in the fields of Earth, too.

Gladia was not waiting for them at the door this time, but she was clearly expecting them. When a robot ushered them in, she did not stand up, but said, with something between crossness and weariness, "Dr. Fastolfe told me you had to see me again. What now?"

She was wearing a robe that clung tightly to her body and was clearly wearing nothing underneath. Her hair was pulled back shapelessly and her face was pallid. She looked more drawn than she had the day before and it was clear that she had had little sleep.

Daneel, remembering what had happened the day before, did not enter the room. Giskard entered, however, glanced keenly about, then retired to a wall niche. One of Gladia's robots stood in another niche.

Baley said, "I'm terribly sorry, Gladia, to have to bother you again."

Gladia said, "I forgot to tell you last night that, after Jander is torched, he will, of course, be recycled for use in the robot factories again. It will be amusing, I suppose, to know that each time I see a newly formed robot, I can take time to realize that many of Jander's atoms form part of him."

Baley said, "We ourselves, when we die, are recycled—and

who knows what atoms of whom are in you and me right now or in whom ours will someday be."

"You are very right, Elijah. And you remind me how easy it is to philosophize over the sorrows of others."

"That is right, too, Gladia, but I did not come to philosophize."

"Do what you came to do, then."

"I must ask questions."

"Weren't yesterday's enough? Have you spent the time since then in thinking up new ones?"

"In part, yes, Gladia. —Yesterday, you said that even after you were with Jander—as wife and husband—there were men who offered themselves to you and that you refused. It is that which I must question you about."

"Why?"

Baley ignored the question. "Tell me," he said, "how many men offered themselves to you during the time you were married to Jander?"

"I don't keep records, Elijah. Three or four."

"Were any of them persistent? Did anyone offer himself more than once?"

Gladia, who had been avoiding his eyes, now looked at him full and said, "Have you talked to others about this?"

Baley shook his head. "I have talked on this subject to no one but you. From your question, however, I suspect that there was at least one who was persistent."

"One. Santirix Gremionis." She sighed. "Aurorans have such peculiar names and he *was* peculiar—for an Auroran. I had never met one as repetitious in the matter as he. He was always polite, always accepted my refusal with a small smile and a stately bow, and then, as like as not, he would try again the next week or even the next day. The mere repetition was a small discourtesy. A decent Auroran would accept a refusal permanently unless the prospective partner made it reasonably plain there was a change of mind."

"Tell me again— Did those who offered themselves to you know of your relationship with Jander?"

"It was not something I mentioned in casual conversation."

"Well, then, consider this Gremionis, specifically. Did *he* know that Jander was your husband?"

"I never told him so."

"Don't dismiss it like that, Gladia. It's not a matter of his being told. Unlike the others, he offered himself repeatedly. How often would you say, by the way? Three times? Four? How many?"

"I did not count," said Gladia wearily. "It might have been a dozen times or more. If he weren't a likable person otherwise, I would have had my robots bar the establishment to him."

"Ah, but you didn't. And it takes time to make multiple offerings. He came to see you. He encountered you. He had time to note Jander's presence and how you behaved to him. Might he not have guessed at the relationship?"

Gladia shook her head. "I don't think so. Jander never intruded when I was with any human being."

"Were those your instructions? I presume they must have been."

"They were. And before you suggest I was ashamed of the relationship, it was merely an attempt to avoid bothersome complications. I have retained some instinct of privacy about sex that Aurorans don't have."

"Think again. Might he have guessed? Here he is, a man in love—"

"In love!" The sound she made was almost a snort. "What do Aurorans know of love?"

"A man who considers himself in love. You are not responsive. Might he not, with the sensitivity and suspicion of a disappointed lover, have guessed? Consider! Did he ever make any roundabout reference to Jander? Anything to cause you the slightest suspicion—"

"No! No! It would be unheard of for any Auroran to comment adversely on the sexual preferences or habits of another."

"Not necessarily adversely. A humorous comment, perhaps. *Any* indication that he suspected the relationship."

"No! If young Gremionis had ever breathed a word of that sort, he would never have seen the inside of my establishment again and I would have seen to it that he never approached me again. —But he wouldn't have done anything of the sort. He was the soul of eager politeness to me."

"You say 'young.' How old is this Gremionis?"

"About my age. Thirty-five. Perhaps even a year or two younger."

"A child," said Baley sadly. "Even younger than I am. But at that age— Suppose he guessed at your relationship with Jander and said nothing—nothing at all. Might he not, nevertheless, have been jealous?"

"Jealous?"

It occurred to Baley that the word might have little meaning on Aurora or Solaria. "Angered that you should prefer another to himself."

Gladia said sharply, "I know the meaning of the word 'jealous.' I repeated it only out of surprise that you should think any Auroran was jealous. On Aurora, people are not jealous over sex. Over other things certainly, but not over sex." There was a definite sneer upon her face. "Even if he were jealous, what would it matter? What could he do?"

"Wasn't it possible he might have told Jander that the relationship with a robot would endanger your position on Aurora—"

"That would not have been true!"

"Jander might have believed it if he were told so—believed he was endangering you, harming you. Might not that have been the reason for the mental freeze-out?"

"Jander would never have believed that. He made me happy every day he was my husband and I told him so."

Baley remained calm. She was missing the point, but he would simply have to make it clearer. "I am sure he believed you, but he might also feel impelled to believe someone else who told him the reverse. If he were then caught in an unbearable First Law dilemma—"

Gladia's face contorted and she shrieked, "That's *mad*. You're just telling me the old fairy tale of Susan Calvin and the mind-reading robot. No one over the age of ten can possibly believe that."

"Isn't it possible that—"

"No, it isn't. I'm from Solaria and I know enough about robots to know it isn't possible. It would take an incredible expert to tie First Law knots in a robot. Dr. Fastolfe might be able to do it, but certainly not Santirix Gremionis. Gremionis is a stylist. He works on human beings. He cuts hair, designs clothing. I do the same, but at least I work on robots. Gremionis has never touched a robot. He knows nothing about them, except to order one to close the window or something like that. Are you trying to tell me that it was the relationship between Jander and me—me"—she tapped herself harshly on the breastbone with one rigid finger, the swells of her small breasts scarcely showing under her robe—"that caused Jander's death?"

"It was nothing you did knowingly," said Baley, wanting to stop but unable to quit probing. "What if Gremionis had learned from Dr. Fastolfe how to—"

"Gremionis didn't know Dr. Fastolfe and couldn't have understood anything Dr. Fastolfe might have told him, anyhow."

"You can't know for certain what Gremionis might or might not understand and, as for not knowing Dr. Fastolfe—Gremionis must have been frequently in your establishment if he hounded you so and—"

"And Dr. Fastolfe was almost never in my establishment. Last night, when he came with you, it was only the second time he had crossed my threshold. He was afraid that to be too close to me would drive me away. He admitted that once. He lost his daughter that way, he thought—something foolish like that. —You see, Elijah, when you live several centuries, you have plenty of time to lose *thousands* of things. Be th-thankful for short life, Elijah." She was weeping uncontrollably.

Baley looked and felt helpless. "I'm sorry, Gladia. I have no more questions. Shall I call a robot? Will you need help?"

She shook her head and waved her hand at him. "Just go away—go away," she said in a strangled voice. "Go away."

Baley hesitated and then strode out of the room, taking one last, uncertain look at her as he walked out the door. Giskard followed in his footsteps and Daneel joined him as he left the house. He scarcely noticed. It occurred to him, abstractedly, that he was coming to accept their presence as he would have that of his shadow or of his clothing, that he was reaching a point where he would feel bare without them.

He walked rapidly back toward the Fastolfe establishment, his mind churning. His desire to see Vasilia had at first been a matter of desperation, a lack of any other object of curiosity, but now things had changed. There was just a chance that he had stumbled on something vital.

*34.*

Fastolfe's homely face was set in grim lines when Baley returned.

"Any progress?" he asked.

"I eliminated part of a possibility. —Perhaps."

"*Part* of a possibility? How do you eliminate the other part? Better yet, how do you *establish* a possibility?"

Baley said, "By finding it impossible to eliminate a possibility, a beginning is made at establishing one."

"And if you find it impossible to eliminate the other part of the possibility you mysteriously mentioned?"

Baley shrugged. "Before we waste our time considering that, I must see your daughter."

Fastolfe looked dejected. "Well, Mr. Baley, I did as you asked me to do and tried to contact her. It was necessary to awaken her."

"You mean she is in part of the planet where it is night? I hadn't thought of that." Baley felt chagrined. "I'm afraid I'm fool enough to imagine I'm on Earth still. In underground Cities, day and night lose their meaning and time tends to be uniform."

"It's not that bad. Eos is the robotics center of Aurora and you'll find few roboticists who live out of it. She was simply sleeping and being awakened did not improve her temper, apparently. She would not speak to me."

"Call again," said Baley urgently.

"I spoke to her secretarial robot and there was an uncomfortable relaying of messages. She made it quite plain she will not speak to me in any fashion. She was a little more flexible with you. The robot announced that she would give you five minutes on her private viewing channel, if you call"—Fastolfe consulted the time-strip on the wall—"in half an hour. She will not see you in person under any conditions."

"The conditions are insufficient and so is the time. I must see her in person for as long as is needed. Did you explain the importance of this, Dr. Fastolfe?"

"I tried. She is not concerned."

"You are her father. Surely—"

"She is less inclined to bend her decision for my sake than for a randomly chosen stranger. I knew this, so I made use of Giskard."

"Giskard?"

"Oh yes. Giskard is a great favorite of hers. When she was studying robotics at the university, she took the liberty of adjusting some minor aspects of his programming—and nothing makes for a closer relationship with a robot than that—except for Gladia's method, of course. It was almost as though Giskard were Andrew Martin—"

"Who is Andrew Martin?"

"Was, not is," said Fastolfe. "You have never heard of him?"

"Never!"

"How odd! These ancient legends of ours all have Earth as their setting, yet on Earth they are not known. —Andrew Martin was a robot who, gradually, step by step, was supposed to have become humaniform. To be sure, there have been humaniform robots before Daneel, but they were all simple toys, little more than automatons. Nevertheless, amazing stories are told of the abilities of Andrew Martin—a sure sign of the legendary nature of the tale. There was a woman who was part of the legends who is usually known as Little Miss. The relationship is too complicated to describe now, but I suppose that every little girl on Aurora has daydreamed of being Little Miss and of having Andrew Martin as a robot. Vasilia did—and Giskard was her Andrew Martin."

"Well, then?"

"I asked her robot to tell her that you would be accompanied by Giskard. She hasn't seen him in years and I thought that might lure her into agreeing to see you."

"But it didn't, I presume."

"It didn't."

"Then we must think of something else. There must be some way of inducing her to see me."

Fastolfe said, "Perhaps you will think of one. In a few minutes, you will view her on trimensic and you will have five minutes to convince her that she ought to see you personally."

"Five minutes! What can I do in five minutes?"

"I don't know. It is better, after all, than nothing."

## 35.

Fifteen minutes later, Baley stood before the trimensional viewing screen, ready to meet Vasilia Fastolfe.

Dr. Fastolfe had left, saying, with a wry smile, that his presence would certainly make his daughter less amenable to persuasion. Nor was Daneel present. Only Giskard remained behind to keep Baley company.

Giskard said, "Dr. Vasilia's trimensic channel is open for reception. Are you ready, sir?"

"As ready as I can be," said Baley grimly. He had refused to sit, feeling he might be more imposing if he were standing. (How imposing could an Earthman be?)

The screen grew bright as the rest of the room dimmed and a woman appeared—in rather uncertain focus, at first. She was standing facing him, her right hand resting on a laboratory bench laden with sets of diagrams. (No doubt *she* planned to be imposing, too.)

As the focus sharpened, the edges of the screen seemed to melt away and the image of Vasilia (if it were she) deepened and became three-dimensional. She was standing in the room with every sign of solid reality, except that the decor of the room she was in did not match the room Baley was in and the break was a sharp one.

She was wearing a dark brown skirt that divided into loose trouser legs that were semitransparent, so that her legs, from midthigh down, were shadowily visible. Her blouse was tight and sleeveless, so that her arms were bare to the shoulder. Her neckline was low and her hair, quite blond, was in tight curls.

She had none of her father's plainness and certainly not his large ears. Baley could only assume she had had a beautiful mother and was fortunate in the allotment of genes.

She was short and Baley could see a remarkable resemblance to Gladia in her facial features, although her expression was far colder and seemed to bear the mark of a dominating personality.

She said sharply, "Are you the Earthman come to solve my father's problems?"

"Yes, Dr. Fastolfe," said Baley in an equally clipped manner.

"You may call me Dr. Vasilia. I do not wish the confusion of being mistaken for my father."

"Dr. Vasilia, I must have a chance to deal with you, face-to-face, for a reasonably extended period."

"No doubt you feel that. You are, of course, an Earthman and a certain source of infection."

"I have been medically treated and I am quite safe to be with. Your father has been constantly with me for over a day."

"My father pretends to be an idealist and must do foolish things at times to support the pretense. I will not imitate him."

"I take it you do not wish him harm. You will bring him harm if you refuse to see me."

"You are wasting time. I will not see you, except in this manner, and half the period I have allotted is gone. If you wish, we can stop this now if you find it unsatisfactory."

"Giskard is here, Dr. Vasilia, and would like to urge you to see me."

Giskard stepped into the field of vision. "Good morning, Little Miss," he said in a low voice.

For a moment, Vasilia looked embarrassed and, when she spoke, it was in a somewhat softer tone. "I am glad to view you, Giskard, and will see you any time you wish, but I will not see this Earthman, even at your urging."

"In that case," said Baley, throwing in all his reserves desperately, "I must take the case of Santirix Gremionis to the public without the benefit of having consulted you."

Vasilia's eyes widened and her hand on the table lifted upward and clenched into a fist, "What is this about Gremionis?"

"Only that he is a handsome young man and he knows you well. Am I to deal with these matters without hearing what you have to say?"

"I will tell you right now that—"

"No," said Baley loudly. "You will tell me nothing unless I see you face-to-face."

Her mouth twitched. "I will see you, then, but I will not remain with you one moment more than I choose. I warn you. —And bring Giskard."

The trimensional connection broke off with a snap and Baley felt himself turn dizzy at the sudden change in background that resulted. He made his way to a chair and sat down.

Giskard's hand was on his elbow, making certain that he reached the chair safely. "Can I help you in any way, sir?" he asked.

"I'm all right," said Baley. "I just need to catch my breath."

Dr. Fastolfe was standing before him. "My apologies, again, for failure in my duties as a host. I listened on an extension that was equipped to receive and not transmit. I wanted to see my daughter, even if she didn't see me."

"I understand," said Baley, panting slightly. "If manners dictate that what you did requires an apology, then I forgive you."

"But what is this about Santirix Gremionis? The name is unfamiliar to me."

Baley looked up at Fastolfe and said, "Dr. Fastolfe, I heard his name from Gladia this morning. I know very little about him, but I took the chance of saying what I did to your daughter anyway. The odds were heavily against me, but the results were what I wanted them to be, nevertheless. As you see, I can make useful deductions, even when I have very little information, so you had better leave me in peace to continue to do so. Please, in the future, cooperate to the full and make no further mention of a Psychic Probe."

Fastolfe was silent and Baley felt a grim satisfaction at having imposed his will first on the daughter, then on the father.

How long he could continue to do so he did not know.

# 9

## Vasilia

### 36.

Baley paused at the door of the airfoil and said firmly, "Giskard, I do *not* wish the windows opacified. I do *not* wish to sit in the back. I want to sit in the front seat and observe the Outside. Since I will be sitting between you and Daneel, I should be safe enough, unless the car itself is destroyed. And, in that case, we will all be destroyed and it won't matter whether I am in front or in back."

Giskard responded to the force of the statement by retreating into greater respectfulness. "Sir, if you should feel ill—"

"Then you will stop the car and I will climb into the back seat and you can opacify the rear windows. Or you needn't even stop. I can climb over the front seat while you are moving. The point is, Giskard, that it is important for me to become as acquainted with Aurora as is possible and it is important for me, in any case, to become accustomed to the Outside. I am stating this as an order, Giskard."

Daneel said softly, "Partner Elijah is quite correct in his request, friend Giskard. He will be reasonably safe."

Giskard, perhaps reluctantly (Baley could not interpret the expression on his not-quite-human face), gave in and took his place at the controls. Baley followed and looked out of the clear glass of the windshield without quite the assurance he had presented in his voice. However, the pressure of a robot on either side was comforting.

The car rose on its jets of compressed air and swayed a bit as though it were finding its footing. Baley felt a queasy sensation in the pit of his stomach and tried not to regret his brave performance of moments before. There was no use trying to tell himself that Daneel and Giskard showed no signs of fear and should be imitated. They were robots and could not feel fear.

And then the car moved forward suddenly and Baley felt himself pushed hard against the seat. Within a minute he was moving at as fast a speed as he had ever experienced on the Expressways of the City. A wide, grassy road stretched out ahead.

The speed seemed the greater for the fact that there were none of the friendly lights and structures of the City on either side but rather wide gulfs of greenery and irregular formations.

Baley fought to keep his breath steady and to talk as naturally as he might of neutral things.

He said, "We don't seem to be passing any farmland, Daneel. This seems to be unused land."

Daneel said, "This is city territory, Partner Elijah. It is privately owned parkland and estates."

"City?" Baley could not accept the word. He knew what a City was.

"Eos is the largest and most important city on Aurora. The first to be established. The Auroran World Legislature sits here. The Chairman of the Legislature has his estate here and we will be passing it."

Not only a city but the largest. Baley looked about to either side. "I was under the impression that the Fastolfe and Gladia establishments were on the outskirts of Eos. I should think we would have passed the city limits by now."

"Not at all, Partner Elijah. We're passing through its center. The limits are seven kilometers away and our destination is nearly forty kilometers beyond that."

"The center of the city? I see no structures."

"They are not meant to be seen from the road, but there's one you can make out between the trees. That is the establishment of Fuad Labord, a well-known writer."

"Do you know all the establishments by sight?"

"They are in my memory banks," said Daneel solemnly.

"There's no traffic on the road. Why is that?"

"Long distances are covered by air-cars or magnetic subcars. Trimensional connections—"

"They call it viewing on Solaria," said Baley.

"And here, too, in informal conversation, but TVC more formally. That takes care of much communication. Finally, Aurorans are fond of walking and it is not unusual to walk several kilometers for social visiting or even for business meetings where time is not of the essence."

"And we have to get somewhere that's too far to walk, too close for air-cars, and trimensional viewing is not wanted—so we use a ground-car."

"An airfoil, more specifically, Partner Elijah, but that qualifies as a ground-car, I suppose."

"How long will it take to reach Vasilia's establishment?"

"Not long, Partner Elijah. She is at the Robotics Institute, as perhaps you know."

There were some moments of silence and then Baley said, "It looks cloudy near the horizon there."

Giskard negotiated a curve at high speed, the airfoil tipping through an angle of some thirty degrees. Baley choked back a moan and clung to Daneel, who flung his left arm about Baley's shoulders and held him in a strong viselike grip, one hand on each shoulder. Slowly, Baley let out his breath as the airfoil righted itself.

Daneel said, "Yes, those clouds will bring precipitation later in the day, as predicted."

Baley frowned. He had been caught in the rain once—*once*—during his experimental work in the field Outside on Earth. It was like standing under a cold shower with his clothes on. There had been sheer panic for a moment when he realized that there was no way in which he could reach for any controls that would turn it off. The water would come down forever! —Then everyone was running and he ran with them, making for the dryness and controllability of the City.

But this was Aurora and he had no idea what one did when it

began to rain and there was no City to escape into. Run into the nearest establishment? Would refugees automatically be welcome?

Then there was another brief turn and Giskard said, "Sir, we are in the parking lot of the Robotics Institute. We can now enter and visit the establishment that Dr. Vasilia maintains on the Institute grounds."

Baley nodded. The trip had taken something between fifteen and twenty minutes (as nearly as he could judge, Earth time) and he was glad it was over. He said, rather breathlessly, "I want to know something about Dr. Fastolfe's daughter before I meet her. You did not know her, did you, Daneel?"

Daneel said, "At the time I came into existence, Dr. Fastolfe and his daughter had been separated for a considerable time. I have never met her."

"But as for you, Giskard, you and she knew each other well. Is that not so?"

"It is so, sir," said Giskard impassively.

"And were fond of each other?"

"I believe, sir," said Giskard, "that it gave Dr. Fastolfe's daughter pleasure to be with me."

"Did it give you pleasure to be with her?"

Giskard seemed to pick his words. "It gives me a sensation that I think is what human beings mean by 'pleasure' to be with any human being."

"But more so with Vasilia, I think. Am I right?"

"Her pleasure at being with me, sir," said Giskard, "did seem to stimulate those positronic potentials that produce actions in me that are equivalent to those that pleasure produces in human beings. Or so I was once told by Dr. Fastolfe."

Baley said suddenly, "Why did Vasilia leave her father?"

Giskard said nothing.

Baley said, with the sudden peremptoriness of an Earthman addressing a robot, "I asked you a question, boy."

Giskard turned his head and stared at Baley, who, for a moment, thought the glow in the robot's eyes might be brightening into a blaze of resentment at the demeaning word.

However, Giskard spoke mildly and there was no readable expression in his eyes when he said, "I would like to answer, sir, but in all matters concerning that separation, Miss Vasilia ordered me at that time to say nothing."

"But I'm ordering you to answer me and I can order you very firmly indeed—if I wish to."

Giskard said, "I am sorry. Miss Vasilia, even at that time, was skilled in robotics and the orders she gave me were sufficiently powerful to remain, despite anything you are likely to say, sir."

Baley said, "She must have been skilled in robotics, since Dr. Fastolfe told me she reprogrammed you on occasion."

"It was not dangerous to do so, sir. Dr. Fastolfe himself could always correct any errors."

"Did he have to?"

"He did not, sir."

"What was the nature of the reprogramming?"

"Minor matters, sir."

"Perhaps, but humor me. Just what was it she did?"

Giskard hesitated and Baley knew what that meant at once. The robot said, "I fear that any questions concerning the reprogramming cannot be answered by me."

"You were forbidden?"

"No, sir, but the reprogramming automatically wipes out what went before. If I am changed in any particular, it would seem to me that I have always been as changed and I would have no memory of what I was before I was changed."

"Then how do you know the reprogramming was minor?"

"Since Dr. Fastolfe never saw any need of correcting what Miss Vasilia did—or so he once told me—I can only suppose the changes were minor. You might ask Miss Vasilia, sir."

"I will," said Baley.

"I fear, however, that she will not answer, sir."

Baley's heart sank. So far he had questioned only Dr. Fastolfe, Gladia, and the two robots, all of whom had overriding reasons to cooperate. Now, for the first time, he would be facing an unfriendly subject.

*37.*

Baley stepped out of the airfoil, which was resting on a grassy plot, and felt a certain pleasure in feeling solidity beneath his feet.

He looked around in surprise, for the structures were rather thickly spread, and to his right was a particularly large one, built plainly, rather like a huge right-angled block of metal and glass.

"Is that the Robotics Institute?" he asked.

Daneel said, "This entire complex is the Institute, Partner Elijah. You are seeing only a portion and it is more thickly built up than is common on Aurora because it is a self-contained political entity. It contains home establishments, laboratories, libraries, communal gymnasia, and so on. The large structure is the administrative center."

"This is so un-Auroran, with all these buildings in view—at least judging from what I saw of Eos—that I should think there would be considerable disapproval."

"I believe there was, Partner Elijah, but the head of the Institute is friendly with the Chairman, who has much influence, and there was a special dispensation, I understand, because of research necessities." Daneel looked about thoughtfully. "It is indeed more compact than I had supposed."

"Than you had *supposed?* Have you never been here before, Daneel?"

"No, Partner Elijah."

"How about you, Giskard?"

"No, sir," said Giskard.

Baley said, "You found your way here without trouble—and you seem to know the place."

"We have been suitably informed, Partner Elijah," said Daneel, "since it was necessary that we come with you."

Baley nodded thoughtfully, then said, "Why didn't Dr. Fastolfe come with us?" and decided, once again, that it made no sense to try to catch a robot off-guard. Ask a question rapidly—

or unexpectedly—and they simply waited until the question was absorbed and then answered. They were never caught off-guard.

Daneel said, "As Dr. Fastolfe said, he is not a member of the Institute and feels it would be improper to visit uninvited."

"But why is he not a member?"

"The reason for that I have never been told, Partner Elijah."

Baley's eyes turned to Giskard, who said at once, "Nor I, sir."

Did not know? Were told not to know? —Baley shrugged. It did not matter which. Human beings could lie and robots be instructed.

Of course, human beings could be browbeaten or maneuvered out of a lie—if the questioner were skillful enough or brutal enough—and robots could be maneuvered out of instruction—if the questioner were skillful enough or unscrupulous enough— but the skills were different and Baley had none at all with respect to robots.

He said, "Where would we be likely to find Dr. Vasilia Fastolfe?"

Daneel said, "This is her establishment immediately before us."

"You have been instructed, then, as to its location?"

"That has been imprinted in our memory banks, Partner Elijah."

"Well, then, lead the way."

The orange sun was well up in the sky now and it was clearly nearing midday. As they approached Vasilia's establishment, they stepped into the shadow of the factory and Baley twitched a little as he felt the temperature drop immediately.

His lips tightened at the thought of occupying and settling worlds without Cities, where the temperature was uncontrolled and subject to unpredictable, idiotic changes. —And, he noted uneasily, the line of clouds at the horizon had advanced somewhat. It could also rain whenever it wished, with water cascading down.

Earth! He longed for the Cities.

Giskard had walked into the establishment first and Daneel held out his arm to prevent Baley from following.

Of course! Giskard was reconnoitering.

So was Daneel, for that matter. His eyes traversed the land-scape with an intentness no human being could have duplicated. Baley was certain that those robotic eyes missed nothing. (He wondered why robots were not equipped with four eyes equally distributed about the perimeter of the head—or an optic strip totally circumnavigating it. Daneel could not be expected to, of course, since he had to be human in appearance, but why not Giskard? Or did that introduce complications of vision that the positronic pathways could not handle? For a moment, Baley had a faint vision of the complexities that burdened the life of a roboticist.)

Giskard reappeared in the doorway and nodded. Daneel's arm exerted a respectful pressure and Baley moved forward. The door stood ajar.

There was no lock on Vasilia's establishment, but there had also been none (Baley suddenly remembered) on those of Gladia and of Dr. Fastolfe. A sparse population and separation helped insure privacy and, no doubt, the custom of noninter-ference helped, too. And, come to think of it, the ubiquitous robot guards were more efficient than any lock could be.

The pressure of Daneel's hand on Baley's upper arm brought the latter to a halt. Giskard, ahead of them, was speaking in a low voice to two robots, who were themselves rather Giskard-like.

A sudden coldness struck the pit of Baley's stomach. What if some rapid maneuver substituted another robot for Giskard? Would he be able to recognize the substitution? Tell two such robots apart? Would he be left with a robot without special in-structions to guard him, one who might innocently lead him into danger and then react with insufficient quickness when protec-tion was necessary?

Controlling his voice, he said calmly to Daneel, "Remarkable the similarity in those robots, Daneel. Can you tell them apart?"

"Certainly, Partner Elijah. Their clothing designs are different and their code numbers are different, as well."

"They don't look different to me."

"You are not accustomed to notice that sort of detail."

Baley stared again. "What code numbers?"

"They are easily visible, Partner Elijah, when you know where to look and when your eyes are sensitive farther into the infrared than human eyes are."

"Well, then, I would be in trouble if I had to do the identifying, wouldn't I?"

"Not at all, Partner Elijah. You had but to ask a robot for its full name and serial number. It would tell you."

"Even if instructed to give me a false one?"

"Why should any robot be so instructed?"

Baley decided not to explain.

Giskard was, in any case, returning. He said to Baley, "Sir, you will be received. Come this way, please."

The two robots of the establishment led. Behind them came Baley and Daneel, the latter retaining his grip protectively.

Following in the rear was Giskard.

The two robots stopped before a double door which opened, apparently automatically, in both directions. The room within was suffused with a dim, grayish light—daylight diffusing through thick drapery.

Baley could make out, not very clearly, a small human figure in the room, half-seated on a tall stool, with one elbow resting on a table that ran the length of the wall.

Baley and Daneel entered, Giskard coming up behind them. The door closed, leaving the room dimmer than ever.

A female voice said sharply, "Come no closer! Stay where you are!"

And the room burst into full daylight.

### 38.

Baley blinked and looked upward. The ceiling was glassed and, through it, the sun could be seen. The sun seemed oddly dim, however, and could be looked at, even though that did not seem to affect the quality of the light within. Presumably, the glass (or whatever the transparent substance was) diffused the light without absorbing it.

He looked down at the woman, who still maintained her pose at the stool, and said, "Dr. Vasilia Fastolfe?"

"Dr. Vasilia Aliena, if you want a full name. I do not borrow the names of others. You may call me Dr. Vasilia. It is the name by which I am commonly known at the Institute." Her voice, which had been rather harsh, softened, "And how are you, my old friend Giskard?"

Giskard said, in tones oddly removed from his usual one, "I greet you—" He paused and then said, "I greet you, Little Miss."

Vasilia smiled. "And this, I suppose, is the humaniform robot of whom I have heard—Daneel Olivaw?"

"Yes, Dr. Vasilia," said Daneel briskly.

"And finally, we have—the Earthman."

"Elijah Baley, Doctor," said Baley stiffly.

"Yes, I'm aware that Earthmen have names and that Elijah Baley is yours," she said coolly. "You don't look one blasted thing like the actor who played you in the hyperwave show."

"I am aware of that, Doctor."

"The one who played Daneel was rather a good likeness, however, but I suppose we are not here to discuss the show."

"We are not."

"I gather we are here, Earthman, to talk about whatever it is you want to say about Santirix Gremionis and get it over with. Right?"

"Not entirely," said Baley. "That is not the primary reason for my coming, though I imagine we will get to it."

"Indeed? Are you under the impression that we are here to engage in a long and complicated discussion on whatever topic you choose to deal with?"

"I think, Dr. Vasilia, you would be well-advised to allow me to manage this interview as I wish."

"Is that a threat?"

"No."

"Well, I have never met an Earthman and it might be interesting to see how closely you resemble the actor who played your role—that is, in ways other than appearance. Are you really the masterful person you seemed to be in the show?"

"The show," said Baley with clear distaste, "was overdramatic and exaggerated my personality in every direction. I would rather you accept me as I am and judge me entirely from how I appear to you right now."

Vasilia laughed. "At least you don't seem overawed by me. That's a point in your favor. Or do you think this Gremionis thing you've got in mind puts you in a position to order me about?"

"I am not here to do anything but uncover the truth in the matter of the dead humaniform robot, Jander Panell."

"Dead? Was he ever alive, then?"

"I use one syllable in preference to phrases such as 'rendered inoperative.' Does saying 'dead' confuse you?"

Vasilia said, "You fence well. —Debrett, bring the Earthman a chair. He will grow weary standing if this is to be a long conversation. Then get into your niche. And you may choose one, too, Daneel. —Giskard, come stand by me."

Baley sat down. "Thank you, Debrett. —Dr. Vasilia, I have no authority to question you; I have no legal means of forcing you to answer my questions. However, the death of Jander Panell has put your father in a position of some—"

"It has put *whom* in a position?"

"Your father."

"Earthman, I sometimes refer to a certain individual as my father, but no one else does. Please use a proper name."

"Dr. Han Fastolfe. He is your father, isn't he? As a matter of record?"

Vasilia said, "You are using a biological term. I share genes with him in a manner characteristic of what *on Earth* would be considered a father-daughter relationship. This is a matter of indifference on Aurora, except in medical and genetic matters. I can conceive of my suffering from certain metabolic states in which it would be appropriate to consider the physiology and biochemistry of those with whom I share genes—parents, siblings, children, and so on. Otherwise these relationships are not generally referred to in polite Auroran society. —I explain this to you because you are an Earthman."

"If I have offended against custom," said Baley, "it is through ignorance and I apologize. May I refer to the gentleman under discussion by name?"

"Certainly."

"In that case, the death of Jander Panell has put Dr. Han Fastolfe into a position of some difficulty and I would assume that you would be concerned enough to desire to help him."

"You assume that, do you? Why?"

"He is your— He brought you up. He cared for you. You had a profound affection for each other. He still feels a profound affection for you."

"Did he tell you that?"

"It was obvious from the details of our conversations—even from the fact that he has taken an interest in the Solarian woman, Gladia Delmarre, because of her resemblance to you."

"Did he tell you *that?*"

"He did, but even if he hadn't, the resemblance is obvious."

"Nevertheless, Earthman, I owe Dr. Fastolfe nothing. Your assumptions can be dismissed."

Baley cleared his throat. "Aside from any personal feelings you might or might not have, there is the matter of the future of the Galaxy. Dr. Fastolfe wishes new worlds to be explored and settled by human beings. If the political repercussions of Jander's death lead to the exploration and settlement of the new worlds by robots, Dr. Fastolfe believes that this will be catastrophic for Aurora and humanity. Surely you would not be a party to such a catastrophe."

Vasilia said indifferently, watching him closely, "Surely not, if I agreed with Dr. Fastolfe. I do not. I see no harm in having humaniform robots doing the work. I am here at the Institute, in fact, to make that possible. I am a Globalist. Since Dr. Fastolfe is a Humanist, he is my political enemy."

Her answers were clipped and direct, no longer than they had to be. Each time there followed a definite silence, as though she were waiting, with interest, for the next question. Baley had the impression that she was curious about him, amused by him, making wagers with herself as to what the next question might be, determined to give him just the minimum information necessary to force another question.

He said, "Have you long been a member of this Institute?"

"Since its formation."

"Are there many members?"

"I should judge about a third of Aurora's roboticists are members, though only about half of these actually live and work on the Institute grounds."

"Do other members of the Institute share your views on the robotic exploration of other worlds? Do they oppose Dr. Fastolfe's views one and all?"

"I suspect that most of them are Globalists, but I don't know that we have taken a vote on the matter or even discussed it formally. You had better ask them all individually."

"Is Dr. Fastolfe a member of the Institute?"

"No."

Baley waited a bit, but she said nothing beyond the negative. He said, "Isn't that surprising? I should think he, of all people, would be a member."

"As it happens, we don't want him. What is perhaps less important, he doesn't want us."

"Isn't that even more surprising?"

"I don't think so." —And then, as though goaded into saying something more by an irritation within herself, she said, "He lives in the city of Eos. I suppose you know the significance of the name, Earthman?"

Baley nodded and said, "Eos is the ancient Greek goddess of the dawn, as Aurora is the ancient Roman goddess of the dawn."

"Exactly. Dr. Han Fastolfe lives in the City of the Dawn on the World of the Dawn, but he is not himself a believer in the Dawn. He does not understand the necessary method of expansion through the Galaxy, of converting the Spacer Dawn into broad Galactic Day. The robotic exploration of the Galaxy is the only practical way to carry the task through and he won't accept it—or us."

Baley said slowly, "Why is it the only practical method? Aurora and the other Spacer worlds were not explored and settled by robots but by human beings."

"Correction. By Earthpeople. It was a wasteful and inefficient

procedure and there are now no Earthpeople that we will allow
to serve as further settlers. We have become Spacers, long-lived
and healthy, and we have robots who are infinitely more versatile and flexible than those available to the human beings who
originally settled our worlds. Times and matters are wholly
different—and *today* only robotic exploration is feasible."

"Let us suppose you are right and Dr. Fastolfe is wrong. Even
so, he has a logical view. Why won't he and the Institute accept
each other? Simply because they disagree on this point?"

"No, this disagreement is comparatively minor. There is a
more fundamental conflict."

Again Baley paused and again she added nothing to her
remark. He did not feel it safe to display irritation, so he said
quietly, almost tentatively, "What is the more fundamental
conflict?"

The amusement in Vasilia's voice came nearer the surface. It
softened the lines of her face somewhat and, for a moment, she
looked more like Gladia. "You couldn't guess, unless it were explained to you, I think."

"Precisely why I am asking, Dr. Vasilia."

"Well, then, Earthman, I have been told that Earthpeople are
short-lived. I have not been misled in that, have I?"

Baley shrugged, "Some of us live to be a hundred years old,
Earth time." He thought a bit. "Perhaps a hundred and thirty or
so metric years."

"And how old are you?"

"Forty-five standard, sixty metric."

"I am sixty-six metric. I expect to live three metric centuries
more at least—if I am careful."

Baley spread his hands wide. "I congratulate you."

"There are disadvantages."

"I was told this morning that, in three or four centuries, many,
many losses have a chance to accumulate."

"I'm afraid so," said Vasilia. "And many, many gains have a
chance to accumulate, as well. On the whole, it balances."

"What, then, are the disadvantages?"

"You are not a scientist, of course."

"I am a plainclothesman—a policeman, if you like."

"But perhaps you know scientists on your world."

"I have met some," said Baley cautiously.

"You know how they work? We are told that on Earth they cooperate out of necessity. They have, at most, half a century of active labor in the course of their short lives. Less than seven metric decades. Not much can be done in that time."

"Some of our scientists had accomplished quite a deal in considerably less time."

"Because they have taken advantage of the findings others have made before them and profit from the use they can make of contemporary findings by others. Isn't that so?"

"Of course. We have a scientific community to which all contribute, across the expanse of space and of time."

"Exactly. It won't work otherwise. Each scientist, aware of the unlikelihood of accomplishing much entirely by himself, is forced into the community, cannot help becoming part of the clearinghouse. Progress thus becomes enormously greater than it would be if this did not exist."

"Is not this the case on Aurora and the other Spacer worlds, too?" asked Baley.

"In theory it is; in practice not so much. The pressures in a long-lived society are less. Scientists here have three or three and a half centuries to devote to a problem, so that the thought arises that significant progress may be made in that time by a solitary worker. It becomes possible to feel a kind of intellectual greed—to *want* to accomplish something on your own, to assume a property right to a particular facet of progress, to be willing to see the general advance slowed—rather than give up what you conceive to be yours alone. And the general advance *is* slowed on Spacer worlds as a result, to the point where it is difficult to outpace the work done on Earth, despite our enormous advantages."

"I assume you wouldn't say this if I were not to take it that Dr. Han Fastolfe behaves in this manner."

"He certainly does. It is his theoretical analysis of the positronic brain that has made the humaniform robot possible. He has used it to construct—with the help of the late Dr. Sarton—your robot friend Daneel, but he has not published the important details of his theory, nor does he make it available to anyone else. In this way, he—and he alone—holds a stranglehold on the production of humaniform robots."

Baley furrowed his brow. "And the Robotics Institute is dedicated to cooperation among scientists?"

"Exactly. This Institute is made up of over a hundred topnotch roboticists of different ages, advancements, and skills and we hope to establish branches on other worlds and make it an interstellar association. All of us are dedicated to communicating our separate discoveries or speculations to the common fund—doing voluntarily for the general good what you Earthpeople do perforce because you live such short lives.

"This, however, Dr. Han Fastolfe will not do. I'm sure you think of Dr. Han Fastolfe as a nobly idealistic Auroran patriot, but he will not put his intellectual property—as he thinks of it—into the common fund and therefore he does not want us. And because he assumes a personal property right upon scientific discoveries, we do not want him. —You no longer find the mutual distaste a mystery, I take it."

Baley nodded his head, then said, "You think this will work—this voluntary giving up of personal glory?"

"It must," said Vasilia grimly.

"And has the Institute, through community endeavor, duplicated Dr. Fastolfe's individual work and rediscovered the theory of the humaniform positronic brain?"

"We will, in time. It is inevitable."

"And you are making no attempt to shorten the time it will take by persuading Dr. Fastolfe to yield the secret?"

"I think we are on the way to persuading him."

"Through the working of the Jander scandal?"

"I don't think you really have to ask that question. —Well, have I told you what you wanted to know, Earthman?"

Baley said, "You have told me some things I didn't know."

"Then it is time for you to tell me about Gremionis. Why have you brought up the name of this barber in connection with me?"

"Barber?"

"He considers himself a hair stylist, among other things, but he is a barber, plain and simple. Tell me about him—or let us consider this interview at an end."

Baley felt weary. It seemed clear to him that Vasilia had enjoyed the fencing. She had given him enough to whet his appetite and now he would be forced to buy additional material with information of his own. —But he had none. Or at least he had only guesses. And if any of them were wrong, vitally wrong, he was through.

He therefore fenced on his own. "You understand, Dr. Vasilia, that you can't get away with pretending that it is farcical to suppose there is a connection between Gremionis and yourself."

"Why not, when it *is* farcical?"

"Oh no. If it were farcical, you would have laughed in my face and shut off trimensional contact. The mere fact that you were willing to abandon your earlier stand and receive me—the mere fact that you have been talking to me at length and telling me a great many things—is a clear admission that you feel that I just possibly might have my knife at your jugular."

Vasilia's jaw muscles tightened and she said, in a low and angry voice, "See here, little Earthman, my position is vulnerable and you probably know it. I *am* the daughter of Dr. Fastolfe and there are some here at the Institute who are foolish enough —or knavish enough—to mistrust me therefor. I don't know what kind of story you may have heard—or made up—but that it's more or less farcical is certain. Nevertheless, no matter how farcical, it might be used effectively against me. So I am willing to trade for it. I have told you some things and I might tell you more, but only if you now tell me what you have in your hand and convince me you are telling me the truth. So tell me *now*.

"If you try to play games with me, I will be in no worse position than at present if I kick you out—and I will at least get pleasure out of that. And I will use what leverage I have with the Chairman to get him to cancel his decision to let you come here and have you sent right back to Earth. There is consid-

erable pressure on him now to do this and you won't want the
addition of mine.

"So talk! Now!"

39.

Baley's impulse was to lead up to the crucial point, feeling his
way to see if he were right. That, he felt, would not work. She
would see what he was doing—she was no fool—and would stop
him. He was on the track of something, he knew, and he didn't
want to spoil it. What she said about her vulnerable position as
the result of her relationship to her father might well be true,
but she still would not have been frightened into seeing him if
she hadn't suspected that some notion he had was not *completely*
farcical.

He had to come out with something, then, with something important that would establish, at once, some sort of domination
over her. Therefore—the gamble.

He said, "Santirix Gremionis offered himself to you." And, before Vasilia could react, he raised the ante by saying, with an
added touch of harshness, "And not once but many times."

Vasilia clasped her hands over one knee, then pulled herself
up and seated herself on the stool, as though to make herself
more comfortable. She looked at Giskard, who stood motionless
and expressionless at her side.

Then she looked at Baley and said, "Well, the idiot offers himself to everyone he sees, regardless of age and sex. I would be
unusual if he paid me no attention."

Baley made the gesture of brushing that to one side. (She had
not laughed. She had not brought the interview to an end. She
had not even put on a display of fury. She was waiting to see
what he would build out of the statement, so he did have *something* by the tail.)

He said, "That is exaggeration, Dr. Vasilia. No one, however
undiscriminating, would fail to make choices and, in the case of
this Gremionis, you were selected and, despite your refusal to

accept him, he continued to offer himself, quite out of keeping with Auroran custom."

Vasilia said, "I am glad you realize I refused him. There are some who feel that, as a matter of courtesy, any offer—or almost any offer—should be accepted, but that is not my opinion. I see no reason why I have to subject myself to some uninteresting event that will merely waste my time. Do you find something objectionable in that, Earthman?"

"I have no opinion to offer—either favorable or unfavorable— in connection with Auroran custom." (She was still waiting, listening to him. What was she waiting for? Would it be for what he wanted to say but yet wasn't sure he dared to?)

She said, with an effort at lightness, "Do you have anything at all to offer—or are we through?"

"Not through," said Baley, who was now forced to take another gamble. "You recognized this non-Auroran perseverance in Gremionis and it occurred to you that you could make use of it."

"Really? How mad! What possible use could I make of it?"

"Since he was clearly attracted to you very strongly, it would not be difficult to arrange to have him attracted by another who resembled you very closely. You urged him to do so, perhaps promising to accept him if the other did not."

"Who is this poor woman who resembles me closely?"

"You do not know? Come now, that is naïve, Dr. Vasilia. I am talking of the Solarian woman, Gladia, whom I already have said has come under the protection of Dr. Fastolfe precisely because she does resemble you. You expressed no surprise when I referred to this at the beginning of our talk. It is too late to pretend ignorance now."

Vasilia looked at him sharply. "And from his interest in her, you deduced that he must first have been interested in me? It was this wild guess with which you approached me?"

"Not entirely a wild guess. There are other substantiating factors. Do you deny all this?"

She brushed thoughtfully at the long desk beside her and Baley wondered what details were carried by the long sheets of paper on it. He could make out, from a distance, complexities of patterns that he knew would be totally meaningless to him, no matter how carefully and thoroughly he studied them.

Vasilia said, "I grow weary. You have told me that Gremionis was interested first in me, and then in my look-alike, the Solarian. And now you want me to deny it. Why should I take the trouble to deny it? Of what importance is it? Even if it were true, how could this damage me in any way? You are saying that I was annoyed by attentions I didn't want and that I ingeniously deflected them. Well?"

Baley said, "It is not so much what you did, as why. You knew that Gremionis was the type of person who would be persistent. He had offered himself to you over and over and he would offer himself to Gladia over and over."

"If she would refuse him."

"She was a Solarian, having trouble with sex, and was refusing everyone, something I dare say you knew, since I imagine that, for all your estrangement from your fa—from Dr. Fastolfe, you have enough feeling to keep an eye on your replacement."

"Well, then, good for her. If she refused Gremionis, she showed good taste."

"You knew there was no 'if' about it. You knew she would."

"Still—what of it?"

"Repeated offers to her would mean that Gremionis would be in Gladia's establishment frequently, that he would cling to her."

"One last time. Well?"

"And in Gladia's establishment was a very unusual object, one of the two humaniform robots in existence, Jander Panell."

Vasilia hesitated. Then, "What are you driving at?"

"I think it struck you that if, somehow, the humaniform robot were killed under circumstances that would implicate Dr. Fastolfe, that could be used as a weapon to force the secret of the humaniform positronic brain out of him. Gremionis, annoyed over Gladia's persistent refusal to accept him and given the opportunity by his constant presence at Gladia's establishment, could be induced to seek a fearful revenge by killing the robot."

Vasilia blinked rapidly. "That poor barber might have twenty such motives and twenty such opportunities and it wouldn't matter. He wouldn't know how to order a robot to shake hands with any efficiency. How would he manage to come within a light-year of imposing mental freeze-out on a robot?"

"Which now," said Baley softly, "finally brings us to the point, a point I think you have been anticipating, for you have some-how restrained yourself from throwing me out because you had to make sure whether I had this point in mind or not. What I'm saying is that Gremionis did the job, with the help of this Robot-ics Institute, *working through you.*"

# 10

## Again Vasilia

40.

It was as though a hyperwave drama had come to a halt in a holographic still.

None of the robots moved, of course, but neither did Baley and neither did Dr. Vasilia Aliena. Long seconds—abnormally long ones—passed, before Vasilia let out her breath and, very slowly, rose to her feet.

Her face had tightened itself into a humorless smile and her voice was low. "You are saying, Earthman, that I am an accessory in the destruction of the humaniform robot?"

Baley said, "Something of the sort had occurred to me, Doctor."

"Thank you for the thought. The interview is over and you will leave." She pointed to the door.

Baley said, "I'm afraid I do not wish to."

"I don't consult your wishes, Earthman."

"You must, for how can you make me leave against my wishes?"

"I have robots who, at my request, will put you out politely but firmly and without hurting anything but your self-esteem—if you have any."

"You have but one robot here. I have two that will not allow that to happen."

"I have twenty on instant call."

Baley said, "Dr. Vasilia, please understand! You were surprised at seeing Daneel. I suspect that, even though you work at the Robotics Institute, where humaniform robots are the first order of business, you have never actually seen a completed and functioning one. Your robots, therefore, haven't seen one, either. Now look at Daneel. He looks human. He looks more human than any robot who has ever existed, except for the dead Jander. To your robots, Daneel will surely look human. He will know how to present an order in such a way that they will obey him in preference, perhaps, to you."

Vasilia said, "I can, if necessary, summon twenty human beings from within the Institute who will put you out, perhaps *with* a little damage, and your robots, even Daneel, will not be able to interfere effectively."

"How do you intend to call them, since my robots are not going to allow you to move? They have extraordinarily quick reflexes."

Vasilia showed her teeth in something that could not be called a smile. "I cannot speak for Daneel, but I've known Giskard for most of my life. I don't think he will do *anything* to keep me from summoning help and I imagine he will keep Daneel from interfering, too."

Baley tried to keep his voice from trembling as he skated on ever-thinner ice—and knew it. He said, "Before you do anything, perhaps you might ask Giskard what he will do if you and I give conflicting orders."

"Giskard?" said Vasilia with supreme confidence.

Giskard's eyes turned full on Vasilia and he said, with an odd timbre to his voice, "Little Miss, I am compelled to protect Mr. Baley. He takes precedence."

"Indeed? By whose order? By this Earthman's? This stranger's?"

Giskard said, "By Dr. Han Fastolfe's order."

Vasilia's eyes flashed and she slowly sat down on the stool again. Her hands, resting in her lap, trembled and she said through lips that scarcely moved, "He's even taken *you* away."

"If that is not enough, Dr. Vasilia," said Daneel, speaking suddenly, of his own accord, "I, too, would place Partner Elijah's welfare above yours."

Vasilia looked at Daneel with bitter curiosity. "Partner Elijah? Is that what you call him?"

"Yes, Dr. Vasilia. My choice in this matter—the Earthman over you—arises not only out of Dr. Fastolfe's instructions, but because the Earthman and I are partners in this investigation and because—" Daneel paused as though puzzled by what he was about to say, and then said it anyway, "—we are friends."

Vasilia said, "Friends? An Earthman and a humaniform robot? Well, there is a match. Neither quite human."

Baley said, sharply, "Nevertheless bound by friendship. Do not, for your own sake, test the force of our—" Now it was he who paused and, as though to his own surprise, completed the sentence impossibly, "—love."

Vasilia turned to Baley. "What do you want?"

"Information. I have been called to Aurora—this World of the Dawn—to straighten out an event that does not seem to have an easy explanation, one in which Dr. Fastolfe stands falsely accused, with the possibility, therefore, of terrible consequences for your world and mine. Daneel and Giskard understand this situation well and know that nothing but the First Law at its fullest and most immediate can take precedence over my efforts to solve the mystery. Since they have heard what I have said and know that you might possibly be an accessory to the deed, they understand that they must not allow this interview to end. Therefore, I say again, don't risk the actions they may be forced to take if you refuse to answer my questions. I have accused you of being an accessory in the murder of Jander Panell. Do you deny that accusation or not? You *must* answer."

Vasilia said bitterly, "I will answer. Never fear! Murder? A robot is put out of commission and that's *murder*? Well, I *do* deny it, murder or whatever! I deny it with all possible force. I have not given Gremionis information on robotics for the purpose of allowing him to put an end to Jander. I don't know enough to do so and I suspect that no one at the Institute knows enough."

Baley said, "I can't say whether you know enough to have helped commit the crime or whether anyone at the Institute knows enough. We can, however, discuss motive. First, you might have a feeling of tenderness for this Gremionis. However much you might reject his offers—however contemptible you might find him as a possible lover—would it be so strange that you would feel flattered by his persistence, sufficiently so to be willing to help him if he turned to you prayerfully and without any sexual demands with which to annoy you?"

"You mean he may have come to me and said, 'Vasilia, dear, I want to put a robot out of commission. Please tell me how to do it and I will be terribly grateful to you.' And I would say, 'Why, certainly, dear, I would just love to help you commit a crime.' —Preposterous! No one except an Earthman, who knows nothing of Auroran ways, could believe anything like this could happen. It would take a particularly *stupid* Earthman, too."

"Perhaps, but all possibilities must be considered. For instance, as a second possibility, might you yourself not be jealous over the fact that Gremionis has switched his affections, so that you might help him not out of abstract tenderness but out of a very concrete desire to win him back?"

"Jealous? That is an Earthly emotion. If I do not wish Gremionis for myself, how can I possibly care whether he offers himself to another woman and she accepts or, for that matter, if another woman offers herself to him and he accepts?"

"I have been told before that sexual jealousy is unknown on Aurora and I am willing to admit that is true in theory, but such theories rarely hold up in practice. There are surely some exceptions. What's more, jealousy is all too often an irrational emotion and not to be dismissed by mere logic. Still, let us leave that for the moment. As a third possibility, you might be jealous of Gladia and wish to do her harm, even if you don't care the least bit for Gremionis yourself."

"Jealous of Gladia? I have never even seen her, except once on the hyperwave when she arrived in Aurora. The fact that people have commented on her resemblance to me, every once in a long while, hasn't bothered me."

"Does it perhaps bother you that she is Dr. Fastolfe's ward, his favorite, almost the daughter that you were once? She has replaced you."

"She is *welcome* to that. I could not care less."

"Even if they were lovers?"

Vasilia stared at Baley with growing fury and beads of perspiration appeared at her hairline.

She said, "There is no need to discuss this. You have asked me to deny the allegation that I was accessory to what you call murder and I have denied it. I have said I lacked the ability and I lacked the motive. You are welcome to present your case to all Aurora. Present your foolish attempts at supplying me with a motive. Maintain, if you wish, that I have the ability to do so. You will get nowhere. Absolutely nowhere."

And even while she trembled with anger, it seemed to Baley that there was conviction in her voice.

She did not fear the accusation.

She had agreed to see him, so he *was* on the track of something that she feared—perhaps feared desperately.

But she did not fear *this*.

Where, then, had he gone wrong?

## 41.

Baley said (troubled, casting about for some way out), "Suppose I accept your statement, Dr. Vasilia. Suppose I agree that my suspicion that you might have been an accessory in this—roboticide—was wrong. Even that would not mean that it is impossible for you to help me."

"Why should I help you?"

Baley said, "Out of human decency. Dr. Han Fastolfe assures us he did not do it, that he is not a robot-killer, that he did not put this particular robot, Jander, out of operation. You've known Dr. Fastolfe better than anyone ever has, one would suppose. You spent years in an intimate relationship with him as a beloved child and growing daughter. You saw him at times and under conditions that no one else saw him. Whatever your present feelings toward him might be, the past is not changed by them. Knowing him as you do, you must be able to bear witness that his character is such that he could not harm a robot, certainly not a robot that is one of his supreme achievements. Would you be willing to bear such witness openly? To all the worlds? It would help a great deal."

Vasilia's face seemed to harden. "Understand me," she said, pronouncing the words distinctly. "I will not be involved."

"You *must* be involved."

"Why?"

"Do you owe nothing to your father? He *is* your father. Whether the word means anything to you or not, there is a biological connection. And besides that—father or not—he took care of you, nurtured and brought you up, for years. You owe him something for that."

Vasilia trembled. It was a visible shaking and her teeth were chattering. She tried to speak, failed, took a deep breath, another, then tried again. She said, "Giskard, do you hear all that is going on?"

Giskard bowed his head. "Yes, Little Miss."

"And you, the humaniform— Daneel?"

"Yes, Dr. Vasilia."

"You hear all this, too?"

"Yes, Dr. Vasilia."

"You both understand the Earthman insists that I bear evidence on Dr. Fastolfe's character?"

Both nodded.

"Then I will speak—against my will and in anger. It is because I have felt that I did owe this *father* of mine some minimum consideration as my gene-bearer and, after a fashion, my upbringer, that I have *not* borne witness. But now I will. Earthman, listen to me. Dr. Han Fastolfe, some of whose genes I share, did not take care of me—*me—me*—as a separate, distinct human being. I was to him nothing more than an experiment, an observational phenomenon."

Baley shook his head. "That is not what I was asking."

She drove furiously over him. "You insisted that I speak and I *will* speak—and it will answer you. —One thing interests Dr. Han Fastolfe. One thing. One thing only. That is the functioning of the human brain. He wishes to reduce it to equations, to a wiring diagram, to a solved maze, and thus found a mathematical science of human behavior which will allow him to predict the human future. He calls the science 'psychohistory.' I can't believe that you have talked to him for as little as an hour without his mentioning it. It is the monomania that drives him."

Vasilia searched Baley's face and cried out in a fierce joy, "I can tell! He *has* talked to you about it. Then he must have told you that he is interested in robots only insofar as they can bring him to the human brain. He is interested in humaniform robots only insofar as they can bring him still closer to the human brain. —Yes, he's told you that, too.

"The basic theory that made humaniform robots possible arose, I am quite certain, out of his attempt to understand the human brain and he hugs that theory to himself and will allow no one else to see it because he wants to solve the problem of the human brain totally by himself in the two centuries or so he has left. Everything is subordinate to that. And that most certainly included me."

Baley, trying to breast his way against the flood of fury, said in a low voice, "In what way did it include you, Dr. Vasilia?"

"When I was born, I should have been placed with others of my kind, with professionals who knew how to care for infants. I should not have been kept by myself in the charge of an amateur—father or not, scientist or not. Dr. Fastolfe should not have been allowed to subject a child to such an environment and would not—if he had been anyone else but Han Fastolfe. He used all his prestige to bring it about, called in every debt he had, persuaded every key person he could, until he had control of me."

"He loved you," muttered Baley.

"Loved me? Any other infant would have done as well, but no other infant was available. What he wanted was a growing child in his presence, a developing brain. He wanted to make a careful study of the method of its development, the fashion of its growth. He wanted a human brain in simple form, growing complex, so that he could study it in detail. For that purpose, he subjected me to an abnormal environment and to subtle experimentation, with no consideration for me as a human being at all."

"I can't believe that. Even if he were interested in you as an experimental object, he could still care for you as a human being."

"*No.* You speak as an Earthman. Perhaps on Earth there is some sort of regard for biological connections. Here there is not. I was an experimental object to him. Period."

"Even if that were so to start with, Dr. Fastolfe couldn't help but learn to love you—a helpless object entrusted to his care. Even if there were no biological connection at all, even if you were an animal, let us say, he would have learned to love you."

"Oh, would he now?" she said bitterly. "You don't know the force of indifference in a man like Dr. Fastolfe. If it would have advanced his knowledge to snuff out my life, he would have done so without hesitation."

"That is ridiculous, Dr. Vasilia. His treatment of you was so kind and considerate that it evoked love from you. I know that. You—you offered yourself to him."

"He told you that, did he? Yes, he would. Not for a moment, even today, would he stop to question whether such a revelation might not embarrass me. —Yes, I offered myself to him and why not? He was the only human being I really knew. He was superficially gentle to me and I didn't understand his true purposes. He was a natural target for me. Then, too, he saw to it that I was introduced to sexual stimulation under controlled conditions—the controls *he* set up. It was inevitable that eventually I would turn to him. I had to, for there was no one else—and he refused."

"And you hated him for that?"

"*No.* Not at first. Not for years. Even though my sexual development was stunted and distorted, with effects I feel to this day, I did not blame him. I did not know enough. I found excuses for him. He was busy. He had others. He needed older women. You would be astonished at the ingenuity with which I uncovered reasons for his refusal. It was only years later that I became aware that something was wrong and I managed to bring it out openly, face-to-face. 'Why did you refuse me?' I asked. 'Obliging me might have put me on the right track, solved everything.'"

She paused, swallowing, and for a moment covered her eyes. Baley waited, frozen with embarrassment. The robots were expressionless (incapable, for all Baley knew, of experiencing any balance or imbalance of the positronic pathways that would produce a sensation in any way analogous to human embarrassment).

She said, calmer, "He avoided the question for as long as he could, but I faced him with it over and over. 'Why did you refuse me?' 'Why did you refuse me?' He had no hesitation in engaging in sex. I knew of several occasions— I remember wondering if he simply preferred men. Where children are not involved, personal preference in such things is not of any importance and some men can find women distasteful or, for that matter, vice versa. It was not so with this man you call my father, however. He enjoyed women—sometimes young women—as young as I was when I first offered myself. 'Why did you refuse me?' He finally answered me—and you are welcome to guess what that answer was."

She paused and waited sardonically.

Baley stirred uneasily and said in a mumble, "He didn't want to make love to his daughter?"

"Oh, don't be a fool. What difference does that make? Considering that hardly any man on Aurora knows who his daughter is, any man making love to any woman a few decades younger might be— But never mind, it's self-evident. —What he answered—and oh, how I remember the words—was 'You great fool! If I involved myself with you in that manner, how could I maintain my objectivity—and of what use would my continuing study of you be?'

"By that time, you see, I knew of his interest in the human brain. I was even following in his footsteps and becoming a roboticist in my own right. I worked with Giskard in this direction and experimented with his programming. I did it very well, too, didn't I, Giskard?"

Giskard said, "So you did, Little Miss."

"But I could see that this man whom you call my father did not view me as a human being. He was willing to see me distorted for life, rather than risk his objectivity. His observations meant more to him than my normality. From that time on, I knew what I was and what he was—and I left him."

The silence hung heavy in the air.

Baley's head was throbbing slightly. He wanted to ask: could you not take into account the self-centeredness of a great scientist? The importance of a great problem? Could you make no allowances for something spoken perhaps in irritation at being forced to discuss what one did not want to discuss? Was not Vasilia's own anger just now much the same thing? Did not Vasilia's concentration on her own "normality" (whatever she meant by that) to the exclusion of perhaps the two most important problems facing humanity—the nature of the human brain and the settling of the Galaxy—represent an equal self-centeredness with much less excuse?

But he could ask none of those things. He did not know how to put it so that it would make real sense to this woman, nor was he sure he would understand her if she answered.

What was he doing on this world? He could not understand their ways, no matter how they explained. Nor could they understand his.

He said wearily, "I am sorry, Dr. Vasilia. I understand that you are angry, but if you would dismiss your anger for a moment and consider, instead, the matter of Dr. Fastolfe and the murdered robot, could you not see that we are dealing with two different things? Dr. Fastolfe might have wanted to observe you in a detached and objective way, even at the cost of your unhappiness, and yet be light-years removed from the desire to destroy an advanced humaniform robot."

Vasilia reddened. She shouted, "Don't you understand what I'm telling you, Earthman? Do you think I have told you what I have just told you because I think you—or anyone—would be interested in the sad story of my life? For that matter, do you think I enjoy revealing myself in this manner?

"I'm telling you this only to show you that Dr. Han Fastolfe— my biological father, as you never tire of pointing out—*did* destroy Jander. Of course he did. I have refrained from saying so because no one—until you—was idiot enough to ask me and because of some foolish remnant of consideration I have for that man. But now that you have asked me, I say so and, by Aurora, I will continue to say so—to anyone and everyone. Publicly, if necessary.

"Dr. Han Fastolfe *did* destroy Jander Panell. I am certain of it. Does that satisfy you?"

## 42.

Baley stared at the distraught woman in horror.

He stuttered and began again. "I don't understand at all, Dr. Vasilia. Please quiet down and consider. Why should Dr. Fastolfe destroy the robot? What has that to do with his treatment of you? Do you imagine it is some kind of retaliation against you?"

Vasilia was breathing rapidly (Baley noted absently and without conscious intention that, although Vasilia was as small-boned as Gladia was, her breasts were larger) and she seemed to wrench at her voice to keep it under control.

She said, "I told you, Earthman, did I not, that Han Fastolfe was interested in observing the human brain? He did not hesitate to put it under stress in order to observe the results. And he preferred brains that were out of the ordinary—that of an infant, for instance—so that he might watch their development. Any brain but a commonplace one."

"But what has that to do—"

"Ask yourself, then, why he gained this interest in the foreign woman."

"In Gladia? I asked *him* and he told me. She reminded him of you and the resemblance is indeed distinct."

"And when you told me this earlier, I was amused and asked if you believed him? I ask again. Do you believe him?"

"Why shouldn't I believe him?"

"Because it's not true. The resemblance may have attracted his attention, but the real key to his interest is that the foreign woman is—foreign. She had been brought up in Solaria, under assumptions and social axioms not like those on Aurora. He could therefore study a brain that was differently molded from ours and could gain an interesting perspective. Don't you understand that? —For that matter, why is he interested in *you*, Earthman? Is he silly enough to imagine that you can solve an Auroran problem when you know nothing about Aurora?"

Daneel suddenly intervened again and Baley started at the sound of the other's voice. Daneel said, "Dr. Vasilia, Partner Elijah solved a problem on Solaria, though he knew nothing of Solaria."

"Yes," said Vasilia sourly, "so all the worlds noted on that hyperwave program. And lightning may strike, too, but I don't think that Han Fastolfe is confident it will strike twice in the same place in rapid succession. No, Earthman, he was attracted to you, in the first place, because you are an Earthman. You possess another alien brain he can study and manipulate."

"Surely you cannot believe, Dr. Vasilia, that he would risk matters of vital importance to Aurora and call in someone he knew to be useless, merely to study an unusual brain."

"Of course he would. Isn't that the whole point of what I am telling you? There is no crisis that could face Aurora that he would believe, for a single moment, to be as important as solving the problem of the brain. I can tell you exactly what he would say if you were to ask him. Aurora might rise or fall, flourish or decay, and that would all be of little concern compared to the problem of the brain, for if human beings really understood the brain, all that might have been lost in the course of a millennium of neglect or wrong decisions would be regained in a decade of cleverly directed human development guided by his dream of 'psychohistory.' He would use the same argument to justify anything—lies, cruelty, *anything*—by merely saying that it is all intended to serve the purpose of advancing the knowledge of the brain."

"I can't imagine that Dr. Fastolfe would be cruel. He is the gentlest of men."

"Is he? How long have you been with him?"

Baley said, "A few hours on Earth three years ago. A day, now, here on Aurora."

"A whole day. A *whole* day. I was with him for thirty years almost constantly and I have followed his career from a distance with some attention ever since. And you have been with him a whole day, Earthman? Well, on that one day, has he done nothing that frightened or humiliated you?"

Baley kept silent. He thought of the sudden attack with the spicer from which Daneel had rescued him; of the Personal that presented him with such difficulty, thanks to its masked nature; the extended walk Outside designed to test his ability to adapt to the open.

Vasilia said, "I see he did. Your face, Earthman, is not quite the mask of disguise you may think it is. Did he threaten you with a Psychic Probe?"

Baley said, "It was mentioned."

"One day—and it was already mentioned. I assume it made you feel uneasy?"

"It did."

"And that there was no reason to mention it?"

"Oh, but there was," said Baley quickly. "I had said that, for a moment, I had a thought which I then lost and it was certainly legitimate to suggest that a Psychic Probe might help me relocate that thought."

Vasilia said, "No, it wasn't. The Psychic Probe cannot be used with sufficient delicacy of touch for that—and, if it were attempted, the chances would be considerable that there would be permanent brain damage."

"Surely not if it were wielded by an expert—by Dr. Fastolfe, for instance."

"By *him?* He doesn't know one end of the Probe from the other. He is a theoretician, not a technician."

"By someone else, then. He did not, in actual fact, specify himself."

"No, Earthman. By *no one*. Think! Think! If the Psychic Probe could be used on human beings safely by *anyone,* and if Han Fastolfe were so concerned about the problem of the inactivation of the robot, then why didn't he suggest the Psychic Probe be used on himself?"

"On himself?"

"Don't tell me this hasn't occurred to you? Any thinking person would come to the conclusion that Fastolfe is guilty. The only point in favor of his innocence is that he himself insists he is innocent. Well, then, why does he not offer to prove his innocence by being psychically probed and showing that no trace of guilt can be dredged up from the recesses of his brain? Has he suggested such a thing, Earthman?"

"No, he hasn't. At least, not to me."

"Because he knows very well that it is deadly dangerous. Yet he does not hesitate to suggest it in your case, merely to observe how your brain works under pressure, how you react to fright. Or perhaps it occurs to him that, however dangerous the Probe is to *you*, it may come up with some interesting data for *him*, as far as the details of your Earth-molded brain are concerned. Tell me, then, isn't that cruel?"

Baley brushed it aside with a tight gesture of his right arm. "How does this apply to the actual case—to the roboticide?"

"The Solarian woman, Gladia, caught my onetime father's eye. She had an interesting brain—for his purposes. He therefore gave her the robot, Jander, to see what would happen if a woman not raised on Aurora were faced with a robot that seemed human in every particular. He knew that an Auroran woman would very likely make use of the robot for sex immediately and have no trouble doing so. I myself would have some trouble, I admit, because I was not brought up normally, but no ordinary Auroran would. The Solarian woman, on the other hand, would have a great deal of trouble because she was brought up on an extremely robotic world and had unusually rigid mental attitudes toward robots. The difference, you see, might be very instructive to my father, who tried, out of these variations, to build his theory of brain functioning. Han Fastolfe waited half a year for the Solarian woman to get to the point where she could perhaps begin making the first experimental approaches—"

Baley interrupted. "Your father knew nothing at all about the relationship between Gladia and Jander."

"Who told you that, Earthman? My father? Gladia? If the for-mer, he was naturally lying; if the latter, she simply didn't know, very likely. You may be sure Fastolfe knew what was going on; he had to, for it must have been part of his study of how a human brain was bent under Solarian conditions.

"And then he thought—and I am as sure of this as I would be if I could read his thoughts—what would happen now, at the point where the woman is just beginning to rely on Jander, if, suddenly, without reason, she lost him. He knew what an Auroran woman would do. She would feel some disappointment and then seek out some substitute, but what would a Solarian woman do? So he arranged to put Jander out of commission—"

"Destroy an immensely valuable robot just to satisfy a trivial curiosity?"

"Monstrous, isn't it? But that's what Han Fastolfe would do. So go back to him, Earthman, and tell him that his little game is over. If the planet, generally, doesn't believe him to be guilty now, they most certainly will after I have had my say."

43.

For a long moment, Baley sat there stunned, while Vasilia looked at him with a kind of grim delight, her face looking harsh and totally unlike that of Gladia.

There seemed nothing to do—

Baley got to his feet, feeling old—much older than his forty-five standard years (a child's age to these Aurorans). So far everything he had done had led to nothing. To worse than nothing, for at every one of his moves, the ropes seemed to tighten about Fastolfe.

He looked upward at the transparent ceiling. The sun was quite high, but perhaps it had passed its zenith, as it was dimmer than ever. Lines of thin clouds obscured it inter-mittently.

Vasilia seemed to become aware of this from his upward glance. Her arm moved on the section of the long bench near which she was sitting and the transparency of the ceiling vanished. At the same time, a brilliant light suffused the room, bearing the same faint orange tinge that the sun itself had.

She said, "I think the interview is over. I shall have no reason to see you again, Earthman—or you me. Perhaps you had better leave Aurora. You have done"—she smiled humorlessly and said the next words almost savagely—"my father enough damage, though scarcely as much as he deserves."

Baley took a step toward the door and his two robots closed in on him. Giskard said in a low voice, "Are you well, sir?"

Baley shrugged. What was there to answer to that?

Vasilia called out, "Giskard! When Dr. Fastolfe finds he has no further use for you, come join my staff?"

Giskard looked at her calmly. "If Dr. Fastolfe permits, I will do so, Little Miss."

Her smile grew warm. "Please do so, Giskard. I've never stopped missing you."

"I often think of you, Little Miss."

Baley turned at the door. "Dr. Vasilia, would you have a Personal I might use?"

Vasilia's eyes widened. "Of course not, Earthman. There are Community Personals here and there at the Institute. Your robots should be able to guide you."

He stared at her and shook his head. It was not surprising that she wanted no Earthman infecting her rooms and yet it angered him just the same.

He said out of anger, rather than out of any rational judgment, "Dr. Vasilia, I would not, were I you, speak of the guilt of Dr. Fastolfe."

"What is there to stop me?"

"The danger of the general uncovering of your dealings with Gremionis. The danger to you."

"Don't be ridiculous. You have admitted there was no conspiracy between myself and Gremionis."

"Not really. I agreed there seemed reason to conclude there was no direct conspiracy between you and Gremionis to destroy Jander. There remains the possibility of an indirect conspiracy."

"You are mad. What is an indirect conspiracy?"

"I am not ready to discuss that in front of Dr. Fastolfe's robots

—unless you insist. And why should you? You know very well what I mean." There was no reason why Baley should think she would accept this bluff. It might simply worsen the situation still further.

But it didn't! Vasilia seemed to shrink within herself, frowning.

Baley thought: There *is* then an indirect conspiracy, whatever it might be, and this might hold her till she sees through my bluff.

Baley said, his spirits rising a little, "I repeat, say nothing about Dr. Fastolfe."

But, of course, he didn't know how much time he had bought —perhaps very little.

# 11

## Gremionis

*44·*

They were sitting in the airfoil again—all three in the front, with Baley once more in the middle and feeling the pressure on either side. Baley was grateful to them for the care they unfailingly gave him, even though they were only machines, helpless to disobey instructions.

And then he thought: Why dismiss them with a word—"machines"? They're *good* machines in a Universe of sometimes-evil people. I have no right to favor the machines vs. people subcategorization over the good vs. evil one. And Daneel, at least, I cannot think of as a machine.

Giskard said, "I must ask again, sir. Do you feel well?"

Baley nodded. "Quite well, Giskard. I am glad to be out here with you two."

The sky was, for the most part, white—off-white, actually. There was a gentle wind and it had felt distinctly cool until they got into the car.

Daneel said, "Partner Elijah, I was listening carefully to the conversation between yourself and Dr. Vasilia. I do not wish to comment unfavorably on what Dr. Vasilia has said, but I must tell you that, in my observation, Dr. Fastolfe is a kind and courteous human being. He has never, to my knowledge, been deliberately cruel, nor has he, as nearly as I can judge, sacrificed a human being's essential welfare to the needs of his curiosity."

Baley looked at Daneel's face, which gave the impression, somehow, of intent sincerity. He said, "Could you say anything against Dr. Fastolfe, even if he were, in fact, cruel and thoughtless?"

"I could remain silent."

"But would you?"

"If, by telling a lie, I were to harm a truthful Dr. Vasilia by casting unjustified doubt on her truthfulness, and if, by remaining silent, I would harm Dr. Fastolfe by lending further color to the true accusations against him, and if the two harms were, to my mind, roughly equal in intensity, then it would be necessary for me to remain silent. Harm through an active deed outweighs, in general, harm through passivity—all things being reasonably equal."

Baley said, "Then, even though the First Law states: 'A robot may not injure a human being or, *through inaction,* allow a human being to come to harm,' the two halves of the law are not equal? A fault of commission, you say, is greater than one of omission?"

"The words of the law are merely an approximate description of the constant variations in positronomotive force along the robotic brain paths, Partner Elijah. I do not know enough to describe the matter mathematically, but I know what my tendencies are."

"And they are always to choose not doing over doing, if the harm is roughly equal in both directions?"

"In general. And always to choose truth over nontruth, if the harm is roughly equal in both directions. In general, that is."

"And, in this case, since you speak to refute Dr. Vasilia and thus do her harm, you can only do so because the First Law is mitigated sufficiently by the fact that you are telling the truth?"

"That is so, Partner Elijah."

"Yet the fact is, you would say what you have said, even though it were a lie—provided Dr. Fastolfe had instructed you, with sufficient intensity, to tell that lie when necessary and to refuse to admit that you had been so instructed."

There was a pause and then Daneel said, "That is so, Partner Elijah."

"It is a complicated mess, Daneel—but you still believe that Dr. Fastolfe did not murder Jander Panell?"

"My experience with him is that he is truthful, Partner Elijah, and that he would not do harm to friend Jander."

"And yet Dr. Fastolfe has himself described a powerful motive for his having committed the deed, while Dr. Vasilia has described a completely different motive, one that is just as powerful and is even more disgraceful than the first." Baley brooded a bit. "If the public were made aware of either motive, belief in Dr. Fastolfe's guilt would be universal."

Baley turned suddenly to Giskard. "How about you, Giskard? You have known Dr. Fastolfe longer than Daneel has. Do you agree that Dr. Fastolfe could not have committed the deed and could not have destroyed Jander, on the basis of your understanding of Dr. Fastolfe's character?"

"I do, sir."

Baley regarded the robot uncertainly. He was less advanced than Daneel. How far could he be trusted as a corroborating witness? Might he not be impelled to follow Daneel in whatever direction Daneel chose to take?

He said, "You knew Dr. Vasilia, too, did you not?"

"I knew her very well," said Giskard.

"And liked her, I gather?"

"She was in my charge for many years and the task did not in any way trouble me."

"Even though she fiddled with your programming?"

"She was very skillful."

"Would she lie about her father—about Dr. Fastolfe, that is?"

Giskard hesitated. "No, sir. She would not."

"Then you are saying that what she says is the truth."

"Not quite, sir. What I am saying is that she herself believes she is telling the truth."

"But why should she believe such evil things about her father to be true if, in actual fact, he is as kind a person as Daneel has just told me he was?"

Giskard said slowly, "She has been embittered by various events in her youth, events for which she considers Dr. Fastolfe to have been responsible and for which he may indeed have

been unwittingly responsible—to an extent. It seems to me it
was not his intention that the events in question should have the
consequences they did. However, human beings are not governed by the straightforward laws of robotics. It is therefore
difficult to judge the complexities of their motivations under
most conditions."

"True enough," muttered Baley.

Giskard said, "Do you think the task of demonstrating Dr.
Fastolfe's innocence to be hopeless?"

Baley's eyebrows moved toward each other in a frown. "It
may be. As it happens, I see no way out—and if Dr. Vasilia
talks, as she has threatened to do—"

"But you ordered her not to talk. You explained that it would
be dangerous to herself if she did."

Baley shook his head. "I was bluffing. I didn't know what else
to say."

"Do you intend to give up, then?"

And Baley said forcefully, "No! If it were merely Fastolfe, I
might. After all, what physical harm would come to him? Roboticide is not even a crime, apparently, merely a civil offense. At
worst, he will lose political influence and, perhaps, find himself
unable to continue with his scientific labors for a time. I would
be sorry to see that happen, but if there's nothing more I can do,
then there's nothing more I can do.

"And if it were just myself, I might give up, too. Failure
would damage my reputation, but who can build a brick house
without bricks? I would go back to Earth a bit tarnished, I
would lead a miserable and unclassified life, but that is the
chance that faces every Earthman and woman. Better men than
I have had to face that as unjustly.

"However, it is a matter of Earth. If I fail, then along with the
grievous loss to Dr. Fastolfe and to myself, there would be an
end for any hope Earthpeople might have to move out of Earth
and into the Galaxy generally. For that reason, I must not fail
and I must keep on somehow, as long as I am not physically
thrust off this world."

Having ended in what was almost a whisper, he suddenly
looked up and said in a peevish tone, "Why are we sitting here

parked, Giskard? Are you running the motor for your own amusement?"

"With respect, sir," said Giskard, "you have not told me where to take you."

"True! —I beg your pardon, Giskard. First, take me to the nearest of the Community Personals that Dr. Vasilia made mention of. You two may be immune to such things, but I have a bladder that needs emptying. After that, find someplace nearby where I can get something to eat. I have a stomach that needs filling. And after that—"

"Yes, Partner Elijah?" asked Daneel.

"To tell you the truth, Daneel, I don't know. However, after I tend to these purely physical needs, I will think of something."

And how Baley wished he could believe that.

## 45.

The airfoil did not skim the ground for long. It came to a halt, swaying a bit, and Baley felt the usual odd tightening of his stomach. That small unsteadiness told him he was in a vehicle and it drove away the temporary feeling of being safe within walls and between robots. Through the glass ahead and on either side (and backward, if he craned his neck) was the whiteness of sky and the greenness of foliage, all amounting to Outside—that is, to nothing. He swallowed uneasily.

They had stopped at a small structure.

Baley said, "Is this the Community Personal?"

Daneel said, "It is the nearest of a number on the Institute grounds, Partner Elijah."

"You found it quickly. Are these structures also included in the map that has been pumped into your memory?"

"That is the case, Partner Elijah."

"Is this one in use now?"

"It may be, Partner Elijah, but three or four may use it simultaneously."

"Is there room for me?"

"Very likely, Partner Elijah."

"Well, then, let me out. I'll go there and see—"

The robots did not move. Giskard said, "Sir, we may not enter with you."

"Yes, I am aware of that, Giskard."

"We will not be able to guard you properly, sir."

Baley frowned. The lesser robot would naturally have the more rigid mind and Baley suddenly recognized the danger that he would simply not be allowed out of their sight and, therefore, not allowed to enter the Personal. He put a note of urgency into his voice and turned his attention to Daneel, who might be expected to more nearly understand human needs. "I can't help that, Giskard. —Daneel, I have no choice in the matter. Let me out of the car."

Giskard looked at Baley without moving and, for one horrid moment, Baley thought the robot would suggest that he unburden himself in the nearby field—in the open, like an animal.

The moment passed. Daneel said, "I think we must allow Partner Elijah to have his way in this respect."

Whereupon Giskard said to Baley, "If you can wait for a short while, sir, I will approach the structure first."

Baley grimaced. Giskard walked slowly toward the building and then, deliberately, circumnavigated it. Baley might have predicted the fact that, once Giskard disappeared, his own sense of urgency would increase.

He tried to distract his own nerve endings by staring around at the prospect. After some study, he became aware of thin wires in the air, here and there—fine, dark hairs against the white sky. He did not see them, to begin with. What he saw first was an oval object sliding along beneath the clouds. He became aware of it as a vehicle and realized that it was not floating but was suspended from a long horizontal wire. He followed that long wire with his eyes, forward and back, noting others of the sort. He then saw another vehicle farther off—and yet another still farther off. The farthest of the three was a featureless speck whose nature he understood only because he had seen the nearer ones.

Undoubtedly, these were cable-cars for internal transportation from one part of the Robotics Institute to another.

How spread out it all was, thought Baley. How needlessly the Institute consumed space.

And yet, in doing so, it did not consume the surface. The structures were sufficiently widely spaced so that the greenery seemed untouched and the plant and animal life continued (Baley imagined) as they might in emptiness.

Solaria, Baley remembered, had been empty. No doubt all the Spacer worlds were empty, since Aurora, the most populous, was so empty, even here in the most built-up region of the planet. For that matter, even Earth—outside the Cities—was empty.

But there *were* the Cities and Baley felt a sharp pang of homesickness, which he had to push to one side.

Daneel said, "Ah, friend Giskard has completed his examination."

Giskard was back and Baley said tartly, "Well? Will you be so kind as to grant me permission—" He stopped. Why expend sarcasm on the impenetrable hide of a robot?

Giskard said, "It seems quite certain that the Personal is unoccupied."

"Good! Then get out of my way." Baley flung open the door of the airfoil and stepped out onto the gravel of a narrow path. He strode rapidly, with Daneel following.

When he reached the door of the structure, Daneel wordlessly indicated the contact that would open it. Daneel did not venture to touch the contact himself. Presumably, thought Baley, to have done so without specific instructions would have indicated an intention to enter—and even the intention was not permitted.

Baley pushed the contact and entered, leaving the two robots behind.

It was not until he was inside that it occurred to him that Giskard could not possibly have entered the Personal to see that it was unoccupied, that the robot must have been judging the matter from external appearance—a dubious proceeding at best.

And Baley realized, with some discomfort, that, for the first time, he was isolated and separated from all protectors—and that the protectors on the other side of the door couldn't easily enter if he were suddenly in trouble. What, then, if he were, at this moment, not alone? What if some enemy had been alerted by Vasilia, who knew he would be in search of a Personal, and what if that enemy was in hiding right now in the structure?

Baley grew suddenly and uncomfortably aware that (as would not have been the case on Earth) he was totally unarmed.

46.

To be sure, the structure was not large. There were small urinals, side by side, half a dozen of them; small washbasins, side by side, again half a dozen. No showers, no clothes-fresheners, no shaving devices.

There were half a dozen stalls, separated by partitions and with small doors to each. Might there not be someone waiting inside one of them—

The doors did not come down to the ground. Moving softly, he bent and glanced under each door, looking for any sign of legs. He then approached each door, testing it, swinging it open tensely, ready to slam it shut at the least sign of anything untoward, and then to dash to the door that led to the Outside.

All the stalls were empty.

He looked around to make sure there were no other hiding places.

He could find none.

He went to the door to the Outside and found no indication of a way of locking it. It occurred to him that there would naturally be no way of locking it. The Personal was clearly for the use of several men at the same time. Others would have to be able to enter at need.

Yet he could not very well leave and try another, for the danger would exist at any—and besides, he could delay no longer.

For a moment, he found himself unable to decide which of the series of urinals he should use. He could approach and use any of them. So could anyone else.

He forced the choice of one upon himself and, aware of openness all around, was afflicted at once with bashful bladder. He felt the urgency, but had to wait impatiently for the feeling of

apprehension at the possible entrance of others to dissipate itself.

He no longer feared the entrance of enemies, just the entrance
of anyone.

And then he thought: The robots will at least delay anyone
approaching.

With that, he managed to relax—

He was quite done, greatly relieved, and about to turn to a
washbasin, when he heard a moderately high-pitched, rather
tense voice. "Are you Elijah Baley?"

Baley froze. After all his apprehension and all his precautions,
he had been unaware of someone entering. In the end, he had
been entirely wrapped up in the simple act of emptying his
bladder, something that should not have taken up even the
tiniest fraction of his conscious mind. (Was he getting old?)

To be sure, there seemed no threat of any kind in the voice he
heard. It seemed empty of menace. It may have been that Baley
simply felt certain—and had the sure confidence within him—
that Daneel, at least, if not Giskard, would not have allowed a
threat to enter.

What bothered Baley was merely the entrance. In his whole
life, he had never been approached—let alone addressed—by a
man in a Personal. On Earth that was the most strenuous taboo
and on Solaria (and, until now, on Aurora) he had used only
one-person Personals.

The voice came again. Impatient. "Come! You *must* be Elijah
Baley."

Slowly, Baley turned. It was a man of moderate height, delicately dressed in well-fitted clothing in various shades of blue.
He was light-skinned, light-haired, and had a small mustache
that was a shade darker than the hair on his head. Baley found
himself staring with fascination at the small strip of hair on the
upper lip. It was the first time he had seen a Spacer with a mustache.

Baley said (and was filled with shame at speaking in a Personal), "I am Elijah Baley." His voice, even in his own ears,
seemed a scratchy and unconvincing whisper.

The Spacer seemed to find it unconvincing, certainly. He said,
narrowing his eyes and staring, "The robots outside said Elijah

Baley was in here, but you don't look at all the way you looked on hyperwave. Not at all."

That foolish dramatization! thought Baley fiercely. No one would meet him to the end of time without having been preliminarily poisoned by that impossible representation. No one would accept him as a human being at the start, as a fallible human being—and when they discovered the fallibility, they would, in disappointment, consider him a fool.

He turned resentfully to the washbasin and splashed water, then shook his hands vaguely in the air, while wondering where the hot-air jet might be found. The Spacer touched a contact and seemed to pluck a thin bit of absorbent fluff out of midair.

"Thank you," said Baley, taking it. "That was not me in the hyperwave show. It was an actor."

"I know that, but they might have picked one that looked more like you, mightn't they?" It seemed to be a source of grievance to him. "I want to speak to you."

"How did you get past my robots?"

That was another source of grievance, apparently. "I nearly didn't," said the Spacer. "They tried to stop me and I only had one robot with me. I had to pretend I had to get in here on an emergency basis and they *searched* me. They absolutely laid *hands* on me to see if I was carrying anything dangerous. I'd have you up on charges—if you weren't an Earthman. You can't give robots the kind of orders that embarrass a human being."

"I'm sorry," said Baley stiffly, "but I am not the one who gave them their orders. What can I do for you?"

"I want to speak to you."

"You *are* speaking to me. —Who are you?"

The other seemed to hesitate, then said, "Gremionis."

"Santirix Gremionis?"

"That's right."

"Why do you want to speak to me?"

For a moment, Gremionis stared at Baley, apparently with embarrassment. Then he mumbled, "Well, as long as I'm here—if you don't mind—I might as well—" and he stepped toward the line of urinals.

Baley realized, with the last refinement of horrified queasiness,

what it was Gremionis intended to do. He turned hastily and
said, "I'll wait for you outside."

"No no, don't go," said Gremionis desperately, in what was almost a squeak. "This won't take a second. Please!"

It was only that Baley now wanted, just as desperately, to talk
to Gremionis and did not want to do anything that might offend
the other and make him unwilling to talk; otherwise he would
not have been willing to accede to the request.

He kept his back turned and squinted his eyes nearly shut in a
sort of horrified reflex. It was only when Gremionis came up
around him, his hands kneading a fluffy towel of his own, that
Baley could relax again, after a fashion.

"Why do you want to speak to me?" he said again.

"Gladia—the woman from Solaria—" Gremionis looked dubious and stopped.

"I know Gladia," said Baley coldly.

"Gladia viewed me—trimensionally, you know—and told me
you had asked about me. And she asked me if I had, in any way,
mistreated a robot she owned—a human-looking robot like one
of those outside—"

"Well, did you, Mr. Gremionis?"

"*No!* I didn't even know she owned a robot like that, until—
Did you tell her I did?"

"I was only asking questions, Mr. Gremionis."

Gremionis had made a fist of his right hand and was grinding
it nervously into his left. He said intensely, "I don't want to be
falsely accused of anything—and especially where such a false
accusation would affect my relationship with Gladia."

Baley said, "How did you find me?"

Gremionis said, "She asked me about that robot and said you
had asked about me. I had heard you had been called to Aurora
by Dr. Fastolfe to solve this—puzzle—about the robot. It was on
the hyperwave news. And—" The words ground out as though
they were emerging from him with the utmost difficulty.

"Go on," said Baley.

"I had to talk to you and explain that I had had nothing to do
with that robot. *Nothing!* Gladia didn't know where you were,
but I thought Dr. Fastolfe would know."

"So you called him?"

"Oh no, I—I don't think I'd have the nerve to— He's such an important scientist. But Gladia called him for me. She's—that kind of person. He told her you had gone to see his daughter, Dr. Vasilia Aliena. That was good because I know her."

"Yes, I know you do," said Baley.

Gremionis looked uneasy. "How did you— Did you ask her about me, too?" His uneasiness seemed to be degenerating to misery. "I finally called Dr. Vasilia and she said you had just left and I'd probably find you at some Community Personal—and this one is the closest to her establishment. I was sure there would be no reason for you to delay in order to find a farther one. I mean why should you?"

"You reason quite correctly, but how is it you got here so quickly?"

"I work at the Robotics Institute and my establishment is on the Institute grounds. My scooter brought me here in minutes."

"Did you come here alone?"

"Yes! With only one robot. The scooter is a two-seater, you see."

"And your robot is waiting outside?"

"Yes."

"Tell me again why you want to see me."

"I've got to make sure you don't think I've had anything to do with that robot. I never even *heard* of him till this whole thing exploded in the news. So can I talk to you *now*?"

"Yes, but not here," said Baley firmly. "Let's get out."

How strange it was, thought Baley, that he was so pleased to get out from behind walls and into the Outside. There was something more totally alien to this Personal than anything else he had encountered on either Aurora or Solaria. Even more disconcerting than the fact of planet-wide indiscriminate use had been the horror of being openly and casually addressed—of behavior that drew no distinction between this place and its purpose and any other place and purpose.

The book-films he had viewed had said nothing of this. Clearly, as Fastolfe had pointed out, they were not written for Earthpeople but for Aurorans and, to a lesser extent, for possible tourists from the other forty-nine Spacer worlds. Earthpeople, after all, almost never went to the Spacer worlds, least of all to

Aurora. They were not welcome there. Why, then, should they be addressed?

And why should the book-films expand on what everyone knew? Should they make a fuss over the fact that Aurora was spherical in shape, or that water was wet, or that one man might address another freely in a Personal?

Yet did that not make a mockery of the very name of the structure? Yet Baley found himself unable to avoid thinking of the Women's Personals on Earth where, as Jessie had frequently told him, women chattered incessantly and felt no discomfort about it. Why women, but not men? Baley had never thought seriously about it before, but had accepted it merely as custom —as unbreakable custom—but if women, why not men?

It didn't matter. The thought only affected his intellect and not whatever it was about his mind that made him feel overwhelming and ineradicable distaste for the whole idea. He repeated, "Let's get out."

Gremionis protested, "But your robots are out there."

"So they are. What of it?"

"But this is something I want to talk about privately, man to m-man." He stumbled over the phrase.

"I suppose you mean Spacer to Earthman."

"If you like."

"My robots are necessary. They are my partners in my investigation."

"But this has nothing to do with the investigation. That's what I'm trying to tell you."

"I'll be the judge of that," said Baley firmly, walking out of the Personal.

Gremionis hesitated and then followed.

47.

Daneel and Giskard were waiting—impassive, expressionless, patient. On Daneel's face, Baley thought he could make out a trace of concern, but, on the other hand, he might merely be reading that emotion into those inhumanly human features.

Giskard, the less human-looking, showed nothing, of course, even to the most willing personifier.

A third robot waited as well—presumably that of Gremionis. He was simpler in appearance even than Giskard and had an air of shabbiness about him. It was clear that Gremionis was not very well-to-do.

Daneel said, with what Baley automatically assumed to be the warmth of relief, "I am pleased that you are well, Partner Elijah."

"Entirely well. I am curious, however, about something. If you had heard me call out in alarm from within, would you have come in?"

"At once, sir," said Giskard.

"Even though you are programmed not to enter Personals?"

"The need to protect a human being—you, in particular— would be paramount, sir."

"That is so, Partner Elijah," said Daneel.

"I'm glad to hear that," said Baley. "This person is Santirix Gremionis. Mr. Gremionis, this is Daneel and this is Giskard."

Each robot bent his head solemnly. Gremionis merely glanced at them and lifted one hand in indifferent acknowledgment. He made no effort to introduce his own robot.

Baley looked around. The light was distinctly dimmer, the wind was brisker, the air was cooler, the sun was completely hidden by clouds. There was a gloom to the surroundings that did not seem to affect Baley, who continued to be delighted at having escaped from the Personal. It lifted his spirits amazingly that he was actually experiencing the feeling of being pleased at being Outside. It was a special case, he knew, but it was a beginning and he could not help but consider it a triumph.

Baley was about to turn to Gremionis to resume the conversation, when his eye caught movement. Walking across the lawn came a woman with an accompanying robot. She was coming toward them but seemed totally oblivious to them. She was clearly making for the Personal.

Baley put out his arm in the direction of the woman, as though to stop her, even though she was still thirty meters away, and muttered, "Doesn't she know that's a Men's Personal?"

"What?" said Gremionis.

The woman continued to approach, while Baley watched in total puzzlement. Finally, the woman's robot stepped to one side to wait and the woman entered the structure.

Baley said helplessly, "But she can't go in there."

Gremionis said, "Why not? It's communal."

"But it's for men."

"It's for people," said Gremionis. He seemed utterly confused.

"Either sex? Surely you can't mean that."

"Any human being. Of course I mean it! How would you want it to be? I don't understand."

Baley turned away. It had not been many minutes before that he had thought that open conversation in a Personal was the acme in bad taste, of Things Not Done.

If he had tried to think of something worse yet, he would have completely failed to dredge up the possibility of encountering a woman in a Personal. Convention on Earth required him to ignore the presence of others in the large Community Personals on that world, but not all the conventions ever invented would have prevented him from knowing whether a person passing him was a man or a woman.

What if, while he had been in the Personal, a woman had entered—casually, indifferently—as this one had just done? Or, worse still, what if he had entered a Personal and found a woman already there?

He could not estimate his reaction. He had never weighed the possibility, let alone met with such a situation, but he found the thought totally intolerable.

And the book-films had told him nothing about that, either.

He had viewed those films in order that he might not approach the investigation in total ignorance of the Auroran way of life—and they had left him in total ignorance of all that was important.

Then how could he handle this triply knotted puzzle of Jander's death, when at every step he found himself lost in ignorance?

A moment before he had felt triumph at a small conquest over the terrors of Outside, but now he was faced with the feeling of being ignorant of everything, ignorant even of the nature of his ignorance.

It was now, while fighting not to picture the woman passing through the airspace lately occupied by himself, that he came near to utter despair.

### 48.

Again Giskard said (and in a way that made it possible to read concern into his words—if not into the tone), "Are you un-well, sir? Do you need help?"

Baley muttered, "No no. I'm all right. —But let's move away. We're in the path of people wishing to use that structure."

He walked rapidly toward the airfoil that was resting in the open stretch beyond the gravel path. On the other side was a small two-wheeled vehicle, with two seats, one behind the other. Baley assumed it to be Gremionis' scooter.

His feeling of depression and misery, Baley realized, was ac-centuated by the fact that he felt hungry. It was clearly past lunchtime and he had not eaten.

He turned to Gremionis. "Let's talk—but if you don't mind, let's do it over lunch. That is, if you haven't already eaten—and if you don't mind eating with me."

"Where are you going to eat?"

"I don't know. Where does one eat at the Institute?"

Gremionis said, "Not at the Community Diner. We can't talk there."

"Is there an alternative?"

"Come to my establishment," said Gremionis at once. "It isn't one of the fancier ones here. I'm not one of your high executives. Still, I have a few serviceable robots and we can set a decent table. —I tell you what. I'll get on my scooter with Brundij—my robot, you know—and you follow me. You'll have to go slowly, but I'm only a little over a kilometer away. It will just take two or three minutes."

He moved away at an eager half-run. Baley watched him and thought there seemed to be a kind of gangly youthfulness about him. There was no easy way of actually judging his age, of course; Spacers didn't show age and Gremionis might easily be fifty. But he *acted* young, almost what an Earthman would consider teenage young. Baley wasn't sure exactly what there was about him that gave that impression.

Baley turned suddenly to Daneel. "Do you know Gremionis, Daneel?"

"I have never met him before, Partner Elijah."

"You, Giskard?"

"I have met him once, sir, but only in passing."

"Do you know anything about him, Giskard?"

"Nothing that is not apparent on the surface, sir."

"His age? His personality?"

"No, sir."

Gremionis shouted, "Ready?" His scooter was humming rather roughly. It was clear that it was not air-jet assisted. The wheels would not leave the ground. Brundij sat behind Gremionis.

Giskard, Daneel, and Baley moved quickly into their airfoil once again.

Gremionis moved outward in a loose circle. Gremionis' hair flew backward in the wind and Baley had a sudden sensation of how the wind must feel when one traveled in an open vehicle such as a scooter. He was thankful he was totally enclosed in an airfoil—which suddenly seemed to him a much more civilized way of traveling.

The scooter straightened out and darted off with a muted roar, Gremionis waving one hand in a follow-me gesture. The robot behind him maintained his balance with almost negligent ease and did not hold on to Gremionis' waist, as Baley was certain a human being would have needed to.

The airfoil followed. Although the scooter's smooth forward progression seemed high-speed, that was apparently the illusion of its small size. The airfoil had some difficulty maintaining a speed low enough to avoid running it down.

"Just the same," said Baley thoughtfully, "one thing puzzles me."

"What is that, Partner Elijah?" asked Daneel.

"Vasilia referred to this Gremionis disparagingly as a 'barber.' Apparently, he deals with hair, clothes, and other matters of personal human adornment. How is it, then, that he has an establishment on the grounds of the Robotics Institute?"

# 12

## Again Gremionis

## 49

It took only a few minutes before Baley found himself in the fourth Auroran establishment he had seen since his arrival on the planet a day and a half before: Fastolfe's, Gladia's, Vasilia's, and now Gremionis'.

Gremionis' establishment appeared smaller and drabber than the others, even though it showed, to Baley's unpracticed eye in Auroran matters, signs of recent construction. The distinctive mark of the Auroran establishment—the robotic niches—were, however, present. On entering, Giskard and Daneel moved quickly into two that were empty and faced the room, unmoving and silent. Gremionis' robot, Brundij, moved into a third niche almost as quickly.

There was no sign of any difficulty in making their choices or of any tendency for any one niche to be the target of two robots, however briefly. Baley wondered how the robots avoided conflict and decided there must be signal communication among them of a kind that was subliminal to human beings. It was something (provided he remembered to do so) concerning which he might consult Daneel.

Gremionis was studying the niches also, Baley noticed.

Gremionis' hand had gone to his upper lip and, for a moment, his forefinger stroked the small mustache. He said, a bit uncertainly, "Your robot, the human-looking one, doesn't seem right in the niche. That's Daneel Olivaw, isn't it? Dr. Fastolfe's robot?"

"Yes," said Baley. "He was in the hyperwave drama, too. Or at least an actor was—one who better fit the part."

"Yes, I remember."

Baley noted that Gremionis—like Vasilia and even like Gladia and Fastolfe—kept a certain distance. There seemed to be a repulsion field—unseen, unfelt, unsensed in any way—around Baley that kept these Spacers from approaching too closely, that sent them into a gentle curve of avoidance when they passed him.

Baley wondered if Gremionis was aware of this or if it was entirely automatic. And what did they do with the chairs he sat in while in their establishments, the dishes he ate from, the towels he used? Would ordinary washing suffice? Were there special sterilizing procedures? Would they discard and replace everything? Would the establishments be fumigated once he left the planet—or every night? What about the Community Personal he used? Would they tear it down and rebuild it? What about the woman who had ignorantly entered it after he had left? Or could she possibly have been the fumigator?

He realized he was getting silly.

To outer space with it. What the Aurorans did and how they dealt with their problems was their affair and he would bother his head no more with them. Jehoshaphat! He had his own problems and, right now, the particular splinter of it was Gremionis —and he would tackle that after lunch.

Lunch was rather simple, largely vegetarian, but for the first time he had a little trouble. Each separate item was too sharply defined in taste. The carrots tasted rather strongly of carrots and the peas of peas, so to speak.

A little too much so, perhaps.

He ate rather reluctantly and tried not to show a slightly rising gorge.

And, as he did so, he became aware that he grew used to it— as though his taste buds saturated and could handle the excess more easily. It dawned on Baley, in a rather sad way, that if his exposure to Auroran food was to continue for any length of time, he would return to Earth missing that distinctiveness of flavor and resenting the flowing together of Earth tastes.

Even the crispness of various items—which had startled him at first, as each closing of his teeth seemed to create a noise that surely (he thought) must interfere with conversation—had already grown to seem exciting evidence that he was, in fact, eating. There would be a silence about an Earth meal that would leave him missing something.

He began to eat with attention, to study the tastes. Perhaps, when Earthpeople established themselves on other worlds, this Spacer-fashion food would be the mark of the new diet, especially if there were no robots to prepare and serve the meals.

And then he thought uncomfortably, not when but *if* Earthpeople established themselves on other worlds—and the ifness of it all depended on him, on Plainclothesman Elijah Baley. The burden of it weighed him down.

The meal was over. A pair of robots brought in the heated, moistened napkins with which one could clean one's hands. Except that they weren't ordinary napkins, for when Baley put his down on the plate, it seemed to move slightly, thin out, and grow cobwebby. Then, quite suddenly, it leaped up insubstantially and was carried into an outlet in the ceiling. Baley jumped slightly and his eyes moved upward, following the disappearing item open-mouthed.

Gremionis said, "That's something new I just picked up. Disposable, you see, but I don't know if I like it yet. Some people say it will clog the disposal vent after a while and others worry about pollution because they say some of it will surely get in your lungs. The manufacturer says not, but—"

Baley realized suddenly that he had said not a word during the meal and that this was the first time either of them had spoken since the short exchange on Daneel before the meal had been served. —And there was no use in small talk about napkins.

Baley said, rather gruffly, "Are you a barber, Mr. Gremionis?"

Gremionis flushed, his light skin reddening to the hairline. He said in a choked voice, "Who told you that?"

Baley said, "If that is an impolite way of referring to your profession, I apologize. It is a common way of speaking on Earth and is no insult there."

Gremionis said, "I am a hair designer and a clothing designer. It is a recognized branch of art. I am, in fact, a personnel artist." His finger went to his mustache again.

Baley said gravely, "I notice your mustache. Is it common to grow them on Aurora?"

"No, it is not. I hope it will become so. You take your masculine face— A great many of them can be strengthened and improved by the artful design of facial hair. Everything is in the design—that's part of my profession. You can go too far, of course. On the world of Pallas, facial hair is common, but it is the practice there to indulge in parti-colored dying. Each individual hair is separately dyed to produce some sort of mixture. —Now, that's foolish. It doesn't last, the colors change with time, and it looks terrible. But even so, it's better than facial baldness in some ways. Nothing is less attractive than a facial desert. —That's my own phrase. I use it in my personal talks with potential clients and it's very effective. Females can get by with no facial hair because they make up for it in other ways. On the world of Smitheus—"

There was a hypnotic quality to his quiet, rapid words and his earnest expression, the way in which his eyes widened and remained fixed on Baley with an intense sincerity. Baley had to shake loose with an almost physical force.

He said, "Are you a roboticist, Mr. Gremionis?"

Gremionis looked startled and a little confused at being interrupted in midflow. "A roboticist?"

"Yes. A roboticist."

"No, not at all. I use robots as everyone does, but I don't know what's inside them. —Don't care really."

"But you live here on the grounds of the Robotics Institute. How is that?"

"Why shouldn't I?" Gremionis' voice was measurably more hostile.

"If you're not a roboticist—"

Gremionis grimaced. "That's stupid! The Institute, when it was designed some years ago, was intended to be a self-contained community. We have our own transport vehicle repair shops, our own personal robot maintenance shops, our own physicians, our own structuralists. Our personnel live here and, if they have use for a personnel artist, that's Santirix Gremionis and I live here, too. —Is there something wrong with my profession that I should not?"

"I haven't said that."

Gremionis turned away with a residual petulance that Baley's hasty disclaimer had not allayed. He pressed a button, then, after studying a varicolored rectangular strip, did something that was remarkably like drumming his fingers briefly.

A sphere dropped gently from the ceiling and remained suspended a meter or so above their heads. It opened as though it were an orange that was unsegmenting and a play of colors began within it, together with a soft wash of sound. The two melted together so skillfully that Baley, watching with astonishment, discovered that, after a short while, it was hard to distinguish one from the other.

The windows opacified and the segments grew brighter.

"Too bright?" asked Gremionis.

"No," said Baley, after some hesitation.

"It's meant for background and I've picked a soothing combination that will make it easier for us to talk in a civilized way, you know." Then he said briskly, "Shall we get to the point?"

Baley withdrew his attention from the—whatever it was (Gremionis had not given it a name)—with some difficulty and said, "If you please. I would like to."

"Have you been accusing me of having anything to do with the immobilization of that robot Jander?"

"I've been inquiring into the circumstances of the robot's ending."

"But you've mentioned me in connection with that ending. —In fact, just a little while ago, you asked me if I were a roboticist. I know what you had in mind. You were trying to get me to admit I knew something about robotics, so that you could build up a case against me as the—as the—ender of the robot."

"You might say the killer."

"The killer? You can't kill a robot. —In any case, I didn't end it, or kill it, or anything you want to call it. I told you, I'm not a roboticist. I know *nothing* about robotics. How can you even *think* that—"

"I must investigate all connections, Mr. Gremionis. Jander belonged to Gladia—the Solarian woman—and you were friendly with her. That's a connection."

"There could be any number of people friendly with her. That's no connection."

"Are you willing to state that you never saw Jander in all the times you may have been in Gladia's establishment?"

"Never! Not once!"

"You never knew she had a humaniform robot?"

"*No!*"

"She never mentioned him."

"She had robots all over the place. All ordinary robots. She said nothing about having anything else."

Baley shrugged. "Very well. I have no reason—so far—to suppose that that is not the truth."

"Then say so to Gladia. *That* is why I wanted to see you. To ask you to do that. To *insist*."

"Has Gladia any reason to think otherwise?"

"Of course. You poisoned her mind. You questioned her about me in that connection and she assumed—she was made uncertain— The fact is, she called this morning and asked me if I had anything to do with it. I told you that."

"And you denied it?"

"Of course I denied it and very strenuously, too, because I *didn't* have anything to do with it. But it's not convincing if *I* do the denying. I want *you* to do it. I want you to tell her that, in your opinion, I had nothing to do with the whole business. You just said I didn't and you can't, without any evidence at all, destroy my reputation. I can report you."

"To whom?"

"To the Committee on Personal Defense. To the Legislature. The head of this Institute is a close personal friend of the Chairman himself and I've already sent a full report to him on this matter. I'm not waiting, you understand. I'm taking action."

Gremionis shook his head with an attitude that might have

been intended for fierceness but that did not entirely carry conviction, considering the mildness of his face. "Look," he said, "this isn't Earth. We are *protected* here. Your planet, with its overpopulation, makes your people exist in so many beehives, so many anthills. You push against each other, suffocate each other —and it doesn't matter. One life or a million lives—it doesn't matter."

Baley, fighting to keep contempt from showing in his voice, said, "You've been reading historical novels."

"Of course I have—and they describe it as it is. You can't have billions of people on a single world without its being so. —On Aurora, we are each a *valuable* life. We are protected physically, each of us, by our robots, so that there is never an assault, let alone murder, on Aurora."

"Except for Jander."

"That's not *murder;* it's only a robot. And we are protected from the kinds of harm more subtle than assault by our Legislature. The Committee on Personal Defense takes a dim view—a very dim view—of any action that unfairly damages the reputation or the social status of any individual citizen. An Auroran, acting as you did, would be in trouble enough. As for an Earthman—well—"

Baley said, "I am carrying on an investigation at the invitation, I presume, of the Legislature. I don't suppose Dr. Fastolfe could have brought me here without Legislative permission."

"Maybe so, but that wouldn't give you the right to overstep the limits of fair investigation."

"Are you going to put this up to the Legislature, then?"

"I'm going to have the Institute head—"

"What is his name, by the way?"

"Kelden Amadiro. I'm going to ask him to put it up to the Legislature—and he's *in* the Legislature, you know—he's one of the leaders of the Globalist party. So I think you had better make it plain to Gladia that I am completely innocent."

"I would like to, Mr. Gremionis, because I suspect that you *are* innocent, but how can I change suspicion to certainty, unless you will allow me to ask you some questions?"

Gremionis hesitated. Then, with an air of defiance, he leaned back in his chair and placed his hands behind his neck, the picture of a man utterly failing to appear at ease. He said, "Ask away. I have nothing to hide. And after you're done, you'll have to call Gladia, right on that trimensional transmitter behind you and say your piece—or you will be in more trouble than you can imagine."

"I understand. But first— How long have you known Dr. Vasilia Fastolfe, Mr. Gremionis? Or Dr. Vasilia Aliena, if you know her by that name?"

Gremionis hesitated, then said in a tense voice, "Why do you ask that? What does that have to do with it?"

Baley sighed and his dour face seemed to sadden further. "I remind you, Mr. Gremionis, that you have nothing to hide and that you want to convince me of your innocence, so that I can convince Gladia of the same. Just tell me how long you have known her. If you have not known her, just say so—but before you do, it is only fair to tell you that Dr. Vasilia has stated that you knew her well—well enough, at least, to offer yourself to her."

Gremionis looked chagrined. He said in a shaky voice, "I don't know why people have to make a big thing out of it. An offer is a perfectly natural social interaction that concerns no one else. —Of course, you're an Earthman, so *you'd* make a fuss about it."

"I understand she didn't accept your offer."

Gremionis brought his hands down upon his lap, fists clenched. "Accepting or rejecting is entirely up to her. There've been people who've offered themselves to me and whom *I've* rejected. It's no large matter."

"Well, then. How long have you known her?"

"For some years. About fifteen."

"Did you know her when she was still living with Dr. Fastolfe?"

"I was just a boy then," he said, flushing.

"How did you get to know her?"

"When I finished my training as a personnel artist, I was called in to design a wardrobe for her. It gave her pleasure and after that she used my services—in that respect—exclusively."

"Was it on her recommendation, then, that you received your

present position as—might we say—official personnel artist for the members of the Robotics Institute?"

"She recognized my qualifications. I was tested, along with others, and won the position on my merits."

"But she did recommend you?"

Briefly and with annoyance, Gremionis said, "Yes."

"And you felt the only decent return you could make was to offer yourself to her."

Gremionis grimaced and drew his tongue across his lips, as though tasting something unpleasant. "That—is—disgusting! I suppose an Earthman would think in such a way. My offer meant only that it pleased me to do so."

"Because she is attractive and has a warm personality?"

Gremionis hesitated. "Well, I wouldn't say she has a warm personality," he said cautiously, "but certainly she's attractive."

"I've been told that you offer yourself to everybody—without distinction."

"That is a lie."

"What is a lie? That you offer yourself to everybody or that I have been told so?"

"That I offer myself to everybody. Who said that?"

"I don't know that it would serve any purpose to answer that question. Would you expect me to quote you as a source of embarrassing information? Would you speak freely to me if you thought I would?"

"Well, whoever said it is a liar."

"Perhaps it was merely dramatic exaggeration. Had you offered yourself to others before you offered yourself to Dr. Vasilia?"

Gremionis looked away. "Once or twice. Never seriously."

"But Dr. Vasilia was someone you were serious about?"

"Well—"

"It is my understanding you offered yourself to her repeatedly, which is quite against Auroran custom."

"Oh, Auroran custom—" Gremionis began furiously. Then he pressed his lips together firmly and his forehead furrowed. "See here, Mr. Baley, can I speak to you confidentially?"

"Yes. All my questions are intended to satisfy myself that you had nothing to do with Jander's death. Once I am satisfied of that, you may be sure I'll keep your remarks in confidence."

"Very well, then. It's nothing wrong—it's nothing I'm ashamed of, you understand. It's just that I have a strong sense of privacy and I have a right to that if I wish, don't I?"

"Absolutely," said Baley consolingly.

"You see, I feel that social sex is best when there is a profound love and affection between partners."

"I imagine that's very true."

"And then there's no need for others, wouldn't you say?"

"It sounds—plausible."

"I've always dreamed of finding the perfect partner and never seeking anyone else. They call it monogamy. It doesn't exist on Aurora, but on some worlds it does—and they have it on Earth don't they, Mr. Baley?"

"In theory, Mr. Gremionis."

"It's what I want. I've looked for it for years. When I experimented with sex sometimes, I could tell something was missing. Then I met Dr. Vasilia and she told me—well, people get confidential with their personnel artists because it's *very* personal work—and this is the *really* confidential part—"

"Well, go on."

Gremionis licked his lips. "If what I say now gets out, I'm ruined. She'll do her best to see to it that I get no further commissions. Are you *sure* this has something to do with the case?"

"I assure you with as much force as I can, Mr. Gremionis, that this can be totally important."

"Well, then"—Gremionis did not look quite convinced—"the fact is, that I gathered from what Dr. Vasilia told me, in bits and pieces, that she is"—his voice dropped to a whisper—"a virgin."

"I see," said Baley quietly (remembering Vasilia's certainty that her father's refusal had distorted her life and getting a firmer understanding of her hatred of her father).

"That excited me. It seemed to me I could have her all to myself and I would be the only one that she would ever have. I can't explain how much that meant to me. It made her look gloriously beautiful in my eyes and I just wanted her so much."

"So you offered yourself to her?"

"Yes."

"Repeatedly. You weren't discouraged by her refusals?"

"It just reinforced her virginity, so to speak, and made me more eager. It was more exciting that it wasn't easy. I can't explain and I don't expect you to understand."

"Actually, Mr. Gremionis, I do understand. —But there came a time when you stopped offering yourself to Dr. Vasilia?"

"Well, yes."

"And began offering yourself to Gladia?"

"Well, yes."

"Repeatedly?"

"Well, yes."

"Why? Why the change?"

Gremionis said, "Dr. Vasilia finally made it clear that there was no chance and then Gladia came along and she looked like Dr. Vasilia and—and—that was it."

Baley said, "But Gladia is no virgin. She was married on Solaria and she experimented rather widely on Aurora, I am told."

"I knew about that, but she—stopped. You see, she's a Solarian by birth, not an Auroran, and she didn't quite understand Auroran customs. But she stopped because she doesn't like what she calls 'promiscuity.'"

"Did she tell you that?"

"Yes. Monogamy is the custom on Solaria. She wasn't happily married, but it is still the custom she's used to, so she never enjoyed the Auroran way when she tried it—and monogamy is what I want, too. Do you see?"

"I see. But how did you meet her in the first place?"

"I just met her. She was on the hyperwave when she arrived in Aurora, a romantic refugee from Solaria. And she played a part in that hyperwave drama—"

"Yes yes, but there was something else, wasn't there?"

"I don't know what else you want."

"Well, let me guess. Didn't there come a point when Dr. Vasilia said she was rejecting you forever—and didn't she suggest an alternative to you?"

Gremionis, in sudden fury, shouted, "Did Dr. Vasilia tell you *that?*"

"Not in so many words, but I think I know what happened, even so. Did she not tell you that it might be advantageous if you looked up a new arrival on the planet, a young lady from Solaria who was a ward or protégée of Dr. Fastolfe—who you know is Dr. Vasilia's father? Did Dr. Vasilia perhaps not tell you that people thought this young lady, Gladia, rather resembled herself, but that she was younger and had a warmer personality? Did Dr. Vasilia not, in short, encourage you to transfer your attentions from herself to Gladia?"

Gremionis was visibly suffering. His eyes flicked to those of Baley and away again. It was the first time that Baley saw in the eyes of any Spacer a look of fright—or was it awe? (Baley shook his head slightly. He must not take too much satisfaction at having overawed a Spacer. It could damage his objectivity.)

He said, "Well? Am I right or wrong?"

And Gremionis said in a low voice. "That hyperwave show was no exaggeration, then. —Do you read minds?"

## 50.

Baley said calmly, "I just ask questions. —And you haven't answered directly. Am I right or wrong?"

Gremionis said, "It didn't quite happen like that. Not just like that. She did talk about Gladia, but—" He bit at his lower lip and then said, "Well, it amounted to what you said. It was just about the way you described it."

"And you were not disappointed? You found that Gladia did resemble Dr. Vasilia?"

"In a way, she did." Gremionis' eyes brightened. "But not really. Stand them side by side and you'll see the difference. Gladia has much greater delicacy and grace. A greater spirit of —of fun."

"Have you offered yourself to Vasilia since you met Gladia?"

"Are you mad? Of course not."

"But you have offered yourself to Gladia?"

"Yes."

"And she rejected you?"

"Well, yes, but you have to understand that she has to be sure, as I would have to be. Think what a mistake I would have made if I had moved Dr. Vasilia to accept me. Gladia doesn't want to make that mistake and I don't blame her."

"But *you* don't think it would be a mistake for her to accept you, so you have offered yourself again—and again—and again."

Gremionis stared vacantly at Baley for a moment and then seemed to shudder. He thrust out his lower lip, as though he were a rebellious child. "You say it in an insulting way—"

"I'm sorry. I don't mean it to be insulting. Please answer the question."

"Well, I have."

"How many times have you offered yourself?"

"I haven't counted. Four times. Well, five. Or maybe more."

"And she has always rejected you."

"Yes. Or I wouldn't have to offer again, would I?"

"Did she reject you angrily?"

"Oh no. That's not Gladia. Very kindly."

"Has it made you offer yourself to anyone else?"

"What?"

"Well, Gladia has rejected you. One way of responding would be to offer yourself to someone else. Why not? If Gladia doesn't want you—"

"*No.* I don't want anyone else."

"Why is that, do you suppose?"

And, strenuously, Gremionis said, "How should I know why that is? I want Gladia. It's a—it's a kind of madness, except that I think it's the best kind of insanity. I'd be mad *not* to have that kind of madness. —I don't expect you to understand."

"Have you tried to explain this to Gladia? She might understand."

"Never. I'd distress her. I'd embarrass her. You don't talk about such things. I should see a mentologist."

"Have you?"

"No."

"Why not?"

Gremionis frowned. "You have a way of asking the rudest questions, Earthman."

"Perhaps because I'm an Earthman. I know no better. But I'm also an investigator and I must know these things. Why have you not seen a mentologist?"

Surprisingly, Gremionis laughed. "I told you. The cure would be greater madness than the disease. I would rather be with Gladia and be rejected than be with anyone else and be accepted. —Imagine having your mind out of whack and wanting it to *stay* out of whack. Any mentologist would put me in for major treatment."

Baley thought awhile, then said, "Do you know whether Dr. Vasilia is a mentologist in any way?"

"She's a roboticist. They say that's the closest thing to it. If you know how a robot works, you've got a hint as to how a human brain works. Or so they say."

"Does it occur to you that Vasilia knows these strange feelings you have in connection with Gladia?"

Gremionis stiffened. "I've never told her. —I mean in so many words."

"Isn't it possible that she understands your feelings without having to ask? Is she aware that you have repeatedly offered yourself to Gladia?"

"Well— She would ask how I was getting along. In the way of long-standing acquaintanceship, you know. I would say certain things. Nothing intimate."

"Are you sure that it was never anything intimate? Surely she encouraged you to continue to offer."

"You know—now that you mention it, I seem to see it all in a new way. I don't see quite how you managed to put it into my head. It's the questions you ask, I suppose, but it seems to me now that she did continue to encourage my friendship with Gladia. She actively supported it." He looked very uneasy. "This never occurred to me before. I never really thought about it."

"Why do you think she encouraged you to make repeated offers to Gladia?"

Gremionis twitched his eyebrows ruefully and his finger went to his mustache. "I suppose some might guess she was trying to get rid of me. Trying to make sure I wouldn't want to bother *her*." He made a small laughing sound. "That's not very complimentary to me, is it?"

"Did Dr. Vasilia cease being friendly with you?"

"Not at all. She was more friendly—if anything."

"Did she try to tell you how to be more successful with Gladia? To show a greater interest in Gladia's work, for example?"

"She didn't have to do that. Gladia's work and mine are very similar. I work with human beings and she with robots, but we're both designers—artists— That does make for closeness, you know. We even help each other at times. When I'm not offering and being rejected, we're good friends. —That's a lot, when you come to think of it."

"Did Dr. Vasilia suggest you show a greater interest in Dr. Fastolfe's work?"

"Why should she suggest that? I don't know anything about Dr. Fastolfe's work."

"Gladia might be interested in her benefactor's work and it might be a way for you to ingratiate yourself with her."

Gremionis' eyes narrowed. He rose with almost explosive force, walked to the other end of the room, came back, stood in front of Baley, and said, "*Now—you—look—here!* I'm not the biggest brain on the planet, not even the second-biggest, but I'm not a blithering idiot. I see what you're getting at, you know."

"Oh?"

"All your questions have served to sort of wriggle me into saying that Dr. Vasilia got me to fall in love— That's it"—he stopped in sudden surprise—"I'm in love, like in the historical novels." He thought about that with the light of wonder in his eyes. Then the anger returned. "That she got me to fall in love and to stay in love, so that I could find out things from Dr. Fastolfe and learn how to immobilize that robot, Jander."

"You don't think that's so?"

"No, it's not!" shouted Gremionis. "I don't know anything about robotics. *Anything.* No matter how carefully anything about robotics were explained to me, I wouldn't understand it. And I don't think Gladia would either. Besides, I never asked anyone about robotics. I was never told—by Dr. Fastolfe or anyone—anything about robotics. No one ever suggested I get involved with robotics. Dr. Vasilia never suggested it. Your whole rotten theory doesn't work." He shot his arms out to either side. "It doesn't work. Forget it."

He sat back, folded his arms rigidly across his chest, and forced his lips together in a thin line, making his small mustache bristle.

Baley looked up at the unsegmented orange, which was still humming its low, pleasantly varying tune and displaying a gentle change of color as it swayed hypnotically through a small, slow arc.

If Gremionis' outburst had upset his line of attack, he showed no sign of it. He said, "I understand what you're saying, but it's still true that you see much of Gladia, isn't it?"

"Yes, I do."

"Your repeated offers do not offend her—and her repeated rejections do not offend you?"

Gremionis shrugged. "My offers are polite. Her refusals are gentle. Why should we be offended?"

"But how do you spend time together? Sex is out, obviously, and you don't talk robotics. What do you do?"

"Is that all there is to companionship—sex and robotics? We do a great deal together. We talk, for one thing. She is very curious about Aurora and I spend hours describing the planet. She's seen very little of it, you know. And she spends hours telling me about Solaria and what a hellhole it is. I'd rather live on Earth— no offense intended. And there's her dead husband. What a miserable character *he* was. Gladia's had a hard life, poor woman.

"We go to concerts, I took her to the Art Institute a few times, and we *work* together. I told you that. We go over my designs— or her designs—together. To be perfectly honest, I don't see that working on robots is very rewarding, but we all have our own notions, you know. For that matter, she seemed to be amused when I explained why it was so important to cut hair correctly— her own hair isn't *quite* right, you know. But mostly, we go for walks."

"Walks? Where?"

"Nowhere particularly. Just walks. That is her habit—because of the way she was brought up on Solaria. Have you ever been on Solaria? —Yes, you have been, of course. I'm sorry. —On Solaria, there are these huge estates with only one or two human beings on them, just robots otherwise. You can walk for miles and be completely alone and Gladia says that it makes you feel as though you owned the entire planet. The robots are always there, of course, keeping an eye on you and taking care of you, but, of course, they keep out of sight. Gladia misses that feeling of world ownership here on Aurora."

"Do you mean that she wants world ownership?"

"You mean a kind of lust for power? Gladia? That's crazy. All she means is that she misses the feeling of being alone with nature. I don't see it myself, you understand, but I like humoring her. Of course, you can't quite get the Solarian feeling in Aurora. There are bound to be people about, especially in the Eos metropolitan area, and robots haven't been programmed to keep out of sight. In fact, Aurorans generally walk *with* robots. —Still, I know some routes that are pleasant and not very crowded and Gladia enjoys them."

"Do you enjoy them, too?"

"Well, only because I would be with Gladia. Aurorans are walkers, too, by and large, but I must admit I'm not. I had protesting muscles at first and Vasilia laughed at me."

"She knew you went on walks, did she?"

"Well, I came in limping one day and creaking at the thighs, so I had to explain. She laughed and said it was a good idea and the best way to get a walker to accept an offer was to walk with them. 'Keep it up,' she said, 'and she'll cancel her rejection before you get a chance to offer again. She'll make the offer herself.' As it happened, Gladia didn't, but eventually I grew to like the walks very much, just the same."

He seemed to have gotten over his flash of anger and was now very much at his ease. He might have been thinking of the walks, Baley thought, for there was a half-smile on his face. He looked rather likable—and vulnerable—with his mind back on who-knew-what conversational passage on a walk that had taken them who-knew-where. Baley almost smiled in response.

"Vasilia knew, then, that you continued the walks."

"I suppose so. I began to take Wednesdays and Saturdays off because that fit in with Gladia's schedule choice—and Vasilia would sometimes joke about my 'WS walks' when I brought in some sketches."

"Did Dr. Vasilia ever join the walks?"

"Certainly not."

Baley shifted in his seat and stared intently at his fingertips as he said, "I presume you had robots accompanying you on your walks."

"Absolutely. One of mine, one of hers. They kept rather out of the way, though. They didn't tag along in what Gladia called Aurora fashion. She wanted Solarian solitude, she said. So I obliged, though at first I got a crick in my neck looking around to see if Brundij was with me."

"And which robot accompanied Gladia?"

"It wasn't always the same one. Whichever he was, he held off, too. I didn't get to talk to him."

"What about Jander?"

Some of the sunniness left Gremionis' expression at once.

"What about him?" he asked.

"Did he ever come along? If he did, you would know, wouldn't you?"

"A humaniform robot? I certainly would. And he did not accompany us—not ever."

"Are you certain?"

"Completely certain." Gremionis scowled. "I imagine she thought him far too valuable to waste on duties any ordinary robot could perform."

"You seem annoyed. Did you think so, too?"

"He was her robot. I didn't worry about it."

"And you never saw him when you were at Gladia's establishment?"

"Never."

"Did she ever say anything about him? Discuss him?"

"Not that I recall."

"Didn't you consider that strange?"

Gremionis shook his head. "No. Why talk about robots?"

Baley's somber eyes fixed on the other's face. "Did you have any idea of the relationship between Gladia and Jander?"

Gremionis said, "Are you going to tell me that there was sex between them?"

Baley said, "Would you be surprised if I did?"

Gremionis said stolidly, "It happens. It's not unusual. You can use a robot sometimes, if you feel like it. And a humaniform robot—completely humaniform, I believe—"

"Completely," said Baley with an appropriate gesture.

Gremionis' lips curved downward. "Well, then, it would be hard for a woman to resist."

"She resisted *you*. Doesn't it bother you that Gladia would prefer a robot to you?"

"Well, if it comes to that, I'm not sure that I believe this is true—but if it is, it's nothing to worry about. A robot is just a robot. A woman and a robot—or a man and a robot—it's just masturbation."

"You honestly never knew of the relationship, Mr. Gremionis? You never suspected?"

"I never gave it any thought," insisted Gremionis.

"Didn't know? Or did know, but paid it no mind?"

Gremionis scowled. "You're pushing again. What do you want me to say? Now that you put it into my head and push, it seems to me, if I look back, that maybe I was wondering about something like that. Just the same, I never felt anything was happening before you started asking questions."

"Are you sure?"

"Yes, I'm sure. Don't badger me."

"I'm not badgering you. I'm just wondering if it were possible that you did know that Gladia was regularly engaging in sex with Jander, that you knew that you would never be accepted as her lover as long as that was so, that you wanted her so much that you would stop at nothing to eliminate Jander, that, in short, you were so jealous that you—"

And at that moment, Gremionis—as though some tightly coiled spring, held back with difficulty for some minutes, had suddenly twitched loose—hurled himself at Baley with a loud

and incoherent cry. Baley, taken completely by surprise, pushed
backward instinctively and his chair went over.

51.

There were strong arms upon him at once. Baley felt himself
lifted, the chair righted, and was aware that he was in the grip
of a robot. How easy it was to forget they were in the room
when they stood silent and motionless in their niches.

It was neither Daneel nor Giskard who had come to his rescue, however. It was Gremionis' robot, Brundij.

"Sir," said Brundij, his voice just a bit unnatural, "I hope you
are not hurt."

Where were Daneel and Giskard?

The question answered itself at once. The robots had divided
the labor neatly and quickly. Daneel and Giskard, estimating instantly that an overturned chair offered less chance of harm to
Daley than a maddened Gremionis, had launched themselves at
the host. Brundij, seeing at once that he was not needed in that
direction, saw to the welfare of the guest.

Gremionis—still standing, his breath heaving—was completely
immobilized in the careful double-grasp of Baley's robots.

Gremionis said, in very little above a whisper, "Release me. I
am in control of myself."

"Yes, sir," said Giskard.

"Of course, Mr. Gremionis," said Daneel with what was almost
suavity.

But although their arms released their hold, neither moved
back for a period of time. Gremionis looked right and left,
adjusted the smoothness of his clothing, and then, deliberately,
sat down. His breathing was still rapid and his hair was, to a
small extent, in disarray.

Baley now stood, one hand on the back of the chair on which
he had been sitting.

Gremionis said, "I am sorry, Mr. Baley, for losing control. It is
something I have not done in my adult life. You accused me of
being j-jealous. It is a word no respectable Auroran would use of

another, but I should have remembered you are an Earthman. It is a word *we* encounter only in historical romances and even then the word is usually spelled with a 'j,' followed by a dash. Of course, that is not so on your world. I understand that."

"I am sorry, too, Mr. Gremionis," said Baley gravely, "that my forgetfulness of Auroran custom led me astray in this instance. I assure you that such a lapse will not happen again." He seated himself and said, "I don't know that there is much more to discuss—"

Gremionis did not seem to be listening. "When I was a child," he said, "I would sometimes push against another, and be pushed, and it would be awhile before the robots would take the trouble to separate us, of course—"

Daneel said, "If I may explain, Partner Elijah. It has been well-established that total suppression of aggression in the very young has undesirable consequences. A certain amount of youthful play involving physical competition is permitted—even encouraged—provided no real hurt is involved. Robots in charge of the young are carefully programmed to be able to distinguish the chances and level of harm that may take place. I, for instance, am not properly programmed in this respect and would not qualify as a guardian of the young except under emergency conditions for brief periods. —Nor would Giskard."

Baley said, "Such aggressive behavior is stopped during adolescence, I suppose."

"Gradually," said Daneel, "as the level of harm that may be inflicted increases and as the desirability of self-control becomes more pronounced."

Gremionis said, "By the time I was ready for higher schooling, I, like all Aurorans, knew quite well that all competition rested on the comparison of mental capacity and talent—"

"No physical competition?" said Baley.

"Certainly, but only in fashions that do not involve deliberate physical contact with intent to injure."

"But since you've been an adolescent—"

"I've attacked no one. Of course I haven't. I've had the urge to do so on a number of occasions, to be sure. I suppose I wouldn't be entirely normal if I hadn't, but until this moment, I've been able to control it. But then, no one ever called me—*that* before."

Baley said, "It would do no good to attack, in any case, if you are going to be stopped by robots, would it? I presume there is always a robot within reach on both sides of both the attacker and the attacked."

"Certainly. —All the more reason for me to be ashamed of having lost my self-control. I trust that this won't have to go into your report."

"I assure you I will tell no one of this. It has nothing to do with the case."

"Thank you. Did you say that the interview is over?"

"I think it is."

"In that case, will you do as I have asked you to do?"

"What is that?"

"To tell Gladia I had nothing to do with Jander's immobilization."

Baley hesitated. "I will tell her that that is my opinion."

Gremionis said, "Please make it stronger than that. I want her to be absolutely certain that I had nothing to do with it; all the more so if she was fond of the robot from a sexual standpoint. I couldn't bear to have her think I was j-j— Being a Solarian, she might think that."

"Yes, she might," said Baley thoughtfully.

'But look," said Gremionis, speaking quickly and earnestly. "I don't know anything about robots and no one—Dr. Vasilia or anyone else—has told me anything about them—how they work, I mean. There is just no way in which I could have destroyed Jander."

Baley seemed, for a moment, to be deep in thought. Then he said, with clear reluctance, "I can't help but believe you. To be sure, I don't know everything. And it is possible—I say this without meaning offense—that either you or Dr. Vasilia—or both—are lying. I know surprisingly little about the intimate nature of Auroran society and I can perhaps be easily fooled. And yet, I can't help but believe you. Nevertheless, I can't do more than tell Gladia that, in my opinion, you are completely innocent. I must say 'in my opinion,' however. I am sure she will find that strong enough."

Gremionis said gloomily, "Then I will have to be satisfied with that. —If it will help, though, I assure you, on the word of an Auroran citizen, that I am innocent."

Baley smiled slightly. "I wouldn't dream of doubting your word, but my training forces me to rely on objective evidence alone."

He stood up, stared solemnly at Gremionis for a moment, then said, "What I am about to say should not be taken amiss, Mr. Gremionis. I take it that you are interested in having me give Gladia this reassurance because you want to retain her friendship."

"I want that very much, Mr. Baley."

"And you intend, on some suitable occasion, to offer yourself again?"

Gremionis flushed, swallowed visibly, then said, "Yes, I do."

"May I then give you a word of advice, sir? Don't do it."

"You may keep your advice, if that's what you're going to tell me. I don't intend ever to give up."

"I mean do not go through the usual formal procedure. You might consider simply"—Baley looked away, feeling unaccountably embarrassed—"putting your arms around her and kissing her."

"*No,*" said Gremionis earnestly. "*Please.* An Auroran woman would not endure that. Nor an Auroran man."

"Mr. Gremionis, won't you remember that Gladia is *not* Auroran? She is Solarian and has other customs, other traditions. I would try it if I were you."

Baley's level gaze masked a sudden internal fury. What was Gremionis to him that he should give such advice? Why tell another to do that which he himself longed to do?

# 13
## Amadiro

### 52.

Baley got back to business, with a somewhat deeper baritone to his voice than was usual. He said, "Mr. Gremionis, you mentioned the name of the head of the Robotics Institute earlier. Could you give me that name again?"

"Kelden Amadiro."

"And would there be some way of reaching him from here?"

Gremionis said, "Well, yes and no. You can reach his receptionist or his assistant. I doubt that you'll reach him. He's a rather standoffish person, I'm told. I don't know him personally, of course. I've seen him now and then, but I've never talked to him."

"I take it, then, he doesn't use you as a clothes designer or for personal grooming?"

"I don't know that he uses anyone and, from the few occasions when I've seen him, I can tell you he looks it, though I'd rather you didn't repeat that remark."

"I'm sure you're right, but I'll keep the confidence," said Baley gravely. "I would like to try to reach him, despite his standoffish reputation. If you have a trimensic outlet, would you mind my making use of it for that purpose?"

"Brundij can make the call for you."

"No, I think my partner, Daneel, should—that is, if you don't mind."

"I don't mind at all," said Gremionis. "The outlet is in there, so just follow me, Daneel. The pattern you must use is 75-30-up-20."

Daneel bowed his head. "Thank you, sir."

The room with the trimensic outlet was quite empty, except for a thin pillar toward one side of the room. It ended waist-high in a flat surface on which there was a rather complicated console. The pillar stood in the center of a circle marked off on the light green floor in a neutral gray. Near it was an identical circle in size and color, but on the second one there stood no pillar.

Daneel stepped to the pillar and, as he did so, the circle on which it stood glowed with a faint white radiance. His hand moved over the console, his fingers flicking too quickly for Baley to make out clearly what it was they did. It only took a second and then the other circle glowed in precisely the same way. A robot appeared on it, three-dimensional in appearance but with a very faint flicker that gave away the fact that it was a holographic image. Next to him was a console like that next to which Daneel stood, but the robot's console also flickered and was also an image.

Daneel said, "I am R. Daneel Olivaw"—he faintly emphasized the "R." so the robot would not mistake him for a human being —"and I represent my partner, Elijah Baley, a plainclothesman from Earth. My partner would like to speak with Master Roboticist Kelden Amadiro."

The robot said, "Master Roboticist Amadiro is in conference. Would it be sufficient to speak to Roboticist Cicis?"

Daneel looked quickly in Baley's direction. Baley nodded and Daneel said, "That will be quite satisfactory."

The robot said, "If you will ask Plainclothesman Baley to take your place, I will try to locate Roboticist Cicis."

Daneel said smoothly, "It would perhaps be better if you were first to—"

But Baley called out, "It's all right, Daneel. I don't mind waiting."

Daneel said, "Partner Elijah, as the personal representative of Master Roboticist Han Fastolfe, you have assimilated his social status, at least temporarily. It is not your place to have to wait for—"

"It's all *right*, Daneel," said Baley, with enough emphasis to preclude further discussion. "I don't wish to create delay by a dispute over social etiquette."

Daneel stepped off the circle and Baley stepped on. He felt a slight tingle as he did so (perhaps a purely imaginary one), but it quickly passed.

The robot's image, standing on the other circle, faded and disappeared. Baley waited patiently and eventually another image darkened and took on apparent three-dimensionality.

"Roboticist Maloon Cicis here," said the figure in a rather sharp, clear voice. He had the close-cut bronze hair that alone sufficed to give him what Baley thought of as a typical Spacer look, though there was a certain un-Spacerlike asymmetry to the line of his nose.

Baley said quietly, "I am Plainclothesman Elijah Baley from Earth. I would like to speak with Master Roboticist Kelden Amadiro."

"Do you have an appointment, Plainclothesman?"

"No, sir."

"You will have to make one if you wish to see him—and there's no time slot available for this week or next."

"I am Plainclothesman Elijah Baley of Earth—"

"So I have been given to understand. It doesn't alter the facts."

Baley said, "At the request of Dr. Han Fastolfe and with the permission of the World Legislature of Aurora, I am investigating the murder of Robot Jander Panell—"

"The *murder* of Robot Jander Panell?" asked Cicis so politely as to indicate contempt.

"Roboticide, if you prefer, then. On Earth, the destruction of a robot would not be so great a matter, but on Aurora, where robots are treated more or less as human beings, it seemed to me that the word 'murder' might be used."

Cicis said, "Nevertheless, whether murder, roboticide, or nothing at all, it is still impossible to see Master Roboticist Amadiro."

"May I leave a message for him?"

"You may."

"Will it be delivered to him instantly? Now?"

"I can try, but obviously I can make no guarantee."

"Good enough. I will make several points and I will number them. Perhaps you would like to make notes."

Cicis smiled faintly. "I think I will be able to remember."

"First, where there is a murder, there is a murderer, and I would like to give Dr. Amadiro a chance to speak in his own defense—"

"What!" said Cicis.

(And Gremionis, watching from the other side of the room, let his jaw drop.)

Baley managed to imitate the faint smile that had suddenly disappeared from the other's lips. "Am I too fast for you, sir? Would you like to make notes after all?"

"Are you accusing the Master Roboticist of having had anything to do with this Jander Panell business?"

"On the contrary, Roboticist. It is because I *don't* want to accuse him that I must see him. I would hate to imply any connection between the Master Roboticist and the immobilized robot on the basis of incomplete information, when a word from him might make everything clear."

"You are mad!"

"Very well. Then tell the Master Roboticist that a madman wants a word with him in order to avoid accusing him of murder. That's my first point. I have a second. Could you tell him that the same madman has just completed a detailed interrogation of Personnel Artist Santirix Gremionis and is calling from Gremionis' establishment. And the third point—am I going too fast for you?"

"No! Finish!"

"The third point is this. It may be that the Master Roboticist, who surely has a great deal on his mind that is of much moment, does not remember who Personnel Artist Santirix Gremionis is.

In that case, please identify him as someone living on the Institute grounds who has, in the last year, taken many long walks with Gladia, a woman from Solaria who now lives on Aurora."

"I cannot deliver a message so ridiculous and offensive, Earthman."

"In that case, would you tell him I will go straight to the Legislature and I will announce that I cannot continue with my investigation because one Maloon Cicis takes it upon himself to assure me that Master Roboticist Kelden Amadiro will not assist me in the investigation of the destruction of Robot Jander Panell and will not defend himself against accusations of being responsible for that destruction?"

Cicis reddened. "You wouldn't *dare* say anything of the sort."

"Wouldn't I? What would I have to lose? On the other hand, how will it sound to the general public? After all, Aurorans are perfectly aware that Dr. Amadiro is second only to Dr. Fastolfe himself in expertise in robotics and that, if Fastolfe himself is not responsible for the roboticide— Is it necessary to continue?"

"You will find, Earthman, that the laws of Aurora against slander are strict."

"Undoubtedly, but if Dr. Amadiro is effectively slandered, his punishment is likely to be greater than mine. But why don't you simply deliver my message *now?* Then, if he explains just a few minor points, we can avoid all question of slander or accusation or anything of the sort."

Cicis scowled and said stiffly, "I will tell Dr. Amadiro this and I will strongly advise him to refuse to see you." He disappeared.

Again, Baley waited patiently, while Gremionis gestured fiercely and said in a loud whisper, "You can't do that, Baley. You can't do it." Baley waved him quiet.

After some five minutes (it seemed much longer to Baley), Cicis reappeared, looking enormously angry. He said, "Dr. Amadiro will take my place here in a few minutes and will talk to you. Wait!"

And Baley said at once, "There is no point in waiting. I will come directly to Dr. Amadiro's office and I will see him there."

He stepped off the gray circle and made a cutting gesture to Daneel, who promptly broke the connection.

Gremionis said, with a kind of strangled gasp, "You can't talk to Dr. Amadiro's people that way, Earthman."

"I just have," said Baley.

"He'll have you thrown off the planet within twelve hours."

"If I don't make progress in straightening out this mess, I may in any case be thrown off the planet within twelve hours."

Daneel said, "Partner Elijah, I fear that Mr. Gremionis is justified in his alarm. The Auroran World Legislature cannot do more than evict you, since you are not an Auroran citizen. Nevertheless, they can insist that the Earth authorities punish you severely and Earth will do so. They could not resist an Auroran demand, in this case. I would not wish you to be punished in this way, Partner Elijah."

Baley said heavily, "Nor do I wish the punishment, Daneel, but I must take the chance. —Mr. Gremionis, I am sorry that I had to tell him I was calling from your establishment. I had to do something to persuade him to see me and I felt he might attach importance to that fact. What I said was, after all, the truth."

Gremionis shook his head. "If I had known what you were going to do, Mr. Baley, I would not have permitted you to call from my establishment. I feel sure that I'm going to lose my position here and"—with bitterness—"what are you going to do for me that will make up for that?"

"I will do my best, Mr. Gremionis, to see that you do not lose your position. I feel confident that you will be in no trouble. If I fail, however, you are free to describe me as a madman who made wild accusations against you and frightened you with threats of slander, so that you had to let me use your viewer. I'm sure Dr. Amadiro will believe you. After all, you have already sent him a memo complaining that I have been slandering you, have you not?"

Baley lifted his hand in farewell. "Good-bye, Mr. Gremionis. Thank you again. Don't worry and—remember what I said about Gladia."

With Daneel and Giskard sandwiching him fore and aft, Baley stepped out of Gremionis' establishment, scarcely conscious of the fact that he was moving out into the open once more.

53.

Once out in the open, it was a different matter. Baley stopped and looked up.

"Odd," he said. "I didn't think that that much time had passed, even allowing for the fact that the Auroran day is a little shorter than standard."

"What is it, Partner Elijah?" asked Daneel solicitously.

"The sun has set. I wouldn't have thought it."

"The sun has not yet set, sir," put in Giskard. "It is about two hours before sunset."

Daneel said, "It is the gathering storm, Partner Elijah. The clouds are thickening, but the storm will not actually break for some time yet."

Baley shivered. Dark, in itself, did not disturb him. In fact, when Outside, night, with its suggestion of enclosing walls, was far more soothing than the day, which broadened the horizons and opened space in every direction.

The trouble was that this was neither day nor night.

Again, he tried to remember what it had been like that time it had rained when he had been Outside.

It suddenly occurred to him that he had never been out when it snowed and that he wasn't even sure what the rain of crystalline solid water was like. Descriptions in words were surely insufficient. The younger ones sometimes went out to go sliding or sledding—or whatever—and returned shrieking with excitement—but always glad to get within the City walls. Ben had once tried to make a pair of skis, according to directions in some ancient book or other, and had gotten himself half-buried in a drift of the white stuff. And even Ben's descriptions of what it was like to see and feel snow were distressingly vague and unsatisfying.

Then, too, no one went out when it was actually snowing, as opposed to having the material merely lying about on the ground. Baley told himself, at this point, that the one thing everyone agreed on was that it only snowed when it was very cold.

It was not very cold now; it was merely cool. Those clouds did *not* mean it was going to snow. —Somehow, he felt only minimally consoled.

This was not like the cloudy days on Earth, which he *had* seen. On Earth, the clouds were lighter; he was sure of that. They were grayish-white, even when they covered the sky solidly. Here, the light—what there was of it—was rather bilious, a ghastly yellowish-slate.

Was that because Aurora's sun was more orange than Earth's was?

He said, "Is the color of the sky—unusual?"

Daneel looked up at the sky. "No, Partner Elijah. It is a storm."

"Do you often have storms like this?"

"At this time of year, yes. Occasional thunderstorms. This is no surprise. It was predicted in the weather forecast yesterday and again this morning. It will be over well before daybreak and the fields can use the water. We've been a bit subnormal in rainfall lately."

"And it gets this cold, too? Is that normal, too?"

"Oh yes. —But let us get into the airfoil, Partner Elijah. It can be heated."

Baley nodded and walked toward the airfoil, which lay on the grassy plot where it had been brought to rest before lunch. He paused.

"Wait. I did not ask Gremionis for directions to Amadiro's establishment—or office."

"No need, Partner Elijah," said Daneel immediately, his hand in the crook of Baley's elbow, propelling him gently but unmistakably onward. "Friend Giskard has the map of the Institute clearly in his memory banks and he will take us to the Administration Building. It is very likely that Dr. Amadiro has his office there."

Giskard said, "My information is to the effect that Dr. Amadiro's office *is* in the Administration Building. If, by some chance, he is not at his office but is in his establishment, that is nearby."

Again, Baley found himself crammed into the front seat between the two robots. He welcomed Daneel particularly, with his humanlike body warmth. Although Giskard's textilelike outermost layer was insulating and not as cold to the touch as bare metal would have been, he was the less attractive of the two in Baley's current chilly state.

Baley caught himself on the verge of putting an arm around Daneel's shoulder, with the intention of finding comfort by drawing him even closer. He brought his arm down to his lap in confusion.

He said, "I don't like the way it looks out there."

Daneel, perhaps in an effort to take Baley's mind off the appearance Outside, said, "Partner Elijah, how is it you knew that Dr. Vasilia had encouraged Mr. Gremionis' interest in Miss Gladia? I did not see that you had received any evidence to that effect."

"I didn't," said Baley. "I've been desperate enough to play long shots—that is, to gamble on events of low probability. Gladia told me that Gremionis was the one person sufficiently interested in her to offer himself repeatedly. I thought he might have killed Jander out of jealousy. I didn't think he could possibly know enough about robotics to do it, but then I heard that Fastolfe's daughter Vasilia was a roboticist and resembled Gladia physically. I wondered if Gremionis, having been fascinated by Gladia, might not have been fascinated by Vasilia earlier— and if the killing might possibly have been the result of a conspiracy between the two. It was by hinting obscurely at the existence of such a conspiracy that I was able to persuade Vasilia to see me."

Daneel said, "But there was no conspiracy, Partner Elijah—at least as far as the destruction of Jander was concerned. Vasilia and Gremionis could not have engineered that destruction, even if they had worked together."

"Granted—and yet Vasilia had been made nervous by the suggestion of having had a connection with Gremionis. Why? When Gremionis told us of having been attracted to Vasilia first, and then to Gladia, I wondered if the connection between the two had been more indirect, if Vasilia might have encouraged the transfer for some reason more distantly connected—but connected nevertheless—to Jander's death. After all, there had to be some connection between the two; Vasilia's reaction to the original suggestion showed that.

"My suspicion was correct. Vasilia had engineered Gremionis' switch from one woman to the other. Gremionis was astonished at my knowing this and that, too, was useful, for if the matter were something completely innocent, there would have been no reason to make a secret of it—and a secret it obviously was. You remember that Vasilia mentioned nothing of urging Gremionis to turn to Gladia. When I told her that Gremionis had offered himself to Gladia, she acted as though that was the first time she had heard of it."

"But, Partner Elijah, of what importance is this?"

"We may find out. It seemed to me that there was no importance in it to either Gremionis or Vasilia. Therefore, if it had any importance at all, it might be that a third person was involved. If it had anything to do with the Jander affair, then it ought to be a roboticist still more skillful than Vasilia—and that might be Amadiro. So I hinted to him of the existence of a conspiracy by deliberately pointing out I had been questioning Gremionis and was calling from his establishment—and that worked, too."

"Yet I still don't know what it all means, Partner Elijah."

"Nor I—except for some speculations. But perhaps we'll find out at Amadiro's. Our situation is so bad, you see, we have nothing to lose by guessing and gambling."

During this exchange, the airfoil has risen on its air-jets, and had moved to a moderate height. It cleared a line of bushes and was now once again speeding along over grassy areas and graveled roads. Baley noticed that, where the grass was taller, it was swept to one side by the wind as though an invisible—and much larger—airfoil were passing over it.

Baley said, "Giskard, you have been recording the conversations which have taken place in your presence, haven't you?"

"Yes, sir."

"And can reproduce them at need?"

"Yes, sir."

"And can easily locate—and reproduce—some particular statement made by some given person?"

"Yes, sir. You would not have to listen to the entire recording."

"And could you, at need, serve as a witness in a courtroom?"

"I, sir? No, sir." Giskard's eyes were fixed firmly on the road. "Since a robot can be directed to lie by a skillful enough command and not all the exhortations or threats of a judge might help, the law wisely considers a robot an incompetent witness."

"But, in that case, of what use are your recordings?"

"That, sir, is a different thing. A recording, once made, cannot be altered on simple command, though it might be erased. Such a recording can, therefore, be admitted as evidence. There are no firm precedents, however, and whether it is—or is not—admitted depends on the individual case and on the individual judge."

Baley could not tell whether that statement was depressing in itself or whether he was influenced by the unpleasant livid light that bathed the landscape. He said, "Can you see well enough to drive, Giskard?"

"Certainly, sir, but I do not need to. The airfoil is equipped with a computerized radar that would enable it to avoid obstacles on its own, even if I were, unaccountably, to fail in my task. It was this that was in operation yesterday morning when we traveled comfortably though all the windows were opacified."

"Partner Elijah," said Daneel, again veering the conversation away from Baley's uncomfortable awareness of the coming storm, "do you have hope that Dr. Amadiro might indeed be helpful?"

Giskard brought the airfoil to rest on a wide lawn before a broad but not very high building, with an intricately-carved façade that was clearly new and yet gave the impression of imitating something quite old.

Baley knew it was the Administration Building without being told. He said, "No, Daneel, I suspect that Amadiro may be far too intelligent to give us the least handle to grasp him by."

"And if that is so, what do you plan to do next?"

"I don't know," said Baley, with a grim feeling of *déjà vu*, "but I'll try to think of something."

54.

When Baley entered the Administration Building, his first feeling was one of relief at removing himself from the unnatural lighting Outside. The second was one of wry amusement.

Here on Aurora, the establishments—the private dwelling places—were all strictly Auroran. He couldn't, for a moment, while sitting in Gladia's living room, or breakfasting in Fastolfe's dining room, or talking in Vasilia's work room, or making use of Gremionis' trimensional viewing device, have thought himself on Earth. All four were distinct from each other, but all fell within a certain genus, widely different from that of the underground apartments on Earth.

The Administration Building, however, breathed officialdom and that, apparently, transcended ordinary human variety. It did not belong to the same genus as the dwelling places on Aurora, any more than an official building in Baley's home City resembled an apartment in the dwelling Sectors—but the two official buildings on the two worlds of such widely different natures strangely resembled each other.

This was the first place on Aurora where, for an instant, Baley might have imagined himself on Earth. Here were the same long cold bare corridors, the same lowest common denominator of design and decoration, with every light source designed so as to irritate as few people as possible and to please just as few.

There were some touches here that would have been absent on Earth—the occasional suspended pots of plants, for instance, flourishing in the light and outfitted with devices (Baley guessed) for controlled and automatic watering. That natural touch was absent on Earth and its presence did not delight him. Might such pots not sometimes fall? Might they not attract insects? Might not the water drip?

There were some things missing here, too. On Earth, when

one was within a City, there was always the vast, warm hum of people and machinery—even in the most coldly official of administrative structures. It was the "Busy Buzz of Brotherhood," to use the phrase popular among Earth's politicians and journalists.

Here, on the other hand, it was quiet. Baley had not particularly noticed the quiet in the establishments he had visited that day and the day before, since everything had seemed so unnatural there that one more oddity escaped his notice. Indeed, he had been more aware of the soft susurration of insect life outside or of the wind through the vegetation than of the absence of the steady "Hum of Humanity" (another popular phrase).

Here, however, where there seemed a touch of Earth, the absence of the "Hum" was as disconcerting as was the distinct orange touch to the artificial light—which was far more noticeable against the blank off-white of the walls here than among the busy decoration that marked the Auroran establishments.

Baley's reverie did not last long. They were standing just inside the main entrance and Daneel had held out his arm to stop the other two. Some thirty seconds passed before Baley, speaking in an automatic whisper in view of the silence everywhere, said, "Why are we waiting?"

"Because it is advisable to do so, Partner Elijah," said Daneel. "There is a tingle field ahead."

"A what?"

"A tingle field, Partner Elijah. Actually, the name is a euphemism. It stimulates the nerve endings and produces a rather sharp pain. Robots can pass, but human beings cannot. Any breach, of course, whether by human or robot, will set off an alarm."

Baley said, "How can you tell there's a tingle field?"

"It can be seen, Partner Elijah, if you know what to look for. The air seems to twinkle a bit and the wall beyond that region has a faint greenish tinge as compared to the wall in front of it."

"I'm not at all sure I see it," said Baley indignantly. "What's to prevent me—or any innocent outsider—from walking into it and experiencing agony?"

Daneel said, "Those who are members of the Institute carry a neutralizing device; those who are visitors are almost always attended by one or more robots who will surely detect the tingle field."

A robot was approaching down the corridor on the other side of the field. (The twinkling of the field was more easily noted against the muted smoothness of his metallic surface.) He seemed to ignore Giskard, but, for a moment, he hesitated as he looked from Baley to Daneel and back. And then, having made a decision, he addressed Baley. (Perhaps, thought Baley, Daneel looks too human to be human.)

The robot said, "Your name, sir?"

Baley said, "I am Plainclothesman Elijah Baley from Earth. I am accompanied by two robots of the establishment of Dr. Han Fastolfe—Daneel Olivaw and Giskard Reventlov."

"Identification, sir?"

Giskard's serial number flared out in soft phosphorescence on the left side of his chest. "I vouch for the other two, friend," he said.

The robot studied the number a moment, as though comparing it with a file in his memory banks. Then he nodded and said, "Serial number accepted. You may pass."

Daneel and Giskard moved forward at once, but Baley found himself edging ahead slowly. He put out one arm as a way of testing the coming of pain.

Daneel said, "The field is gone, Partner Elijah. It will be restored after we have passed through."

Better safe than sorry, thought Baley, and continued his shuffle till he was well past the point where the barrier of the field might have existed.

The robots, showing no sign of impatience or condemnation, waited for Baley's reluctant steps to catch up with them.

They then stepped onto a helical ramp that was only two people wide. The robot was first, by himself; Baley and Daneel stood side by side behind him (Daneel's hand rested lightly, but almost possessively, on Baley's elbow); and Giskard brought up the rear.

Baley was conscious of his shoes pointing upward just a bit uncomfortably and felt vaguely that it would be a little tiresome mounting this too-steep ramp and having to lean forward in order to avoid a clumsy slip. Either the soles of his shoes or the surface of the ramp—or both—ought to be ridged. In fact, neither was.

The robot in the lead said, "Mr. Baley," as though warning of something, and the robot's hand then visibly tightened on the railing that it held.

At once, the ramp divided into sections that slid against each other to form steps. Immediately thereafter, the whole ramp began to move upward. It made a complete turn, passing up through the ceiling, a section of which had retracted, and, when it came to a halt, they were on what was (presumably) the second floor. The steps disappeared and the four stepped off.

Baley looked back curiously. "I suppose it will service those who want to go down as well, but what if there is a period where more people want to go up than down? It would end up sticking half a kilometer into the sky—or into the ground, in reverse."

"That is an up-helix," said Daneel in a low voice. "There are separate down-helices."

"But it has to get down again, doesn't it?"

"It collapses at the top—or the bottom—depending on which we're speaking of, Partner Elijah, and, in periods of nonuse, it unwinds, so to speak. This up-helix is descending now."

Baley looked back. The smooth surface might be sliding downward, but it showed no irregularity or mark whose motion he could notice.

"And if someone should want to use it when it has moved up as far as it can?"

"Then one must wait for the unwinding, which would take less than a minute. —There are ordinary flights of stairs as well, Partner Elijah, and most Aurorans are not reluctant to use them. Robots almost always use the stairs. Since you are a visitor, you are being offered the courtesy of the helix."

They were walking down a corridor again, toward a door more ornate than the others. "They are offering me courtesy, then," said Baley. "A hopeful sign."

It was perhaps another hopeful sign that an Auroran now ap-

peared in the ornate doorway. He was tall, at least eight centimeters taller than Daneel, who was some five centimeters taller
than Baley. The man in the doorway was broad as well, somewhat heavyset, with a round face, a somewhat bulbous nose,
curly dark hair, a swarthy complexion, and a smile.

It was the smile that was most noticeable. Wide and apparently unforced, it revealed prominent teeth that were white
and well-shaped.

He said, "Ah, it is Mr. Baley, the famous investigator from
Earth, who has come to our little planet to show that I am a
dreadful villain. Come in, come in. You are welcome. I am sorry
if my able aide, Roboticist Maloon Cicis, gave you the impression that I would be unavailable, but he is a cautious fellow and
is a great deal more concerned about my time than I myself
am."

He stepped to one side as Baley walked in and tapped him
lightly with the flat of his hand on the shoulder blade as he
passed. It seemed to be a gesture of friendship of a kind that
Baley had not yet experienced on Aurora.

Baley said, cautiously (was he assuming too much?), "I take
it you are Master Roboticist Kelden Amadiro?"

"Exactly. Exactly. The man who intends to destroy Dr. Han
Fastolfe as a political force upon this planet—but that, as I hope
to persuade you, does not really make me a villain. After all, I
am not trying to prove that it is Fastolfe who is a villain simply
because of the foolish vandalism he committed on the structure
of his own creation—poor Jander. Let us say only that I will
demonstrate that Fastolfe is—mistaken."

He gestured lightly and the robot who had guided them in
stepped forward and into a niche.

As the door closed, Amadiro gestured Baley jovially to a well-
upholstered armchair and, with admirable economy, indicated,
with his other arm, wall niches for Daneel and Giskard as well.

Baley noticed that Amadiro stared with a moment's hunger at
Daneel and that, for that moment, his smile disappeared and a
look that was almost predatory appeared on his face. It was
gone quickly and he was smiling again. Baley was left to wonder

if, perhaps, that momentary change of expression was an invention of his own imagination.

Amadiro said, "Since it looks as though we're in for some mildly nasty weather, let's do without the ineffective daylight we are now dubiously blessed with."

Somehow (Baley did not follow exactly what it was that Amadiro did on the control-panel of his desk) the windows opacified and the walls glowed with gentle daylight.

Amadiro's smile seemed to broaden. "We do not really have much to talk about, you and I, Mr. Baley. I took the precaution of speaking to Mr. Gremionis while you were coming here. From what he said, I decided to call Dr. Vasilia as well. Apparently, Mr. Baley, you have more or less accused both of complicity in the destruction of Jander and, if I can understand the language, you have also accused me."

"I merely asked questions, Dr. Amadiro, as I intend to do now."

"No doubt, but you are an Earthman, so you are not aware of the enormity of your actions and I am really sorry that you must nonetheless suffer the consequences of them. —You know perhaps that Gremionis sent me a memo concerning your slander of him."

"He told me he had, but he misinterpreted my action. It was not slander."

Amadiro pursed his lips as though considering the statement. "I dare say you are right from your standpoint, Mr. Baley, but you don't understand the Auroran definition of the word. I was forced to send Gremionis' memo on to the Chairman and, as a result, it is very likely that you'll be ordered off the planet by tomorrow morning. I regret this, of course, but I fear that your investigation is about to come to an end."

# 14

## Again Amadiro

### 55.

Baley was taken aback. He did not know what to make of Amadiro and he had not expected this confusion within himself. Gremionis had described him as "standoffish." From what Cicis had said, he expected Amadiro to be autocratic. In person, however, Amadiro seemed jovial, outgoing, even friendly. Yet if his words were to be trusted, Amadiro was calmly moving to end the investigation. He was doing it pitilessly—and yet with what seemed to be a commiserating smile.

What was he?

Automatically, Baley glanced toward the niches where Giskard and Daneel were standing, the primitive Giskard of course without expression, the advanced Daneel calm and quiet. That Daneel had ever met Amadiro in his short existence was, on the face of it, unlikely. Giskard, on the other hand, in his—how many?—decades of life might very well have met him.

Baley's lips tightened as he thought he might have asked Giskard in advance what Amadiro might be like. He might, in that case, be now better able to judge how much of this roboticist's present persona was real and how much was cleverly calculated.

Why on Earth—or off it, Baley wondered, didn't he use these robotic resources of his more intelligently? Or why didn't Gis-

kard volunteer information—but no, that was unfair. Giskard
clearly lacked the capacity for independent activity of that sort.
He would yield information on request, Baley thought, but
would produce none on his own initiative.

Amadiro followed the brief flicking of Baley's eyes and said,
"I'm one against three, I think. As you see, I have none of my robots here in my office—although any number are on instant call,
I admit—while you have two of Fastolfe's robots: the old reliable Giskard and that marvel of design, Daneel."

"You know them both, I see," said Baley.

"By reputation only. I actually see them—I, a roboticist, was
about to say 'in the flesh'—I actually see them physically for the
first time now, although I saw Daneel portrayed by an actor in
that hyperwave show."

"Everyone in all the worlds has apparently seen that hyperwave show," said Baley glumly. "It makes my life—as a real and
limited individual—difficult."

"Not with me," said Amadiro, his smile broadening. "I assure
you I did not take your fictional representation with any
seriousness whatever. I assumed you were limited in real life.
And so you are—or you would not have indulged so freely in
unwarranted accusations on Aurora."

"Dr. Amadiro," said Baley, "I assure you I was making no formal accusations. I was merely pursuing an investigation and
considering possibilities."

"Don't misunderstand me," said Amadiro with sudden ear-
nestness. "I don't blame you. I am sure that you were behav-
ing perfectly by Earth standards. It is just that you are up
against Auroran standards now. We treasure reputation with unbelievable intensity."

"If that were so, Dr. Amadiro, then haven't you and other
Globalists been slandering Dr. Fastolfe with suspicion, to a far
greater extent than any small thing I have done?"

"Quite true," agreed Amadiro, "but I am an eminent Auroran
and have a certain influence, while you are an Earthman and
have no influence whatever. That is most unfair, I admit, and I
deplore it, but that is the way the worlds are. What can we do?
Besides, the accusation against Fastolfe can be maintained—and

*will* be maintained—and slander isn't slander when it is the truth. Your mistake was to make accusations that simply can't be maintained. I'm sure you must admit that neither Mr. Gremionis nor Dr. Vasilia Aliena—nor both together—could possibly have disabled poor Jander."

"I did not formally accuse either."

"Perhaps not, but you can't hide behind the word 'formally' on Aurora. It's too bad Fastolfe didn't warn you of this when he brought you in to take up this investigation, this—as it now is, I'm afraid—ill-fated investigation."

Baley felt the corner of his mouth twitch as he thought that Fastolfe might indeed have warned him.

He said, "Am I to get a hearing in the matter or is it all settled?"

"Of course you will get a hearing before being condemned. We are not barbarians here on Aurora. The Chairman will consider the memo I have sent him, together with my own suggestions in the matter. He will probably consult Fastolfe as the other party intimately concerned and then arrange to meet with all three of us, perhaps tomorrow. Some decision might be reached then—or later—and it would be ratified by the full Legislature. All due process of law will be followed, I assure you."

"The letter of the law will be followed, no doubt, but what if the Chairman has already made up his mind, what if nothing I say will be accepted, and what if the Legislature simply rubber-stamps a foregone decision? Is that possible?"

Amadiro did not exactly smile at that, but he seemed subtly amused. "You are a realist, Mr. Baley. I am pleased with that. People who dream of justice are so apt to be disappointed—and they are usually such wonderful people that one hates to see that happen."

Amadiro's glance fixed itself on Daneel again. "A remarkable job, this humaniform robot," he said. "It is astonishing how close to his vest Fastolfe has kept things. And it is a shame that Jander was lost. There Fastolfe did the unforgivable."

"Dr. Fastolfe, sir, denies that he was in any way implicated."

"Yes, Mr. Baley, of course he would. Does he say that *I* am implicated? Or is my implication entirely your own idea?"

Baley said deliberately, "I have no such idea. I merely wish to question you on the matter. As for Dr. Fastolfe, he is not a candidate for one of your accusations of slander. He is certain you have had nothing to do with what happened to Jander because he is quite certain you lack the knowledge and capacity to immobilize a humaniform robot."

If Baley hoped to stir things up in that manner, he failed. Amadiro accepted the slur with no loss of good humor and said, "In that he is right, Mr. Baley. Sufficient ability is not to be found in any roboticist—alive or dead—except for Fastolfe himself. Isn't that what he says, our modest master of masters?"

"Yes, he does."

"Then whatever does he say happened to Jander, I wonder?"

"A random event. Purely chance."

Amadiro laughed. "Has he calculated the probability of such a random event?"

"Yes, Master Roboticist. Yet even an extremely unlikely chance might happen, especially if there were incidents that bettered the odds."

"Such as what?"

"That is what I am hoping to find out. Since you have already arranged to have me thrown off the planet, do you now intend to forestall any questioning of yourself—or may I continue my investigation until such time as my activity in that respect is legally ended? —Before you answer, Dr. Amadiro, please consider that the investigation has *not* as yet been legally ended and, in any hearing that may come up, whether tomorrow or later, I will be able to accuse you of refusing to answer my questions if you should insist on now ending this interview. That might influence the Chairman in his decision."

"It would not, my dear Mr. Baley. Don't imagine you can in any way interfere with me. —However, you may interview me for as long as you wish. I will cooperate fully with you, if only to enjoy the spectacle of the good Fastolfe trying uselessly to disentangle himself from his unfortunate deed. I am not extraordinarily vindictive, Mr. Baley, but the fact that Jander was Fastolfe's own creation does not give him the right to destroy it."

Baley said, "It is not legally established that this is what he has done, so that what you have just said is, at least potentially, slander. Let us put that to one side, therefore, and get on with this interview. I need information. I will ask my questions briefly and directly and, if you answer in the same way, this interview may be completed quickly."

"No, Mr. Baley. It is not you who will set the conditions for this interview," said Amadiro. "I take it that one or both of your robots is equipped to record our conversation in full."

"I believe so."

"I know so. I have a recording device of my own as well. Don't think, my good Mr. Baley, that you will lead me through a jungle of short answers to something that will serve Fastolfe's purpose. I will answer as I choose and make certain I am not misinterpreted. And my own recording will help me make it certain that I am not misinterpreted." Now, for the first time, there was the suggestion of the wolf behind Amadiro's attitude of friendliness.

"Very well, then, but if your answers are deliberately long-winded and evasive, that, too, will show up in the recording."

"Obviously."

"With that understood, may I have a glass of water, to begin with?"

"Absolutely. —Giskard, will you oblige Mr. Baley?"

Giskard was out of his niche at once. There was the inevitable tinkle of ice at the bar at one end of the room and a tall glass of water was on the desk immediately before Baley.

Baley said, "Thank you, Giskard," and waited for him to move back into his niche.

He said, "Dr. Amadiro, am I correct in considering you the head of the Robotics Institute?"

"Yes, you are."

"And its founder?"

"Correct. —You see, I answer briefly."

"How long has it been in existence?"

"As a concept—decades. I have been gathering like-minded people for at least fifteen years. Permission was obtained from the Legislature twelve years ago. Building began nine years ago and active work began six years ago. In its present completed form, the Institute is two years old and there are long-range plans for further expansion, eventually. —There you have a long answer, sir, but presented reasonably concisely."

"Why did you find it necessary to set up the Institute?"

"Ah, Mr. Baley. Here you surely expect nothing but a long-winded answer."

"As you please, sir."

At this point, a robot brought in a tray of small sandwiches and still smaller pastries, none of which were familiar to Baley. He tried a sandwich and found it crunchy and not exactly unpleasant but odd enough for him to finish it only with an effort. He washed it down with what was left of his water.

Amadiro watched with a kind of gentle amusement and said, "You must understand, Mr. Baley, that we Aurorans are unusual people. So are Spacers generally, but I speak of Aurorans in particular now. We are descended from Earthpeople—something most of us do not willingly think about—but we are self-selected."

"What does that mean, sir?"

"Earthpeople have long lived on an increasingly crowded planet and have drawn together into still more crowded cities that finally became the beehives and anthills you call Cities with a capital 'C.' What kind of Earthpeople, then, would leave Earth and go to other worlds that are empty and hostile so that they might build new societies from nothing, societies that they could not enjoy in completed form in their own lifetime—trees that would still be saplings when they died, so to speak."

"Rather unusual people, I suppose."

"Quite unusual. Specifically, people who are not so dependent on crowds of their fellows as to lack the ability to face emptiness. People who even prefer emptiness, who would like to work on their own and face problems by themselves, rather than hide in the herd and share the burden so that their own load is virtually nothing. Individualists, Mr. Baley. Individualists!"

"I see that."

"And our society is founded on that. Every direction in which the Spacer worlds have developed further emphasizes our individuality. We are proudly human on Aurora, rather than being

huddled sheep on Earth. —Mind you, Mr. Baley, I use the meta-
phor not as a way of deriding Earth. It is simply a different society which I find unadmirable but which you, I suppose, find
comforting and ideal."

"What has this to do with the founding of the Institute, Dr.
Amadiro?"

"Even proud and healthy individualism has its drawbacks.
The greatest minds—working singly, even for centuries—cannot
progress rapidly if they refuse to communicate their findings. A
knotty puzzle may hold up a scientist for a century, when it may
be that a colleague has the solution already and is not even
aware of the puzzle that it might solve. —The Institute is an attempt, in the narrow field of robotics at least, to introduce a certain community of thought."

"Is it possible that the particular knotty puzzle you are attacking is that of the construction of a humaniform robot?"

Amadiro's eyes twinkled. "Yes, that is obvious, isn't it? It was
twenty-six years ago that Fastolfe's new mathematical system,
which he calls 'intersectional analysis,' made it possible to design
humaniform robots—but he kept the system to himself. Years afterward, when all the difficult technical details were worked out,
he and Dr. Sarton applied the theory to the design of Daneel.
Then Fastolfe alone completed Jander. But all of those details
were kept secret, also.

"Most roboticists shrugged and felt that this was natural. They
could only try, individually, to work out the details for themselves. I, on the other hand, was struck by the possibility of an
Institute in which efforts would be pooled. It wasn't easy to persuade other roboticists of the usefulness of the plan, or to persuade the Legislature to fund it against Fastolfe's formidable opposition, or to persevere through the years of effort, but here we
are."

Baley said, "Why was Dr. Fastolfe opposed?"

"Ordinary self-love, to begin with—and I have no fault to find
with that, you understand. All of us have a very natural self-
love. It comes with the territory of individualism. The point is
that Fastolfe considers himself the greatest roboticist in history
and also considers the humaniform robot his own particular

achievement. He doesn't want that achievement duplicated by a group of roboticists, individually faceless compared to himself. I imagine he viewed it as a conspiracy of inferiors to dilute and deface his own great victory."

"You say that was his motive for opposition 'to begin with.' That means there were other motives. What were they?"

"He also objects to the uses to which we plan to put the humaniform robots."

"What uses are these, Dr. Amadiro?"

"Now now. Let's not be ingenuous. Surely Dr. Fastolfe has told you of the Globalist plans for settling the Galaxy?"

"That he has and, for that matter, Dr. Vasilia has spoken to me of the difficulties of scientific advance among individualists. However, that does not stop me from wanting to hear your views on these matters. Nor should it stop you from wanting to tell me. For instance, do you want me to accept Dr. Fastolfe's interpretation of Globalist plans as unbiased and impartial—and would you state that for the record? Or would you prefer to describe your plans in your own words?"

"Put that way, Mr. Baley, you intend to give me no choice."

"None, Dr. Amadiro."

"Very well. I—we, I should say, for the people at the Institute are like-minded in this—look into the future and wish to see humanity opening ever more and ever newer planets to settlement. We do not, however, want the process of self-selection to destroy the older planets or to reduce them to moribundity, as in the case—pardon me—of Earth. We don't want the new planets to take the best of us and to leave behind the dregs. You see that, don't you?"

"Please go on."

"In any robot-oriented society, as in the case of our own, the easy solution is to send out robots as settlers. The robots will build the society and the world and we can then all follow later without selection, for the new world will be as comfortable and as adjusted to ourselves as the old worlds were, so that we can go on to new worlds without leaving home, so to speak."

"Won't the robots create robot worlds rather than human worlds?"

"Exactly, if we send out robots that are nothing but robots. We have, however, the opportunity of sending out humaniform robots like Daneel here, who, in creating worlds for themselves, would automatically create worlds for us. Dr. Fastolfe, however, objects to this. He finds some virtue in the thought of human beings carving a new world out of a strange and forbidding planet and does not see that the effort to do so would not only cost enormously in human life, but would also create a world molded by catastrophic events into something not at all like the worlds we know."

"As the Spacer worlds today are different from Earth and from each other?"

Amadiro, for a moment, lost his joviality and looked thoughtful. "Actually, Mr. Baley, you touch an important point. I am discussing Aurora only. The Spacer worlds do indeed differ among themselves and I am not overly fond of most of them. It is clear to me—though I may be prejudiced—that Aurora, the oldest among them, is also the best and most successful. I don't want a variety of new worlds of which only a few might be really valuable. I want many Auroras—uncounted millions of Auroras—and for that reason I want new worlds carved into Auroras *before* human beings go there. That's why we call ourselves 'Globalists' by the way. We are concerned with *this* globe of ours—Aurora—and no other."

"Do you see no value in variety, Dr. Amadiro?"

"If the varieties were equally good, perhaps there would be value, but if some—or most—are inferior, how would that benefit humanity?"

"When do you start this work?"

"When we have the humaniform robots with which to do it. So far there were Fastolfe's two, of which he destroyed one, leaving Daneel the only specimen." His eyes strayed briefly to Daneel as he spoke.

"When will you have humaniform robots?"

"That is difficult to say. We have not yet caught up with Dr. Fastolfe."

"Even though he is one and you are many, Dr. Amadiro?"

Amadiro twitched his shoulders slightly. "You waste your sarcasm, Mr. Baley. Fastolfe was well ahead of us to begin with and, though the Institute has been in embryo for a long time, we have been fully at work for only two years. Besides, it will be necessary for us not only to catch up with Fastolfe but to move ahead of him. Daneel is a good product, but he is only a prototype and is not good enough."

"In what way must the humaniform robots be improved beyond Daneel's mark?"

"They must be even more human, obviously. They must exist in both sexes and there must be the equivalent of children. We must have a generational spread if a sufficiently human society is to be built up on the planets."

"I think I see difficulties, Dr. Amadiro."

"No doubt. There are many. Which difficulties do you foresee, Mr. Baley?"

"If you produce humaniform robots who are so humaniform they can produce a human society, and if they are produced with a generational spread in both sexes, how will you be able to distinguish them from human beings?"

"Will that matter?"

"It might. If such robots are too human, they might melt into Auroran society and become part of human family groups—and might not be suitable for service as pioneers."

Amadiro laughed. "That thought clearly entered your head because of Gladia Delmarre's attachment to Jander. You see, I know something of your interview with that woman from my conversations with Gremionis and with Dr. Vasilia. I remind you that Gladia is from Solaria and her notion of what constitutes a husband is not necessarily Auroran in nature."

"I was not thinking of her in particular. I was thinking that sex on Aurora is broadly interpreted and that robots as sex partners are tolerated even now, with robots who are only approximately humaniform. If you really cannot tell a robot from a human being—"

"There's the question of children. Robots can neither father nor mother children."

"But that brings up another point. The robots will be long-lived, since the proper building of the society may take centuries."

"They would, in any case, have to be long-lived if they are to resemble Aurorans."

"And the children—also long-lived?"

Amadiro did not speak.

Baley said, "These will be artificial robot children and will never grow older—they will not age and mature. Surely this will create an element sufficiently nonhuman to cast the nature of the society into doubt."

Amadiro sighed. "You are penetrating, Mr. Baley. It is indeed our thought to devise some scheme whereby robots can produce babies who can in some fashion grow and mature—at least long enough to establish the society we want."

"And then, when human beings arrive, the robots can be restored to more robotic schemes of behavior."

"Perhaps—if that seems advisable."

"And this production of babies? Clearly, it would be best if the system used were as close to the human as possible, wouldn't it?"

"Possibly."

"Sex, fertilization, birth?"

"Possibly."

"And if these robots form a society so human that they cannot be differentiated from human, then, when true human beings arrive, might it not be that the robots would resent the immigrants and try to keep them off? Might the robots not react to Aurorans as you react to Earthpeople?"

"Mr. Baley, the robots would still be bound by the Three Laws."

"The Three Laws speak of refraining from injuring human beings and of obeying human beings."

"Exactly."

"And what if the robots are so close to human beings that they regard *themselves* as the human beings they should protect and obey? They might, very rightly, place themselves above the immigrants."

"My good Mr. Baley, why are you so concerned with all these things? They are for the far future. There will be solutions, as we progress in time and as we understand, by observation, what the problems really are."

"It may be, Dr. Amadiro, that Aurorans may not very much approve what you are planning, once they understand what it is. They may prefer Dr. Fastolfe's views."

"Indeed? Fastolfe thinks that, if Aurorans cannot settle new planets directly and without the help of robots, then Earthpeople should be encouraged to do so."

Baley said, "It seems to me that that makes good sense."

"Because you are an Earthman, my good Baley. I assure you that Aurorans would not find it pleasant to have Earthpeople swarming over the new worlds, building new beehives and forming some sort of Galactic Empire in their trillions and quadrillions and reducing the Spacer worlds to what? To insignificance at best and to extinction at worst."

"But the alternative to that is worlds of humaniform robots, building quasi-human societies and allowing no true human beings among themselves. There would gradually develop a robotic Galactic Empire, reducing the Spacer worlds to insignificance at best and to extinction at worst. Surely Aurorans would prefer a human Galactic Empire to a robotic one."

"What makes you so sure of that, Mr. Baley?"

"The form your society takes now makes me sure. I was told, on my way to Aurora, that no distinctions are made between robots and human beings on Aurora, but that is clearly wrong. It may be a wished-for ideal that Aurorans flatter themselves truly exists, but it does not."

"You've been here—what?—less than two days and you can already tell?"

"Yes, Dr. Amadiro. It may be precisely because I'm a stranger that I can see clearly. I am not blinded by custom and ideals. Robots are not permitted to enter Personals and that's one distinction that is clearly made. It permits human beings to find one place where they can be alone. You and I sit at our ease, while robots remain standing in their niches, as you see"—Baley waved his arm toward Daneel—"which is another distinction. I think that human beings—even Aurorans—will always be eager to make distinctions and to preserve their own humanity."

"Astonishing, Mr. Baley."

"Not astonishing at all, Dr. Amadiro. You have lost. Even if you manage to foist your belief that Dr. Fastolfe destroyed Jander upon Aurorans generally, even if you reduce Dr. Fastolfe to political impotence, even if you get the Legislature and the Auroran people to approve your plan of robot settlement, you will only have gained time. As soon as the Aurorans see the implications of your plan, they will turn against you. It might be better, then, if you put an end to your campaign against Dr. Fastolfe and meet with him to work out some compromise whereby the settlement of new worlds by Earthmen can be so arranged as to represent no threat to Aurora or to the Spacer worlds in general."

"Astonishing, Mr. Baley," said Amadiro a second time.

"You have no choice," said Baley flatly.

But Amadiro answered, in a leisurely and amused tone, "When I say your remarks are astonishing, I do not refer to the content of your statements but only to the fact that you make them at all —and that you think they are worth something."

## 56.

Baley watched Amadiro forage for one last piece of pastry and put half of it into his mouth, clearly enjoying it.

"Very good," said Amadiro, "but I am a little too fond of eating. What was I saying? —Oh yes. Mr. Baley, do you think you have discovered a secret? That I have told you something that our world does not already know? That my plans are dangerous, but that I blab them to every newcomer? I imagine you may think that, if I talk to you long enough, I will surely produce some verbal folly that you will be able to make use of. Be assured that I am not likely to. My plans for ever more humaniform robots, for robot families, and for as human a culture as possible are all on record. They are available to the Legislature and to anyone who is interested."

Baley said, "Does the general public know?"

"Probably not. The general public has its own priorities and is more interested in the next meal, the next hyperwave show, the next space-soccer contest than in the next century and the next millennium. Still, the general public will be as glad to accept my plans, as are the intellectually minded who already know. Those who object will not be numerous enough to matter."

"Can you be certain of that?"

"Oddly enough, I can be. You don't understand, I'm afraid, the intensity of the feelings that Aurorans—and Spacers generally—have toward Earthpeople. I don't share those feelings, mind you, and I am, for instance, quite at ease with you. I don't have that primitive fear of infection, I don't imagine that you smell bad, I don't attribute to you all sorts of personality traits that I find offensive, I don't think that you and yours are plotting to take our lives or steal our property—but the large majority of Aurorans have all these attitudes. It may not be very close to the surface and Aurorans may bring themselves to be very polite to individual Earthpeople who seem harmless, but put them to the test and all their hatred and suspicion will emerge. Tell them that Earthpeople are swarming over new worlds and will preempt the Galaxy and they will howl for Earth's destruction before such a thing can happen."

"Even if the alternative was a robot society?"

"Certainly. You don't understand how we feel about robots, either. We are familiar with them. We are at home with them."

"No. They are your servants. You feel superior to them and are at home with them only while that superiority is maintained. If you are threatened by an overturn, by having *them* become your superiors, you will react with horror."

"You say that only because that is how Earthpeople would react."

"No. You keep them out of the Personals. It is a symptom."

"They have no use for those rooms. They have their own facilities for washing and they do not excrete. —Of course, they are not truly humaniform. If they were, we might not make that distinction."

"You would fear them the more."

"Truly?" said Amadiro. "That's foolish. Do you fear Daneel? If I can trust that hyperwave show—and I admit I do not think I can—you developed a considerable affection for Daneel. You feel it now, don't you?"

Baley's silence was eloquent and Amadiro pursued his advantage.

"Right now," he said, "you are unmoved by the fact that Giskard is standing, silent and unresponsive, in an alcove, but I can tell by small examples of body language that you are uneasy over the fact that Daneel is doing so, too. You feel he is too human in appearance to be treated as a robot. You don't fear him the more because he looks human."

"I am an Earthman. We have robots," said Baley, "but not a robot culture. You cannot judge from my case."

"And Gladia, who preferred Jander to human beings—"

"She is a Solarian. You cannot judge from her case, either."

"What case can you judge from, then? You are only guessing. To me, it seems obvious that, if a robot is human enough, he would be accepted as human. Do you demand proof that *I* am not a robot? The fact that I *seem* human is enough. In the end, we will not worry whether a new world is settled by Aurorans who are human in fact or in appearance, if no one can tell the difference. But—human or robot—the settlers will be *Aurorans* either way, not Earthpeople."

Baley's assurance faltered. He said unconvincingly, "What if you never learn how to construct a humaniform robot?"

"Why would you expect we would not? Notice that I say 'we.' There are many of us involved here."

"It may be that any number of mediocrities do not add up to one genius."

Amadiro said shortly, "We are not mediocrities. Fastolfe may yet find it profitable to come in with us."

"I don't think so."

"I do. He will not enjoy being without power in the Legislature and, when our plans for settling the Galaxy move ahead and he sees that his opposition does not stop us, he will join us. It will be only human of him to do so."

"I don't think you will win out," said Baley.

"Because you think that somehow this investigation of yours will exonerate Fastolfe and implicate me, perhaps, or someone else."

"Perhaps," said Baley desperately.

Amadiro shook his head. "My friend, if I thought that anything you could do would spoil my plans, would I be sitting still and waiting for destruction?"

"You are not. You are doing everything you can to have this investigation aborted. Why would you do that if you were confident that nothing I could do would get in your way?"

"Well," said Amadiro, "you *can* get in my way by demoralizing some of the members of the Institute. You can't be dangerous, but you can be annoying—and I don't want that either. So, if I can, I'll put an end to the annoyance—but I'll do that in reasonable fashion, in gentle fashion, even. If you were actually *dangerous*—"

"What could you do, Dr. Amadiro, in that case?"

"I could have you seized and imprisoned until you were evicted. I don't think Aurorans generally would worry overmuch about what I might do to an Earthman."

Baley said, "You are trying to browbeat me and that won't work. You know very well you could not lay a hand on me with my robots present."

Amadiro said, "Does it occur to you that I have a hundred robots within call? What would yours do against *them?*"

"All hundred could not harm me. They cannot distinguish between Earthmen and Aurorans. I am human within the meaning of the Three Laws."

"They could hold you quite immobilized—without harming you—while your robots were destroyed."

"Not so," said Baley. "Giskard can hear you and, if you make a move to summon your robots, Giskard will have *you* immobilized. He moves very quickly and, once that happens, your robots will be helpless, even if you manage to call them. They will understand that any move against me will result in harm to you."

"You mean that Giskard will hurt me?"

"To protect me from harm? Certainly. He will kill you, if absolutely necessary."

"Surely you don't mean that."

"I do," said Baley. "Daneel and Giskard have orders to protect me. The First Law, in this respect, has been strengthened with all the skill Dr. Fastolfe can bring to the job—and with respect to me, specifically. I haven't been told this in so many words, but I'm quite sure it's true. If my robots must choose between harm to you and harm to me, Earthman though I am, it will be easy for them to choose harm to you. I imagine you are well aware that Dr. Fastolfe is not very eager to ensure *your* well-being."

Amadiro chuckled and a grin wreathed his face. "I'm sure you're right in every respect, Mr. Baley, but it *is* good to have you say so. You know, my good sir, that I am recording this conversation also—I told you so at the start—and I'm glad of it. It is possible that Dr. Fastolfe will erase the last part of this conversation, but I assure you I won't. It is clear from what you have said that he is quite prepared to devise a robotic way of doing harm to me—even kill me, if he can manage that—whereas it cannot be said from anything in this conversation—or any other—that I plan any physical harm to him whatever or even to you. Which of us is the villain, Mr. Baley? —I think you have established that and I think, then, that this is a good place at which to end the interview."

He rose, still smiling, and Baley, swallowing hard, stood up as well, almost automatically.

Amadiro said, "I still have one thing to say, however. It has nothing to do with our little contretemps here on Aurora—Fastolfe's and mine. Rather, with your own problem, Mr. Baley."

"My problem?"

"Perhaps I should say Earth's problem. I imagine that you feel very anxious to save poor Fastolfe from his own folly because you think that will give your planet a chance for expansion. —Don't think so, Mr. Baley. You are quite wrong, rather arsy-varsy, to use a vulgar expression I've come across in some of your planet's historical novels."

"I'm not familiar with that phrase," said Baley stiffly.

"I mean you have the situation reversed. You see, when my view wins out in the Legislature—and note that I say 'when' and not 'if'—Earth will be forced to remain in her own planetary system, I admit, but that will actually be to her benefit. Aurora will have the prospect of expansion and of establishing an endless empire. If we then know that Earth will merely be Earth and never anything more, of what concern will she be to us? With the Galaxy at our disposal, we will not begrudge Earthpeople their one world. We would even be disposed to make Earth as comfortable a world for her people as would be practical.

"On the other hand, Mr. Baley, if Aurorans do what Fastolfe asks and allow Earth to send out settling parties, then it won't be long before it will occur to an increasing number of us that Earth will take over the Galaxy and that we will be encircled and hemmed in, that we will be doomed to decay and death. After that, there will be nothing I can do. My own quite kindly feeling toward Earthmen will not be able to withstand the general kindling of Auroran suspicion and prejudice and it will then be *very* bad for Earth.

"So if, Mr. Baley, you are truly concerned for your own people, you should be very anxious indeed for Fastolfe *not* to succeed in foisting upon this planet his very misguided plan. You should be a strong ally of mine. Think about it. I tell you this, I assure you, out of a sincere friendship and liking for you and for your planet."

Amadiro was smiling as broadly as ever, but it was all wolf now.

57.

Baley and his robots followed Amadiro out the room and along the corridor.

Amadiro stopped at one inconspicuous door and said, "Would you care to use the facilities before leaving?"

For a moment, Baley frowned in confusion, for he did not understand. Then he remembered the antiquated phrase Amadiro had used, thanks to his own reading of historical novels.

He said, "There was an ancient general, whose name I have forgotten, who, mindful of the exigencies of sudden absorption in military affairs, once said, 'Never turn down a chance to piss.'"

Amadiro smiled broadly and said, "Excellent advice. Quite as good as my advice to think seriously about what I have said. —But I notice that you hesitate, even so. Surely you don't think I am laying a trap for you. Believe me, I am not a barbarian. You are my guest in this building and, for that reason alone, you are perfectly safe."

Baley said cautiously, "If I hesitate, it is because I am considering the propriety of using your—uh—facilities, considering that I am not an Auroran."

"Nonsense, my dear Baley. What is your alternative? Needs must. Please make use of it. Let that be a symbol that I myself am not subject to the general Auroran prejudices and wish you and Earth well."

"Could you go a step further?"

"In what way, Mr. Baley?"

"Could you show me that you are also superior to this planet's prejudice against robots—"

"There is no prejudice against robots," said Amadiro quickly.

Baley nodded his head solemnly in apparent acceptance of the remark and completed his sentence. "—by allowing them to enter the Personal with me. I have grown to feel uncomfortable without them."

For one moment, Amadiro seemed shaken. He recovered almost at once and said, with what was almost a scowl, "By all means, Mr. Baley."

"Yet whoever is now inside might object strenuously. I would not want to create scandal."

"No one is in there. It is a one-person Personal and, if someone were making use of it, the in-use signal would indicate that."

"Thank you, Dr. Amadiro," said Baley. He opened the door and said, "Giskard, please enter."

Giskard clearly hesitated, but said nothing in objection and entered. At a gesture from Baley, Daneel followed, but as he passed through the door, he took Baley's elbow and pulled him in as well.

Baley said, as the door closed behind him, "I'll be out again soon. Thank you for allowing this."

He entered the room with as much unconcern as he could manage and yet he felt a tightness in the pit of his abdomen. Might it contain some unpleasant surprise?

58.

Baley found the Personal empty, however. There was not even much to search. It was smaller than the one in Fastolfe's establishment.

Eventually, he noticed Daneel and Giskard standing silently side by side, backs against the door, as though endeavoring to have entered the room by the least amount possible.

Baley tried to speak normally, but what came out was a dim croak. He cleared his throat with unnecessary noise and said, "You can come farther into the room—and you needn't remain silent, Daneel." (Daneel had been on Earth. He knew the Earthly taboo against speech in the Personal.)

Daneel displayed that knowledge at once. He put his forefinger to his lips.

Baley said, "I know, I know, but forget it. If Amadiro can forget the Auroran taboo about robots in Personals, I can forget the Earthly taboo about speech there."

"Will it not make you uncomfortable, Partner Elijah?" asked Daneel in a low voice.

"Not a bit," said Baley in an ordinary one. (Actually, speech felt different with Daneel—a robot. The sound of speech in a room such as this when, actually, no *human being* was present was not as horrifying as it might be. In fact, it was not horrifying at all when only robots were present, however humaniform one of them might be. Baley could not say so, of course. Though Daneel had no feelings a human being could hurt, Baley had feelings on his behalf.)

And then Baley thought of something else and felt, quite intensely, the sensation of being a thoroughgoing fool.

"Or," he said to Daneel, in a voice that was suddenly very low indeed, "are you suggesting silence because this room is bugged?" The last word came out merely as a shaping of the mouth.

"If you mean, Partner Elijah, that people outside this room can detect what is spoken inside this room through some sort of eavesdropping device, that is quite impossible."

"Why impossible?"

The toilet device flushed itself with quick and silent efficiency and Baley advanced toward the washbasin.

Daneel said, "On Earth, the dense packing of the Cities makes privacy impossible. Overhearing is taken for granted and to use a device to make overhearing more efficient might seem natural. If an Earthman wishes not to be overheard, he simply doesn't speak, which may be why silence is so mandatory in places where there is a pretense of privacy, as in the very rooms you call Personals.

"On Aurora, on the other hand, as on all the Spacer worlds, privacy is a true fact of life and is greatly valued. You remember Solaria and the diseased extremes to which it was carried there. But even on Aurora, which is no Solaria, every human being is insulated from every other human being by the kind of space extension unthinkable on Earth and by a wall of robots, in addition. To break down that privacy would be an unthinkable act."

Baley said, "Do you mean it would be a crime to bug this room?"

"Much worse, Partner Elijah. It would not be the act of a civilized Auroran gentleman."

Baley looked about. Daneel, mistaking the gesture, plucked a towel out of the dispenser, which might not have been instantly apparent to the other's unaccustomed eyes, and offered it to Baley.

Baley accepted the towel, but that was not the object of his questing glance. It was a bug for which his eyes searched, for he found it difficult to believe that someone would forego an easy advantage on the ground that it would not be civilized behavior. It was, however, useless and Baley, rather despondently, knew it would be. He would not be able to detect an Auroran bug, even if one were there. He wouldn't know what to look for in a strange culture.

Whereupon he followed the course of another strand of suspicion in his mind. "Tell me, Daneel, since you know Aurorans better than I do, why do you suppose Amadiro is taking all this trouble with me? He talks to me at his leisure. He sees me out. He offers me the use of this room—something Vasilia would not have done. He seems to have all the time in the world to spend on me. Politeness?"

"Many Aurorans pride themselves on their politeness. It may be that Amadiro does. He has several times stressed that he is not a barbarian."

"Another question. Why do you think he was willing to have me bring you and Giskard into this room?"

"It seemed to me that that was to remove your suspicions that the offer of this room might conceal a trap."

"Why should he bother? Because he was concerned over the possibility of my experiencing unnecessary anxiety?"

"Another gesture of a civilized Auroran gentleman, I should imagine."

Baley shook his head. "Well, if this room is bugged and Amadiro can hear me, let him hear me. I don't consider him a civilized Auroran gentleman. He made it quite clear that, if I did not abandon my investigation, he would see to it that Earth as a whole would suffer. Is that the act of a civilized gentleman? Or of an incredibly brutal blackmailer?"

Daneel said, "An Auroran gentleman may find it necessary to utter threats, but if so, he would do it in a gentlemanly manner."

"As Amadiro did. It is, then, the manner and not the content of speech that marks the gentleman. But then, Daneel, you are a robot and therefore can not really criticize a human being, can you?"

Daneel said, "It would be difficult for me to do so. But may I ask a question, Partner Elijah? Why did you ask permission to bring friend Giskard and me into this room? It had seemed to me that you were reluctant, earlier, to believe you were in danger. Have you now decided that you are not safe except in our presence?"

"No, not at all, Daneel. I am now quite convinced that I am not in danger and have not been."

"Yet there was a distinctly suspicious cast about your actions when you entered this room, Partner Elijah. You searched it."

Baley said, "Of course! I said I am not in danger, but I do not say there is no danger."

"I do not think I see the distinction, Partner Elijah," said Daneel.

"We will discuss it later, Daneel. I am still not certain as to whether this room is bugged or not."

Baley was by now quite done. He said, "Well, Daneel, I've been leisurely about this; I haven't rushed at all. Now I'm ready to go out again and I wonder if Amadiro is still waiting for us after all this time or whether he has delegated an underling to do the rest of the job of showing us out. After all, Amadiro is a busy man and cannot spend all day with me. What do you think, Daneel?"

"It would be more logical if Dr. Amadiro had delegated the task."

"And you, Giskard? What do you think?"

"I agree with friend Daneel, though it is my experience that human beings do not always make what would seem the logical response."

Baley said, "For my part, I suspect Amadiro is waiting for us quite patiently. If something has driven him to waste this much time on us, I rather think that the driving force—whatever it might be—has not yet weakened."

"I do not know what might be the driving force you speak of, Partner Elijah," said Daneel.

"Nor I, Daneel," said Baley, "which bothers me a great deal. But let us open the door now and see."

59.

Amadiro was waiting outside the door for them, precisely where Baley had left him. He smiled at them, showing no sign of impatience. Baley could not resist shooting a quiet I-told-you-so glance at Daneel, who responded with bland impassivity.

Amadiro said, "I rather regretted, Mr. Baley, that you had not left Giskard outside when you entered the Personal. I might have known him in times past, when Fastolfe and I were on better terms but somehow never did. Fastolfe was my teacher once, you know."

"Was he?" said Baley. "I didn't know that, as a matter of fact."

"No reason you should, unless you had been told—and, in the short time you've been on the planet, you can scarcely have had time to learn much in the way of this sort of trivia, I suppose. —Come now, it has occurred to me that you can scarcely think me hospitable if I do not take advantage of your being at the Institute to show you around."

"Really," said Baley, stiffening a bit. "I must—"

"I insist," said Amadiro, with something of a note of the imperious entering his voice. "You arrived on Aurora yesterday morning and I doubt that you will be staying on the planet much longer. This may be the only chance you will ever have of getting a glimpse of a modern laboratory doing research work on robotics."

He linked arms with Baley and continued to speak in familiar terms. ("Prattled" was the term that occurred to the astonished Baley.)

"You've washed," said Amadiro. "You've taken care of your needs. There may be other roboticists here whom you will wish to question and I would welcome that, since I am determined to show I have put no barriers in your way during the short time in which you will yet be permitted to conduct your investigation. In fact, there is no reason you can't have dinner with us."

Giskard said, "If I may interrupt, sir—"

"You may not!" said Amadiro with unmistakable firmness and the robot fell silent.

Amadiro said, "My dear Mr. Baley, I understand these robots. Who should know them better? —Except for the unfortunate Fastolfe, of course. Giskard, I am sure, was going to remind you of some appointment, some promise, some business—and there is no point in any of that. Since the investigation is about over, I promise you, none of what he was going to remind you of will have any significance. Let us forget all such nonsense and, for a brief time, be friends.

"You must understand, my good Mr. Baley," he went on, "that I am quite an aficionado of Earth and its culture. It is not the most popular of subjects on Aurora, but I find it fascinating. I am particularly interested in Earth's past history, the days when it had a hundred languages and Interstellar Standard had not yet been developed. —May I compliment you, by the way, on your own handling of Interstellar?

"This way, this way," he said, turning a corner. "We'll be coming to the pathway-simulation room, which has its own weird beauty, and we may have a mock-up in operation. Quite symphonic, actually. —But I was talking about your handling of Interstellar. It is one of the many Auroran superstitions concerning Earth, that Earthpeople speak an all-but-incomprehensible version of Interstellar. When the show about you was produced, there were many who said that the actors could not be Earthpeople because they could be understood, yet I can understand you." He smiled as he said that.

"I've tried reading Shakespeare," he continued with a confidential air, "but I can't read him in the original, of course, and the translation is curiously flat. I can't help but believe that the fault lies with the translation and not with Shakespeare. I do better with Dickens and Tolstoy, perhaps because that is prose, although the names of the characters are, in both cases, virtually unpronounceable to me.

"What I'm trying to say, Mr. Baley, is that I'm a friend of Earth. I really am. I want what is best for it. Do you understand?" He looked at Baley and again the wolf showed in his twinkling eyes.

Baley raised his voice, forcing it between the softly running sentences of the other. "I'm afraid I *cannot* oblige you, Dr. Amadiro. I must be about my business and I have no further questions to ask of either you or anyone else here. If you—"

Baley paused. There was a faint and curious rumble of sound in the air. He looked up, startled. "What is that?"

"What is what?" asked Amadiro. "I sense nothing." He looked at the robots, who had been following the two human beings in grave silence. "Nothing!" he said forcefully. "Nothing."

Baley recognized that as the equivalent of an order. Neither robot could now claim to have heard the rumble in direct con-

tradiction to a human being, unless Baley himself applied a
counter-pressure—and he was sure he could not manage to do it
skillfully enough in the face of Amadiro's professionalism.

Nevertheless, it didn't matter. He had heard something and he
was not a robot; he would not be talked out of it. He said, "By
your own statement, Dr. Amadiro, I have little time left me.
That is all the more reason that I must—"

The rumble again. Louder.

Baley said, with a sharp, cutting edge to his voice, "That, I
suppose, is precisely what you didn't hear before and what you
don't hear now. Let me go, sir, or I will ask my robots for help."

Amadiro loosened his grip on Baley's upper arm at once. "My
friend, you had but to express the wish. Come! I will take you to
the nearest exit and, if ever you are on Aurora again, which
seems unlikely in the extreme, please return and you may have
the tour I promised you."

They were walking faster. They moved down the spiral ramp,
out along a corridor to the commodious and now empty anteroom and the door by which they had entered.

The windows in the anteroom showed utterly dark. Could it
be night already?

It wasn't. Amadiro muttered to himself, "Rotten weather!
They've opacified the windows."

He turned to Baley, "I imagine it's raining. They predicted it
and the forecasts can usually be relied on—always, when they're
unpleasant."

The door opened and Baley jumped backward with a gasp. A
cold wind gusted inward and against the sky—not black but a
dull, dark gray—the tops of trees were whipping back and forth.

There was water pouring from the sky—descending in
streams. And as Baley watched, appalled, a streak of light
flashed across the sky with blinding brilliance and then the rumble came again, this time with a cracking report, as though the
light-streak had split the sky and the rumble was the noise it
had made.

Baley turned and fled back the way he had come, whimper-
ing.

# 15

---

# Again Daneel and Giskard

## 60.

Baley felt Daneel's strong grip on his arms, just beneath his shoulders. He halted and forced himself to stop making that infantile sound. He could feel himself trembling.

Daneel said with infinite respect, "Partner Elijah, it is a thunderstorm—expected—predicted—normal."

"I know that," whispered Baley.

He did know it. Thunderstorms had been described innumerable times in the books he had read, whether fiction or nonfiction. He had seen them in holographs and on hyperwave shows—sound, sight, and all.

The real thing, however, the actual sound and sight, had never penetrated into the bowels of the City and he had never in his life actually experienced such a thing.

With all he knew—intellectually—about thunderstorms, he could not face—viscerally—the actuality. Despite the descriptions, the collections of words, the sight in small pictures and on small screens, the sounds captured in recordings; despite all that, he had no idea the flashes were so bright and streaked so across the sky; that the sound was so vibratorily bass in sound when it rattled across a hollow world; that both were so *sudden;* and that rain could be so like an inverted bowl of water, endlessly pouring.

He muttered in despair, "I can't go out in that."

"You won't have to," said Daneel urgently. "Giskard will get the airfoil. It will be brought right to the door for you. Not a drop of rain will fall on you."

"Why not wait until it's over?"

"Surely that would not be advisable, Partner Elijah. Some rain, at least, will continue past midnight and if the Chairman arrives tomorrow morning, as Dr. Amadiro implied he might, it might be wise to spend the evening in consultation with Dr. Fastolfe."

Baley forced himself to turn around, face in the direction from which he wanted to flee, and look into Daneel's eyes. They seemed deeply concerned, but Baley thought dismally that that was merely the result of his own interpretation of the appearance of those eyes. The robot had no feelings, only positronic surges that mimicked those feelings. (And perhaps human beings had no feelings, only neuronic surges that were interpreted as feelings.)

He was somehow aware that Amadiro was gone. He said, "Amadiro delayed me deliberately—by ushering me into the Personal, by his senseless talk, by his preventing you or Giskard from interrupting and warning me about the storm. He would even have tried to persuade me to tour the building or dine with him. He desisted only at the sound of the storm. That was what he was waiting for."

"It would seem so. If the storm now keeps you here, *that* may be what he was waiting for."

Baley drew a deep breath. "You are right. I must leave—somehow."

Reluctantly, he took a step toward the door, which was still open, still filled with a dark gray vista of whipping rain. Another step. And still another—leaning heavily on Daneel.

Giskard was waiting quietly at the door.

Baley paused and closed his eyes for a moment. Then he said in a low voice, to himself rather than to Daneel, "I must do it," and moved forward again.

61.

"Are you well, sir?" asked Giskard.

It was a foolish question, dictated by the programming of the robot, thought Baley, though, at that, it was no worse than the questions asked by human beings, sometimes with wild inappropriateness, out of the programming of etiquette.

"Yes," said Baley in a voice he tried—and failed—to raise above a husky whisper. It was a useless answer to the foolish question, for Giskard, robot though he was, could surely see that Baley was unwell and that Baley's answer was a palpable lie.

The answer was, however, given and accepted and that freed Giskard for the next step. He said, "I will now leave to get the airfoil and bring it to the door."

"Will it work—in all this—this water, Giskard?"

"Yes, sir. This is not an uncommon rain."

He left, moving steadily into the downpour. The lightning was flickering almost continuously and the thunder was a muted growl that rose to a louder crescendo every few minutes.

For the first time in his life, Baley found himself envying a robot. Imagine being able to walk through *that;* to be indifferent to water, to sight, to sound; to be able to ignore surroundings and to have a pseudo-life that was absolutely courageous; to know no fear of pain or of death, because there was no pain or death.

And yet to be incapable of originality of thought, to be incapable of unpredictable leaps of intuition—

Were such gifts worth what humanity paid for them?

At the moment, Baley could not say. He knew that, once he no longer felt terror, he would know that no price was too high to pay for being human. But now that he experienced nothing but the pounding of his heart and the collapse of his will, he could not help but wonder of what use it might be to be a human being if one could not overcome these deep-seated terrors, this intense agoraphobia.

Yet he had been in the open for much of two days and had managed to be almost comfortable.

But the fear had not been conquered. He knew that now. He had suppressed it by thinking intensely of other things, but the storm overrode all intensity of thought.

He could not allow this. If all else failed—thought, pride, will —then he would have to fall back on shame. He could not collapse under the impersonal, superior gaze of the robots. Shame would have to be stronger than fear.

He felt Daneel's steady arm about his waist and shame prevented him from doing what, at the moment, he most wanted to do—to turn and hide his face against the robotic chest. He might have been unable to resist if Daneel had been human—

He had lost contact with reality, for he was becoming aware of Daneel's voice as though it were reaching him from a long distance. It sounded as though Daneel was feeling something akin to panic.

"Partner Elijah, do you hear me?"

Giskard's voice, from an equal distance, said, "We must carry him."

"No," mumbled Baley. "Let me walk."

Perhaps they did not hear him. Perhaps he did not really speak, but merely thought he did. He felt himself lifted from the ground. His left arm dangled helplessly and he strove to lift it, to push it against someone's shoulder, to lift himself upright again from the waist, to grope for the floor with his feet and stand upright.

But his left arm continued to dangle helplessly and his striving went for nothing.

He was somehow aware that he was moving through the air and he felt a wash of spray against his face. Not actually water but the sifting of damp air. Then there was the pressure of a hard surface against his left side, a more resilient one against his right side.

He was in the airfoil, wedged in once more between Giskard and Daneel. What he was most conscious of was that Giskard was very wet.

He felt a jet of warm air cascading over him. Between the

near-darkness outside and the film of trickling water upon the glass, they might as well have been opacified—or so Baley thought till opacification actually took place and total darkness descended. The soft noise of the jet, as the airfoil rose above the grass and swayed, muted the thunder and seemed to draw its teeth.

Giskard said, "I regret the discomfort of my wet surface, sir. I will dry quickly. We will wait here a short while till you recover."

Baley was breathing more easily. He felt wonderfully and comfortably enclosed. He thought: Give me back my City. Wipe out all the Universe and let the Spacers colonize it. Earth is all we need.

And even as he thought it, he knew it was his madness that believed it, not he.

He felt the need to keep his mind busy.

He said weakly, "Daneel."

"Yes, Partner Elijah?"

"About the Chairman. Is it your opinion that Amadiro was judging the situation correctly in supposing that the Chairman would put an end to the investigation or was he perhaps allowing his wishes to do his thinking for him?"

"It may be, Partner Elijah, that the Chairman will indeed interview Dr. Fastolfe and Amadiro on the matter. It would be a standard procedure for settling a dispute of this nature. There are ample precedents."

"But why?" asked Baley weakly. "If Amadiro was so persuasive, why should not the Chairman simply order the investigation stopped?"

"The Chairman," said Daneel, "is in a difficult political situation. He agreed originally to allow you to be brought to Aurora at Dr. Fastolfe's urging and he cannot so sharply reverse himself so soon without making himself look weak and irresolute—and without angering Dr. Fastolfe, who is still a very influential figure in the Legislature."

"Then why did he not simply turn down Amadiro's request?"

"Dr. Amadiro is also influential, Partner Elijah, and likely to grow even more so. The Chairman must temporize by hearing both sides and by giving at least the appearance of deliberation before coming to a decision."

"Based on what?"

"On the merits of the case, we must presume."

"Then by tomorrow morning, I must come up with something that will persuade the Chairman to side with Fastolfe, rather than against him. If I do that, will that mean victory?"

Daneel said, "The Chairman is not all-powerful, but his influence is great. If he comes out strongly on Dr. Fastolfe's side, then, under the present political conditions, Dr. Fastolfe will probably win the backing of the Legislature."

Baley found himself beginning to think clearly again. "That would seem explanation enough for Amadiro's attempt to delay us. He might have reasoned that I had nothing yet to offer the Chairman and he needed only to delay to keep me from getting anything in the time that remained to me."

"So it would seem, Partner Elijah."

"And he let me go only when he thought he could rely on the storm continuing to keep me."

"Perhaps so, Partner Elijah."

"In that case, we cannot allow the storm to stop us."

Giskard said calmly, "Where do you wish to be taken, sir?"

"Back to the establishment of Dr. Fastolfe."

Daneel said, "May we have one moment's more pause, Partner Elijah? Do you plan to tell Dr. Fastolfe that you cannot continue the investigation?"

Baley said sharply, "Why do you say that?" It was a measure of his recovery that his voice was loud and angry.

Daneel said, "It is merely that I fear you might have forgotten for a moment that Dr. Amadiro urged you to do so for the sake of Earth's welfare."

"I have not forgotten," said Baley grimly, "and I am surprised, Daneel, that you should think that that would influence me. Fastolfe must be exonerated and Earth must send its settlers outward into the Galaxy. If there is danger in that from the Globalists, that danger must be chanced."

"But, in that case, Partner Elijah, why go back to Dr. Fastolfe? It doesn't seem to me that we have anything of moment to report to him. Is there no direction in which we can further continue our investigation *before* reporting to Dr. Fastolfe?"

Baley sat up in his seat and placed his hand on Giskard, who was now entirely dry. He said, in quite a normal voice, "I am satisfied with the progress I have already made, Daneel. Let's get moving, Giskard. Proceed to Fastolfe's establishment."

And then, tightening his fists and stiffening his body, Baley added, "What's more, Giskard, clear the windows. I want to look out into the face of the storm."

## 62.

Baley held his breath in preparation for transparency. The small box of the airfoil would no longer be entirely enclosed; it would no longer have unbroken walls.

As the windows clarified, there was a flash of light that came and went too quickly to do anything but darken the world by contrast.

Baley could not prevent his cringe as he tried to steel himself for the thunder which, after a moment or two, rolled and grumbled.

Daneel said pacifyingly, "The storm will get no worse and soon enough it will recede."

"I don't care whether it recedes or not," said Baley through trembling lips. "Come on. Let's go." He was trying, for his own sake, to maintain the illusion of a human being in charge of robots.

The airfoil rose slightly in the air and at once underwent a sideways movement that tilted it so that Baley felt himself pushing hard against Giskard.

Baley cried out (gasped out, rather), "Straighten the vehicle, Giskard!"

Daneel placed his arm around Baley's shoulder and pulled him gently back. His other arm was braced about a hand-grip attached to the frame of the airfoil.

"That cannot be done, Partner Elijah," Daneel said. "There is a fairly strong wind."

Baley felt his hair bristle. "You mean—we're going to be blown away?"

"No, of course not," said Daneel. "If the car were antigrav—a form of technology that does not, of course, exist—and if its mass and inertia were eliminated, then it would be blown like a feather high into the air. However, we retain our full mass even when our jets lift us and poise us in the air, so our inertia resists the wind. Nevertheless, the wind makes us sway, even though the car remains completely under Giskard's control."

"It doesn't feel like it." Baley was conscious of a thin whine, which he imagined to be the wind curling around the body of the airfoil as it cut its way through the protesting atmosphere. Then the airfoil lurched and Baley, who could not for his life have helped it, seized Daneel in a desperate grip around the neck.

Daneel waited a moment. When Baley had caught his breath and his grip grew less rigid, Daneel released himself easily from the other's embrace, while somewhat tightening the pressure of his own arm around Baley.

He said, "In order to maintain course, Partner Elijah, Giskard must counter the wind by an asymmetric ordering of the airfoil's jets. They are sent to one side so as to cause the airfoil to lean into the wind and these jets have to be adjusted in force and direction as the wind itself changes force and direction. There are none better at this than Giskard, but, even so, there are occasional jiggles and lurches. You must excuse Giskard, then, if he does not participate in our conversation. His attention is fully on the airfoil."

"Is it—it safe?" Baley felt his stomach contract at the thought of playing with the wind in this fashion. He was devoutly glad he had not eaten for some hours. He could not—dared not—be sick in the close confines of the airfoil. The very thought unsettled him further and he tried to concentrate on something else.

He thought of running the strips back on Earth, of racing from one moving strip to its neighboring faster strip, and then to its neighboring still faster strip, and then back down into the slower regions, leaning expertly into the wind either way; in one direction as one fastered (an odd word used by no one but strip-racers) and in the other direction, as one slowered. In his younger days, Daneel could do it without pause and without error.

Daneel had adjusted to the need without trouble and, the one time they had run the strips together, Daneel had done it perfectly. Well, this was just the same! The airfoil was running strips. Absolutely! It was the same!

Not quite the same, to be sure. In the City, the speed of the strips was a fixed quantity. What wind there was blew in absolutely predictable fashion, since it was only the result of the movement of the strips. Here in the storm, however, the wind had a mind of its own or, rather, it depended on so many variables (Baley was deliberately striving for rationality) that it seemed to have a mind of its own—and Giskard had to allow for that. That was all. Otherwise, it was just running the strips with an added complication. The strips were moving at variable—and sharply changing—speeds.

Baley muttered, "What if we blow into a tree?"

"Very unlikely, Partner Elijah. Giskard is far too skillful for that. And we are only very slightly above the ground, so that the jets are particularly powerful."

"Then we'll hit a rock. It will cave us in underneath."

"We will not hit a rock, Partner Elijah."

"Why not? How on Earth can Giskard see where he's going, anyway?" Baley stared at the darkness ahead.

"It is just about sunset," said Daneel, "and some light is making its way through the clouds. It is enough for us to see by with the help of our headlights. And as it grows darker, Giskard will brighten the headlights."

"What headlights?" asked Baley rebelliously.

"You do not see them very well because they have a strong infrared component, to which Giskard's eyes are sensitive but yours are not. What's more, the infrared is more penetrating than shorter wave light is and, for that reason, is more effective in rain, mist, and fog."

Baley managed to feel some curiosity, even amid his uneasiness. "And *your* eyes, Daneel?"

"My eyes, Partner Elijah, are designed to be as similar to

those of human beings as possible. That is regrettable, perhaps, at this moment."

The airfoil trembled and Baley found himself holding his breath again. He said in a whisper, "Spacer eyes are still adapted to Earth's sun, even if robot eyes aren't. A good thing, too, if it helps remind them they're descended from Earthpeople."

His voice faded out. It was getting darker. He could see nothing at all now and the intermittent flashes lighted nothing, either. They were merely blinding. He closed his eyes and that didn't help. He was the more conscious of the angry, threatening thunder.

Should they not stop? Should they not wait for the worst of the storm to pass?

Giskard suddenly said, "The vehicle is not reacting properly."

Baley felt the ride become ragged as though the machine was on wheels and was rolling over ridges.

Daneel said, "Can it be storm damage, friend Giskard?"

"It does not have the feel of that, friend Daneel. Nor does it seem likely that this machine would suffer from this kind of damage in this or any other storm."

Baley absorbed the exchange with difficulty. "Damage?" he muttered. "What kind of damage?"

Giskard said, "I should judge the compressor to be leaking, sir, but slowly. It's not the result of an ordinary puncture."

"How did it happen, then?" Baley asked.

"Deliberate damage, perhaps, while it was outside the Administration Building. I have known, now, for some little time that we are being followed and carefully not being overtaken."

"Why, Giskard?"

"A possibility, sir, is that they are waiting for us to break down completely." The airfoil's motion was becoming more ragged.

"Can you make it to Dr. Fastolfe's?"

"It would not seem so, sir."

Baley tried to fling his reeling mind into action. "In that case, I've completely misjudged Amadiro's reason for delaying us. He was keeping us there to have one or more of his robots damage the airfoil in such a way as to bring us down in the midst of desolation and lightning."

"But why should he do that?" said Daneel, sounding shocked. "To get you? —In a way, he already had you."

"He doesn't want me. No one wants *me*," said Baley with a somewhat feeble anger. "The danger is to you, Daneel."

"To me, Partner Elijah?"

"Yes, *you!* Daneel. —Giskard, choose a safe place to come down and, as soon as you do, Daneel must get out of the car and be off to a place of safety."

Daneel said, "That is impossible, Partner Elijah. I could not leave you when you are feeling ill—and most especially if there are those who pursue us and might do you harm."

Baley said, "Daneel, they're pursuing *you*. You *must* leave. As for me, I will stay in the airfoil. I am in no danger."

"How can I believe that?"

"Please! Please! How can I explain the whole thing with everything spinning— Daneel"—Baley's voice grew desperately calm—"you are the most important individual here, far more important than Giskard and I put together. It's not just that I care for you and want no harm to come to you. All of humanity depends on you. Don't worry about me; I'm one man; worry about *billions*. Daneel—please—"

63.

Baley could feel himself rocking back and forth. Or was it the airfoil? Was it breaking up altogether? Or was Giskard losing control? Or was he taking evasive action?

Baley didn't care. He didn't *care!* Let the airfoil crash. Let it smash to bits. He would welcome oblivion. Anything to get rid of this terrible fright, this total inability to come to terms with the Universe.

Except that he had to make sure that Daneel got away—safely away. But how?

Everything was unreal and he was not going to be able to explain anything to these robots. The situation was so clear to him, but how was he to transfer this understanding to these robots, to these nonmen, who understood nothing but their Three Laws and who would let all of Earth and, in the long run, all of humanity go to hell because they could only be concerned with the one man under their noses?

Why had robots ever been invented?

And then, oddly enough, Giskard, the lesser of the two, came to his aid.

He said in his contentless voice, "Friend Daneel, I cannot keep this airfoil in motion much longer. Perhaps it will be more suitable to do as Mr. Baley suggests. He has given you a very strong order."

"Can I leave him when he is unwell, friend Giskard?" said Daneel, perplexed.

"You cannot take him out into the storm with you, friend Daneel. Moreover, he seems so anxious for you to leave that it may do him harm for you to stay."

Baley felt himself reviving. "Yes—yes—" he managed to croak out. "As Giskard says. Giskard, you go with him, hide him, make sure he doesn't return—then come back for me."

Daneel said forcefully, "That cannot be, Partner Elijah. We cannot leave you alone, untended, unguarded."

"No danger—I am in no danger. Do as I say—"

Giskard said, "Those following are probably robots. Human beings would hesitate to come out in the storm. And robots would not harm Mr. Baley."

Daneel said, "They might take him away."

"Not into the storm, friend Daneel, since that would work obvious harm to him. I will bring the airfoil to a halt now, friend Daneel. You must be ready to do as Mr. Baley orders. I, too."

"Good!" whispered Baley. "Good!" He was grateful for the simpler brain that could more easily be impressed and that lacked the ability to get lost and uncertain in ever-expanding refinements.

Vaguely, he thought of Daneel trapped between his perception of Baley's ill-being and the urgency of the order—and of his brain snapping under the conflict.

Baley thought: No no, Daneel. Just do as I say and don't question it.

He lacked the strength, almost the will, to articulate it and he let the order remain a thought.

The airfoil came down with a bump and a short, harsh, scraping noise.

The doors flew open, one on either side, and then closed with a soft, sighing noise. At once, the robots were gone. Having come to their decision, there was no hesitation and they moved with a speed that human beings could not duplicate.

Baley took a deep breath and shuddered. The airfoil was rock-steady now. It was part of the ground.

He was suddenly aware of how much of his misery had been the result of the swaying and bucking of the vehicle, the feeling of insubstantiality, of not being connected to the Universe but of being at the mercy of inanimate, uncaring forces.

Now, however, it was still and he opened his eyes.

He had not been aware that they had been closed.

There was still lightning on the horizon and the thunder was a subdued mutter, while the wind, meeting a more resistant and less yielding object now than it had hitherto, keened a higher note than before.

It was dark. Baley's eyes were no more' than human and he saw no light of any kind, other than the occasional blip of lightning. The sun must surely have set and the clouds were thick.

And for the first time since Baley had left Earth, he was alone!

## 64.

Alone!

He had been too ill, too beside himself, to make proper sense. Even now, he found himself struggling to understand what it was he should have done and would have done—if he had had room in his tottering mind for more than the one thought that Daneel must leave.

For instance, he had not asked where he now was, what he

was near, where Daneel and Giskard were planning to go. He did not know how any portion of the grounded airfoil worked. He could not, of course, make it move, but he might have had it supply heat if he felt cold or turn off the heat if there were too much—except that he did not know how to direct the machine to do either.

He did not know how to opacify the windows if he wanted to be enclosed or how to open a door if he wanted to leave.

The only thing he could do now was to wait for Giskard to come back for him. Surely that was what Giskard would expect him to do. The orders to him had simply been: Come back for me.

There had been no indication that Baley would change position in any way and Giskard's clear and uncluttered mind would surely interpret the "Come back" with the assumption that he was to come back to the airfoil.

Baley tried to adjust himself to that. In a way, it was a relief merely to wait, to have to make no decisions for a while, because there were no decisions he could possibly make. It was a relief to be steady and to feel at rest and to be rid of the terrible light flashes and the disturbing crashes of sound.

Perhaps he might even allow himself to go to sleep.

And then he stiffened. —Dare he do that?

They were being pursued. They were under observation. The airfoil, while parked and waiting for them outside the Administration Building of the Robotics Institute, had been tampered with and no doubt the tamperers would soon be upon him.

He was waiting for them, too, and not for Giskard only.

Had he thought it out clearly in the midst of his misery? The machine had been tampered with outside the Administration Building. That might have been done by anyone, but most likely by someone who knew it was there—and who would know that better than Amadiro?

Amadiro had intended delay until the storm. That was obvious. He was to travel in the storm and he was to break down in the storm. Amadiro had studied Earth and its population; he boasted of that. He would know quite clearly just what difficulty

Earthpeople would have with the Outside generally and with a thunderstorm in particular.

He would be quite certain that Baley would be reduced to complete helplessness.

But why should he want that?

To bring Baley back to the Institute? He had already had him, but he had had a Baley in the full possession of his faculties and along with him he had had two robots perfectly capable of defending Baley physically. It would be different now!

If the airfoil were disabled in a storm, Baley would be disabled emotionally. He would even be unconscious, perhaps, and would certainly not be able to resist being brought back. Nor would the two robots object. With Baley clearly ill, their only appropriate reaction would be to assist Amadiro's robots in rescuing him.

In fact, the two robots would have to come along with Baley and would do so helplessly.

And if anyone ever questioned Amadiro's action, he could say that he had feared for Baley in the storm; that he had tried to keep him at the Institute and failed; that he had sent his robots to trail him and assure his safety; and that, when the airfoil came to grief in the storm, those robots brought Baley back to haven. Unless people understood that it had been Amadiro who had ordered the airfoil tampered with (and who would believe that—and how could one prove it?), the only possible public reaction would be to praise Amadiro for his humanitarian feelings —all the more astonishing for having been expressed toward a subhuman Earthman.

And what would Amadiro do with Baley then?

Nothing, except to keep him quiet and helpless for a time. Baley was not himself the quarry. That was the point.

Amadiro would also have two robots and they would now be helpless. Their instructions forced them, in the strongest manner, to guard Baley and, if Baley were ill and being cared for, they could only follow Amadiro's orders if those orders were clearly and apparently for Baley's benefit. Nor would Baley be (perhaps) sufficiently himself to protect them with further orders—certainly not if he were kept under sedation.

It was clear! It was clear! Amadiro had had Baley, Daneel, and Giskard—but in unusable fashion. He had sent them out into the storm in order to bring them back and have them again —in usable fashion. Especially Daneel! It was Daneel who was the key.

To be sure, Fastolfe would be searching for them eventually and would find them, too, and retrieve them, but by then it would be too late, wouldn't it?

And what did Amadiro want with Daneel?

Baley, his head aching, was sure he knew—but how could he possibly prove it?

He could think no more. —If he could opacify the windows, he could make a little interior world again, enclosed and motionless, and then maybe he could continue his thoughts.

But he did not know how to opacify the windows. He could only sit there and look at the flagging storm beyond those windows, hear the whip of rain against the windows, watch the fading lightning, and listen to the muttering thunder.

He closed his eyes tightly. The eyelids made a wall, too, but he dared not sleep.

The car door on his right opened. He heard the sighing noise it made. He felt the cool, damp breeze enter, the temperature drop, the sharp smell of things green and wet enter and drown out the faint and friendly smell of oil and upholstery that reminded him somehow of the City that he wondered if he would ever see again.

He opened his eyes and there was the odd sensation of a robotic face staring at him—and drifting sideways, yet not really moving. Baley felt dizzy.

The robot, seen as a darker shadow against the darkness, seemed a large one. He had, somehow, an air of capability about him. He said, "Your pardon, sir. Did you not have the company of two robots?"

"Gone," muttered Baley, acting as ill as he could and aware that it did not require acting. A brighter flash of the heavens made its way through the eyelids that were now half-open.

"Gone! Gone where, sir?" And then, as he waited for an answer, he said, "Are you ill, sir?"

Baley felt a distant twinge of satisfaction within the inner scrap of himself that was still capable of thinking. If the robot had been without special instruction, he would have responded to Baley's clear signs of illness before doing anything else. To have asked first about the robots implied hard and close-pressed directions as to their importance.

It fit.

He tried to assume a strength and normality he did not possess and said, "I am well. Don't concern yourself with me."

It could not possibly have convinced an ordinary robot, but this one had been so intensified in connection with Daneel (obviously) that he accepted it. He said, "Where have the robots gone, sir?"

"Back to the Robotics Institute."

"To the Institute? Why, sir?"

"They were called by Master Roboticist Amadiro and he ordered them to return. I am waiting for them."

"But why did you not go with them, sir?"

"Master Roboticist Amadiro did not wish me to be exposed to the storm. He ordered me to wait here. I am following Master Roboticist Amadiro's orders."

He hoped the repetition of the prestige-filled name with the inclusion of the honorific, together with the repetition of the word "order," would have its effect on the robot and persuade him to leave Baley where he was.

On the other hand, if they had been instructed, with particular care, to bring back Daneel, and if they were convinced that Daneel was already on his way back to the Institute, there would be a decline in the intensity of their need in connection with that robot. They would have time to think of Baley again. They would say—

The robot said, "But it appears you are not well, sir."

Baley felt another twinge of satisfaction. He said, "I am well."

Behind the robot, he could vaguely see a crowding of several other robots—he could not count them—with their faces gleaming in the occasional lightning flash. As Baley's eyes adapted to the return of darkness, he could see the dim shine of *their* eyes.

He turned his head. There were robots at the left door, too, though that remained closed.

How many had Amadiro sent? Were they to have been returned by force, if necessary?

He said, "Master Roboticist Amadiro's orders were that my robots were to return to the Institute and I was to wait. You see that they are returning and that I am waiting. If you were sent to help, if you have a vehicle, find the robots, who are on their way back, and transport them. This airfoil is no longer operative." He tried to say it all without hesitation and firmly, as a well man would. He did not entirely succeed.

"They have returned on foot, sir?"

Baley said, "Find them. Your orders are clear."

There was hesitation. Clear hesitation.

Baley finally remembered to move his right foot—he hoped properly. He should have done it before, but his physical body was not responding properly to his thoughts.

Still the robots hesitated and Baley grieved over that. He was not a Spacer. He did not know the proper words, the proper tone, the proper air with which to handle robots with the proper efficiency. A skilled roboticist could, with a gesture, a lift of an eyebrow, direct a robot as though it were a marionette of which he held the strings. —Especially if the robot were of his own design.

But Baley was only an Earthman.

He frowned—that was easy to do in his misery—and whispered a weary "Go!" and motioned with his hands.

Perhaps that added the last small and necessary quantity of weight to his order—or perhaps an end had simply been reached to the time it took for the robots' positronic pathways to determine, by voltage and counter-voltage, how to sort out their instructions according to the Three Laws.

Either way, they had made up their minds and, after that, there was no further hesitation. They moved back to their vehicle, whatever and wherever it was, with such determined speed that they seemed simply to disappear.

The door the robot had held open now closed of its own accord. Baley had moved his foot in order to place it in the pathway of the closing door. He wondered distantly if his foot would be cut off cleanly or if its bones would be crushed, but he didn't move it. Surely no vehicle would be designed to make such a misadventure possible.

He was alone again. He had forced robots to leave a patently unwell human being by playing on the force of the orders given them by a competent robot master who had been intent on strengthening the Second Law for his own purposes—and had done it to the point where Baley's own quite apparent lies had subordinated the First Law to it.

How well he had done it, Baley thought with distant self-satisfaction—and became aware that the door which had swung shut was still ajar, held so by his foot, and that that foot had not been the least bit damaged as a result.

### 65.

Baley felt cool air curling about his foot and a sprinkle of cool water. It was a frighteningly abnormal thing to sense, yet he could not allow the door to close, for he would then not know how to open it. (How did the robots open those doors? Undoubtedly, it was no puzzle to members of the culture, but in his reading on Auroran life, there was no careful instruction of just how one opens the door of a standard airfoil. Everything of importance is taken for granted. You're supposed to *know*, even though you are, in theory, being informed.)

He was groping in his pockets as he thought this and even the pockets were not easy to find. They were not in the right places and they were sealed, so that they had to be opened by fumbles till he found the precise motion that caused the seal to part. He pulled out a handkerchief, balled it, and placed it between the door and jamb so that the door would not entirely close. He then removed his foot.

Now to think—if he could. There was no point to keeping the door open unless he meant to get out. Was there, however, any purpose in getting out?

If he waited where he was, Giskard would eventually come back for him and, presumably, lead him to safety.

Dare he wait?

He did not know how long it would take Giskard to see Daneel to safety and then return.

But neither did he know how long it would take the pursuing robots to decide they would not find Daneel and Giskard on any road leading back to the Institute. (Surely it was impossible that Daneel and Giskard had actually moved backward toward the Institute in search of sanctuary. Baley had not actually ordered them not to—but what if that were the only feasible route? —No! Impossible!)

Baley shook his head in silent denial of the possibility and felt it ache in response. He put his hands to it and gritted his teeth.

How long would the pursuing robots continue to search before they would decide that Baley had misled them—or had been himself misled? Would they then return and take him in custody, very politely and with great care not to harm him? Could he hold them off by telling them he would die if exposed to the storm?

Would they believe that? Would they call the Institute to report? Surely they would do *that*. And would human beings then arrive? *They* would not be overly concerned about his welfare.

If Baley got out of the car and found some hiding place in the surrounding trees, it would be that much harder for the pursuing robots to locate him—and that would gain him time.

It would also be harder for Giskard to locate him, but Giskard would be under a much more intense instruction to guard Baley than the pursuing robots were to find him. The primary task of the former would be to locate Baley—and of the latter, to locate Daneel.

Besides, Giskard was programmed by Fastolfe himself and Amadiro, however skillful, was no match for Fastolfe.

Surely, then, all things being equal, Giskard would be back before the other robots could possibly be.

But would all things be equal? With a faint attempt at cynicism, Baley thought: I'm worn-out and can't really think. I'm merely seizing desperately at whatever will console me.

Still, what could he do but play the odds, as he conceived the odds to be?

He leaned against the door and was out into the open. The handkerchief fell out into the wet, rank grass and he automatically bent down to pick it up, holding it in his hands as he staggered away from the car.

He was overwhelmed by the gusts of rain that soaked his face and hands. After a short while, his wet clothes were clinging to his body and he was shivering with cold.

There was a piercing splitting of the sky—too quick for him to close his eyes against—and then a sharp hammering that stiffened him in terror and made him clap his hands over his ears.

Had the storm returned? Or did it sound louder only because he was out in the open?

He had to move. He had to move away from the car, so that the pursuers would not find him too easily. He must not waver and remain in its vicinity or he might as well have stayed inside —and dry.

He tried to wipe his face with the handkerchief, but it was as wet as his face was and he let it go. It was useless.

He moved on, hands outstretched. Was there a moon that circled Aurora? He seemed to recall there had been mention of such a thing and he would have welcomed its light. —But what did it matter? Even if it existed and were in the sky now, the clouds would obscure it.

He felt something. He could not see what it was, but he knew it to be the rough bark of a tree. Undoubtedly a tree. Even a City man would know that much.

And then he remembered that lightning might hit trees and might kill people. He could not remember that he had ever read a description of how it felt to be hit by lightning or if there were any measures to prevent it. He knew of no one on Earth who had been hit by lightning.

He felt his way about the tree and was in an agony of apprehension and fear. How much was halfway around, so that he would end up moving in the same direction?

Onward!

The underbrush was thick now and hard to get through. It was like bony, clutching fingers holding him. He pulled petulantly and he heard the tearing of cloth.

Onward!

His teeth were chattering and he was trembling.

Another flash. Not a bad one. For a moment, he caught a glimpse of his surroundings.

Trees! A number of them. He was in a grove of trees. Were many trees more dangerous than one tree where lightning was concerned?

He didn't know.

Would it help if he didn't actually touch a tree?

He didn't know that, either. Death by lightning simply wasn't a factor in the Cities and the historical novels (and sometimes histories) that mentioned it never went into detail.

He looked up at the dark sky and felt the wetness coming down. He wiped at his wet eyes with his wet hands.

He stumbled onward, trying to step high. At one point, he splashed through a narrow stream of water, sliding over the pebbles underlaying it.

How strange! It made him no wetter than he was.

He went on again. The robots would not find him. Would Giskard?

He didn't know where he was. Or where he was going. Or how far he was from anything.

If he wanted to return to the car, he couldn't.

If he was trying to find himself, he couldn't.

And the storm would continue forever and he would finally dissolve and pour down in a little stream of Baley and no one would ever find him again.

And his dissolved molecules would float down to the ocean.

Was there an ocean on Aurora?

Of course there was! It was larger than Earth's, but there was more ice at the Auroran poles.

Ah, he would float to the ice and freeze there, glistening in the cold orange sun.

His hands were touching a tree again—wet hands—wet tree—

rumble of thunder—funny he didn't see the flash of lightning—lightning came first—was he hit?

He didn't feel anything—except the ground.

The ground was under him because his fingers were scrabbling into cold mud. He turned his head so he could breathe. It was rather comfortable. He didn't have to walk anymore. He could wait. Giskard would find him.

He was suddenly very sure of it. Giskard would have to find him because—

No, he had forgotten the because. It was the second time he had forgotten something. Before he went to sleep— Was it the same thing he had forgotten each time?— The same thing?—

It didn't matter. ·

It would be all right—all—

And he lay there, alone and unconscious, in the rain at the base of a tree, while the storm beat on.

# 16

## Again Gladia

66.

Afterward, looking back and estimating times, it would appear that Baley had remained unconscious not less than ten minutes and not more than twenty.

At the time, though, it might have been anything from zero to infinity. He was conscious of a voice. He could not hear the words it spoke, just a voice. He puzzled over the fact that it sounded odd and solved the matter to his satisfaction by recognizing it as a woman's voice.

There were arms around him, lifting him, heaving him. One arm—his arm—dangled. His head lolled.

He tried feebly to straighten out, but nothing happened. The woman's voice again.

He opened his eyes wearily. He was aware of being cold and wet and suddenly realized that water was not striking him. And it was not dark, not entirely. There was a dim suffusing of light and, by it, he saw a robot's face.

He recognized it. "Giskard," he whispered and with that he remembered the storm and the flight. And Giskard had reached him first; he had found him before the other robots had.

Baley thought contentedly: I knew he would.

He let his eyes close again and felt himself moving rapidly but with the slight—yet definite—unevenness that meant he was being carried by someone who was walking. Then a stop and a slow adjustment until he was resting on something quite warm and comfortable. He knew it was the seat of a car covered, perhaps, with toweling, but did not question how he knew.

Then there was the sensation. of smooth motion through the air and the feeling of soft absorbent fabric over his face and hands, the tearing open of his blouse, cold air upon his chest, and then the drying and blotting again.

After that, the sensations crowded in upon him.

He was in an establishment. There were flashes of walls, of illumination, of objects (miscellaneous shapes of furnishings) which he saw now and then when he opened his eyes.

He felt his clothes being stripped off methodically and made a few feeble and useless attempts to cooperate, then he felt warm water and vigorous scrubbing. It went on and on and he didn't want it to stop.

At one point, a thought occurred to him and he seized the arm that was holding him. "Giskard! Giskard!"

He heard Giskard's voice, "I am here, sir."

"Giskard, is Daneel safe?"

"He is quite safe, sir."

"Good." Baley closed his eyes again and made no effort whatever in connection with the drying. He felt himself turned over and over in the stream of dry air and then he was being dressed again in something like a warm robe.

Luxury! Nothing like this had happened to him since he was an infant and he was suddenly sorry for the babies for whom everything was done and who were not sufficiently conscious of it to enjoy it.

Or did they? Was the hidden memory of that infant luxury a determinant of adult behavior? Was his own feeling now just an expression of the delight of being an infant again?

And he had heard a woman's voice. Mother?

No, that couldn't possibly be.

—Mamma?

He was sitting in a chair now. He could sense as much and he could also feel, somehow, that the short, happy period of renewed infancy was coming to an end. He had to return to the sad world of self-consciousness and self-help.

But there had been a woman's voice. —What woman?

Baley opened his eyes. "Gladia?"

### 67.

It was a question, a surprised question, but deep within himself he was not really surprised. Thinking back, he had, of course, recognized her voice.

He looked around. Giskard was standing in his alcove, but he ignored him. First things first.

He said, "Where's Daneel?"

Gladia said, "He has cleaned and dried himself in the robot's quarters and he has dry clothing. He is surrounded by my household staff and they have their instructions. I can tell you that no outsider will approach within fifty meters of my establishment in any direction without our all knowing it at once. —Giskard is cleaned and dried as well."

"Yes, I can see that," said Baley. He was not concerned with Giskard, only with Daneel. He was relieved that Gladia seemed to accept the necessity of guarding Daneel and that he would not have to face the complications of explaining the matter.

Yet there was one breach in the wall of security and a note of querulousness entered in his voice as he said, "Why did you leave him, Gladia? With you gone, there was no human being in the house to stop the approach of a band of outside robots. Daneel could have been taken by force."

"Nonsense," said Gladia with spirit. "We were not gone long and Dr. Fastolfe had been informed. Many of his robots had joined mine and he could be on the spot in minutes if needed— and I'd like to see any band of outside robots withstand *him*."

"Have you seen Daneel since you returned, Gladia?"

"Of course! He's safe, I tell you."

"Thank you!" Baley relaxed and closed his eyes. Oddly enough, he thought: It wasn't so bad.

Of course it wasn't. He had survived, hadn't he? When he thought that, something inside himself grinned and was happy.

He had survived, hadn't he?

He opened his eyes and said, "How did you find me, Gladia?"

"It was Giskard. They had come here—both of them—and Giskard explained the situation to me quickly. I set right about securing Daneel, but he wouldn't budge until I had promised to order Giskard out after you. He was very eloquent. His responses with respect to you are very intense, Elijah.

"Daneel remained behind, of course. It made him very unhappy, but Giskard insisted that I order him to stay at the very top of my voice. You must have given Giskard some mighty strict orders. Then we got in touch with Dr. Fastolfe and, after that, we took my personal airfoil."

Baley shook his head wearily. "You should not have come along, Gladia. Your place was here, making sure Daneel was safe."

Gladia's face twisted into scorn. "And leave you dying in the storm, for all we knew? Or being taken up by Dr. Fastolfe's enemies? I have a little holograph of myself letting that happen. No, Elijah, I might have been needed to keep the other robots away from you if they had gotten to you first. I may not be much good in most ways, but any Solarian can handle a mob of robots, let me tell you. We're used to it."

"But how did you find me?"

"It wasn't so terribly hard. Actually, your airfoil wasn't far away, so that we could have walked it, except for the storm. We—"

Baley said, "You mean we had almost made it to Fastolfe's?"

"Yes," said Gladia. "Either your airfoil, in being damaged, wasn't damaged sufficiently to force you to a standstill sooner or Giskard's skill kept it going for longer than the vandals had anticipated. Which is a good thing. If you had come down closer to the Institute, they might have gotten you all. Anyway, we took my airfoil to where yours had come down. Giskard knew where it was, of course, and we got out—"

"And you got all wet, didn't you, Gladia?"

"Not a bit," she replied. "I had a large rain shade and a light sphere, too. My shoes got muddy and my feet got a little damp because I didn't have time to spray on Latex, but there's no harm in that. —Anyway, we were back at your airfoil less than half an hour after Giskard and Daneel had left you and, of course, you weren't there."

"I had tried—" began Baley.

"Yes, we know. I thought they—the others—had taken you away because Giskard said you were being followed. But Giskard found your handkerchief about fifty meters from the airfoil and he said that you must have wandered off in that direction. Giskard said it was an illogical thing to do, but that human beings were often illogical, so that we should search for you. —So we looked—both of us—using the lightsphere, but it was he found you. He said he saw the infrared glimmer of your body heat at the base of the tree and we brought you back."

Baley said, with a spark of annoyance, "Why was my leaving an illogical thing to do?"

"He didn't say, Elijah. Do you wish to ask him?" She gestured toward Giskard.

Baley said, "Giskard, what's this?"

Giskard's impassivity was disrupted at once and his eyes focused on Baley. He said, "I felt that you had exposed yourself to the storm unnecessarily. If you had waited, we would have brought you here sooner."

"The other robots might have gotten to me first."

"They did—but you had sent them away, sir."

"How do you know that?"

"There were many robotic footprints around the doors on either side, sir, but there was no sign of dampness within the airfoil, as there would have been if wet arms had reached in to lift you out. I judged you would not have gotten out of the airfoil of your own accord in order to join them, sir. And, having sent them away, you need not have feared they would return very quickly, since it was Daneel they were after—by your own estimate of the situation—and not you. In addition, you might have been certain that I would have been back quickly."

Baley muttered, "I reasoned precisely in that manner but I felt that confusing the issue might help further. I did what seemed best to me and you did find me, even so."

"Yes, sir."

Baley said, "But why bring me here? If we were close to Gladia's establishment, we were just as close, perhaps closer, to Dr. Fastolfe's."

"Not quite, sir. This residence was somewhat closer and I judged, from the urgency of your orders, that every moment counted in securing Daneel's safety. Daneel concurred in this, though he was most reluctant to leave you. Once he was here, I felt you would want to be here, too, so that you could, if you desired, assure yourself of his safety firsthand."

Baley nodded and said grumpily (he was still annoyed at that remark concerning his illogicality), "You did well, Giskard."

Gladia said, "Is it important that you see Dr. Fastolfe, Elijah? I can have him summoned here. Or you can view him trimensionally."

Baley leaned back in his chair again. He had leisure to realize that his thought processes were blunted and that he was very tired. It would do him no good to face Fastolfe now. He said, "No. I'll see him tomorrow after breakfast. Time enough. And then I think I'll be seeing this man, Kelden Amadiro, the head of the Robotics Institute. And a high official—what d'you call him? —the Chairman. *He* will be there, too, I suppose."

"You look terribly tired, Elijah," said Gladia. "Of course, we don't have those microorganisms—those germs and viruses—that you have on Earth and you've been cleaned out, so you won't get any of the diseases they have all over your planet, but you're clearly tired."

Baley thought: After all that, no cold? No flu? No pneumonia? —There was something to being on a Spacer world at that.

He said, "I admit I'm tired, but that can be cured by a bit of rest."

"Are you hungry? It's dinnertime."

Baley made a face. "I don't feel like eating."

"I'm not sure that's wise. You don't want a heavy meal, perhaps, but how about some hot soup? It will do you good."

Baley felt the urge to smile. She might be Solarian, but given the proper circumstances she sounded exactly like an Earth-woman. He suspected that this would be true of Aurorans as well. There are some things that differences in culture don't touch.

He said, "Do you have soup available? I don't want to be a problem."

"How can you be a problem? I have a staff—not a large one, as on Solaria, but enough to prepare any reasonable item of food on short order. —Now you just sit there and tell me what kind of soup you would like. It will all be taken care of."

Baley couldn't resist. "Chicken soup?"

"Of course." Then innocently, "Just what I would have suggested—and with lumps of chicken, so that it will be sub-stantial."

The bowl was put before him with surprising speed. He said, "Aren't you going to eat, Gladia?"

"I've eaten already, while you were being bathed and treated."

"Treated?"

"Only routine biochemical adjustment, Elijah. You had been rather psychic-damaged and we wanted no repercussions. —Do eat!"

Baley lifted an experimental spoonful to his lips. It was not bad chicken soup, though it had the queer tendency of Auroran food to be rather spicier than Baley would prefer. Or perhaps it was prepared with different spices than those he was used to.

He remembered his mother suddenly—a sharp thrust of mem-ory that made her appear younger than he himself was right now. He remembered her standing over him when he rebelled at eating his "nice soup."

She would say to him, "Come, Lije. This is real chicken and very expensive. Even the Spacers don't have anything better."

They didn't. He called to her in his mind across the years: They don't, Mom!

Really! If he could trust memory and allow for the power of youthful taste buds, his mother's chicken soup, when it wasn't dulled by repetition, was far superior.

He sipped again and again—and when he finished, he mut-tered in a shamefaced way, "Would there be a little more?"

"As much as you want, Elijah."

"Just a little more."

Gladia said to him, as he was finishing, "Elijah, this meeting tomorrow morning—"

"Yes, Gladia?"

"Does it mean that your investigation is over? Do you know what happened to Jander?"

Baley said judiciously, "I have an idea as to what might have happened to Jander. I don't think I can necessarily persuade anyone that I am right."

"Then why are you having the conference?"

"It's not my idea, Gladia. It's Master Roboticist Amadiro's idea. He objects to the investigation and he's going to try to have me sent back to Earth."

"Is he the one who tampered with your airfoil and tried to have his robots take Daneel?"

"I think he is."

"Well, can't he be tried and convicted and punished for that?"

"He certainly could," said Baley feelingly, "except for the very small problem that I can't prove it."

"And can he do all that and get away with it—and stop the investigation, too?"

"I'm afraid he has a good chance of being able to do so. As he himself says, people who don't expect justice don't have to suffer disappointment."

"But he mustn't. You mustn't let him. You've got to complete your investigation and find out the truth."

Baley sighed. "What if I can't find out the truth? Or what if I can—but can't make people listen to me?"

"You *can* find out the truth. And you *can* make people listen to you."

"You have a touching faith in me, Gladia. Still, if the Auroran World Legislature wants to send me back and orders the investigation ended, there's nothing I'm going to be able to do about it."

"Surely you won't be willing to go back with nothing accomplished."

"Of course I won't. It's worse than just accomplishing nothing,

Gladia. I'll go back with my career ruined and with Earth's future destroyed."

"Then don't let them do that, Elijah."

And he said, "Jehoshaphat, Gladia, I'm going to try not to, but I can't lift a planet with my bare hands. You can't ask me for miracles."

Gladia nodded and, eyes downcast, put her fist to her mouth, sitting there motionlessly, as though in thought. It took a while for Baley to realize that she was weeping soundlessly.

### 68.

Baley stood up quickly and walked around the table to her. He noted absently—and with some annoyance—that his legs were trembling and that there was a tic in the muscle of his right thigh.

"Gladia," he said urgently, "don't cry."

"Don't bother, Elijah," she whispered. "It will pass."

He stood helplessly at her side, reaching out to her yet hesitating. "I'm not touching you," he said. "I don't think I had better do so, but—"

"Oh, touch me. Touch me. I'm not all that fond of my body and I won't catch anything from you. I'm not—what I used to be."

So Baley reached out and touched her elbow and stroked it very slightly and clumsily with his fingertips. "I'll do what I can tomorrow, Gladia," he said. "I'll give it my very best try."

She rose at that, turned toward him, and said, "Oh, Elijah."

Automatically, scarcely knowing what he was doing, Baley held out his arms. And, just as automatically, she walked into them and he was holding her while her head cradled against his chest.

He held her as lightly as he could, waiting for her to realize that she was embracing an Earthman. (She had undoubtedly embraced a humaniform robot, but he had been no Earthman.)

She sniffed loudly and spoke while her mouth was half-obscured in Baley's shirt.

She said, "It isn't fair. It's because I'm a Solarian. No one really cares what happened to Jander and they would if I were an Auroran. It just boils down to prejudice and politics."

Baley thought: Spacers are *people*. This is exactly what Jessie would say in a similar situation. And if it were Gremionis who was holding Gladia, he'd say exactly what I'll say—if I knew what I would say.

And then he said, "That's not entirely so. I'm sure Dr. Fastolfe cares what happened to Jander."

"No, he doesn't. Not really. He just wants to have his way in the Legislature, and that Amadiro wants to have *his* way, and either one would trade Jander for his way."

"I promise you, Gladia, I won't trade Jander for anything."

"No? If they tell you that you can go back to Earth with your career saved and no penalty for your world, provided you forget all about Jander, what would you do?"

"There's no use setting up hypothetical situations that can't possibly come to pass. They're not going to give me anything in return for abandoning Jander. They're just going to try to send me back with nothing at all except ruin for me and my world. But, if they were to let me, I would get the man who destroyed Jander and see to it that he was adequately punished."

"What do you mean *if* they were to let you? *Make* them let you!"

Baley smiled bitterly. "If you think Aurorans pay no attention to you because you're a Solarian, imagine how little you would get if you were from Earth, as I am."

He held her closer, forgetting he was from Earth, even as he said the word. "But I'll try, Gladia. It's no use raising hopes, but I don't have a completely empty hand. I'll try—" His voice trailed off.

"You keep saying you'll try. —But *how?*" She pushed away from him a bit to look up into his face.

Baley said, bewildered, "Why, I may—"

"Find the murderer?"

"Whatever. —Gladia, please, I must sit down."

He reached out for the table, leaning on it.

She said, "What is it, Elijah?"

"I've had a difficult day, obviously, and I haven't quite recovered, I think."

"You'd better go to bed, then."

"To tell the truth, Gladia, I would like to."

She released him, her face full of concern and with no further room in it for tears. She lifted her arm and made a rapid motion and he was (it seemed to him) surrounded by robots at once.

And when he was in bed eventually and the last robot had left him, he found himself staring up at darkness.

He could not tell whether it was still raining Outside or whether some feeble lightning flashes were still making their last sleepy sparks, but he knew he heard no thunder.

He drew a deep breath and thought: Now what is it I have promised Gladia? What will happen tomorrow?

Last act: Failure?

And as Baley drifted into the borderland of sleep, he thought of that unbelievable flash of illumination that had come before sleep.

69.

Twice before, it had happened. Once the night before when, as now, he was falling asleep and once earlier this evening when he had slipped into unconsciousness beneath the tree in the storm. Each time, something had occurred to him, some enlightenment that had unmystified the problem as the lightning had undarkened the night.

And it had stayed with him as briefly as the lightning had.

What was it?

Would it come to him again?

This time, he tried consciously to seize it, to catch the elusive truth. —Or was it the elusive illusion? Was it the slipping away of conscious reason and the coming of attractive nonsense that one couldn't analyze properly in the absence of a properly thinking brain?

The search for whatever it was, however, slid slowly away. It would no more come on call than a unicorn would in a world in which unicorns did not exist.

It was easier to think of Gladia and of how she had felt. There had been the direct touch of the silkiness of her blouse, but beneath it were the small and delicate arms, the smooth back.

Would he have dared to kiss her if his legs had not begun to buckle beneath him? Or would that have been going too far?

He heard his breath exhale in a soft snore and, as always, that embarrassed him. He flogged himself awake and thought of Gladia again. Before he left, surely—but not if he could gain nothing for her in ret— Would that be payment for services ren— He heard the soft snore again and cared less this time.

Gladia— He had never thought he would see her again—let alone touch her—let alone hold her—hold her—

And he had no way of telling at what point he passed from thought to dream.

He was holding her again, as before— But there was no blouse—and her skin was warm and soft—and his hand moved slowly down the slope of shoulder blade and down the hidden ridges of her ribs—

There was a total aura of reality about it. All of his senses were engaged. He smelled her hair and his lips tasted the faint, faint salt of her skin—and now somehow they were no longer standing. Had they lain down or were they lying down from the start? And what had happened to the light?

He felt the mattress beneath him and the cover over him—darkness—and she was still in his arms and her body was bare.

He was shocked awake. "Gladia?"

Rising inflection—disbelieving—

"Shh. Elijah." She placed the fingers of one hand gently on his lips. "Don't say anything."

She might as well have asked him to stop the current of his blood.

He said, "What are you *doing?*"

She said, "Don't you *know* what I'm doing? I'm in bed with you."

"But why?"

"Because I want to." Her body moved against his.

She pinched the top of his night garment and the seam that held it together fell apart.

"Don't move, Elijah. You're tired and I don't want you to wear yourself out further."

Elijah felt a warmth stirring within him. He decided not to protect Gladia against herself. He said, "I'm not *that* tired, Gladia."

"No," she said sharply. "Rest! I want you to rest. Don't move."

Her mouth was on his as though intent on forcing him to keep quiet. He relaxed and the small thought flitted past him that he was following orders, that he *was* tired and was willing to be done to rather than to do. And, tinged with shame, it occurred to him that it rather diluted his guilt. (I couldn't help it, he heard himself say. She made me.) Jehoshaphat, how cowardly! How unbearably demeaning!

But those thoughts washed away, too. Somehow there was soft music in the air and the temperature had risen a bit. The cover had vanished and so had his nightclothes. He felt his head moved into the cradle of her arms and pressed against softness.

With a detached surprise, he knew, from her position, that the softness was her left breast and that it was centered, contrastingly, with its nipple hard against his lips.

Softly, she was singing to the music, a sleepily joyful tune he did not recognize.

She rocked gently back and forth and her fingertips grazed his chin and neck. He relaxed, content to do nothing, to let her initiate and carry through every activity. When she moved his arms, he did not resist and let them rest wherever she placed them.

He did not help and, when he did respond with heightened excitement and climax, it was only out of helplessness to do otherwise.

She seemed tireless and he did not want her to stop. Aside from the sensuality of sexual response, he felt again what he had felt earlier, the total luxury of the infant's passivity.

And, finally, he could respond no more and, it seemed, she could do no more and she lay with her head in the hollow where his left shoulder met his chest and her left arm lay across his ribs, her fingers stroking the short, curling hairs tenderly.

He seemed to hear her murmuring, "Thank you— Thank you—"

For what? he wondered.

He was scarcely conscious of her now, for this utterly soft end of a hard day was as soporific as the fabled nepenthe and he could feel himself slipping away, as though his fingertips were relaxing from the edge of the cliff of harsh reality in order that he might drop—drop—through the soft clouds of gathering sleep into the slowly swaying ocean of dreams.

And as he did so, what had not come on call came of itself. For the third time, the curtain was lifted and all the events since he had left Earth shuffled once more into hard focus. Again, it was all clear. He struggled to speak, to hear the words he needed to hear, to fix them and make them part of his thought processes, but though he clutched at them with every tendril of his mind, they slipped past and through and were gone.

So that, in this respect, Baley's second day on Aurora ended very much as his first had.

# 17

## The Chairman

*70.*

When Baley opened his eyes, it was to find sunlight streaming through the window and he welcomed it. To his still-sleepy surprise, he welcomed it.

It meant the storm was over and it was as though the storm had never happened. Sunlight—when viewed only as an alternative to the smooth, soft, warm, controlled light of the Cities—could only be considered harsh and uncertain. But compare it with the storm and it was the promise of peace itself. Everything, Baley thought, is relative and he knew he would never think of sunshine as entirely evil again.

"Partner Elijah?" Daneel was standing at the side of the bed. A little behind him stood Giskard.

Baley's long face dissolved in a rare smile of pure pleasure. He held out his hands, one to each. "Jehoshaphat, men"—and he was totally unaware, at the moment, of any inappropriateness in the word—"when I last saw you two together, I wasn't in the least sure I would ever see either of you again."

"Surely," said Daneel softly, "none of us would have been harmed under any circumstances."

"With the sunlight coming in, I see that," said Baley. "But last night, I felt as though the storm would kill me and I was certain you were in deadly danger, Daneel. It even seemed possible that

Giskard might be damaged in some way, trying to defend me against overwhelming odds. Melodramatic, I admit, but I wasn't quite myself, you know."

"We were aware of that, sir," said Giskard. "That was what made it difficult for us to leave you, despite your urgent order. We trust that this is not a source of displeasure for you at present."

"Not at all, Giskard."

"And," said Daneel, "we also know that you have been well cared for since we left you."

It was only then that Baley remembered the events of the night before.

Gladia!

He looked about in sudden astonishment. She was not anywhere in the room. Had he imagined—

No, of course not. That would be impossible.

And then he looked at Daneel with a frown, as though suspecting his remark to bear a libidinous character.

But no, that would be impossible, too. A robot, however humaniform, would not be designed to take lubricious delight in innuendo.

He said, "*Quite* well cared for. But what I need at the moment is to be shown to the Personal."

"We are here, sir," said Giskard, "to direct you and help you through the morning. Miss Gladia felt you would be more comfortable with us than with any of her own staff and she stressed that we were to leave nothing wanting for your comfort."

Baley looked doubtful. "How far did she instruct you to go? I feel pretty well now, so I don't have to have anyone wash and dry me. I can take care of myself. She does understand that, I hope."

"You need fear no embarrassment, Partner Elijah," said Daneel, with the small smile that (it seemed to Baley) came at those moments when, in a human being, it might be judged that a feeling of affection would have arisen. "We are merely to see to your comfort. If, at any time, you are most comfortable in privacy, we will wait at some distance."

"In that case, Daneel, we're all set." Baley scrambled out of bed. It pleased him to see that he felt quite steady on his legs. The night's rest and the treatment when he was brought back (whatever it might have been) had done marvels. —And Gladia, too.

### 71.

Still nude and just damp enough from his shower to feel thoroughly fresh, Baley, having brushed his hair, studied the result critically. It seemed natural that he would have breakfast with Gladia and he wasn't certain how he might be received. It might be best, perhaps, to take the attitude that nothing had happened and to be guided by her attitude. And somehow, he thought, it might help if he looked reasonably good—provided that was within the realm of the possible. He made a dissatisfied face at his reflection in the mirror.

"Daneel!" he called.

"Yes, Partner Elijah."

Speaking through and around toothpaste, Baley said, "Those are new clothes you are wearing, it seems."

"Not mine originally, Partner Elijah. They had been friend Jander's."

Baley's eyebrows climbed. "She let you have Jander's?"

"Miss Gladia did not wish me to be unclothed while waiting for my storm-drenched items to be washed and to dry. Those are ready now, but Miss Gladia says I may keep these."

"When did she say that?"

"This morning, Partner Elijah."

"She's awake, then?"

"Indeed. And you will be joining her at breakfast when you are ready."

Baley's lips tightened. It was odd that, at the moment, he was more concerned with having to face Gladia than, a little later on, the Chairman. The matter of the Chairman was, after all, in the lap of the Fates. He had decided on his strategy and it would either work or it would not work. As for Gladia—he simply had no strategy.

Well, he would have to face her.

He said, with as careful an air of indifference as he might manage, "And how is Miss Gladia this morning?"

Daneel said, "She seems well."

"Cheerful? Depressed?"

Daneel hesitated. "It is difficult to judge the inner attitude of a human being. There is nothing in her behavior to indicate internal turmoil."

Baley cast a quick eye on Daneel and again he wondered if he were referring to the events of last night. —And again he dismissed the possibility.

Nor did it do any good to study Daneel's face. One could not stare at a robot to guess thoughts from expression, for there were no thoughts in the human sense.

He stepped out into the bedroom and looked at the clothes that had been laid out for him, considering them thoughtfully and wondering if he could put them on without error and without requiring robotic help. The storm and the night were over and he wanted to assume the mantle of adulthood and independence once again.

He said, "What is this?" He held up a long sash covered with an intricately colored arabesque.

"It is a pajama sash," said Daneel. "It is purely ornamental. It passes over the left shoulder and is tied at the right side of the waist. It is traditionally worn at breakfast on some Spacer worlds but is not very popular on Aurora."

"Then why should I wear it?"

"Miss Gladia thought it would become you, Partner Elijah. The method of tieing is rather intricate and I will be glad to help you."

Jehoshaphat, thought Baley ruefully, she wants me to be pretty. What does she have in mind?

Don't think about it!

Baley said, "Never mind. I'll manage with a simple bowknot. —But listen, Daneel, after breakfast I will be going over to Fastolfe's, where I will meet with him, with Amadiro, and with the Chairman of the Legislature. I don't know if there will be any others present."

"Yes, Partner Elijah. I am aware of that. I don't think there will be others present."

"Well, then," said Baley, beginning to put on his undergarments and doing it slowly so as to make no mistake and thus find it unnecessary to appeal for help to Daneel, "tell me about the Chairman. I know from my reading that he is the nearest thing to an executive officer that there is on Aurora, but I gathered from that same reading that the position is purely honorary. He has no power, I take it."

Daneel said, "I am afraid, Partner Elijah—"

Giskard interrupted. "Sir, I am more aware of the political situation on Aurora than friend Daneel is. I have been in operation for much longer. Would you be willing to have me answer the question?"

"Why, certainly, Giskard. Go ahead."

"When the government of Aurora was first set up, sir," began Giskard in a didactic way, as though an information reel within him were methodically spinning, "it was intended that the executive officer fulfill only ceremonial duties. He was to greet dignitaries from other worlds, open all meetings of the Legislature, preside over its deliberations, and vote only to break a tie. After the River Controversy, however—"

"Yes, I read about that," said Baley. It had been a particularly dull episode in Auroran history, in which impenetrable arguments over the proper division of hydroelectric power had led to the nearest approach to civil war the planet had ever seen. "You needn't go into details."

"No, sir," said Giskard. "After the River Controversy, however, there was a general determination never to allow controversy to endanger Auroran society again. It has become customary, therefore, to settle all disputes in a private and peaceable manner outside the Legislature. When the legislators finally vote, it is in an agreed-upon fashion, so that there is always a large majority on one side or the other.

"The key figure in the settlement of disputes is the Chairman of the Legislature. He is held to be above the struggle and his power—which, although nil in theory, is considerable in practice —only holds as long as he is seen to be so. The Chairman there-

fore jealously guards his objectivity and, as long as he succeeds
in this, it is he who usually makes the decision that settles any
controversy in one direction or another."

Baley said, "You mean that the Chairman will listen to me, to
Fastolfe, and to Amadiro, and then come to a decision?"

"Possibly. On the other hand, sir, he may remain uncertain
and require further testimony, further thought—or both."

"And if the Chairman does come to a decision, will Amadiro
bow to it if it is against him—or will Fastolfe bow if it is against
*him?*"

"That is not an absolute necessity. There are almost always
some who will not accept the Chairman's decision and both Dr.
Amadiro and Dr. Fastolfe are headstrong and obstinate individuals—if one may judge from their actions. Most of the legislators, however, will go along with the Chairman's decision,
whatever that might be. Dr. Fastolfe or Dr. Amadiro—
whichever it may be who will be decided against by the Chairman—will then be sure to find himself in a small minority when
the vote is taken."

"How sure, Giskard?"

"Almost sure. The Chairman's term of office is ordinarily thirty
years, with the opportunity for reelection by the Legislature for
another thirty years. If, however, a vote were to go against the
Chairman's recommendation, the Chairman would be forced to
resign forthwith and there would be a governmental crisis while
the Legislature tried to find another Chairman under conditions
of bitter dispute. Few legislators are willing to risk that and the
chance of getting a majority to vote against the Chairman, when
that is the consequence, is almost nil."

"Then," said Baley ruefully, "everything depends on this morning's conference."

"That is very likely."

"Thank you, Giskard."

Gloomily, Baley arranged and rearranged his line of thought.
It seemed hopeful to him, but he did not have any idea what
Amadiro might say or what the Chairman might be like. It was
Amadiro who had initiated the meeting and *he* must feel
confident, sure of himself.

It was then that Baley remembered that once again, when he was falling asleep, with Gladia in his arms, he had seen—or thought he had seen—or imagined he had seen—the meaning of all the events on Aurora. Everything had seemed clear—obvious —certain. And once more, for the third time, it was gone as though it had never been.

And with that thought, his hopes seemed to go, too.

## 72.

Daneel led Baley into the room where breakfast was being served—it seemed more intimate than an ordinary dining room. It was small and plain, with no more in the way of furnishings than a table and two chairs and when Daneel retired, he did not move into a niche. In fact, there were no niches and, for a moment, Baley found himself alone—entirely alone—in the room.

That he was not really alone, he was certain. There would be robots on instant call. Still, it was a room for two—a no-robots room—a room (Baley hesitated at the thought) for lovers.

On the table there were two stacks of pancakelike objects that did not smell like pancakes but smelled good. Two containers of what looked like melted butter (but might not be) flanked them. There was a pot of the hot drink (which Baley had tried and had not liked very much) that substituted for coffee.

Gladia walked in, dressed in rather prim fashion and with her hair glistening, as though freshly conditioned. She paused a moment, her face wearing a half-smile. "Elijah?"

Baley, caught a little by surprise at the sudden appearance, jumped to his feet. "How are you, Gladia?" He stuttered a bit.

She ignored that. She seemed cheerful, carefree. She said, "If you're worried about Daneel not being in sight, don't be. He's completely safe and he'll stay so. As for us—" She came to him, standing close, and put a hand slowly to his cheek, as once, long ago, she had done in Solaria.

She laughed lightly. "That was all I did then, Elijah. Do you remember?"

Elijah nodded silently.

"Did you sleep well, Elijah? —Sit down, dear."

He sat down. "Very well. —Thank you, Gladia." He hesitated before deciding not to return the endearment in kind.

She said, "Don't thank *me*. I've had my best night's sleep in *weeks* and I wouldn't have if I. hadn't gotten out of bed after I was sure you were sleeping soundly. If I had stayed—as I wanted to—I would have been annoying you before the night was over and you would not have gotten *your* rest."

He recognized the need for gallantry. "There are some things more important than r-rest, Gladia," he said, but with such formality that she laughed again.

"Poor Elijah," she said. "You're embarrassed."

The fact that she recognized that embarrassed him even more. Baley had been prepared for contrition, disgust, shame, affected indifference, tears—everything but the frankly erotic attitude she had assumed.

She said, "Well, don't suffer so. You're hungry. You hardly ate last night. Get some calories inside you and you'll feel more carnal."

Baley looked doubtfully at the pancakes that weren't.

Gladia said, "Oh! You've probably never seen these. They're Solarian delicacies. Pachinkas! I had to reprogram my chef before he could make them properly. In the first place, you have to use imported Solarian grain. It won't work with the Auroran varieties. And they're stuffed. Actually, there are a thousand stuffings you can use, but this is my favorite and I *know* you'll like it, too. I won't tell you what's in it, except for chestnut puree and a touch of honey, but try it and tell me what you think. You can eat it with your fingers, but be careful how you bite into it."

She picked one up, holding it daintily between the thumb and middle finger of each hand, then took a small bite, slowly, and licked at the golden, semiliquid filling that flowed out.

Baley imitated her action. The pachinka was hard to the touch and not too hot to hold. He put one end cautiously in his mouth and found it resisted biting. He put more muscle into it and the pachinka cracked and he found the contents flowing over his hands.

"The bite was too large and too forceful," said Gladia, rushing to him with a napkin. "Now lick at it. No one eats a pachinka neatly. There's no such thing. You're supposed to wallow in it. Ideally, you're supposed to eat it in the nude, then take a shower."

Baley tried a hesitant lick and his expression was clear enough.

"You like it, don't you?" said Gladia.

"It's delicious," said Baley and he bit away at it slowly and gently. It wasn't too sweet and it seemed to soften and melt in the mouth. It scarcely required swallowing.

He ate three pachinkas and it was only shame that kept him from asking for more. He licked at his fingers without urging and eschewed the use of napkins, for he wanted none of it to be wasted on an inanimate object.

"Dip your fingers and hands in the cleanser, Elijah," and she showed him. The "melted butter" was a finger bowl, obviously.

Baley did as he was shown and then dried his hands. He sniffed at them and there was no odor whatever.

She said, "*Are* you embarrassed about last night, Elijah? Is that all you feel?"

What did one say? Baley wondered.

Finally, he nodded. "I'm afraid I am, Gladia. It's not all I feel, by twenty kilometers or more, but I *am* embarrassed. Stop and think. I'm an Earthman and you know that, but for the time being you're repressing it and 'Earthman' is only a meaningless disyllabic sound to you. Last night you were sorry for me, concerned over my problem with the storm, feeling toward me as you would toward a child, and—sympathizing with me, perhaps, out of the vulnerability produced in you by your own loss—you came to me. But that feeling will pass—I'm surprised it hasn't passed already—and then you will remember that I am an Earthman and you will feel ashamed, demeaned, and dirtied. You will hate me for what I have done for you and I don't want to be hated. —I don't want to be hated, Gladia." (If he looked as unhappy as he felt, he looked unhappy indeed.)

She must have thought so, for she reached out to him and stroked his hand. "I won't hate you, Elijah. Why should I? You did nothing to me that I can object to. I did it to you and I'll be glad for the rest of my life that I did. You freed me by a touch two years ago, Elijah, and last night you freed me again. I needed to know, two years ago, that I could feel desire—and last night I needed to know that I could feel desire *again* after Jander. Elijah—stay with me. It would be—"

He cut her off earnestly. "How can that be, Gladia? I must go back to my own world. I have duties and goals there and you cannot come with me. You could not live the kind of life that is lived on Earth. You would die of Earthly diseases—if the crowds and enclosure did not kill you first. Surely you under-stand."

"I understand about Earth," said Gladia with a sigh, "but surely you needn't leave immediately."

"Before the morning is over, I may be ordered off the planet by the Chairman."

"You won't be," said Gladia energetically. "You won't let your-self be. —And if you are, we can go to another Spacer world. There are dozens we can choose from. Does Earth mean so much to you that you wouldn't live on a Spacer world?"

Baley said, "I could be evasive, Gladia, and point out that no other Spacer world would let me make my home there per-manently—and you know that's so. The greater truth is, though, that even if some Spacer world *would* accept me, Earth means so much to me that I would have to return. —Even if it meant leaving you."

"And never visiting Aurora again? Never seeing me again?"

"If I could see you again, I would," Baley said, wishing. "Over and over again, believe me. But what's the use of saying so? You know I'm not likely to be invited back. And you know I can't return without an invitation."

Gladia said in a low voice, "I don't want to believe that, Elijah."

Baley said, "Gladia, don't make yourself unhappy. Something wonderful happened between us, but there are other wonderful things that will happen to you, too—many of them, of all kinds, but not the *same* wonderful thing. Look forward to the others."

She was silent.

"Gladia," he said urgently, "need anyone know what has happened between us?"

She looked up at him, a pained expression on her face. "Are you *that* ashamed?"

"Of what happened, certainly not. But even though I am not ashamed, there could be consequences that would be discomforting. The matter would be talked about. Thanks to that hateful hyperwave drama, which included a distorted view of our relationship, we are news. The Earthman and the Solarian woman. If there is the slightest reason to suspect that there is— love between us, it will get back to Earth at the speed of hyperspatial drive."

Gladia lifted her eyebrows with a touch of hauteur. "And Earth will consider you demeaned? You will have indulged in sex with someone beneath your station?"

"No, of course not," said Baley uneasily, for he knew that that would certainly be the view of billions of Earthpeople. "Has it occurred to you that my wife would hear of it? I'm married."

"And if she does? What of it?"

Baley took a deep breath. "You don't understand. Earth ways are not Spacer ways. We have had times in our history when sexual mores were fairly loose, at least in some places and for some classes. This is not one of those times. Earthmen live crowded together and it takes a puritan ethic to keep the family system stable under such conditions."

"Everyone has one partner, you mean, and no other?"

"No," said Baley. "To be honest, that's not so. But care is taken to keep irregularities sufficiently quiet, so that everyone can—can—"

"Pretend they don't know?"

"Well, yes, but in this case—"

"It will all be so public that no one could pretend not to know —and your wife will be angry with you and will strike you."

"No, she won't strike me, but she will be shamed, which is worse. I will be shamed as well and so will my son. My social position will suffer and— Gladia, if you don't understand, you don't understand, but tell me that you will not speak freely of this thing as Aurorans do." He was conscious of making a rather miserable show of himself.

Gladia said thoughtfully, "I do not mean to tease you, Elijah. You have been kind to me and I would not be unkind to you, but"—she threw her arms up hopelessly—"your Earth ways are so nonsensical."

"Undoubtedly. Yet I must live with them—as you have lived with Solarian ways."

"Yes." Her expression darkened with memory. Then, "Forgive me, Elijah. Really and honestly, I apologize. I want what I can't have and I take it out on you."

"It's all right."

"No, it's not all right. Please, Elijah, I must explain something to you. I don't think you understand what happened last night. Will you be all the more embarrassed if I do?"

Baley wondered how Jessie would feel and what she would do if she could hear this conversation. Baley was quite aware that his mind should be on the confrontation with the Chairman that was looming immediately up ahead and not on his own personal marital dilemma. He should be thinking of Earth's danger and not of his wife's, but, in actual fact, he was thinking of Jessie.

He said, "I'll probably be embarrassed, but explain it anyway."

Gladia moved her chair, refraining from calling one of her robotic staff to do it for her. He waited for her nervously, not offering to move it himself.

She put her chair immediately next to his, facing it in the other direction, so that she was looking at him directly when she sat down. And as she did so, she put out her small hand and placed it in his and he felt his own hand press it.

"You see," she said, "I no longer fear contact. I'm no longer at the stage where all I can do is brush your cheek for an instant."

"That may be, but this does not affect you, Gladia, does it, as that bare touch did then?"

She nodded. "No, it doesn't affect me that way, but I like it anyway. I think that's an advance, actually. To be turned inside out just by a single moment of touch shows how abnormally I had lived and for how long. Now it is better. May I tell you how? What I have just said is actually prologue."

"Tell me."

"I wish we were in bed and it was dark. I could talk more freely."

"We are sitting up and it is light, Gladia, but I am listening."

"Yes. —On Solaria, Elijah, there was no sex to speak of. You know that."

"Yes, I do."

"I experienced none, in any real sense. On a few occasions— only a few—my husband approached me out of duty. I won't even describe how that was, but you will believe me when I tell you that, looking back on it, it was worse than none."

"I believe you."

"But I knew about sex. I read about it. I discussed it with other women sometimes, all of whom pretended it was a hateful duty that Solarians must undergo. If they had children to the limit of their quota, they always said they were delighted they would never have to deal with sex again."

"Did you believe them?"

"Of course I did. I had never heard anything else and the few non-Solarian accounts I read were denounced as false distortions. I believed that, too. My husband found some books I had, called them pornography, and had them destroyed. Then, too, you know, people can make themselves believe anything. I think Solarian women believed what they said and really *did* despise sex. They certainly sounded sincere enough and it made me feel there was something terribly wrong with me because I had a kind of curiosity about it—and odd feelings I could not understand."

"You did not, at that time, use robots for relief in any way?"

"No, it didn't occur to me. Or any inanimate object. There were occasional whispers of such things, but with such horror— or pretended horror—that I would never *dream* of doing anything like that. Of course, I had dreams and sometimes something that, as I look back on it, must have been incipient orgasms, would wake me. I never understood them, of course, or dared talk of it. I was bitterly ashamed of it, in fact. Worse, I was frightened of the pleasure they brought me. And then, of course, I came to Aurora."

"You told me of that. Sex with Aurorans was unsatisfactory."

"Yes. It made me think that Solarians were right after all. Sex was not like my dreams at all. It was not until Jander that I understood. It is not sex that they have on Aurora; it is, it is— choreography. Every step of it is dictated by fashion, from the method of approach to the moment of departure. There is nothing unexpected, nothing spontaneous. On Solaria, since there was so little sex, nothing was given or taken. And on Aurora, sex was so stylized that, in the end, nothing was given or taken either. Do you understand?"

"I'm not sure, Gladia, never having experienced sex with an Auroran woman or, for that matter, never having been an Auroran man. But it's not necessary to explain. I have a dim notion of what you mean."

"You're terribly embarrassed, aren't you?"

"Not to the point of being unable to listen."

"But then I met Jander and learned to use him. He was not an Auroran man. His only aim, his *only* possible aim, was to please me. He gave and I took and, for the first time, I experienced sex as it should be experienced. Do you understand *that*? Can you imagine what it must be like suddenly to know that you are not mad, or distorted, or perverted, or even simply wrong—but to know that you are a woman and have a satisfying sex partner?"

"I think I can imagine that."

"And then, after so short a time, to have it all taken away from me. I thought—I thought—that that was the end. I was doomed. I was never again, through centuries of life, to have a good sexual relationship again. Not to have had it to start with— and then never to have had it at all—was bad enough. But to get it against all expectation and to have it, then suddenly to *lose* it and go back to nothing—*that* was unbearable. —You see how important, therefore, last night was."

"But why me, Gladia? Why not someone else?"

"No, Elijah, it *had* to be you. We came and found you, Giskard and I, and you were helpless. Truly helpless. You were not unconscious, but you did not rule your body. You had to be lifted and carried and placed in the car. I was there when you were warmed and treated, bathed and dried, helpless throughout. The robots did it all with marvelous efficiency, intent on caring for you and preventing harm from coming to you but totally without actual feeling. I, on the other hand, watched and I *felt*."

Baley bent his head, gritting his teeth at the thought of his public helplessness. He had luxuriated in it when it had happened, but now he could only feel the disgrace of being observed under such conditions.

She went on. "I wanted to do it all for you. I resented the robots for reserving for themselves the right to be kind to you—and to give. And as I thought of myself doing it, I felt a growing sexual excitement, something I hadn't felt since Jander's death. —And it occurred to me then that, in my only successful sex, what I had done was to take. Jander gave whatever I wished, but he never took. He was incapable of taking, since his only pleasure lay in pleasing me. And it never occurred to me to give because I was brought up with robots and knew they couldn't take.

"And as I watched, it came to me that I knew only half of sex and I desperately wanted to experience the other half. But then, at the dinner table with me afterward, when you were eating your hot soup, you seemed recovered, you seemed strong. You were strong enough to console me and because I had had that feeling for you, when you were being cared for, I no longer feared your being from Earth and I was willing to move into your embrace. I *wanted* it. But even as you held me, I felt a sense of loss, for I was taking again and not giving.

"And you said to me, 'Gladia, please, I must sit down.' Oh, Elijah, it was the most wonderful thing you could have said to me."

Baley felt himself flush. "It embarrassed me hideously at the time. Such a confession of weakness."

"It was just what I wanted. It drove me wild with desire. I forced you to bed and came to you and, for the first time in my life, I gave. I took nothing. And the spell of Jander passed, for I knew that he had not been enough, either. It must be possible to take and give, *both*. —Elijah, stay with me."

Baley shook his head. "Gladia, if I tore my heart in two, it wouldn't change the facts. I cannot remain on Aurora. I must return to Earth. You cannot come to Earth."

"Elijah, what if I *can* come to Earth?"

"Why do you say such a foolish thing? Even if you could, I would age quickly and soon be useless to you. In twenty years, thirty at the most, I will be an old man, probably dead, while you will stay as you are for centuries."

"But that is what I mean, Elijah. On Earth, I will catch your infections and I will grow old quickly, too."

"You wouldn't want that. Besides, old age isn't an infection. You will merely grow sick, very quickly, and die. Gladia, you can find another man."

"An Auroran?" She said it with contempt.

"You can teach. Now that you know how to take and to give, teach them how to do both as well."

"If I teach, will they learn?"

"Some will. Surely some will. You have so much time to find the one who will. There is—" (No, he thought, it is not wise to mention Gremionis now, but perhaps if he comes to her—less politely and with a little more determination—)

She seemed thoughtful. "Is it possible?" Then, looking at Baley, with her gray-blue eyes moist, "Oh, Elijah, do you remember anything at all of what happened last night?"

"I must admit," said Baley a little sadly, "that some of it is distressingly hazy."

"If you remembered, you would not want to leave me."

"I don't want to leave you as it is, Gladia. It is just that I must."

"And afterward," she said, "you seemed so quietly happy, so rested. I lay nestled on your shoulder and felt your heart beat rapidly at first, then more and more slowly, except when you sat up so suddenly. Do you remember that?"

Baley started and leaned a little away from her, gazing into her eyes wildly. "No, I don't remember that. What do you mean? What did I do?"

"I told you. You sat up suddenly."

"Yes, but what else?" His heart was beating rapidly now, as rapidly as it must have in the wake of last night's sex. Three times, something that had seemed the truth had come to him, but the first two times he had been entirely alone. The third time, last night, however, Gladia had been with him. He had had a witness.

Gladia said, "Nothing else, really. I said, 'What is it, Elijah?' but you paid no attention to me. You said, 'I have it. I have it.' You didn't speak clearly and your eyes were unfocused. It was a little frightening."

"Is that all I said? Jehoshaphat, Gladia! Didn't I say anything more?"

Gladia frowned. "I don't remember. But then you lay back and I said, 'Don't be frightened, Elijah. Don't be frightened. You're safe now.' And I stroked you and you settled back and fell asleep—and *snored.* —I never heard anyone snore before, but that's what it must have been—from the descriptions." The thought clearly amused her.

Baley said, "Listen to me, Gladia. What did I say? 'I have it. I have it.' Did I say what it was I had?"

She frowned again. "No. I don't remember— Wait, you did say one thing in a very low voice. You said, 'He was there first.'"

"'He was there first.' That's what I said?"

"Yes. I took it for granted that you meant Giskard was there before the other robots, that you were trying to overcome your fears of being taken away, that you were reliving that time in the storm. Yes! That's why I stroked you and said, 'Don't be frightened, Elijah. You're safe now,' till you relaxed."

"'He was there first.' 'He was there first.' —I won't forget it now. Gladia, thanks for last night. Thanks for talking to me now."

Gladia said, "Is there something important about you saying that Giskard found you first. He *did.* You know that."

"It can't be that, Gladia. It must be something I *don't* know but manage to discover only when my mind is totally relaxed."

"But what does it mean, then?"

"I'm not sure, but if that's what I said, it must mean something. And I have an hour or so to figure it out." He stood up. "I must leave now."

He had taken a few steps toward the door, but Gladia flew to him and put her arms around him. "Wait, Elijah."

Baley hesitated, then lowered his head to kiss her. For a long moment, they clung together.

"Will I see you again, Elijah?"

Baley said sadly, "I can't say. I hope so."

And he went off to find Daneel and Giskard, so that he could make the necessary preparations for the confrontation about to come.

### 73·

Baley's sadness persisted as he walked across the long lawn to Fastolfe's establishment.

The robots walked on either side. Daneel seemed at his ease, but Giskard, faithful to his programming and apparently unable to relax it, maintained his close watch on the surroundings.

Baley said, "What is the name of the Chairman of the Legislature, Daneel?"

"I cannot say, Partner Elijah. On the occasions when he has been referred to in my hearing, he has been referred to only as 'the Chairman.' He is addressed as 'Mr. Chairman.'"

Giskard said, "His name is Rutilan Horder, sir, but it is never mentioned officially. The title alone is used. That serves to impress continuity on the government. Human holders of the position have, individually, fixed terms, but 'the Chairman' always exists."

"And this particular individual Chairman—how old is he?"

"Quite old, sir. Three hundred and thirty-one," said Giskard, who typically had statistics on tap.

"In good health?"

"I know nothing to the contrary, sir."

"Any outstanding personal characteristics it might be well for me to be prepared for?"

That seemed to stop Giskard. He said, after a pause, "That is difficult for me to say, sir. He is in his second term. He is considered an efficient Chairman who works hard and gets results."

"Is he short-tempered? Patient? Domineering? Understanding?"

Giskard said, "You must judge such things for yourself, sir."

Daneel said, "Partner Elijah, the Chairman is above partisanship. He is just and evenhanded, by definition."

"I'm sure of that," muttered Baley, "but definitions are abstract, as is 'the Chairman,' while individual Chairmen—with names—are concrete and may have minds to match."

He shook his head. His own mind, he would swear, had a strong measure of concrete itself. Having three times thought of something and three times lost it, he was now presented with his own comment at the time of having the thought and it *still* didn't help.

"He was there first."

Who was there first? When?

Baley had no answer.


*74.*


Baley found Fastolfe waiting for him at the door of his establishment, with a robot behind him who seemed most unrobotically restless, as though unable to perform his proper function of greeting a visitor and upset by the fact.

(But then, one was always reading human motivations and responses into robots. What was more likely true was no upsettedness—no feeling of any kind—merely a slight oscillation of positronic potentials resulting from the fact that his orders were to greet and inspect all visitors and he could not quite perform the task without pushing past Fastolfe, which he also could not do, in the absence of overriding necessity. So he made false starts, one after the other, and that made him seem restless.)

Baley found himself staring at the robot absently and only with difficulty managing to bring his eyes back to Fastolfe. (He was thinking of robots, but he didn't know why.)

"I'm glad to see you again, Dr. Fastolfe," he said and thrust his hand forward. After his encounter with Gladia, it was rather difficult to remember that Spacers were reluctant to make physical contact with an Earthman.

Fastolfe hesitated a moment and then, as manners triumphed over prudence, he took the hand offered him, held it lightly and briefly, and let it go. He said, "I am even more delighted to see you, Mr. Baley. I was quite alarmed over your experience last evening. It was not a particularly bad storm, but to an Earthman it must have seemed overwhelming."

"You know about what happened, then?"

"Daneel and Giskard have brought me fully up to date in that respect. I would have felt better if they had come here directly and, eventually, brought you here with them, but their decision was based on the fact that Gladia's establishment was closer to the breakdown point of the airfoil and that your orders had been extremely intense and had placed Daneel's safety ahead of your own. They did not misinterpret you?"

"They did not. I forced them to leave me."

"Was that wise?" Fastolfe led the way indoors and pointed to a chair.

Baley sat down. "It seemed the proper thing to do. We were being pursued."

"So Giskard reported. He also reported that—"

Baley intervened. "Dr. Fastolfe, please. I have very little time and I have questions that I must ask you."

"Go ahead, please," said Fastolfe at once, with his usual air of unfailing politeness.

"It has been suggested that you place your work on brain function above everything else, that you—"

"Let me finish, Mr. Baley. That I will let nothing stand in my way, that I am totally ruthless, oblivious to any consideration of immorality or evil, would stop at nothing, would excuse everything, all in the name of the importance of my work."

"Yes."

"Who told you this, Mr. Baley?" asked Fastolfe.

"Does it matter?"

"Perhaps not. Besides, it's not difficult to guess. It was my daughter Vasilia. I'm sure of that."

Baley said, "Perhaps. What I want to know is whether this estimate of your character is correct."

Fastolfe smiled sadly. "Do you expect an honest answer from me about my own character? In some ways, the accusations against me are true. I *do* consider my work the most important matter there is and I *do* have the impulse to sacrifice anything and everything to it. I *would* ignore conventional notions of evil and immorality if these got in my way. —The thing is, however, that I don't. I can't bring myself to. And, in particular, if I have been accused of killing Jander because that would in some way advance my study of the human brain, I deny it. It is not so. I did not kill Jander."

Baley said, "You suggested I submit to a Psychic Probe to get some information that I can't reach otherwise out of my brain. Has it occurred to you that, if *you* submitted to a Psychic Probe, your innocence could be demonstrated?"

Fastolfe nodded his head thoughtfully, "I imagine Vasilia suggested that my failure to offer to submit to one was proof of my guilt. Not so. A Psychic Probe is dangerous and I am as nervous about submitting myself to one as you are. Still, I would have done so, despite my fears, were it not for the fact that is what my opponents would most like to have me do. They would argue against any evidence to my innocence and the Psychic Probe is not delicate enough an instrument to demonstrate innocence beyond argument. But what they *would* get by use of the Probe is information about the theory and design of humaniform robots. *That* is what they are after and *that* is what I am not going to give them."

Baley said, "Very well. Thank you, Dr. Fastolfe."

Fastolfe said, "You are welcome. And now, if I may get back to what I was saying, Giskard reported that, after you were left alone in the airfoil, you were accosted by strange robots. At least, you spoke of strange robots, rather disjointedly, after you were found unconscious and exposed to the storm."

"The strange robots *did* accost me, Dr. Fastolfe. I managed to deflect them and send them away, but I thought it wise to leave the airfoil rather than await their return. I may not have been thinking clearly when I reached that decision. Giskard said I was not."

Fastolfe smiled. "Giskard has a simplistic view of the Universe. Have you any idea whose robots they were?"

Baley moved about restlessly and seemed to find no way of adjusting himself to the seat in a comfortable manner. He said, "Has the Chairman arrived yet?"

"No, but he will be here momentarily. So will Amadiro, the head of the Institute, whom, the robots told me, you met yesterday. I am not sure that was wise. You irritated him."

"I had to see him, Dr. Fastolfe, and he did not seem irritated."

"That is no guide with Amadiro. As a result of what he calls your slanders and your unbearable sullying of professional reputation, he has forced the Chairman's hand."

"In what way?"

"It is the Chairman's job to encourage the meeting of contending parties and to work for a compromise. If Amadiro wishes to meet with me, the Chairman could not, by definition, discourage it, much less forbid it. He must hold the meeting and, if Amadiro can find enough evidence against you—and it is easy to find evidence against an Earthman—that will end the investigation."

"Perhaps, Dr. Fastolfe, you should not have called on an Earthman to help, considering how vulnerable we are."

"Perhaps not, Mr. Baley, but I could think of nothing else to do. I still can't, so I must leave it up to you to persuade the Chairman to our point of view—if you can."

"The responsibility is mine?" said Baley glumly.

"Entirely yours," said Fastolfe smoothly.

Baley said, "Are we four to be the only ones present?"

Fastolfe said, "Actually, we three: the Chairman, Amadiro, and myself. We are the two principals and the compromising agent, so to speak. You will be there as a fourth party, Mr. Baley, only on sufferance. The Chairman can order you to leave at will, so I hope you will not do anything to upset him."

"I'll try not to, Dr. Fastolfe."

"For instance, Mr. Baley, do not offer him your hand—if you will forgive my rudeness."

Baley felt himself grow warm with retroactive embarrassment at his earlier gesture. "I will not."

"And be unfailingly polite. Make no angry accusations. Do not insist on statements for which there is no support—"

"You mean don't try to stampede anyone into betraying himself. Amadiro, for instance."

"Yes, do not do so. You will be committing slander and it will be counterproductive. Therefore, be polite! If the politeness masks an attack, we won't quarrel with that. And try not to speak unless you are spoken to."

Baley said, "How is it, Dr. Fastolfe, that you are so full of careful advice now and yet you never warned me about the dangers of slander earlier."

"The fault is indeed mine," said Dr. Fastolfe. "It was a matter of such basic knowledge to me that it never occurred to me that it had to be explained."

Baley grunted. "Yes, I thought so."

Fastolfe raised his head suddenly. "I hear an airfoil outside. More than that, I can hear the steps of one of my staff, heading for the entrance. I presume the Chairman and Amadiro are at hand."

"Together?" asked Baley.

"Undoubtedly. You see, Amadiro suggested my establishment as the meeting place, thus granting me the advantage of home ground. He will therefore have the chance of offering, out of apparent politeness, to call for the Chairman and bring him here. After all, they must both come here. This will give him a few minutes to talk privately with the Chairman and push his point of view."

"That is scarcely fair," said Baley. "Could you have stopped that?"

"I didn't want to. Amadiro takes a calculated risk. He may say something that will irritate the Chairman."

"Is the Chairman particularly irritable by nature?"

"No. No more so than any Chairman in the fifth decade of his term of office. Still, the necessity of strict adherence to protocol, the further necessity of never taking sides, and the actuality of arbitrary power all combine toward making a certain irritability inevitable. And Amadiro is not always wise. His jovial smile, his white teeth, his exuding bonhomie can be extremely irritating when those upon whom he lavishes it are not in a good mood, for some reason. —But I must go meet them, Mr. Baley, and supply what I hope will be a more substantial version of charm. Please stay here and don't move from that chair."

Baley could do nothing but wait now. He thought, irrelevantly, that he had been on Aurora for just a bit short of fifty standard hours.

# 18

---

# Again the Chairman

### 75.

The Chairman was short, surprisingly short. Amadiro towered over him by nearly thirty centimeters.

However, since most of his shortness was in his thighs, the Chairman, when all were seated, was not noticeably inferior in height to the others. Indeed, he was thickset, with a massive chest and shoulders, and looked almost overpowering under those conditions.

His head was large, too, but his face was lined and marked by age. Nor were its wrinkles the kindly type carved by laughter. They were impressed into his cheeks and forehead, one felt, by the exercise of power. His hair was white and sparse and he was bald in the spot where the hairs would have met in a whorl.

His voice suited him—deep and decisive. Age had robbed it of some of its timbre, perhaps, and lent it a bit of harshness, but in a Chairman (Baley thought) that might help rather than hinder.

Fastolfe went through the full ritual of greeting, exchanged stroking remarks without meaning, and offered food and drink. Through all of this, no mention was made of the outsider and no notice was taken of him.

It was only when the preliminaries were finished and when all were seated that Baley (a little farther from the center than the others) was introduced.

He said, "Mr. Chairman," without holding out his hand. Then, with an offhand nod, he said, "And, of course, I have met Dr. Amadiro."

Amadiro's smile did not waver at the touch of insolence in Baley's voice.

The Chairman, who had not acknowledged Baley's greeting, placed his hands on each knee, fingers spread apart, and said, "Let us get started and let us see if we can't make this as brief and as productive as possible.

"Let me stress first that I wish to get past this matter of the misbehavior—or possible misbehavior—of an Earthman and strike instantly to the heart of the matter. Nor, in dealing with the heart of the matter, are we speaking of this overblown matter of the robot. Disrupting the activity of a robot is a matter for the civil courts; it can result in a judgment of the infringement of property rights and the inflicting of a penalty of costs but nothing more than that. What's more, if it should be proved that Dr. Fastolfe had rendered the robot, Jander Panell, inoperable, it is a robot who, after all, he helped design, whose construction he supervised, and the ownership of whom he held at the time of the inoperability. No penalty is likely to apply, since a person may do what he likes with his own.

"What is really at issue is the matter of the exploration and settlement of the Galaxy: whether we of Aurora carry it through alone, whether we do it in collaboration with the other Spacer worlds, or whether we leave it to Earth. Dr. Amadiro and the Globalists favor having Aurora shoulder the burden alone; Dr. Fastolfe wishes to leave it to Earth.

"If we can settle this matter, then the affair of the robot can be left to the civil courts, and the question of the Earthman's behavior will probably become moot, and we can simply get rid of him.

"Therefore, let me begin by asking whether Dr. Amadiro is prepared to accept Dr. Fastolfe's position in order to achieve unity of decision or whether Dr. Fastolfe is prepared to accept Dr. Amadiro's position with the same end in view."

He paused and waited.

Amadiro said, "I am sorry, Mr. Chairman, but I must insist that Earthmen be confined to their planet and that the Galaxy be settled by Aurorans only. I would be willing to compromise, however, to the extent of allowing other Spacer worlds to share in the settlement if that would prevent needless strife among us."

"I see," said the Chairman. "Will you, Dr. Fastolfe, in view of this statement, abandon your position?"

Fastolfe said, "Dr. Amadiro's compromise has scarcely anything of substance in it, Mr. Chairman. I am willing to offer a compromise of greater significance. Why should not the worlds of the Galaxy be thrown open to Spacers and Earthpeople alike? The Galaxy is large and there would be room for both. I would be willing to accept such an arrangement."

"No doubt," said Amadiro quickly, "for it is no compromise. The over eight billion population of Earth is more than half again the population of all the Spacer worlds combined. Earth's people are short-lived and are used to replacing their losses quickly. They lack our regard for individual human life. They will swarm over the new worlds at any cost, multiplying like insects, and will preempt the Galaxy even while we are making a bare beginning. To offer Earth a supposedly equal chance at the Galaxy is to *give* them the Galaxy—and that is not equality. Earthpeople must be confined to Earth."

"And what have you to say to that, Dr. Fastolfe?" asked the Chairman.

Fastolfe sighed. "My views are on record. I'm sure I don't need to repeat them. Dr. Amadiro plans to use humaniform robots to build the settled worlds that human Aurorans will then enter, ready-made, yet he doesn't even have humaniform robots. He cannot construct them and the project would not work, even if he did have them. No compromise is possible unless Dr. Amadiro consents to the principle that Earthpeople may at least share in the task of the settlement of new worlds."

"Then no compromise is possible," said Amadiro.

The Chairman looked displeased. "I'm afraid that one of you

two *must* give in. I do not intend Aurora to be torn apart in an emotional orgy on a question this important."

He looked at Amadiro blankly, his expression carefully signifying neither favor nor disfavor. "You intend to use the inoperability of the robot, Jander, as an argument against Fastolfe's view, do you not?"

"I do," said Amadiro.

"A purely emotional argument. You are going to claim that Fastolfe is trying to destroy your view by falsely making human-iform robots appear less useful than they, in effect, are."

"That is exactly what he *is* trying to do—"

"Slander!" put in Fastolfe in a low voice.

"Not if I can prove it, which I can," said Amadiro. "The argument may be an emotional one, but it will be effective. You see that, Mr. Chairman, don't you? My view will surely win, but left to itself it will be messy. I would suggest that you persuade Dr. Fastolfe to accept inevitable defeat and spare Aurora the enormous sadness of a spectacle that will weaken our position among the Spacer worlds and shake our own belief in ourselves."

"How can you prove that Dr. Fastolfe rendered the robot inoperative?"

"He himself admits he is the only human being who could have done so. You know this."

"I know," said the Chairman, "but I wanted to hear you say this, not to your constituency, not to the media, but to me—in private. And you have done so."

He turned to Fastolfe. "And what do you say, Dr. Fastolfe? Are you the only man who could have destroyed the robot?"

"Without leaving physical marks? I am, as far as I know. I don't believe that Dr. Amadiro has the skill in robotics to do so and I am constantly amazed that, after having founded his Robotics Institute, he is so eager to proclaim his own incapacity, even with all his associates at his back—and to do so publicly." He smiled at Amadiro, not entirely without malice.

The Chairman sighed. "No, Dr. Fastolfe. No rhetorical tricks now. Let us dispense with sarcasm and clever thrusts. What is your defense?"

"Why, only that I did no harm to Jander. I do not say anyone did. It was chance—the uncertainty principle at work on the positronic pathways. It can happen every so often. Let Dr. Amadiro merely admit that it was chance, that no one be accused without evidence, and we can then argue the competing proposals about settlement on their own merits."

"No," said Amadiro. "The chance of accidental destruction is too small to be considered, far smaller than the chance that Dr. Fastolfe is responsible—so much smaller that to ignore Dr. Fastolfe's guilt is irresponsible. I will not back down and I will win. Mr. Chairman, you know I will win and it seems to me that the only rational step to be taken is to force Dr. Fastolfe to accept his defeat in the interest of global unity."

Fastolfe said quickly, "And that brings me to the matter of the investigation I have asked Mr. Baley of Earth to undertake."

And Amadiro said, just as quickly, "A move I opposed when it was first suggested. The Earthman may be a clever investigator, but he is unfamiliar with Aurora and can accomplish nothing here. Nothing, that is, except to strew slander and to hold Aurora up to the Spacer worlds in an undignified and ridiculous light. There have been satirical pieces on the matter in half a dozen important Spacer hyperwave news programs on as many different worlds. Recordings of these have been sent to your office."

"And have been brought to my attention," said the Chairman.

"And there has been murmuring here on Aurora," Amadiro drove on. "It would be to my selfish interest to allow the investigation to continue. It is costing Fastolfe support among the populace and votes among the legislators. The longer it continues, the more certain I am of victory, but it is damaging Aurora and I do not wish to add to my certainty at the cost of harm to my world. I suggest—with respect—that you end the investigation, Mr. Chairman, and persuade Dr. Fastolfe to submit gracefully now to what he will eventually have to accept—at much greater cost."

The Chairman said, "I agree that to have permitted Dr. Fastolfe to set up this investigation *may* have been unwise. I say '*may*.' I admit I am tempted to end it. And yet the Earthman"—

he gave no indication of knowing that Baley was in the room—"has already been here for some time—"

He paused, as though to give Fastolfe a chance for corroboration, and Fastolfe took it, saying, "This is the third day of his investigation, Mr. Chairman."

"In that case," said the Chairman, "before I end that investigation, it would be fair, I believe, to ask if there have been any significant findings so far."

He paused again. Fastolfe glanced quickly at Baley and made a small motion of his head.

Baley said in a low voice, "I do not wish, Mr. Chairman, to obtrude, unasked, any observations. Am I being asked a question?"

The Chairman frowned. Without looking at Baley, he said, "I am asking Mr. Baley of Earth to tell us whether he has any findings of significance."

Baley took a deep breath. This was it.

## 76.

"Mr. Chairman," he began. "Yesterday afternoon, I was interrogating Dr. Amadiro, who was most cooperative and useful to me. When my staff and I left—"

"Your staff?" asked the Chairman.

"I was accompanied by two robots on all phases of my investigation, Mr. Chairman," said Baley.

"Robots who belong to Dr. Fastolfe?" asked Amadiro. "I ask this for the record."

"For the record, they do," said Baley. "One is Daneel Olivaw, a humaniform robot, and the other is Giskard Reventlov, an older nonhumaniform robot."

"Thank you," said the Chairman. "Continue."

"When we left the Institute grounds, we found that the airfoil we used had been tampered with."

"Tampered with?" asked the Chairman, startled. "By whom?"

"We don't know, but it happened on Institute grounds. We were there by invitation, so it was known by the Institute personnel that we would be there. Moreover, no one else would be likely to be there without the invitation and knowledge of the Institute staff. If it were at all thinkable, it would be necessary to conclude that the tampering could only have been done by someone on the Institute staff and that would, in any case, be impossible—except at the direction of Dr. Amadiro himself, which would also be unthinkable."

Amadiro said, "You seem to think a great deal about the unthinkable. Has the airfoil been examined by a qualified technician to see if it has indeed been tampered with? Might there not have been a natural failing?" asked Amadiro.

"No, sir," said Baley, "but Giskard, who is qualified to drive an airfoil and who has frequently driven that particular one, maintains that it was tampered with."

"And he is one of Dr. Fastolfe's staff and is programmed by him and receives his daily orders from him," said Amadiro.

"Are you suggesting—" began Fastolfe.

"I am suggesting nothing." Amadiro held up his hand in a benign gesture. "I am merely making a statement—for the record."

The Chairman stirred. "Will Mr. Baley of Earth please continue?"

Baley said, "When the airfoil broke down, there were others in pursuit."

"Others?" asked the Chairman.

"Other robots. They arrived and, by that time, my robots were gone."

"One moment," said Amadiro. "What was your condition at the time, Mr. Baley?"

"I was not entirely well."

"Not entirely well? You are an Earthman and unaccustomed to life except in the artificial setting of your Cities. You are uneasy in the open. Is that not so, Mr. Baley?" asked Amadiro.

"Yes, sir."

"And there was a severe thunderstorm in progress last evening, as I am sure the Chairman recalls. Would it not be accurate to say that you were quite ill? Semiconscious, if not worse?"

"I was quite ill," said Baley reluctantly.

"Then how is it your robots were gone?" asked the Chairman sharply. "Should they not have been with you in your illness?"

"I ordered them away, Mr. Chairman."

"Why?"

"I thought it best," said Baley, "and I will explain—if I may be allowed to continue."

"Continue."

"We were indeed being pursued, for the pursuing robots arrived shortly after my robots had left. The pursuers asked me where my robots were and I told them I had sent them away. It was only after that that they asked if I were ill. I said I wasn't ill and they left me in order to continue a search for my robots."

"In search of Daneel and Giskard?" asked the Chairman.

"Yes, Mr. Chairman. It was clear to me that they were under intense orders to find the robots."

"In what way was that clear?"

"Although I was obviously ill, they asked about the robots before they asked about me. Then, later, they abandoned me in my illness to search for my robots. They must have received enormously intense orders to find those robots or it would not have been possible for them to disregard a patently ill human being. As a matter of fact, I had anticipated this search for my robots and that was why I had sent them away. I felt it all-important to keep them out of unauthorized hands."

Amadiro said, "Mr. Chairman, may I continue to question Mr. Baley on this point, in order to show the worthlessness of this statement?"

"You may."

Amadiro said, "Mr. Baley. You were alone after your robots had left, were you not?"

"Yes, sir."

"Therefore you have no recording of events? You are not yourself equipped to record them? You have no recording device?"

"No to all three, sir."

"And you were ill?"

"Yes, sir."

"Distraught? Possibly too ill to remember clearly?"

"No, sir. I remember quite clearly."

"You would think so, I suppose, but you may well have been delirious and hallucinating. Under those conditions, it seems clear that what the robots said or, indeed, whether robots appeared at all would seem highly dubious."

The Chairman said thoughtfully, "I agree. Mr. Baley of Earth, assuming that what you remember—or claim to remember—is accurate, what is your interpretation of the events you are describing?"

"I hesitate to give you my thoughts on the matter, Mr. Chairman," said Baley, "lest I slander the worthy Dr. Amadiro."

"Since you speak at my request and since your remarks are confined to this room"—the Chairman looked around; the wall niches were empty of robots—"there is no question of slander, unless it seems to me you speak with malice."

"In that case, Mr. Chairman," said Baley, "I had thought it possible that Dr. Amadiro detained me in his office by discussing matters with me at greater length than was perhaps necessary, so that there would be time for the damaging of my machine, then detained me further in order that I might leave after the thunderstorm had begun, thus making sure that I would be ill in transit. He had studied Earth's social conditions, as he told me several times, so he would know what my reaction to the storm might be. It seemed to me that it was his plan to send his robots after us and, when they came upon our stalled airfoil, to have them take us all back to the Institute grounds, presumably so that I might be treated for my illness but actually so that he might have Dr. Fastolfe's robots."

Amadiro laughed gently. "What motive am I supposed to have for all this. You see, Mr. Chairman, that this is supposition joined to supposition and would be judged slander in any court on Aurora."

The Chairman said severely, "Has Mr. Baley of Earth anything to support these hypotheses?"

"A line of reasoning, Mr. Chairman."

The Chairman stood up, at once losing some of his presence, since he scarcely unfolded to a greater than sitting height. "Let me take a short walk, so that I might consider what I have heard so far. I will be right back." He left for the Personal.

Fastolfe leaned in the direction of Baley and Baley met him halfway. (Amadiro looked on in casual unconcern, as though it scarcely mattered to him what they might have to say to each other.)

Fastolfe whispered, "Have you anything better to say?"

Baley said, "I think so, if I get the proper chance to say it, but the Chairman does not seem to be sympathetic."

"He is not. So far you have merely made things worse and I would not be surprised if, when he comes back, he calls these proceedings to a halt."

Baley shook his head and stared at his shoes.

## 77.

Baley was still staring at his shoes when the Chairman returned, reseated himself, and turned a hard and rather baleful glance at the Earthman.

He said, "Mr. Baley of Earth?"

"Yes, Mr. Chairman."

"I think you are wasting my time, but I do not want it said that I did not give either side a full hearing, *even* when it seemed to be wasting my time. Can you offer me a motive that would account for Dr. Amadiro acting in the mad way in which you accuse him of acting."

"Mr. Chairman," said Baley in a tone approaching desperation, "there is indeed a motive—a very good one. It rests on the fact that Dr. Amadiro's plan for settling the Galaxy will come to nothing if he and his Institute cannot produce humaniform robots. So far he has produced none and can produce none. Ask him if he is willing to have a legislative committee examine his Institute for any indication that successful humaniform robots are being produced or designed. If he is willing to maintain that successful humaniforms are on the assembly lines or even on the drawing boards—or even in adequate theoretical formulation—

and if he is prepared to demonstrate that fact to a qualified committee, I will say nothing more and admit that my investigation has achieved nothing." He held his breath.

The Chairman looked at Amadiro, whose smile had faded.

Amadiro said, "I will admit that we have no humaniform robots in prospect at the moment."

"Then I will continue," said Baley, resuming his interrupted breathing with something very much like a gasp. "Dr. Amadiro can, of course, find all the information he needs for his project if he turns to Dr. Fastolfe, who has the information in his head, but Dr. Fastolfe will not cooperate in this matter."

"No, I will not," murmured Fastolfe, "under any conditions."

"But, Mr. Chairman," Baley continued, "Dr. Fastolfe is *not* the only individual who has the secret of the design and construction of humaniform robots."

"No?" said the Chairman. "Who else would know? Dr. Fastolfe himself looks astonished at your comment, Mr. Baley." (For the first time, he did not add "of Earth.")

"I am indeed astonished," said Fastolfe. "To my knowledge, I am certainly the only one. I don't know what Mr. Baley means."

Amadiro said, with a small curling of the lip, "I suspect Mr. Baley doesn't know, either."

Baley felt hemmed in. He looked from one to the other and felt that not one of them—not one—was on his side.

He said, "Isn't it true that any humaniform robot would know? Not consciously perhaps, not in such a way as to be able to give instructions in the matter—but the information would surely be there within him, wouldn't it? If a humaniform robot was properly questioned, his answers and responses would betray his design and construction. Eventually, given enough time and given questions properly framed, a humaniform robot would yield information that would make it possible to plan the design of other humaniform robots. —To put it briefly, no machine can be of secret design if the machine itself is available for sufficiently intense study."

Fastolfe seemed struck. "I see what you mean, Mr. Baley, and you are right. I had never thought of that."

"With respect, Dr. Fastolfe," said Baley, "I must tell you that, like all Aurorans, you have a peculiarly individualistic pride. You are entirely too satisfied with being the best roboticist, the *only* roboticist who can construct humaniforms—so you blind yourself to the obvious."

The Chairman relaxed into a smile. "He has you there, Dr. Fastolfe. I have wondered why you were so eager to maintain that you were the only one with the know-how to destroy Jander when that so weakened your political case. I see clearly now that you would rather have your political case go down than your uniqueness."

Fastolfe chafed visibly.

As for Amadiro, he frowned and said, "Has this anything to do with the problem under discussion?"

"Yes, it does," said Baley, his confidence rising. "You cannot force any information from Dr. Fastolfe directly. Your robots cannot be ordered to do him harm, to torture him into revealing his secrets, for instance. You can't harm him directly yourself against the protection of Dr. Fastolfe by his staff. However, you can isolate a robot and have it taken by other robots when the human being present is too ill to take the necessary action to prevent you. All the events of yesterday afternoon were part of a quickly improvised plan to get your hands on Daneel. You saw your opportunity as soon as I insisted on seeing you at the Institute. If I had not sent my robots away, if I had not been just well enough to insist I was well and to send your robots in the wrong direction, you would have had him. And eventually you might have worked out the secret of humaniform robots by some long-sustained analysis of Daneel's behavior and responses."

Amadiro said, "Mr. Chairman, I protest. I have never heard slander so viciously expressed. This is all based on the fancies of an ill man. We don't know—and perhaps can't ever know— whether the airfoil was really damaged; and if it was, by whom; whether robots really pursued the airfoil and really spoke to Mr. Baley or not. He is merely piling inference on inference, all based on dubious testimony concerning events of which he is the only witness—and that at a time when he was half-mad with fear and may have been hallucinating. None of this can stand up for one moment in a courtroom."

"This is not a courtroom, Dr. Amadiro," said the Chairman, "and it is my duty to listen to everything that may be germane to a question under dispute."

"This is not germane, Mr. Chairman. It is a cobweb."

"Yet it hangs together, somehow. I do not seem to catch Mr. Baley in a clear-cut illogicality. If one admits what he claims to have experienced, then his conclusions make a kind of sense. Do you deny all this, Dr. Amadiro? The airfoil damage, the pursuit, the intention to appropriate the humaniform robot?"

"I do! Absolutely! None of it is true!" said Amadiro. It had been a noticeable while since he had smiled. "The Earthman can produce a recording of our entire conversation and no doubt he will point out that I was delaying him by speaking at length, by inviting him to tour the Institute, by inviting him to have dinner —but all that can equally well be interpreted as my stretching a point to be courteous and hospitable. I was misled by a certain sympathy I have for Earthmen, perhaps, and that's all there is to that. I deny his inferences and nothing of what he says can stand up against my denial. My reputation is not such that a mere speculation can persuade anyone that I am the kind of devious plotter this Earthman says I am."

The Chairman scratched at his chin thoughtfully and said, "Certainly, I am not of a mind to accuse you on the basis of what the Earthman has said so far. —Mr. Baley, if this is all you have, it is interesting but insufficient. Is there anything more you have to say of substance? I warn you that, if not, I have now spent all the time on this that I can afford to."

## 78.

Baley said, "There is but one more subject I wish to bring up, Mr. Chairman. You have perhaps heard of Gladia Delmarre—or Gladia Solaria. She calls herself simply Gladia."

"Yes, Mr. Baley," said the Chairman with a testy edge to his voice. "I have heard of her. I have seen the hyperwave show in which you and she play such remarkable parts."

"She was associated with the robot, Jander, for many months. In fact, toward the end, he was her husband."

The Chairman's unfavorable stare at Baley became a hard glare. "Her *what*?"

"Husband, Mr. Chairman."

Fastolfe, who half-rose, sat down again, looking perturbed.

The Chairman said harshly, "That is illegal. Worse, it is ridiculous. A robot could not impregnate her. There could be no children. The status of a husband—or of a wife—is never granted without some statement as to willingness to have a child if permitted. Even an Earthman, I should think, would know that."

Baley said, "I am aware of this, Mr. Chairman. So, I am certain, was Gladia. She did not use the word 'husband' in its legal sense but in an emotional one. She considered Jander the equivalent of a husband. She felt toward him as though he were a husband."

The Chairman turned to Fastolfe. "Did you know of this, Dr. Fastolfe? He was a robot on your staff."

Fastolfe, clearly embarrassed, said, "I knew she was fond of him. I suspected she made use of him sexually. I knew nothing of this illegal charade, however, until Mr. Baley told me of it."

Baley said, "She was a Solarian. Her concept of 'husband' was not Auroran."

"Obviously not," said the Chairman.

"But she did have enough of a sense of reality to keep it to herself, Mr. Chairman. She never told of this charade, as Dr. Fastolfe calls it, to any Auroran. She told me the day before yesterday because she wanted to urge me on in the investigation of something that meant so much to her. Yet even so, I imagine she would not have used the word if she had not known I was an Earthman and would understand it in her sense—and not in an Auroran's."

"Very well," said the Chairman. "I'll grant her a bare minimum of good sense—for a Solarian. Is that the one more subject you wanted to bring up?"

"Yes, Mr. Chairman."

"In that case, it is totally irrelevant and can play no part in our deliberations."

"Mr. Chairman, there is one question I must still ask. One question. A dozen words, sir, and then I will be through." He said it as earnestly as he could, for everything depended on this.

The Chairman hesitated. "Agreed. One last question."

"Yes, Mr. Chairman." Baley would have liked to bark out the words, but he refrained. Nor did he raise his voice. Nor did he even point his finger. Everything depended on this. Everything had led up to this and yet he remembered Fastolfe's warning and said it almost casually. "How is it that Dr. Amadiro knew that Jander was Gladia's husband?"

"*What?*" The Chairman's white and bushy eyebrows raised themselves in surprise. "Who said he knew anything of this?"

Asked a direct question, Baley could continue. "Ask him, Mr. Chairman."

And he merely nodded in the direction of Amadiro, who had risen from his seat and was staring at Baley in obvious horror.

79.

Baley said again, very softly, reluctant to draw attention away from Amadiro, "Ask him, Mr. Chairman. He seems upset."

The Chairman said, "What is this, Dr. Amadiro? Did you know anything about the robot as supposed husband of this Solarian woman?"

Amadiro stuttered, then pressed his lips together for a moment and tried again. The paleness which had struck him had vanished and was replaced by a dull flush. He said, "I am caught by surprise at this meaningless accusation, Mr. Chairman. I do not know what it is all about."

"May I explain, Mr. Chairman? Very briefly?" said Baley. (Would he be cut off?)

"You had better," said the Chairman grimly. "If you have any explanation, I would certainly like to hear it."

"Mr. Chairman," said Baley. "I had a conversation with Dr. Amadiro yesterday afternoon. Because it was his intention to keep me until the storm broke, he spoke more lengthily than he intended and, apparently, more carelessly. In referring to Gladia, he casually referred to the robot, Jander, as her husband. I'm curious as to how he knew that fact."

"Is this true, Dr. Amadiro?" asked the Chairman.

Amadiro was still standing, bearing almost the appearance of a prisoner before a judge. He said, "Whether it is true or not has no bearing on the question under discussion."

"Perhaps not," said the Chairman, "but I was astonished at your reaction to the question when it was put. It occurs to me that there is a meaning to this that Mr. Baley and you both understand and that I do not. I therefore want to understand also. Did you or did you not know of this impossible relationship between Jander and the Solarian woman?"

Amadiro said in a choking voice, "I could not possibly have."

"That is no answer," said the Chairman. "That is an equivocation. You are making a judgment when I am asking you to hand me a memory. Did you or did you not make the statement imputed to you?"

"Before he answers," said Baley, feeling more certain of his ground now that the Chairman was governed by moral outrage, "it is only fair to Dr. Amadiro for me to remind him that Giskard, a robot who was also present at the meeting, can, if asked to do so, repeat the entire conversation, word for word, using the voice and intonation of both parties. In short, the conversation is recorded."

Amadiro burst into a kind of rage. "Mr. Chairman, the robot, Giskard, was designed, constructed, and programmed by Dr. Fastolfe, who announces himself to be the best roboticist who exists and who is bitterly opposed to me. Can we trust a recording produced by such a robot?"

Baley said, "Perhaps you ought to hear the recording and come to your own decision, Mr. Chairman."

"Perhaps I ought," said the Chairman. "I am not here, Dr. Amadiro, to have my decisions made for me. But let us put that aside for a moment. Regardless of what the recording says, Dr. Amadiro, do you wish to state for the record that you did not know that the Solarian woman considered her robot to be her husband and that you never referred to him as her husband? Please remember (as you both, being legislators, should) that, although no robot is present, this entire conversation is being recorded in my own device." He tapped a small bulge at his breast pocket. "Flatly, then, Dr. Amadiro. Yes or no."

Amadiro said, with an edge of desperation in his voice, "Mr. Chairman, I honestly cannot remember what I said in casual conversation. If I did mention the word—and I don't admit I did —it may have been the result of some other casual conversation in which someone mentioned the fact that Gladia acted as love-struck toward her robot as though he were her husband."

The Chairman said, "And with whom did you have this other casual conversation? Who made this statement to you?"

"At the moment, I cannot say."

Baley said, "Mr. Chairman, if Dr. Amadiro will be so kind as to list anyone and everyone who *might* have used the word to him, we can question every one of them to discover which one can remember making such a remark."

Amadiro said, "I hope, Mr. Chairman, you will consider the effect on the morale of the Institute if anything of this sort is done."

The Chairman said, "I hope you will consider it, too, Dr. Amadiro, and come up with a better answer to our question, so that we are not forced to extremes."

"One moment, Mr. Chairman," said Baley, as obsequiously as he could manage, "there remains a question."

"Again? Another one?" The Chairman looked at Baley without favor. "What is it?"

"Why is Dr. Amadiro struggling so to avoid admitting he knew of Jander's relation to Gladia? He says it is irrelevant. In that case, why not say he knew of the relationship and be done with it? *I* say it *is* relevant and that Dr. Amadiro knows that his admission could be used to demonstrate criminal activity on his part."

Amadiro thundered, "I resent the expression and I demand an apology!"

Fastolfe smiled thinly and Baley's lips pressed together grimly. He had forced Amadiro over the edge.

The Chairman turned an almost alarming red and said with passion, "You demand? You *demand?* To whom do you demand? I am the Chairman. I hear all views before deciding what to suggest as best to be done. Let me hear what the Earthman has to say about his interpretation of your action. If he is slandering you, he shall be punished, you may be sure, and I will take the broadest view of the slander statutes, too, you may be sure. But *you*, Amadiro, may make no demands upon me. Go on, Earthman. Say what you have to say, but be extraordinarily careful."

Baley said, "Thank you, Mr. Chairman. Actually, there is one Auroran to whom Gladia *did* tell the secret of her relationship with Jander."

The Chairman interrupted. "Well, who is that? Do not play your hyperwave tricks on me."

Baley said, "I have no intention of anything but a straightforward statement, Mr. Chairman. The one Auroran is, of course, Jander himself. He may have been a robot, but he is an inhabitant of Aurora and might be viewed as an Auroran. Gladia must surely, in her passion, have addressed him as 'my husband.' Since Dr. Amadiro has admitted he might possibly have heard from someone else some statement to the effect of Jander's husbandly relationship to Gladia, isn't it logical to suppose that he heard of the matter from Jander? Would Dr. Amadiro be willing, right now, to state for the record that he never spoke to Jander during the period when Jander formed part of Gladia's staff?"

Twice Amadiro's mouth opened as though he would speak. Twice he did not utter a sound.

"Well," said the Chairman, "did you speak to Jander during that period, Dr. Amadiro?"

There was still no answer.

Baley said softly, "If he did, it is entirely relevant to the matter at hand."

"I'm beginning to see that it must be, Mr. Baley. Well, Dr. Amadiro, once again—yes or no."

And Amadiro burst forth, "What evidence does this Earthman have against me in this matter? Does he have a recording of any conversation I have had with Jander? Does he have witnesses who are willing to say they have seen me with Jander? What does he have anything at all besides mere self-serving statements?"

The Chairman turned to look at Baley and Baley said, "Mr. Chairman, if I have nothing at all, then Dr. Amadiro should not hesitate to deny, for the record, any contact with Jander—but he does not do so. As it happens, in the course of my investigation, I spoke to Dr. Vasilia Aliena, the daughter of Dr. Fastolfe. I spoke also to a young Auroran named Santirix Gremionis. In the recordings of both interviews, it will be plain that Dr. Vasilia encouraged Gremionis to pay court to Gladia. You may question Dr. Vasilia as to her purpose in so doing and as to whether this course of action had been suggested to her by Dr. Amadiro. It also appears that it was Gremionis' custom to take long walks with Gladia, which both enjoyed, and on which they were not accompanied by the robot, Jander. You might check on this, if you wish, sir."

The Chairman said dryly, "I may do so, but if all is as you say, what does this show?"

Baley said, "I have stated that, failing Dr. Fastolfe himself, the secret of the humaniform robot could be obtained only from Daneel. Before Jander's death, it could, with equal facility, have been obtained from Jander. Whereas Daneel was part of Dr. Fastolfe's establishment and could not easily be reached, Jander was part of Gladia's establishment and she was not as sophisticated as Dr. Fastolfe in seeing to a robot's protection.

"Isn't it likely that Dr. Amadiro took the occasion of Gladia's periodic absences from her establishment, when she was walking with Gremionis, to converse with Jander, perhaps by trimensional viewing, to study his responses, to subject him to various tests, and then to erase any sign of his visit with Jander, so that he could never inform Gladia of it? It may be that he came close to finding what he wanted to know—before the attempt ended when Jander went out of action. His concentration then shifted to Daneel. He felt perhaps that he had only a few tests and observations left to make and so he set up the trap of yesterday evening, as I said earlier in my—my testimony."

The Chairman said, in what was almost a whisper, "Now it all hangs together. I am almost forced to believe."

"Plus one final point and then I will truly have nothing more to say," said Baley. "In his examination and testing of Jander, it is entirely possible that Dr. Amadiro accidentally—and without any deliberate intention whatever—immobilized Jander and thus committed roboticide."

And Amadiro, maddened, shouted, "No! Never! Nothing I did to that robot could possibly have immobilized him!"

Fastolfe interposed. "I agree. Mr. Chairman, I, too, think that Dr. Amadiro did not immobilize Jander. However, Mr. Chairman, Dr. Amadiro's statement just now would seem an implicit admission that he was working with Jander—and that Mr. Baley's analysis of the situation is essentially accurate."

The Chairman nodded. "I am forced to agree with you, Dr. Fastolfe. —Dr. Amadiro, you may insist on a formal denial of all this and that may force me into a full-fledged investigation, which could do you a great deal of damage, however it turned out—and I rather suspect, at this stage, it is likely to turn out to your great disadvantage. My suggestion is that you do not force this—that you do not cripple your own position in the Legislature and, perhaps, cripple Aurora's ability to continue along a smooth political course.

"As I see it, before the matter of Jander's immobilization came up, Dr. Fastolfe had a majority of the legislators—not a large majority, admittedly—on his side in the matter of Galactic settlement. You would have swung enough legislators to your side by pushing the matter of Dr. Fastolfe's supposed responsibility for Jander's immobilization and thus have gained the majority. But now Dr. Fastolfe, if he wishes, can turn the tables by accusing *you* of the immobilization and, moreover, of having tried to hang a false accusation upon your opponent as well—and you would lose.

"If I do not interfere, then it may be that you, Dr. Amadiro, and you, Dr. Fastolfe, actuated by stubbornness or even vindictiveness, will both marshal your forces and accuse each other of all sorts of things. Our political forces and public opinion, too, will be hopelessly divided—even fragmented—to our infinite harm.

"I believe that, in that case, Fastolfe's victory, while inevitable, would be a very costly one, so that it would be my task as the Chairman to swing the votes in his direction to begin with, and to place pressure upon you and your faction, Dr. Amadiro, to accept Fastolfe's victory with as much grace as you can manage, and to do it right now—for the good of Aurora."

Fastolfe said, "I am not interested in a crushing victory, Mr. Chairman. I propose again a compromise whereby Aurora, the other Spacer worlds, and Earth, too, all have the freedom of settlement in the Galaxy. In return, I will be glad to join the Robotics Institute, put my knowledge of humaniform robots at its disposal, and thus facilitate Dr. Amadiro's plan, in return for his solemn agreement to abandon all thought of retaliation against Earth at any time in the future and to put this into treaty form, with ourselves and Earth as signatories."

The Chairman nodded. "A wise and statesmanlike suggestion. May I have your acceptance of this, Dr. Amadiro?"

Amadiro now sat down. His face was a study in defeat. He said, "I have not wanted personal power or the satisfaction of victory. I wanted what I know to be best for Aurora and I am convinced that this plan of Dr. Fastolfe's means an end to Aurora someday. However, I recognize that I am now helpless against the work of this Earthman"—he shot a quick venomous glance toward Baley—"and I am forced to accept Dr. Fastolfe's suggestion—though I will ask for permission to address the Legislature on the subject and to state, for the record, my fears of the consequences."

"We will, of course, allow that," said the Chairman. "And if you'll be guided by me, Dr. Fastolfe, you'll get this Earthman off our world as fast as possible. He has won your viewpoint for you, but it will not be a very popular one if Aurorans have too long a time to brood over it as an Earthly victory over Aurorans."

"You are quite right, Mr. Chairman, and Mr. Baley will be gone quickly—with my thanks and, I trust, with yours as well."

"Well," said the Chairman, not with the best of grace, "since his ingenuity has saved us from a bruising political battle, he has my thanks. —Thank you, Mr. Baley."

# 19

---

# Again Baley

80.

Baley watched them leave from a distance. Though Amadiro and the Chairman had come together, they now left separately.

Fastolfe came back from seeing them off, making no attempt to hide his intense relief.

"Come, Mr. Baley," he said, "you will have lunch with me and then, as soon after that as possible, you will leave for Earth again."

His robotic staff was clearly in action with that in mind.

Baley nodded and said sardonically, "The Chairman managed to thank me, but it seemed to stick in his throat."

Fastolfe said, "You have no idea how you have been honored. The Chairman rarely thanks anyone, but then no one ever thanks the Chairman. It is always left to history to praise Chairmen and this one has served for over forty years. He has grown cranky and ill-tempered, as Chairmen always do in their final decades.

"However, Mr. Baley, once again *I* thank you and, through me, Aurora will thank you. You will live to see Earthmen move outward into space, even in your short lifetime, and we will help you with our technology.

"How you have managed to untie this knot of ours, Mr. Baley, in two and a half days—less—I can't imagine. You are a wonder.

—But, come, you will want to wash and freshen up. I know I do."

For the first time since the Chairman arrived, Baley had time to think of something besides his next sentence.

He still didn't know what it was that had come to him three times, first on the point of sleep, then on the point of unconsciousness, and finally in postcoital relaxation.

"He was there first!"

It was still meaningless, yet he had made his point to the Chairman and carried all before him without it. Could it have any meaning at all, then, if it was a part of a mechanism that didn't fit and didn't seem needed? Was it nonsense?

It chafed at the corner of his mind and he came to lunch a victor without the proper sensation of victory. Somehow, he felt as though he had missed the point.

For one thing, would the Chairman stick to his resolve? Amadiro had lost the battle, but he didn't seem the kind of person who would give up altogether under any circumstances. Give him credit and assume he meant what he said, that he was driven not by personal vainglory but by his concept of Auroran patriotism. If that were so, he *could not* give up.

Baley felt it necessary to warn Fastolfe.

"Dr. Fastolfe," he said, "I don't think it's over. Dr. Amadiro will continue the fight to exclude Earth."

Fastolfe nodded as the dishes were served. "I know he will. I expect him to. However, I have no fear as long as the matter of Jander's immobilization is set to rest. With that aside, I'm sure I can always outmaneuver him in the Legislature. Fear not, Mr. Baley, Earth will move along. Nor need you fear personal danger from a vengeful Amadiro. You will be off this planet and on your way back to Earth before sunset—and Daneel will escort you, of course. What's more, the report we'll send with you will ensure, once more, a healthy promotion for you."

"I am eager to go," said Baley, "but I hope I will have time to say my good-byes. I would like to—to see Gladia once more and I would like to say good-bye to Giskard, who may have saved my life last night."

"No question of that, Mr. Baley. But please eat, won't you?"

Baley went through the motions of eating, but didn't enjoy it. Like the confrontation with the Chairman and the victory that ensued, the food was oddly flavorless.

He should not have won. The Chairman should have cut him off. Amadiro, if necessary, should have made a flat denial. It would have been accepted over the word—or the reasoning—of an Earthman.

But Fastolfe was jubilant. He said, "I had feared the worst, Mr. Baley. I feared the meeting with the Chairman was premature and that nothing you could say would help the situation. Yet you managed it so well. I was lost in admiration, listening to you. At any moment, I expected Amadiro to demand that his word be taken against an Earthman who, after all, was in a constant state of semimadness at finding himself on a strange planet in the open—"

Baley said frigidly, "With all respect, Dr. Fastolfe, I was not in a constant state of semimadness. Last night was exceptional, but it was the only time I lost control. For the rest of my stay on Aurora, I may have been uncomfortable from time to time, but I was always in my perfect mind." Some of the anger he had suppressed at considerable cost to himself in the confrontation with the Chairman was expressing itself now. "Only during the storm, sir—except, of course"—recollecting—"for a moment or two on the approaching spaceship—"

He was not conscious of the manner in which the thought—the memory, the interpretation—came to him or at what speed. One moment it did not exist, the next moment it was full-blown in his mind, as though it had been there all the time and needed only the bursting of a soap-bubble veil to show it.

"Jehoshaphat!" he said in an awed whisper. Then, with his fist coming down on the table and rattling the dishes, "*Jehoshaphat!*"

"What is it, Mr. Baley?" asked Fastolfe, startled.

Baley stared at him and heard the question only belatedly. "Nothing, Dr. Fastolfe. I was just thinking of Dr. Amadiro's infernal gall in doing the damage to Jander and then laboring to fix the blame on you, in arranging to have me go half-mad in the

storm last night and then using that as a way of casting doubt
on my statements. I was just—momentarily—angry."

"Well, no need to be, Mr. Baley. And actually, it is quite impossible for Amadiro to have immobilized Jander. It remains
purely a chance event. —To be sure, it is possible that Amadiro's
investigation may have increased the odds of such a chance
event taking place, but I would not argue the matter."

Baley heard the statement with half of one ear. What he had
just said to Fastolfe was fiction and what Fastolfe was saying
didn't matter. It was (as the Chairman would have said) irrelevant. In fact, everything that had happened—everything that
Baley had explained—was irrelevant. —But nothing had to be
changed because of that.

Except one thing—after a while.

Jehoshaphat! he whispered in the silence of his mind and
turned suddenly to the lunch, eating with gusto and with joy.


81.


Once again, Baley crossed the lawn between Fastolfe's establishment and Gladia's. He would be seeing Gladia for the fourth
time in three days—and (his heart seemed to compress into a
hard knot in his chest) now for the last time.

Giskard was with him but at a distance, more intent than ever
on the surroundings. Surely, with the Chairman in full possession of the facts, there should be a relaxation of any concern for
Baley's safety—if there ever had been any, by rights, when it
was Daneel who had been in danger. Presumably, Giskard had
not yet been reinstructed in the matter.

Only once did he approach Baley and that was when the latter
called out, "Giskard, where's Daneel?"

Swiftly, Giskard covered the ground between them, as though
reluctant to speak in anything but a quiet tone. "Daneel is on
his way to the spaceport, sir, in the company of several others of
the staff, in order to make arrangements for your transportation
to Earth. When you are taken to the spaceport, he will meet you

there and be on the ship with you, taking his final leave of you at Earth."

"Good news. I treasure every day of companionship with Daneel. And you, Giskard? Will you accompany us?"

"No, sir. I am instructed to remain on Aurora. However, Daneel will serve you well, even in my absence."

"I am sure of that, Giskard, but I will miss you."

"Thank you, sir," said Giskard and retreated as rapidly as he had come. Baley gazed after him speculatively for a moment or so. —No, first things first. He had to see Gladia.

### 82.

She advanced to greet him—and what a world of change had taken place in two days. She was not joyous, she was not dancing, she was not bubbling; there was still the grave look of one who had suffered a shock and a loss—but the troubled aura around her was gone. There was a kind of serenity now, as though she had grown aware of the fact that life continued after all and might even, on occasion, be sweet.

She managed a smile, warm and friendly, as she advanced to him and held out her hand.

"Oh, take it, take it, Elijah," she said when he hesitated. "It's ridiculous for you to hang back and pretend you don't want to touch me after last night. You see, I still remember it and I haven't come to regret it. Quite the contrary."

Baley performed the unusual operation (for him) of smiling in return. "I remember it, too, Gladia, and I don't regret it either. I would even like to do it again, but I have come to say good-bye."

A shade fell across her face. "Then you'll be going back to Earth. Yet the report I got by way of the robot network that always operates between Fastolfe's establishment and my own is that all went well. You *can't* have failed."

"I did not fail. Dr. Fastolfe, has, in fact, won completely. I don't believe there will be any suggestion at all that he was in any way involved in Jander's death."

"Because of what you had to say, Elijah?"

"I believe so."

"I knew it." There was a tinge of self-satisfaction to that. "I knew you would do it when I told them to get you on the case. —But then why are you being sent home?"

"Precisely because the case is solved. If I remain here longer, I will be a foreign irritant in the body politic, apparently."

She looked at him dubiously for a moment and said, "I'm not sure what you mean by that. It sounds like an Earth expression to me. But never mind. Were you able to find out who killed Jander? That is the important part."

Baley looked around. Giskard was standing in one niche, one of Gladia's robots in another.

Gladia interpreted the look without trouble. She said, "Now, Elijah, you must learn to stop worrying about robots. You don't worry about the presence of the chair, do you, or of these drapes?"

Baley nodded. "Well, then, Gladia, I'm sorry—I'm terribly sorry—but I had to tell them of the fact that Jander was your husband."

Her eyes opened wide and he hastened on. "I *had* to. It was essential to the case, but I promise it won't affect your status on Aurora." As briefly as he might, he summarized the events of the confrontation and concluded, "So, you see, no one killed Jander. The immobilization was the result of a chance change in his positronic pathways, though the probabilities of that chance change may have been enhanced by what had been going on."

"And I never knew," she moaned. "I never knew. I *connived* at this Amadiro's foul plan. —And he is the one responsible just as much, as though he had deliberately hacked away at him with a sledgehammer."

"Gladia," said Baley earnestly, "that is uncharitable. He had no intention of doing harm to Jander and what he was doing was, in his own eyes, for the good of Aurora. As it is, he is punished. He is defeated, his plans are in shambles, and the Robotics Institute will come under the domination of Dr. Fastolfe. You yourself could not work out a more suitable punishment, no matter how you tried."

She said, "I'll think about that. —But what do I do with Santirix Gremionis, this good-looking young lackey whose job it was to lure me away? No wonder he appeared to cling to hope despite my repeated refusal. Well, he'll come here again and I will have the pleasure of—"

Baley shook his head violently. "Gladia, *no*. I have interviewed him and I *assure* you he had no knowledge of what was going on. He was as much deceived as you were. In fact, you have it reversed. He was not persistent because it was important to lure you away. He was useful to Amadiro *because* he was so persistent—and that persistence was out of regard for you. Out of love, if the word means on Aurora what it means on Earth."

"On Aurora, it is choreography. Jander was a robot and you are an Earthman. It is different with the Aurorans."

"So you have explained. But Gladia, you learned from Jander to take; you learned from me—not that I meant it—to give. If you benefit by learning, is it not only right and fair that you should teach in your turn? Gremionis is sufficiently attracted to you to be willing to learn. He already defies Auroran convention by persisting in the face of your refusal. He will defy more. You can teach him to give and take and you will learn to do both in alternation or together, in company with him."

Gladia looked searchingly into his eyes. "Elijah, are you trying to get rid of me?"

Slowly, Baley nodded. "Yes, Gladia, I am. It's your happiness I want at this moment, more than I have ever wanted anything for myself or for Earth. I can't give you happiness, but if Gremionis can give it to you, I will be as happy—*almost* as happy as if it were I myself who were making the gift.

"Gladia, he may surprise you with how eagerly he will break through the choreography when you show him how. And the word will somehow spread, so that others will come to swoon at your feet—and Gremionis may find it possible to teach other women. Gladia, it may be that you will revolutionize Auroran sex before you are through. You will have three centuries in which to do so."

Gladia stared at him and then broke into a laugh. "You are teasing. You are being deliberately foolish. I wouldn't have

thought it of you, Elijah. You always look so long-faced and
grave. Jehoshaphat!" (And, with the last word, she tried to imitate his somber baritone.)

Baley said, "Perhaps I'm teasing a little, but I mean it in essence. Promise me that you will give Gremionis his chance."

She came closer to him and, without hesitation, he put his arm
around her. She placed her finger on his lips and he made a
small kissing motion. She said softly, "Wouldn't you rather have
me for yourself, Elijah?"

He said, just as softly (and unable to become unaware of the
robots in the room), "Yes, I would, Gladia. I am ashamed to say
that at this moment I would be content to have the Earth fall to
pieces if I could have you—but I can't. In a few hours, I'll be off
Aurora and there's no way you will be allowed to go with me.
Nor do I think I will ever be allowed to come back to Aurora, nor
is it possible that you will ever visit Earth.

"I will never see you again, Gladia, but I will never forget you,
either. I will die in a few decades and when I do you will be as
young as you are now, so we would have to say good-bye soon
whatever we could imagine as happening."

She put her head against his chest. "Oh, Elijah, twice you
came into my life, each time for just a few hours. Twice you've
done so much for me and then said good-bye. The first time all I
could do was touch your face, but what a difference that made.
The second time, I did so much more—and again what a
difference that made. I'll never forget you, Elijah, if I live more
centuries than I can count."

Baley said, "Then let it not be the kind of memory that cuts
you off from happiness. Accept Gremionis and make *him* happy
—and let him make you happy as well. And, remember, there is
nothing to prevent you from sending me letters. The hyperpost
between Aurora and Earth exists."

"I will, Elijah. And you will write to me as well?"

"I will, Gladia."

Then there was silence and, reluctantly, they moved apart. She
remained standing in the middle of the room and when he went
to the door and turned back, she was still standing there with a
little smile. His lips shaped: *Good-bye.* And then because there

was no sound—he could not have done it with sound—he added,
*my love.*

And her lips moved, too. *Good-bye, my dearest love.*

And he turned and walked out and knew he would never see
her in tangible form, never touch her again.

### 83.

It was a while before Elijah could bring himself to consider
the task that still lay before him. He had walked in silence perhaps half the distance back to Fastolfe's establishment before he
stopped and lifted his arm.

The observant Giskard was at his side in a moment.

Baley said, "How much time before I must leave for the
spaceport, Giskard?"

"Three hours and ten minutes, sir."

Baley thought a moment. "I would like to walk over to that
tree there and sit down with my back against the trunk and
spend some time there alone. With you, of course, but away
from other human beings."

"In the open, sir?" The robot's voice was unable to express
surprise and shock, but somehow Baley had the feeling that, if
Giskard were human, those words would express those feelings.

"Yes," said Baley. "I have to think and, after last night, a
calm day like this—sunny, cloudless, mild—scarcely seems dangerous. I'll go indoors if I get agoraphobic. I promise. So will
you join me?"

"Yes, sir."

"Good." Baley led the way. They reached the tree and Baley
touched the trunk gingerly and then stared at his finger, which
remained perfectly clean. Reassured that leaning against the
trunk would not dirty him, he inspected the ground and then sat
down carefully and rested his back against the tree.

It was not nearly as comfortable as the back of a chair would
have been, but there was a feeling of peace (oddly enough) that
perhaps he would not have had inside a room.

Giskard remained standing and Baley said, "Won't you sit down, too?"

"I am as comfortable standing, sir."

"I know that, Giskard, but I will think better if I don't have to look up at you."

"I could not guard you against possible harm as efficiently if I were seated, sir."

"I know that, too, Giskard, but there is no reasonable danger at the moment. My mission is over, the case is solved, Dr. Fastolfe's position is secure. You can risk being seated and I order you to sit down."

Giskard at once sat down, facing Baley, but his eyes continued to wander in this direction and that and were ever alert.

Baley looked at the sky, through the leaves of the tree, green against blue, listened to the susurration of insects and to the sudden call of a bird, noted a disturbance of grass nearby that might have meant a small animal passing by, and again thought how oddly peaceful it all was and how different this peacefulness was from the clamor of the City. This was a quiet peace, an unhurried peace, a removed peace.

For the first time, Baley caught a faint suggestion of how it might be to prefer Outside to the City. He caught himself being thankful to his experiences on Aurora, to the storm most of all—for he knew now that he would be able to leave Earth and face the conditions of whatever new world he might settle on, he and Ben—and perhaps Jessie.

He said, "Last night, in the darkness of the storm, I wondered if I might have seen Aurora's satellite were it not for the clouds. It has a satellite, if I recall my reading correctly."

"Two, actually, sir. The larger is Tithonus, but it is still so small that it appears only as a moderately bright star. The smaller is not visible at all to the unaided eye and is simply called Tithonus II, when it is referred to at all."

"Thank you. —And thank you, Giskard, for rescuing me last night." He looked at the robot. "I don't know the proper way of thanking you."

"It is not necessary to thank me at all. I was merely following the dictates of the First Law. I had no choice in the matter."

"Nevertheless, I may even owe you my life and it is important that you know I understand this. —And now, Giskard, what ought I to do?"

"Concerning what matter, sir?"

"My mission is over. Dr. Fastolfe's views are secure. Earth's future may be assured. It would seem I have nothing more to do and yet there is the matter of Jander."

"I do not understand, sir."

"Well, it seems settled that he died by a chance shift of positronic potential in his brain, but Fastolfe admits the chance of that is infinitesimally small. Even with Amadiro's activities, the chance, though possibly greater, would remain infinitesimally small. At least, so Fastolfe thinks. It continues to seem to me, then, that Jander's death was one of deliberate roboticide. Yet I don't dare raise this point now. I don't want to unsettle matters that have been brought to such a satisfactory conclusion. I don't want to put Fastolfe in jeopardy again. I don't want to make Gladia unhappy. I don't know what to do. I can't talk to a human being about this, so I'm talking to you, Giskard."

"Yes, sir."

"I can always order you to erase whatever I have said and to remember it no more."

"Yes, sir."

"In your opinion, what ought I to do?"

Giskard said, "If there is a roboticide, sir, there must be someone capable of committing the act. Only Dr. Fastolfe is capable of committing it and he says he did not do it."

"Yes, we started with that situation. I believe Dr. Fastolfe and am quite certain he did not do it."

"Then how could there have been a roboticide, sir?"

"Suppose that someone else knew as much about robots as Dr. Fastolfe does, Giskard."

Baley drew up his knees and clasped his hands around them. He did not look at Giskard and seemed lost in thought.

"Who might that be, sir?" asked Giskard.

And finally, Baley reached the crucial point.

He said, "You, Giskard."

## 84.

If Giskard had been human, he might have simply stared, silent and stunned; or he might have raged angrily; or shrunk back in terror; or had any of a dozen responses. Because he was a robot, he showed no sign of any emotion whatever and simply said, "Why do you say so, sir?"

Baley said, "I am quite certain, Giskard, that you know exactly how I have come to this conclusion, but you will do me a favor if you allow me, in this quiet place and in this bit of time before I must leave, to explain the matter for my own benefit. I would like to hear myself talk about it. And I would like you to correct me where I am wrong."

"By all means, sir."

"I suppose my initial mistake was to suppose that you are a less complicated and more primitive robot than Daneel is, simply because you look less human. A human being will always suppose that, the more human a robot is, the more advanced, complicated, and intelligent he will be. To be sure, a robot like you is easily designed and one like Daneel is a great problem for men like Amadiro and can be handled only by a robotics genius such as Fastolfe. However, the difficulty in designing Daneel lies, I suspect, in reproducing all the human aspects such as facial expression, intonation of voice, gestures and movements that are extraordinarily intricate but have nothing really to do with complexity of mind. Am I right?"

"Quite right, sir."

"So I automatically underestimated you, as does everyone. Yet you gave yourself away even before we landed on Aurora. You remember, perhaps, that during the landing, I was overcome by an agoraphobic spasm and was, for a moment, even more helpless than I was last night in the storm."

"I do, sir."

"At the time, Daneel was in the cabin with me, while you

were outside the door. I was falling into a kind of catatonic state, noiselessly, and he was, perhaps, not looking at me and so knew nothing of it. You were outside the cabin and yet it was you who dashed in and turned off the viewer I was holding. You got there first, ahead of Daneel, though his reflexes are as fast as yours, I'm sure—as he demonstrated when he prevented Dr. Fastolfe from striking me."

"Surely it cannot be that Dr. Fastolfe was striking you."

"He wasn't. He was merely demonstrating Daneel's reflexes. —And yet, as I say, in the cabin you got there first. I was scarcely in condition to observe that fact, but I have been trained to observe and I am not put entirely out of action even by agoraphobic terror, as I showed last night. I did notice you were there first, though I tended to forget the fact. There is, of course, only one logical solution."

Baley paused, as though expecting Giskard to agree, but the robot said nothing.

(In later years, this was what Baley pictured first when thinking of his stay on Aurora. Not the storm. Not even Gladia. It was, rather, the quiet time under the tree, with the green leaves against the blue sky, the mild breeze, the soft sound of animals, and Giskard opposite him with faintly glowing eyes.)

Baley said, "It would seem that you could somehow detect my state of mind and, even through the closed door, tell that I was having a seizure of some sort. Or, to put it briefly and perhaps simplistically, you can read minds."

"Yes, sir," said Giskard quietly.

"And you can somehow influence minds, too. I believe you noted that I had detected this and you obscured it in my mind, so that I somehow did not remember or did not see the significance—if I did casually recall the situation. Yet you did not do that entirely efficiently, perhaps because your powers are limited—"

Giskard said, "Sir, the First Law is paramount. I had to come to your rescue, although I quite realized that would give me away. And I had to obscure your mind minimally, in order not to damage it in any way."

Baley nodded. "You have your difficulties, I see. Obscured

minimally—so I did remember it when my mind was sufficiently relaxed and could think by free association. Just before I lost consciousness in the storm, I knew you would find me first, as you had on the ship. You may have found me by infrared radiation, but every mammal and bird was radiating as well and that might be confusing—but you could also detect mental activity, even if I were unconscious, and that would help you to find me."

"It certainly helped," said Giskard.

"When I did remember, close to sleep or unconsciousness, I would forget again when fully conscious. Last night, however, I remembered for the third time and I was not alone. Gladia was with me and could repeat what I had said, which was 'He was there first.' And even *then* I could not remember the meaning, until a chance remark of Dr. Fastolfe's led to a thought that worked its way past the obscuration. Then, once it dawned on me, I remembered other things. Thus, when I was wondering if I were really landing on Aurora, you assured me that our destination was Aurora before I actually asked. —I presume you allow no one to know of your mind-reading ability."

"That is true, sir."

"Why is that?"

"My mind reading gives me a unique ability to obey the First Law, sir, so I value its existence. I can prevent harm to human beings far more efficiently. It seemed to me, however, that neither Dr. Fastolfe—nor any other human being—would long tolerate a mind-reading robot, so I keep the ability secret. Dr. Fastolfe loves to tell the legend of the mind-reading robot who was destroyed by Susan Calvin and I would not want him to duplicate Dr. Calvin's feat."

"Yes, he told the legend to me. I suspect that he knows, subliminally, that you read minds or he wouldn't harp on the legend so. And it is dangerous for him to do so, as far as you are concerned, I should think. Certainly, it helped put the matter in my mind."

"I do what I can to neutralize the danger without unduly tampering with Dr. Fastolfe's mind. Dr. Fastolfe invariably stresses the legendary and impossible nature of the story when he tells it."

"Yes, I remember that, too. But if Fastolfe does not know you can read minds, it must be that you were not designed originally with these powers. How, then, do you come to have them? —No, don't tell me, Giskard. Let me suggest something. Miss Vasilia was particularly fascinated with you when she was a young woman first becoming interested in robotics. She told me that she had experimented by programming you under Fastolfe's distant supervision. Could it be that, at one time, quite by accident, she did something that gave you the power? Is that correct?"

"That is correct, sir."

"And do you know what that something is?"

"Yes, sir."

"Are you the only mind-reading robot that exists?"

"So far, yes, sir. There will be others."

"If I asked you what it was that Dr. Vasilia did to you to give you such powers—or if Dr. Fastolfe did—would you tell us by virtue of the Second Law?"

"No, sir, for it is my judgment that it would do you harm to know and my refusal to tell you under the First Law would take precedence. The problem would not arise, however, for I would know that someone was going to ask the question and give the order and I would remove the impulse to do so from the mind before it could be done."

"Yes," said Baley. "Evening before last, as we were walking from Gladia's to Fastolfe's, I asked Daneel if he had had any contact with Jander during the latter's stay with Gladia and he answered quite simply that he had not. I then turned to ask you the same question and, somehow, I never did. You quashed the impulse for me to do so, I take it."

"Yes, sir."

"Because if I had asked, you would have had to say that you knew him well at that time and you were not prepared to have me know that."

"I was not, sir."

"But during this period of contact with Jander, you knew he was being tested by Amadiro because, I presume, you could read Jander's mind or detect his positronic potentials—"

"Yes, sir, the same ability covers both robotic and human mental activity. Robots are far easier to understand."

"You disapproved of Amadiro's activities because you agreed with Fastolfe on the matter of settling the Galaxy."

"Yes, sir."

"Why did you not stop Amadiro? Why did you not remove from his mind the impulse to test Jander?"

Giskard said, "Sir, I do not lightly tamper with minds. Amadiro's resolve was so deep and complex that, to remove it, I would have had to do much—and his mind is an advanced and important one that I would be reluctant to damage. I let the matter continue for a great while, during which I pondered on which action would best fulfill my First Law needs. Finally, I decided on the proper manner to correct the situation. It was not an easy decision."

"You decided to immobilize Jander before Amadiro could work out the method for designing a true humaniform robot. You knew how to do so, since you had, over the years, gained a perfect understanding of Fastolfe's theories from Fastolfe's mind. Is that right?"

"Exactly, sir."

"So that Fastolfe was not the only one, after all, expert enough to immobilize Jander."

"In a sense, he was, sir. My own ability is merely the reflection —or the extension—of his."

"But it will do. Did you not see that this immobilization would place Fastolfe in great danger? That he would be the natural suspect? Did you plan on admitting your action and revealing your abilities if that were necessary to save him?"

Giskard said, "I did indeed see that Dr. Fastolfe would be in a painful situation, but I did not intend to admit my guilt. I had hoped to utilize the situation as a wedge for getting you to Aurora."

"Getting *me* here? Was that *your* idea?" Baley felt rather stupefied.

"Yes, sir. With your permission, I would like to explain."

Baley said, "Please do."

Giskard said, "I knew of you from Miss Gladia and from Dr.

Fastolfe, not only from what they said but from what was in their minds. I learned of the situation on Earth. Earthmen, it was clear, live behind walls, which they find difficult to escape from, but it was just as clear to me that Aurorans live behind walls, too.

"Aurorans live behind walls made of robots, who shield them from all the vicissitudes of life and who, in Amadiro's plans, would build up shielded societies to wall up Aurorans settling new worlds. Aurorans also live behind walls made up of their own extended lives, which forces them to overvalue individuality and keeps them from pooling their scientific resources. Nor do they indulge in the rough-and-tumble of controversy, but, through their Chairman, demand a short-circuiting of all uncertainty and that decisions on solutions be reached before problems are aired. They could not be bothered with actually thrashing out best solutions. What they wanted were *quiet* solutions.

"The Earthman's walls are crude and literal, so that their existence is obtrusive and obvious—and there are always some who long to escape. The Aurorans' walls are immaterial and aren't even seen as walls, so that none can even conceive of escaping. It seemed to me, then, that it must be Earthmen and not Aurorans—or any other Spacers—who must settle the Galaxy and establish what will someday become a Galactic Empire.

"All this was Dr. Fastolfe's reasoning and I agreed with it. Dr. Fastolfe was, however, satisfied with the reasoning, while I, given my own abilities, could not be. I had to examine the mind of at least one Earthman directly, in order that I might check my conclusions, and you were the Earthman I thought I could bring to Aurora. The immobilization of Jander served both to stop Amadiro and to be the occasion for your visit. I pushed Miss Gladia very slightly to have her suggest your coming to Dr. Fastolfe; I pushed him in turn, very slightly, to have him suggest it to the Chairman; and I pushed the Chairman, very slightly, to have him agree. Once you arrived, I studied you and was pleased with what I found."

Giskard stopped speaking and became robotically impassive again.

Baley frowned. "It occurs to me that I have earned no credit in what I have done here. You must have seen to it that I found my way to the truth."

"No, sir. On the contrary. I placed barriers in your way— reasonable ones, of course. I refused to let you recognize my abilities, even though I was forced to give myself away. I made sure that you felt dejection and despair at odd times. I encouraged you to risk the open, in order to study your responses. Yet you found your way through and over all these obstacles and I was pleased.

"I found that you longed for the walls of your City but recognized that you must learn to do without them. I found that you suffered from the view of Aurora from space and from your exposure to the storm, but that neither prevented you from thinking nor drove you from your problem. I found that you accept your shortcomings and your brief life—and that you do not dodge controversy."

Baley said, "How do you know I am representative of Earthpeople generally?"

"I know you are not. But from your mind, I know there are some like you and we will build with those. I will see to it—and now that I know clearly the path that must be followed, I will prepare other robots like myself—and they will see to it, too."

Baley said suddenly, "You mean that mind-reading robots will come to Earth?"

"No, I do not. And you are right to be alarmed. Involving robots directly will mean the construction of the very walls that are dooming Aurora and the Spacer worlds to paralysis. Earthmen will have to settle the Galaxy without robots of any kind. It will mean difficulties, dangers, and harm without measure— events that robots would labor to prevent if they were present— but, in the end, human beings will be better off for having worked on their own. And perhaps someday—some long-away day in the future—robots can intervene once more. Who can tell?"

Baley said curiously, "Do you see the future?"

"No, sir, but studying minds as I do, I can tell dimly that there are laws that govern human behavior as the Three Laws of

Robotics govern robotic behavior; and with these it may be that the future will be dealt with, after a fashion—someday. The human laws are far more complicated than the Laws of Robotics are and I do not have any idea as to how they may be organized. They may be statistical in nature, so that they might not be fruitfully expressed except when dealing with huge populations. They may be very loosely binding, so that they might not make sense unless those huge populations are unaware of the operation of those laws."

"Tell me, Giskard, is this what Dr. Fastolfe refers to as the future science of 'psychohistory'?"

"Yes, sir. I have gently inserted it into his mind, in order that the process of working it out begin. It will be needed someday, now that the existence of the Spacer worlds as a long-lived robotized culture is coming to an end and a new wave of human expansion by short-lived human beings—without robots—will be beginning.

"And now"—Giskard rose to his feet—"I think, sir, that we must go to Dr. Fastolfe's establishment and prepare for your leavetaking. All that we have said here will not be repeated, of course."

"It is strictly confidential, I assure you," said Baley.

"Indeed," said Giskard calmly. "But you need not fear the responsibility of having to remain silent. I will allow you to remember, but you will never have the urge to repeat the matter —not the slightest."

Baley lifted his eyebrows in resignation over that and said, "One thing, though, Giskard, before you clamp down on me. Will you see to it that Gladia is not disturbed on this planet, that she is not treated unkindly because she is a Solarian and has accepted a robot as her husband, and—and that she will accept the offers of Gremionis?"

"I heard your final conversation with Miss Gladia, sir, and I understand. It will be taken care of. Now, sir, may I take my leave of you while no other is watching?" Giskard thrust out his hand in the most human gesture Baley had ever seen him make.

Baley took it. The fingers were hard and cool in his grip. "Good-bye—friend Giskard."

Giskard said, "Good-bye, friend Elijah, and remember that, although people apply the phrase to Aurora, it is, from this point on, Earth itself that is the true World of the Dawn."